Mr Impossible

By Edward Payne

Dearest Kat,

Hope you enjoy the foul language and bodily fluids as much as I've enjoyed yours.

❤ Ed
xxx.

ABOUT THE AUTHOR

Edward Payne is an award winning Radio Presenter, Drama School Graduate and Author. He graduated from drama school in 2009 and began writing his first novel "Mr Impossible". In that time, as a Presenter on Whitechapel AM, he won Silver in the Best Newcomer category of the Hospital Broadcasting Association awards in 2011. In 2012 he won Bronze in the Best Male category.

He currently lives and works in Cheltenham, presenting on Radio Winchcombe and writing. "Hell Wears A Neckerchief" is his first short story, released in 2015 and a new novel is currently in the works to be released in 2017.

For the Class of 09 and Peter Khalil: there at the beginning when it seemed like there was no end.

I sighed.

Most of my days had dwindled into this, mindlessly trawling through various websites just to pass the time. Logging onto Pintpage.com, the UK public house review page, was always a good diversion from doing anything more productive, so I typed a pub name into the search engine:

T-H-E C-A-S-T-L-E.

I loved reading the posts on here; especially if I had visited said dive myself and empathised with the sentiments of the acerbic online reviewer. It wasn't the most exciting pastime, but I had run out of ideas on the internet procrastination front and this was a bit more fun than most, mainly because there are so many wry, sarcastic drunks out there.

A prime example presented itself to me on Tuesday. The unhappy pub-goer, aleforsale73, had described the food at our office local, The Princess, as "more to die from, than to die for."

This week, the satire of Pintpage had filled the long hours. Last week, it had been sneakypeek.com; the webpage that sought the answers to urban legends the world over. Before that the Paranormal Pics Page on realghosts.com had been my favourite. This page is a gallery for those amateur photographers who swear blind that their picture of a deserted autumnal backdrop has the ghostly apparition of someone in a crinoline drifting past in the background.

The likelihood of most of these pics actually containing anything close to paranormal was questionable and, although entertaining, I was far too affected by them. After three hours of squinting at these bloody things, as I did with those magic eye pictures of the late nineties, I was temporarily fooled into thinking I had some sort of sixth sense and would start to see the spooky manifestations of dead people hanging from the boughs of the Maccy D's on the York Way junction.

This was what an administration job at Eco Scene had done to me, turned me into some junk website aficionado. During my two years in the office, I had visited virtually every internet page going, no matter how bizarre, primarily because there was bugger all else to do. The hours of internet perusal had been long, and had at times veered between the surprisingly interesting and the sublimely ridiculous. I had already virtually maimed Keira Knightley on celebrityslap.com and drooled over pictures of a young Morten Harket at welovethe80s.net. I'd even grabbed the rare opportunity of rating a few cocks at bigorwhat.com on the day the server crashed and the firewall took two hours to be reinstalled.

Last Thursday, I completed a thirty-minute online survey, time that would have ordinarily been spent gormlessly watching a fly buzz around my desk with my mouth open, just to browse a gadget site for a wall-mounted tin opener that I didn't even want; eventually admitting that the rusty old-school one I had at home was sufficient in carrying out my limited personal tin-opening needs.

Gradually, though it pained me to admit it, abusing the flexible internet privileges of Eco Scene had grown somewhat monotonous. I was beginning to feel as though my computer had no real relevance anymore. It had, in fact, become one big doodle book with a keyboard. Obsolete. Much like my position in the organisation.

It comes to something when even trying to find, on Facebook, topless beach photos of the boys you used to fancy at school becomes yawn-inducing.

"Right: The Castle," I snapped myself back to the task in hand. "Interior smells fuse the comforting aroma of fresh linen with the fetid stench of an old man's balls. The barmaid looks like she's been smacked repeatedly with the gypsy stick and décor expertly demonstrates how an amateur designer might replicate the inside of Fritzl's basement."

This one was obviously not written by a fan.

In truth, The Castle wasn't *that* bad; I'd been there with my mate, Beez, a few weeks ago. Granted, it's not a place you'd take the in-laws or, in fact, anyone with a pulse and a conscience, but we'd had an okay night. We'd minced in, sat together around a window table, ordered a Pinot Grigio and clucked away quite happily, tackling many important subjects. Subjects such as how we were now able to fancy Andy from *Emmerdale* since he'd lost the school uniform and gained a ripped torso with enormous, deliciously chewable nipples. The thick-armed (alleged) BNP supporters lining the perimeter of the bar barely even flinched.

Upon continued reading, I deduced that I certainly wasn't as pedantic as some of the members of Pintpage.com who graded their pub's worth on the colour of the Bombardier stout or the diversity of the jukebox. My set of criteria was far better. I *always* graded a straight pub's worth solely on the reaction of the punters when faced with two obvious homosexuals. If there was unavoidable tension but they were decent enough to keep themselves to themselves, then it was a triumphant find and bound to get a revisit. If, however, the hostility was palpable from the start and showed no signs of easing up then you supped up quick, shimmied the wine bottle up your sleeve and prepared yourselves for a dramatic exit.

Beez wouldn't have given a toss about any musical credentials, especially if there was at least one Blondie song played per outing. And he certainly wouldn't ever pander to the pernickety views of the English bitter specialist.

"If there's one thing worse than a picky old queen," he'd say with biting vitriol, "it's a picky old queen who drinks real fucking ale."

We both knew the truth in this, having witnessed it first-hand many times. The years we spent working together behind the bar of one of the oldest gay pubs in London, the Queen Boadicea in Hampstead, had exposed us to every type of queen imaginable. Picky, nonplussed, cheery, vile. We never thought that we would end up like any of them, though I feared I was now dangerously close to becoming the former and the latter simultaneously. My time at the Boadicea had been a carefree one in that blissful season between the end of university and the start of something better and more interesting. After that stolen summer, I had meant to use my degree to hunt for a more substantial career prospect. Beez, on the other hand, had no such aspirations. He had stayed stubbornly put, continuing to live above the pub and have fantastic sex with some of the less-obvious customers. He would spend hours swanning confidently up and down Hampstead High Street like the cock of the walk with a cock that was so overworked it had its own tax code.

"Darling," he'd boast, "whether they like it or not, the Hampsteadians are my fucking neighbours. Therefore, Bonham Carter is my fucking neighbour; Joanna Lumley is also my fucking neighbour. All the rich, hot, City boys who own apartments in Heath Street are my fucking neighbours and since we all share the same postcode we are all of equal status. Okay, the pub subsidises my council tax, but that doesn't mean that I don't deserve a place in this community. After all, I provide a service. I am the one who most of my fucking neighbours are quite happy to keep on fucking."

Good point well made. This sort of thing would never happen to me, of course, living in Hackney. Getting fucked by your neighbours in east London meant getting your post stolen by the crazies next door.

So where next? I'd exhausted all my go-to websites, so I would have to venture into the realm of surfing that had much more scope for cynicism: the online dating services. Maybe I would find a man while simultaneously wasting my own time. Some might say that it was an economical decision.

I logged on, but after twenty minutes with no result, I found myself exhaling tragically and scrolling my mouse down the endless list of headshots. It was like a *Who's Who* catalogue of facial imperfections.

Malik89: looks too desperate, pauly_sunshine: too happy; karlthedarl: too... (what's the best word?) toothy; sammyboy7: massive forehead alert; and muttonjeff_4u: well, if he didn't wash his hair, who knows which of his other body parts had yet to be introduced to soap?

I wished I'd never signed up to this bloody dating website in the first place. Granted, it was free, but it was so depressingly lousy that I couldn't help thinking that *they* (the website) should be paying *me* (the hopeful).

The more I searched, it became painfully clear that in order to snag yourself a guy who wasn't so criminally visibly retarded, you had no other option than to throw money at the problem. Thirty-six pounds fifty a month to be precise, if the more established sites' going rates were anything to go by.

Glancing at this one, the old adage that if you paid peanuts, you got monkeys, had never rung so true.

Take the user, happyboy_27, for instance. He had teeth like the corroded gravestones of the *Wizard of Oz* Munchkins on a face that was so small for his head that it looked like it had been drawn on a balloon. I also noticed that, as if he wasn't unfortunate enough, he was also the proud owner of a morbidly oily t-zone. Yet, somehow happyboy_27 had the brass bollocks to look at my page and ignore it completely.

This made me think; I wondered what sweeping judgements other users made when they looked at *my* profile.

I thought I looked quite passable in the photo. It was, however, taken on the prehistoric office digital camera about three years ago and the yucca plant teetering on the shelf behind me looked like it was growing out of my crown. I also looked much thinner in the jowls *then* than I do now.

Oh well. If the barrage of potential daters were so easily pleased that they were reeled in by this odd portrait, then there was no real need to rely on any of my other assets, so that was something. And if they were that easily pleased, it was all to the good; I didn't have many hobbies of interest and I certainly wasn't what one might class as sex on a stick.

God, being single and hunting for a date in London was soul-destroying. And worse still there was no real comfort in knowing that I wasn't alone in this camp. In fact I'm sure that I was very much in the majority. Right across the capital, I imagined leagues of other fretful hopefuls flicking daily through pages and pages of disparate personal profiles in a ruthless attempt to hand-select a possible soulmate. Sitting there, unchecking the personality adjective boxes as the dates got less and less frequent, with more and more desperados. Just-like-me.

But it was tough, and getting more like job-hunting by the minute. *Man seeking man with brown hair, blue eyes, nothing under five foot eight, with good interpersonal and communication skills. Salary negotiable.*

It was hardly the stuff I imagined great romance novels to be based on. And trying to find true, unequivocal love with someone that you've whittled down from the faces of hundreds of total strangers isn't very Mills and Boon either.

I could always give up and just buy a husband. You know, like those sad, lonely, aging individuals who literally *purchase* another human being in order to disprove the notion that they are repellent to all those who are willing to give it for free. They fill in their card details and days later some poor, broke Taiwanese woman turns up at the door. And, being unaware of our national customs and basic human rights laws, she reluctantly agrees to the verbal contract that she will keep her mouth shut when *Millionaire* is on, give her best shot at a Sunday roast week after week and "close her eyes then if she doesn't like it" in the bedroom.

I continued on and got myself into another lather.

I mean, for God's sake, whoever dreamed up the personal profile template as an effective selection tool on dating websites? Titbits of information that are supposed to summarise each human being as if they are a product on eBay and categorised to make it easier to match theirs with your own. It's like a game of Snap, but with added desperation. The website also suggests you fill the great big comments box with a personal statement. A process which is so demeaning that you feel like scrubbing yourself clean afterwards; washing off the shame that the lone paragraph of ambiguous sales patter greases onto your skin. You know the one; it's so shamefully censored to sound so coolly aloof that it doesn't sound like you at all.

If that wasn't bad enough, you are then required to select one picture to illustrate the text, which always turns out to be a *best of a bad bunch* snap from some filthy holiday on one of the cheaper Greek islands, the only one where you look brown and all your friends have been cleverly Photoshopped out.

And, even more humiliating, you must give a title to your page before going live; one sentence in which to sell yourself in forty characters or less. *Dead Horse, Up For One Last Flog.*

"Found somewhere yet?" Sandra asked without looking up from what appeared to be a pile of company bank statements.

Oh fuck, THAT's what I was meant to be doing; NOT looking for dates or reminiscing about days long since passed, but searching for a venue for next Friday's staff party.

"Not yet," I tentatively replied. "They're all a bit shit around here."

"Well of course they are. This is the City. Every bar here is a soulless meat market, where Brylcreem and brothel creepers are allowed to run amuck. You want to look further up the road in Hoxton if you want somewhere decent. There's nothing worse than a roomful of calculator cock-ends in pressed Armani, jerking themselves off over your peanuts."

Sandra was silver-tongued, as ever.

"Hoxton? With this lot?" I scoffed, nodding towards the back of the office where the Project Managers sat scrutinising whatever plagued their dull computer screens with the same enthusiasm that I did with the ASOS summer sale. "They're all eco-warriors, Sandra; the muesli brigade. They're going to want somewhere where they can use words like *Zen* and *groovy* freely and without irony. I think we're better off going to the Organic Café or something."

"I'm not going anywhere you can eat the furniture." She looked up, coral pink lipstick glistening in the energy-saving light. "So think on."

Her head shot back down and her pencil began to dart frantically across the paper once again. I craned my neck up to see what she was really working on. Not the office finances as I first suspected but, instead, scribing yet another witty anecdote for her precious *Coffee Break* magazine.

"What are you writing?" I asked, knowing full well what the answer would be.

"Look," she said, half-focused on me, half on her script, "if *Coffee Break* didn't want to shell out fifty quid for the story of how my sister caught shingles off the handrail on the London Eye then I'm gonna have to come up with a better one aren't I? And quick – Leon's after some new Nike trainers."

Sandra had thousands upon thousands of carefully constructed, if not slightly embellished, yarns, all perfectly worthy of inclusion within the *air your family laundry for cold, hard cash* pages in the aforementioned rag. The problem was that among the disastrous gastric band horror stories (*it came off inside me and I waited days to poo it out*) and the sob stories of some half-witted, middle-aged, fat woman who gave all her life savings to an eighteen-year-old Turkish busboy, there wasn't really enough space for Sandra.

I suggested that she would do better to proffer some kind of brainwave, like a money-saving idea, or a make-up tip, but apparently waxing your own crack with a bag of IKEA tea lights was a bit too inappropriate for their aged sixty-five and up readership.

Sandra and I had worked together for well over a year in Eco Scene. She as the Finance Assistant and me the Senior Administrator. We got on famously. I didn't know how old she was, in fact no one dared ask, but I would hazard a guess at mid-forties. She always came to work disguised under layers of warpaint so you could never tell and she seemed incredibly young at heart so it didn't seem to matter. She was ageless to me, even though I was, fairly obviously, still relatively "new to thirty".

Sandra's fashion sense, however, was even less easy to pin down to any sort of era, being more experimental than it was of any specific period.

Her clothes, though interesting, were repeatedly soaring over the boundaries of good taste. While residing in the tropical climes of Trinidad in the late nineties, Sandra had been used to wearing bright, garish, dramatically designed garments in all the colours of the free world, but these items clearly didn't transpose all that well to London in the late noughties.

Today, she was sporting one of her more regular outfits; citrus green lamé stretch pants and a bright bat-winged blouse. I suspected it was *meant* to be tiger print. It reminded me more of the weathered rug that we used to have in the hall of my childhood house: splattered with the ancient mud from the tread of a thousand wellington boots.

At the centre of the ensemble was a shell necklace that hung round her neck in defiance; all misshapen and off-colour, as though it were made from some Chilean miner's toenail clippings. Truly inspired or terrifically odd? I had no idea.

Sandra's nails were usually the crowning glory of the look, without ever being cohesive with the rest of it. Unless the cohesion was, indeed, a lack of cohesion. Often, I would sit, amazed at how the Asian technician at Mimi's Nail Emporium on the Holloway Road had managed to detail such an intricate portrait of a lazy Caribbean sunset onto such a small and fiddly piece of acrylic. On this particular day, each nail depicted the same West Indian horizon; an orange sky fading into blue sea with a palm tree silhouette and a white star shooting across the top left corner. I had seen that design time and time again emblazoned on the side of low-rent, tropical-flavoured alcopop bottles in the minimart under my flat. Today, however, I couldn't help feeling that I would rather be living that backdrop for real and not just daydreaming about it while gawping at the paint on Sandra's cuticles in a stuffy office on Old Street.

Clothing aside, Sandra was a real giggle, a good friend and, best of all, she didn't care what anyone thought about her appearance. Even when some kids sang "Private Dancer" at her as she sashayed down the High Street. She just sucked her teeth and soldiered on, not even batting a heavily bejewelled eyelid.

I admired that in a person. I was always fiercely self-conscious if I thought people were talking about me. But then, I was a creative you see. That was part of the reason I was deigning to spend a big portion of my day in this office and the reason why, on any other day, I would be dreading the Windows XP clock in the bottom left corner of my screen ticking up to 17:00.

But thank the sweet Lord that today was Friday, and on Friday there would be no such dread. I could quite happily saunter up Old Compton Street tonight, blissfully incognito, without a second thought of next week, or even tomorrow for that matter. And that was exactly what I would do.

Next website then, I thought, suddenly filled with a minor rush of elation. I returned to the monitor in front of me. *Manz*, the gay online magazine, was my next port of call. I had to decide which bar I should accompany Beez to this evening. Pintpage wouldn't be able to help me with their suggestions as I was pretty sure they didn't review bars where baby-oiled men danced suggestively on the tables.

*

The bottle of cheap vodka clinked against my bag; pay day was two weeks away so I needed to get as pissed as was humanly possible before I went out, to save on beer money in town. I jumped off the number fifty-five bus and onto the pavement opposite my local kebab house. To my delight, the semi-attractive kebab guy was on shift tonight so I flashed him a timid smile. I was actually the least timid person ever, but he didn't need to know that. Cute and bashful was the angle I was going for with this particular target, and it seemed to be working. The irony was that I didn't know whether he was even interested in members of the same sex, but that wasn't going to stop me whoring myself out across the entire length of the kebab house window, just in case I got lucky.

He smiled back, blissfully ignorant that I was mentally replaying that same old mucky little fantasy in my head like so many times before; the hot and sweaty one where I lay in submission while my tight-fitting t-shirt was hacked off by the gargantuan knife he would be wielding, shredding the cotton with the same fervour that he applied to carving ribbons off animal carcass. I say "he" because I genuinely didn't know the guy's name. "He" gives him a certain sexual authority, a being greater than myself, which might upset some humanists. Perhaps, for these purposes, I should give him a name, something non-stereotypical, like Emir.

Emir's smile was always genuine, albeit a little greasy. But in my fantasy his smile was devastating, a knowing grin warning me that within the next two seconds I'd be forced over one of the wobbly Formica restaurant tables, my face planted into the Astroturf and my backside fucked until the table legs underneath us buckled from the pure ferocity of his animal lust. God, that was good.

He was, I guess, moderately attractive, if you like monobrows and pocked skin, and he had (what looked like) a well-toned body underneath those filthy chef's whites. But, while perfect for a dirty little daydream, we could never have a stable future. And, yes, my daily hardcore perving was exciting, but I could never seriously date a man whose main life's achievement involved manoeuvring a great husk of flesh around a four-foot spike; even if he *could* cook. What would I tell my mother, that I'm dating a restaurateur?

An even more earth-shattering image entered my head at that point. One of him at the spike, working and frowning as he cast a glance over his shoulder to me. I was in a hideous apron, up to my elbows in folded paper napkins that are so cheap that they don't seem to absorb anything, frantically Febrezing the dead animal smell out of my skinny jeans.

Shudder.

The more I thought about it, the more intense the shudder.

I think I'd rather go out with a vegetarian than wait in bed for the aroma of chip fat and garlic sauce to slide in next to me of a Saturday night. And Turkish men are notoriously hairy: a condition that would ruin every Dove soap I ever purchased.

I turned the corner into our little driveway and up the small steps to the main door.

Once again the bloody recycling box had been stolen from the front step. Who in the name of sanity would want to steal a big green box full of *Heat* magazines and Sauvignon Blanc bottles? The lunacy of it! I would have to call the council again on Monday. *Monday.* Another shiver shot down my spine, Monday was the last thing I wanted to think about. There were two whole days between that day and this, why couldn't I just block it out? I had bags of time before the old Monday death bell knelled for another week.

"Don't think about it." I scolded myself for the umpteenth time. "Live in the moment and enjoy your evening."

The sentiment was wobbly, but I nodded to myself in affirmation. I slipped the key into the lock and pushed the stiff door open hard, hitting something on the other side. A loud clunk reverberated around the deserted hallway, followed by an even louder smash. I tentatively peered behind the door to see what it was that created such a din. Expecting no less than a hammer in the face from the axe murderer who I may or may not have just de-weaponised, my relief turned to frustration as I gazed upon the scattered glass of a Sauvignon Blanc bottle that had been precariously teetering atop a well-hidden pile of dumped *Heat* magazines. Bloody kids!

Once in, the sound of the vodka bottle unscrewing was like the opening riff to a fantastic pop song; one that you know you're going to enjoy, right to the last, even if you have to repeat it again and again. The flat was empty and I had a whole hour to myself in which to get slowly wankered. I'd have a cheeky one, shower, then a few more while getting ready and listening to some of my old house music singles (I thought 1995 would be tonight's choice year) then I'd call Beez. Beez was certain to be working tonight and I would probably have to travel to Hampstead en route, but that was cool. I had a long and loyal relationship with the Queen Boadicea pub and didn't mind popping in for a bit. Over the years, I had gone from being a mainstay customer to employee (reaching the dizzy heights of Bar Manager, no less) and back to mainstay customer again; something I vowed I would never do when I was twenty and behind that bar. Now, at thirty-one, and as a result of complacency, I'd gone full circle before I'd even had a chance to think about stopping myself.

Oh, it was all right really; I still had friends there, the bar staff were cute and they put up with my banter.

I just had a crippling thought: what if they adopted the same tricks that I did when I was behind that bar? Naming each customer after their favourite tipple and sneering as they leered over at me: *Oh God, Jason don't look now, but Little Miss Kronenbourg with the nipple ring is wearing a t-shirt so tight you can see her Aids.*

I hoped that when they called me Simon to my face they weren't whispering, *Frigid old vodka and coke, cranberry juice on payday, is scratting around for the right change again* to each other.

18

Hell, if they did, I didn't care anyway. I had been all lip at that age too. But *I* can admit that I had been absolutely clueless, totally petrified of other men and had used my bitchiness against others to mask both of these rather sad discrepancies. Now, I wasn't *that* much different, but at least I was in on their little secret.

The vodka was strong but mighty welcome as it slipped down my throat. While I selected appropriate getting-ready music (Livin Joy's "Dreamer" was my old faithful), I reminisced on how much my life had changed since my working days at the Boadicea.

Okay, my social butterfly whirl was slightly less colourful now, but at least my friends *were* friends and not just acquaintances, and my job now wasn't up to much but I guess it paid a lot more. And I was happier... or let's say more content, for argument's sake. I still looked young, one might even say a touch cuter now I'd filled out a bit and was no more the white and pasty, ill-looking boy that I had been all those years ago. I had all my own hair and teeth and a good sense of humour. I got on with most people, granted, some through gritted teeth. I wasn't short of mates both in and out of work and I rented a sizeable flat in a funky area of east London. On paper, life was pretty good, apart from the nagging thing that I wasn't supposed to be thinking about. Not till tomorrow at least when I would have to. The thing that was supposed to be my life's work; my calling that hung over my head like a badly made halo from a kids' nativity play.

I poured more vodka in desperation. I needed a distraction; I was going to need a fat tune, and quick! As I pulled on my skinny jeans and chose what t-shirt to wear, I took another slug of my drink, which was proving to be a comforting friend in my hour of need.

Now, what top? Should it be the Porn Star-sloganed t-shirt, the *Mr. Men* parodying Mr. Sleazy t-shirt (why Simon, why?) or the vintage Sonic the Hedgehog?

Seriously? This was all I had to choose from?

I was half-tempted to fish my expensive Zara one out of the laundry basket for the night, but it was a bit stinky. And even if those on the outside couldn't tell, I would still know that it had spent the last twenty-four hours in a close relationship with one of my pairs of sweaty, used briefs.

Okay, well this was what I had to work with, so what statement did I want to make tonight? I was definitely intending to get pissed; the rapid fall of the vodka tidemark on the inside of the bottle demonstrated *that* plan.

Did I really want to pull?

Would I get the chance if Beez was with me, holding himself with so much sexual confidence that I looked practically Amish. On "pull nights", I would often stand there nervously wringing my hands while he led the men astray like a paedophile at Legoland.

Maybe I should just play it down. I didn't really know if I fancied a stranger hanging round my neck like a cheap necklace; I just wanted a few beers. No awkward goose or quick gobble around the back of a taxi-rank tonight, thanks.

Pulling loses all its appeal after the age of twenty-five anyway. Once you pass that age you only ever attract the old, the lonely and the pitiful. The tragedies who crowbar their moobs into tight-fitting neon singlets with suggestive slogans scrawled across them in lipstick-style fonts. The ones who are still sporting a nineties eyebrow piercing because they're convinced it's a cutting-edge and timeless fashion accessory. Those who know the entire bar staff in the Admiral Duncan by the pet names they've branded them with (all unfunny and crass, I might add). They lech over the flyer boys outside G-A-Y who are only standing in the pissing rain in gold hot pants so they can fund themselves through some nondescript dance academy and join the other hundred or so emaciated chickens who look just like them.

I was far too young to be hanging around that type of guy when sober, but God, were they easy pickings when I was leathered enough.

Tonight, however, I would resist, so the Mr. Sleazy t-shirt went back in the drawer. It should really have gone in the bin.

Porn Star: I only bought this truly vile garment because it had been an overspill from the great sloganed tops influx of 2006. I'd kept it because the stitching and cotton was of a higher quality than that of your common or garden shirt and it did well under a hoodie on a frosty afternoon. I don't even know why I selected it. This type of top was a definite no-no to wear out nowadays, especially if the nightmare scenario presented itself and you got abandoned by your pulling partner while he was getting his Calippo licked in the disabled toilets. There you were, a loner with a grimace on your face and a cry for help across your chest. That one went back in the drawer too.

Although now classed as vintage in some of the East End fashion periodicals, my Sonic the Hedgehog t-shirt still fitted me from the first time around and, therefore, made me feel less *on trend* and more *my age*. I couldn't stand there chatting to a younger guy, knowing that I had not purchased my top from somewhere as fancy as the Hoxton Boutique. Instead it had come free with a Sega Master System from 1994. And the fading frontage wasn't distressed, it was butchered from years of washing with Radion Automatic – now discontinued.

I decided on a plain shirt; white, simple, classic, appropriately adult, just like the blank canvas I was going to be tonight. No plans to do anything other than to have a good time; and if I got teabagged at the end of it, well, it was all to the good.

After my fourth, yes *fourth*, vodka and a quick blast of one of my favourite singles of all time ("Don't Give Me Your Life", Alex Party) I was ready to go. The weather was bound to be cold outside so I reluctantly grabbed my black cardie. It didn't really go but I was *not* going to take my big, cumbersome Superdry coat, which would follow me round like a dead relative, slumped in the corner all night. I grabbed my keys and set out into the hazy, orange, street-lit London night.

Turning the corner, I searched over the road for my kebab guy. I was a little pissed up so a quick smile fix might get me set for the evening's activities. I was snubbed. His focus was forward; far more interested in the girl at the front of the huge queue before him than he was in me, sharpening his knife in the vain hope that she might mistake him for Hugh Jackman's Wolverine in the dim light of the doner grill. Her look was fairly textbook; a face full of slag slap, dirty, crispy blonde hair extensions and a cheap, burnt-orange crop top. From underneath, her bosoms looked like two inflated Sainsbury's bags tethered to a single mattress. Her clothes were a size too small, spilling her flesh out in every direction, just how a blancmange might look if someone threw a kiwi fruit into the middle of it.

She was laughing coarsely at everything he was saying. I wasn't aware that he spoke any English, certainly not to a stand-up comedian's level, and she certainly didn't look intelligent enough to understand Turkish. All the same, he seemed to enjoy watching her bosom, bouncing up and down like two grapefruits in a string bag abandoned on a busy trampoline as she chortled.

What would she look like later on? Not so appealing *then*, I'll bet: plonked in front of some nasty eighties Brat Pack film, scratching her fanny and stuffing chips into her face like a paper shredder with Superdrug lip gloss on. Girls could be so vile, much viler than me; I was far more demure. Or maybe Emir preferred fat, gluttonous women over attractive thirty-something men. What did I care anyway? It wasn't like I was going out with him or anything, but I was pissed off all the same.

*

Hampstead tube was full of the usual: suited barbarians, rich kids out spending mummy's and daddy's money, a few gays and a few tramps – the homeless sort *and* the female sort. It was an eclectic mix of people from various social pecking orders, all moving through the cramped station foyer and filing off in separate directions like trains out of Kings Cross station.

The city elite are all off to Toast, the socialites are off to Quango, the gays to the Queen Boadicea and the tramps off to beg for pocket change outside The Coffee Cup.

The High Street at this time of night had a sort of Parisian feel about it. I'd never actually been to Paris, but I could imagine the lit-up bars and coffee shops full of tourists and locals alike, enjoying the crisp February evening under the pleasant buzz of a busy city offshoot.

A few kids darted in and out of McDonald's, young couples strolled up and down the streets, arm in arm, looking into the windows of Baby Gap and smiling at each other expectantly. Sickening.

For all its bravado, Hampstead still managed to feel homely, safe and, therefore, a comforting place to be on a Friday night. It was almost like a little village oasis situated between the chaotic milieu of Camden and the orthodox Jewish community of Golders Green.

As I neared the Queen Boadicea, I waved to Emma behind the crepe stand located to the side of the building. Emma was a hard-working French girl who'd been making those damned crepes since long before my time. You might say her life was as crepe as they came. She shot me a withered smile back and nodded towards the snakelike queue before her, extending all the way down the road.

It was always the same, give a wealthy community a bit of the continent in London and they'll queue up with their bowls out like starving Victorian children. I rolled my eyes in mock disbelief, climbed the steps and pushed open the door to the pub. Emma and I had performed that same dance of mute exchange for years now, it was a routine.

The Friday night gay Hampstead heat hit me immediately as the bustling sounds of the busy bar filled my ears. Every time I entered the Boadicea, I appreciated it more than I thought I would. I had spent a fair chunk of my adult life within these four walls so it was like a home from home with many memories.

There was the time Beez and I took two Ecstasy pills and tried to put the Christmas decorations up. The result was so disastrous that the manager, Jason, came downstairs in the morning and thought we'd been ransacked. If it weren't for the two bodies curled up on the floor before him, chins sticking out and covered in pine needles, he would have alerted the authorities.

And the day when two skinheads came in for a pint, looked suspicious the whole time and then tried to run off with a wodge of cash from the opened till. Their play was so amateur that they only managed to trip clean over a customer's dog's lead. And though we were pleased to get the money back, it was a sad end for the low-flying Chihuahua who no one thought to seize.

I had grown up as a gay man alongside these people and that is a very powerful connection. Without ever living together or working together, we had developed a different kind of family bond, one that was almost unspoken but always present. Everybody knew me, everybody knew my name: kind of like *Cheers* but without the theme music.

Also like *Cheers* was the bone fide all-star cast.

Over in his usual corner, underneath the nicotine-stained chandelier, was Giles, resplendent in a tweed herringbone county jacket with brown suede elbows. Giles was probably about forty-three and very attractive: daily lager and cigarette smoke intake had greyed his pallor and wrinkled his once taut, pink features but the good looks were still there. He was a very intelligent man, who worked as a senior lab technician in some kind of global conglomerate, testing Aquafresh or something of that ilk. He was a decent guy compared to most of the regulars. He was also the biggest old woman I'd ever met and got so unnecessarily upset over the smallest of issues. And like many of the regulars, he never left the Boadicea for fear that he would fall off the edge of the world.

Back when I'd worked here all those years ago, if the real ale had ever been off for whatever reason, Giles would flap his arms like a psychotic seagull and start to gnaw furiously on the lid of whatever tablets he was taking at the time. That said, he had that sort of reliable security on offer that one associates with a handsome, well-groomed professional with a good job, posh flat and all his own hair and teeth. This was one of the reasons why I had become totally obsessed with him in my first year of employment. I was nineteen, he was thirty-seven. I was smitten, he wasn't.

We ended up kissing a few times before it became obvious that he wasn't going to be introducing me to his friends or presenting me with his spare toothbrush anytime soon. He had a string of meaningful relationships under his belt; each one with a bitter memory, each one with its own soundtrack, each one with a handful of regrets. I, not being long out of the closet and ever so slightly frigid, had only had a hand job on the night bus and that was about it. The fact that we didn't fit was an understatement.

Sitting with Giles was Quinton, a successful barrister who had all the charm and discretion of a sledgehammer to the face. Quinton was the epitome of a dirty old man even though he was only in his mid-thirties. His behaviour towards the younger bar staff after a few beers or a line of coke could only be described as cringe-worthy and hopelessly despairing – a trait which seemed to age him massively. Quinton had the most distinctive laugh in the whole of North London; a noise that a child might make when asked to mimic the sound of a motorbike revving its engine. When you heard that laugh across the hubbub of a Saturday night, you just knew that some poor good-looking, but terribly naïve, foreign visitor was being accosted over by the fag machine and would probably end up face down with a courgette down his boxers in some central London Chambers six hours from now.

Standing next to the bar was Paul. Paul Chisholm was possibly one of the sharpest and wittiest men this side of Watford Gap, but he was also one of the meanest and most poisonous arseholes you could ever wish to meet. He had the ability to reduce anyone to a quivering wreck with a mere slice of his acerbic tongue. This was both infuriating and admirable at the same time but, unfortunately, not the slightest bit enjoyable to witness or experience. Paul was the kind of queen that all of us hoped we would never turn into; one whose ferocious bark masked a rather sad and lonely existence. He was a bitter old Mary whose days comprised sitting at home with the curtains drawn before trudging to the Queen Boadicea to get annihilated. Like the fixtures and fittings in the Boadicea, most of the regulars would shrug off Paul's insults as impersonal twaddle spouted by someone whose battle with his own demons was far worse than anything you were likely to throw into the pot. It was also common knowledge that he was gravely ill and making other people feel like shit was his way of coping and dealing with it. Therefore, hard as it was, one should never take his vitriol seriously.

There he was, regular as clockwork at nine-fifty, slurring into his vodka in a bulky leather coat that looked like the dog had slept on it, offending yet another minority group and laughing at his own jokes.

I sidestepped him to make my usual round of air kissing and catching up with a few of the other habitants before spotting Beez behind the bar, chatting away to Blanche and Alice (or Graham and Freddie to give them their true names).

Blanche and Alice were also regular features of the Boadey, forever holed up in the same position at the bar, punter watching and bitching like two old women manning the bake sale table at a suburban village fete. They were so regular, in fact, that I expected, when one or both of them snuffed it, they would be replaced with two brass replica statues – ones with eyeballs that moved independently, following your arse around the room as if they were still with us.

As well as perving and moaning, Blanche and Alice were also infamous for their historical knowledge of all things Hampstead. Between them, they harboured an extensive mental archive of the most ridiculous, unbelievable gossip ever told. Tales which they both claimed were based on fact but, in truth, were so farfetched that even the *Daily Star* would think twice before printing them, even on a slow news day.

Both well into their sixties, Blanche and Alice (their fishwife aliases) would invariably order an ice-cold bottle of chardonnay that was carefully selected from the bottom shelf. This was so that you had to bend right down to retrieve it while they ogled your posterior from over the tops of their glasses. For one week only, Jason decided to rotate the stock and the chardonnay got moved to the upper shelf, only to be replaced by the Bacardi

Breezers. Blanche and Alice were thus faced with a dilemma, to give up the wine, or give up the free porn. In true fighting spirit, however, rather than forfeit gaping at the various cheeks of each member of staff in turn, they relented and were forced to gulp down the "citrus muck" regardless. They were commendable in defeat, but we never heard the end of it and we were forced to rearrange soon after, for fear of World War Three erupting.

In appearance, they couldn't have been more different. Graham (Blanche) was rotund with a ruddy complexion. He had a little mop of grey hair, perfectly styled like a squirrel's tail on his head, and tiny little currant eyes which looked more like giant, genetically modified grapes behind his big, round, thick-rimmed glasses. His little bristled moustache nestled comfortably beneath his red, hooked nose. Even on the coldest of days, he had little beads of sweat running down his rosy forehead, which he mopped regularly with a perfectly folded handkerchief. He reminded me of a picture of Humpty Dumpty from one of my old colouring books – a little rouge egg in a pair of plaid cotton trousers with a lascivious grin on his face.

In his youth, Graham had been in the army but had his kneecap blasted by a sniper rifle fairly early on. Because of his injury, he was partially mobile and now hobbled along with the aid of a wooden cane. This too was responsible for his weight gain which put more pressure on his damaged knee and so he was honoured by management to have first refusal of the seat nearest to the bar. It was a spot in which he could keep his stick close, his injured leg supported and his panoramic gaze fixed on the beings and doings of the expanse before him. I'd seen Graham out in the street, *sans* stick, chasing an escaped McDonald's voucher up the road quite easily before now, but I kept schtum and humoured his Oscar-winning limping trick all the same.

Freddie (Alice), in contrast, was decidedly smaller. Dressed in sensible corduroys, moccasins and with a jumper tied around his shoulders, he was like a dandy garden gnome. Compared to gentle giant Graham, Freddie was a docile dwarf when perched on his chair and chatting away to all and sundry about any old crap that they were willing to listen to. But Freddie's look was deceptive; he was also known for having a much darker, venomous side. If you were ever unfortunate enough to fall foul of his unpredictable temper, the most vicious, odious comments would come spitting out of his mouth as soon as your back was turned. I'd witnessed this before and it wasn't palatable. I did, however, think that words seemed to come cheap to Freddie, so his scorn was rarely more than glorified bitching. Beez and I, however, had a lifetime get out of jail free card as we always lavished him with the necessary carefully monitored attention, tailor-made to keep the wolf from any kind of door.

Beez spotted me emerging from the throng of bodies.

"Sweetheart," he cooed, jumping up and interrupting the aforementioned spectators who were mentally sizing up Beez's backside like two glacial-eyed kittens might two balls of wool. "What's going on with my darling this evening?"

"Hello babes, not much this end, bit pissed. What time are you here till?" I smiled sweetly at Blanche and Alice, who had decided that they were now part of the conversation.

"I'm off at nine actually, thank God," Beez said, "got some new guy coming in for an introductory thingy and there'll be too many bods. Besides, I want to get off and buy you a drink. You sound like you need one after yesterday. What a shit!"

"We're not talking about that tonight, Beez, I need to erase it from my mind while I've got some time to myself, I'll worry about it tomorrow," I grimaced.

Blanche and Alice's eyes widened at the thought of the Holy Grail: new gossip that was shrouded in mystery.

"No worries love, totally get it. Take a pew, chat with Hinge and Bracket here, I'll get you a Smirnoff. Double? Lime? Soda?"

"Yes, yes and yes, please." I smiled, I'd sobered up somewhat since the last four so a double would really hit the spot.

I moved round and kissed Blanche and Alice respectively on each cheek. Freddie's skin was soft like my grandmother's hands after a lifetime of using Imperial Leather soap. Graham's was more like a Triceratops.

"Alright girl, how are ya?" Graham asked in his regional drawl.

"Not bad." I slid in between them as Freddie turned his chair round, his hands clasped in his lap to signify that he was mid-story.

"Evening Aunty Freddie. Any news?" I asked.

"Not really. Our local, The Swan, is having a refurb. The apartment in Spain has dropped a bit on the buyers' market. Doris Day is doing a new record. The usual stuff," Freddie said. I didn't know whether I found it usual or unusual: none of it meant anything whatsoever to me.

"So no gossip then?" I had to ask. It was like a red rag to a tiny, queer bull.

"Well, since you ask," his pace slowed down before he revved the engine, "I was just telling Graham about the new manager of the Shufflewicks Bar in Camden."

"The one above the Black Cap. What about him?"

"Rumour has it," Freddie continued, leaning forward as if it were a piece of government-protected information that should not be disclosed at any cost, "he's a dog."

"Not very good-looking then?" I screwed up my face in disgust.

"No, I mean he's an actual dog."

30

My least dumbfounded face came into its own.

"Apparently the previous sleeping partner died very suddenly, concussed by his own electric hair-clippers. Anyway, it was written in his will and testament that all his worldly belongings, including the pub, should be left to his Alsatian."

"No!" Graham had a genuine look of surprise on his face. He got in closer so as not to miss a second while I worked overtime to try and hide my amusement.

"Apparently, when the staff have gone home at night, the dog's given a set of keys and left to lock up on its own."

*

"Fuck off!" Beez said, straightening up the line of coke on the CD case with my Blockbuster rental card.

"I shit you not," I laughed. "They actually believe that this dog has its own set of keys and checks the toilets and locks up the pub on its own at night."

"And then what, catches the last half-hour in the club downstairs?"

"Well, it wouldn't be *that* out of place; sniffing bumholes and licking itself in public. That's normal practice in there."

Beez snorted. "I'm sorry I missed that one; it's another Alice classic."

He rolled a ten pound note into a straw before bending over and snorting the line up his right nostril. He lifted his head up and back, holding his sinuses.

"I had to keep on smiling and nodding as though I *actually* believed them; it's so difficult when they talk such crap."

I accepted the straw and also bent down to snort my line. It slid up my nostril with ease and settled with a slight tingle at the bridge of my nose.

"It's good stuff this, got it off Paul's guy and he's always fucked."

Beez unravelled the note and stuffed it in his back pocket, standing up to scan the room for the various ingredients he needed to make up the night.

His bedroom was a simple, sparsely decorated space that was only really used for sleeping off hangovers and entertaining the odd visitor. It wasn't really decked out for any other activity, save for a bit of drug paraphernalia which was stored away in the goody cupboard for special occasions like tonight. To his credit, there were a few pictures of him on the wall in various states of undress to brighten the place up. One of him at his brother's graduation, one of him and a group outside some dilapidated African combi van and one of him at Glastonbury wearing a Rasta hat toking on a big spliff, surrounded by similar youths with dreadlocks and bongo drums of varying sizes. Beez had managed to fuck the chief bongo player senseless that night; he'd been impressed by both the size of his hands and the dexterity of his wrists while he watched him play a Gypsy Kings set around the fire. Beez had downed two bottles of warm cider and pounced instantly. "Came like a fucking garden sprinkler babes."

There were also a few random clothes scattered here and there, but he didn't really have the furniture or inclination to kit out a room. Beez always said that if he ever needed to pack up and fuck off somewhere then he could probably fit all his worldly possessions onto a small homemade raft, with enough room left over for a second-hand bass guitar and a hot oarsman to go down on. Beez was a total nomad, preferring the fat of the land to the bleak shadow of the concrete city. Hampstead, however, was a suitable compromise. As long as he was near a substantial stretch of green (the

Heath) where he could escape to when things got heavy, life would sort itself out.

Though he had the soul of a drifter, Beez actually had a brilliant academic brain, which was something he preferred to play down. He'd been sent away to private college when he was eleven before reading Environmental Science at Oxford. Now, at thirty-two, and after a string of unsuccessful career moves on the environmental charity circuit, he decided that he wasn't interested in holding down a full-time office job. Instead he settled for the flexibility of bar work which kept a roof over his head, money in his pocket and time to go to festivals, marches and day-long benders.

Beez, Nathaniel Beasley, was tall and devastatingly handsome with a big explosion of curly, golden blonde hair, untidily placed atop a beautifully structured face. He had the kind of hair that I liked to call Tower Hamlets since no matter how rough round the edges it was, it just seemed to work. His skin was the universally envied olive kind that looked permanently sun-kissed and he wore simple, unkempt clothes of an earthy hue. His straw hats, deck shoes and linen blazers were all slightly off-colour and peppered with holes of disparate sizes. His look was a sort of *Brideshead Revisited* chic, which guys fell over themselves for, and his eyes were a bright, electrifying blue. He was an utter vision – a picture of rugged masculinity mixed with an effortless cool that left a trail of broken hearts stretching from Camden to Camberwell. To me, he was just my mate, Beez.

I can't remember ever fancying him; I had always admired him more. The moment I clapped eyes on him, I had mentally selected him as my best friend. It had been a different kind of love at first sight and I was more than happy with this arrangement. I was the only one who would ever be truly loved by Beez. Greater men had tried, but when it came down to it, I would always be in his affections.

In my first week at the pub, Beez had been there for at least six months already and had graciously taken me under his wing. I'd had no previous bar experience and was forever making schoolboy errors, which meant I was berated continuously by the impatient harridans over the other side of the bar. Beez, like a white knight, would always rush to my aid.

"Hey, lay off bitches, the snakes on your heads are making him nervous," he would snarl.

Ever since, we had become inseparable. Nowadays, although we led very different lives and often had conflicting schedules, we still made the utmost effort to meet up at least once a week, something I looked forward to more than anything else in my sorry little life.

"Come on," Beez said, stuffing his phone into his pocket. "Let's get going, Old Compton Street will be like Hillsborough tonight."

I stood up, enjoying the cokey head rush.

"Where first?" I asked, the druggy euphoria trickling down through my system. "Hey, this IS good shit. Much better than that washing powder you scored last week."

"I can't get it right every time, bitch. I should never have listened to that Scottish prick anyway. I don't usually buy off people I don't know. Besides, when does Miss Critical ever score for the team, eh?"

"My connections aren't dodgy enough! Where shall we start anyway?"

"Tube to Tottenham Court Road, Rupert Street, The Yard and The Duke of Wellington. If we're still standing then we can go to CXR and laugh at the paedos."

"Not on the pull tonight then?"

"What, in CXR? Darling, if I wanted to board a sad old cruiser, I'd book a week on Jane McDonald's. Anyway, it's not high on the agenda tonight sweetheart, YOU are. Are you sure everything's okay?"

"We're not talking about it tonight, I've already told you." I seemed to be pleading with him for some reason.

"Aw, Peach," Beez stroked my head. "Another line?"

I smiled.

2

Old Compton Street on a Friday night was a great place to be anyway, but it was even better when you were off your head. The music pumped through each open doorway, the guys, from all colours of the gay rainbow, strutting up and down the pavement. The Queens, the Bears, the Twinks, all labelled and ready for a good time.

Me? I was already having a good night. We'd stayed at the Boadicea for two more lines, a shot of Sambuca and a dance to Ultra Nate ("Free: Mood 2 Swing Edit") and now I was buzzing and up for it. Every time we partied in Old Compton Street it was fairly inevitable that Beez would know at least three people from separate (or grouped) intimate encounters, either walking past or supping a pint outside one of the many watering holes.

I knew a few by face from the Boadicea but no one really to say hello to. I just puffed on my B&H Silver, taking in the sights and sounds of England's most cosmopolitan gay street. I walked alongside him, gurning like a village idiot through the copious amounts of booze and Charlie that I had consumed.

Beez led the way, smiling at cuties and nodding at the doormen, his charm and confidence shining out of him as if he were some kind of ethereal prince. Some people sniped that Beez reckoned he owned this street, but he wasn't that arrogant. He was everyone's buddy and no objection to that fact would change that in him. And as we both sashayed towards Rupert Street, I could clearly see heads turning in Beez's direction – the skinhead outside Prowler, the twink walking towards us. Hell, even the drag queen bumming a light outside of Madame Jojo's did a pavement dance to hide her oncoming erection. I let out a slight and rather pathetic sigh.

"If only they were looking at me," I thought.

I didn't dare consider that somewhere, in the distance, someone might have been.

*

Rupert Street was absolutely packed with the Old Compton Queen elite, resplendent in Superdry, Ted Baker and Diesel, all holding puny glasses with barely a shot of vodka in them, two mini-straws and a slice of lime. I hated that. If you're going out for a drink, get a real bloody drink! Not some fancy-schmancy bollocks that takes three hours to make, when in reality it's just a shot of vodka with some apricot preserve in it.

The customers were looking me up and down as I entered, being their usual welcoming selves. Even though I was over thirty, I still felt like a kid in here. It was the kind of place where you felt as though you were always upsetting people by not acting in a responsible enough manner. There they were, scanning each new arrival with their eyes and casting aspersions on the spot. They were so merciless with their judgement that I had to hold myself back from apologising to the doorman for being there in the first place.

There was no love in this room. It was as if the Stonewall riots had never happened.

Beez made a beeline for the bar and I made a getaway for downstairs. I knew the waterfall in the gent's toilets might chill my now actually quite wired head. As I descended the stairs, I passed a guy who tossed a confident, cock-eyed leer in my direction. Me being me, I couldn't resist a closer inspection. His hair was shoulder-length and blonde, scraped back with hard gel and moulded into a kind of Johnny Bravo quiff. It looked quite funky.

At first his pin-striped trousers, black braces and white vest combo looked kind of sexy in a deconstructed gangster sort of way; his rock-hard nipples were protruding through the cotton so I could see that he definitely had a shapely, ripped torso underneath. A tremor began to ripple through my underpants. However, when I stepped a little further in, to bat back with an equally testosterone-fuelled leer, the details close up weren't as flattering. I could actually see where this guy had plucked his eyebrows; the pallor of the skin below the brow was white when compared to the orange foundation that had been haphazardly trowelled onto the rest of his face. He looked like a clown who'd packed the wrong make-up bag. I turned away immediately. In a split second I'd been aroused then repulsed and it was too much to handle on coke.

I wrenched open the toilet door and sat on the lid, jamming my spinning head into my clammy hands. God, 2012 and look what the world has come to, grown men plucking their eyebrows and then slathering themselves with so much fake tan that they look like a glass of Tropicana with stick-on eyes. I expected to see that kind of beauty regime on the women who thumbed a lift down Whitechapel, but not in Rupert Street. Maybe I was wrong; perhaps he had a skin condition.

"Hello?" There was a rap at the door.

"Someone's in here," I said.

"Sorry, I thought my mate was in there," the voice said on the other side of the door.

I was rushing now and before I knew what I was doing I'd forced open the lock and swung open the door.

"Who's your mate?" What the hell was I doing?

A guy stood there, aghast.

"Hey, man, I didn't mean for you to come out, you can finish up."

"No, I'm not using it; it's just a bit busy upstairs. I've just come down to sort my head out."

He was tall and had clippered hair, fairly average-looking, nice eyes I guess. God, now *I* was scanning. It must have been the environment.

"Had a bit too much have you?" he asked; the statement was clear of criticism.

"A little bit of vodka, far too much coke."

"Oh I see." As he said this, his smile broadened across his face showing the most beautiful set of pearly whites I'd ever seen. In fact, the smile was beautiful all round. "I plan to be that way soon, only just got out of work though." His accent was definitely local.

"Yeah, what do you do?" I think I was flirting. If you call leaning into one hip flirting.

"I'm a personal trainer."

"And you've just finished? Were you wiping down the handlebars and replacing the barbells?"

The guy laughed. "That's a gym instructor. I only train personal clients."

I raised an eyebrow.

"Well now, that's a form of prostitution." Not funny. Eeek! He laughed. Phew. It was a warm laugh, sincere and masculine. The more he laughed, the more he smiled; the more he smiled, the more attractive he became. Being a personal trainer too, must mean that the present was as good as the wrapping.

It suddenly occurred to both of us that we were conducting a flirtatious exchange in a toilet doorway, which was a bit grim, so I shuffled over to the sink. As I did, I brushed past him, detecting a hit of Polo Sport – how appropriate, I thought. I bet he doesn't drink alcohol, just a protein shake with a cocktail cherry in it. I forgot that I couldn't stand people who don't drink alcohol.

"So, are you here on your own?" He turned to face me.

"I'm here with one mate, he's upstairs with my drink," I splashed water cack-handedly onto my hands, soaking my t-shirt.

"Cool, you staying here or..."

"We'll go to a few places in this area I expect." Subconsciously, I wiped my hands on my jeans in a most unladylike fashion, completely forgetting where I was. The guy leant over to kiss me lightly on the cheek, which took me by complete surprise and I inadvertently touched his cock. He didn't flinch.

"Well it was nice to meet you, I'm Scott." As he pulled away, I felt slightly awkward, I needed to go.

"And I'm ... late,"

I smiled and gingerly motioned away, but I could feel his eyes boring into my back as I left and walked down the small corridor. I couldn't do it, I had to turn back. He quickly looked down as if he'd been busted.

"Simon, my name's Simon." I gave a small smile, turned on my heel and carried on walking without looking back.

If I'd learnt anything from Blanche and Alice then I'd have a fair idea where Scott was now looking. These kinds of scenes never happen in real life, only in chick-flicks with a strong female lead. As far as I remember, it happened just like that...

*

After a round of free Sambucas in Rupert Street (Beez had blown the barman once and been very honest in giving him his diamante Prince Albert back when it came off in his mouth) and a few more in The Yard, we settled for a line and a last few in the Duke of Wellington. By now I was starting to slur and wobble as I picked my way through the smokers on the steps outside. I didn't very much like stabilising myself against exposed brick so we made our way indoors.

We managed to steal a table from a group who had just left and sat looking out of the window. The conversation had beached somewhat and we found ourselves both focusing on a rather large lady, dressed in fuchsia, who was waiting in the rain under a similarly pink umbrella at the stage door of the Queen's Theatre opposite. She seemed like some kind of annoying tourist type, waiting expectantly for one of the star turns from *Les Miserables* to reluctantly scrawl their name across her programme. The thing about *Les Miserables* is that there *are* no star turns. A passer-by could sign it and she wouldn't know the difference. She was much taller than the majority of the crowd of three that had formed in front of her and, it seemed, she'd have no trouble in batting them out of the way when the situation presented itself.

"It's sad isn't it," Beez observed through a squinted eye. "That woman there is stood, expecting a load of nineteenth-century French townsfolk to come out of that door. The cast are all walking past her in jeans and she's not even noticed. She's also dressed like a big cock."

"Well, some people believe that the characters they see on stage are real people don't they? They're gutted when they realise they've just been watching everyday actors play out a fictitious story in silly wigs and funny shoes."

I was just about managing my sentences at a slower pace but the word fictitious had proved to be a bit of a challenge. I don't know why I chose it, trying to be clever as per.

"What about those dullards who watch *EastEnders* and think that Pat is a real person and that a puny east London square is big enough to hold a bookie's, a minimart, a launderette, a café, a boxing ring…"

"A nightclub…"

"Restaurant, car lot…"

"The Arches, Queen Vic…"

"Beauty salon…. Stupid isn't it?"

"I can see why people do it." Beez wound the tip of his finger around the rim of his glass.

"People need escape from their boring lives, they take comfort in the belief that a more entertaining parallel universe is happening out there somewhere."

I mused a while.

"I want to be an entertainer." My eyelashes were practically resting on my glass at this point. "I always have."

"What? Just so people like that heifer out there can throw themselves at you?"

"Fuck off, Beez! You know I'm a born entertainer. There's nothing like the thrill of an audience reaction. It's better than sex to me."

I purposefully ignored Beez's audible scoff.

"It is the truth and that's why I'm going to stick it out." I tapped my glass affirmatively to reinforce my point.

"I thought we weren't talking about that tonight."

"No, I know I said that but I want to be able to talk about it if I want to, with you, coz you're my best friend and I…"

"And you're mine, but I think I might need another line if you're going to plunge into this sentimental old yak." He winked.

Beez slid off his stool and made for the toilet door on unsteady footing. I continued to stare gormlessly through the window at the driving rain and at Mrs. Pink who was commendably braving the weather and clutching her programme, committed to the cause. Something had clearly moved her in that theatre and I concurred: *Les Miserables* was very moving. I once went with my friend and totally pissed her off by blubbing into her shoulder throughout the entire final hour.

Was it the songs that had spurred this woman on, the majesty of a West End show, the costumes or the hammy acting? Whatever it was, she was managing to single-handedly affirm the reason why I was putting myself through the self-proclaimed hell that I was currently trying my damnedest to ignore. Her kind of people were responsible for the career choices I had made, the path that I was meant to be carving out for myself, my sanity, my life. Shit this coke was good!

Beez came back to the table looking a bit more bright-eyed and sprightly.

"Go on then cupcake, tell all."

I waved my hand in the air, signifying my shift in focus. "I don't want to talk about it. I couldn't. It will kill my buzz. I'm going for a fag now since the rain's holding off."

I slumped off the barstool onto a new-born calf's legs, apparently, just managing to stagger over to the side door and fling it open. The cold air hit me clean in the face and sobered me up just enough to feel the second rush of the latter cocaine hit. Pulling out a cigarette from my jeans pocket, I stole a quick look back at Mrs. Pink – my new fascination who was, thankfully, now triumphant in having her programme autographed by some guy who looked so desperate to get away he was practically hopping from foot to foot.

I hadn't noticed them at first, but little more than three metres away from this scene stood an older-looking guy and a teenage boy, both huddled together under a smaller umbrella, presumably waiting for Mrs. Pink to hurry up with her schoolgirl pantomime. They were both visibly shivering as they attempted to seek shelter from the last few drops of the previous downpour, yet they waited patiently, smiling away. They must have spent a good ten minutes in that monsoon, waiting for a dumb autograph off some bloke who could have been the lighting guy for all they knew; he certainly didn't have the gait of someone acting as principal cast. A three-person-strong family standing in the pissing rain for the sole purpose of leaving with a piece of Les Miserables to call their own, no doubt to show friends and neighbours, to wheel out at family gatherings and have framed and placed over the mantelpiece in their modest suburban townhouse. It would be hard evidence of how being present at such a fantastic show had been the best birthday gift ever for all involved. With a cigarette loosely hanging out of my mouth, I watched as she waddled excitedly back to her family, clutching the signed book with both hands like a prize trophy.

At that moment, and as if by some strange gravitational pull, her head slowly rotated in my direction and her eyes met mine. Without any kind of interjection, she allowed herself to stare right at me, smiling like a little girl on Christmas Day.

It was an exuberant, sincere smile that seemed to stretch, unwavering through the curls of smoke from the cigarettes around us and the final little droplets of rain. She gripped the booklet tighter as the exhilaration spread further across her face, her eyes never moving from their fixation into mine. It was so bizarre that I found myself grinning back at her like a simpleton without a thought in his head. From across the sodden London backdrop, we shared an electric moment. Me agog; her overjoyed that she had singled out a kindred spirit from all the other people littering the busy street. As the time passed, my mouth still hanging open like a dead mackerel, I felt the world halt: everything just slowed down, colours and images around me blurred and sounds all but stopped. It was like Mrs. Pink and I were the only people on earth.

"Simon?" A familiar voice made me jump nearly three feet into the air. Oh God, it was that guy from before.

"Oh shit, Scott."

I fought to regain composure but failed miserably. I couldn't ignore that in the corner of my eye Mrs. Pink and family were waddling away from me, like a line of happy mallards. What had just happened? I shook myself.

"I mean, Scott. Fancy seeing you here" I noticed that I was still wrestling a lighter from my front pocket with little success. The thrill of seeing him and his award-winning smile had catapulted the druggy euphoria back into my conscious, along with all the necessary adrenaline-laced side effects. A lurch from my belly descended into my groin. I won the lighter battle and finally lit my cigarette. Scott remained silent as I flapped about like an agitated flamingo before him.

"You," I said without thinking, allowing my big mouth to run away without my brain, "have the most fucking beautiful smile I have ever, ever, seen."

What-did-I-just-say? In panic, I sucked hard on my cigarette, the smoke hitting the back of my throat like liquid fire. Oh God, not the Sambuca.

"Thanks." He blushed, though he looked more uncomfortable than anything else. "I really don't know what to..."

But it was too late, I felt ill suddenly and could not hold back any longer. I spun round and vomited all over the steps and, I realised quickly, over the shoes of at least three unhappy looking punters behind me.

3

It was normally around 4pm on a Saturday afternoon when what I called "the fear" descended upon me. Fear being the perfect word to describe the dread that comes with recalling the grim details of what had happened the night before while under the influence of booze and/or recreational drugs. Fortunately, at only half ten, I was still feeling the effects of said narcotics and, though delicate, I was also surprisingly cheery. The taste of stale vodka flavoured my mouth with a rancid film, coating every taste bud. My head was awash with erratic, blurred memories of last night and I mentally tried to tape back together those that the demon drink had knocked out of sequence.

I remembered vomiting quite violently up against the wall of the Duke of Wellington, scrutinised by the cuter-by-the-minute guy, Scott, who had stooped over me to check that I was okay and ask if I wanted water. He'd also been good enough to defuse the tension between me and the prissy bitch behind who'd shrieked as he narrowly dodged the spray of undigested slurry that poured from my mouth straight towards his brogues. I was pretty sure that afterwards I had started (oh no) *crying* but, thankfully, I don't remember looking up and revealing the hysteria written in tear tracks down my big red face. Scott must have thought that, not only could I not hold my drink but that I clearly couldn't hold my Class As either. Maybe he had fancied me up to that point, but once he had seen my pavement pizza slithering into the drainage system of Old Compton Street, any possibility of an attraction between us had been snuffed out there and then. Oh God, he could have thought anything; I didn't really care, he was only a good-looking stranger. I was more concerned about vomming in the middle of Soho in front of a *group* of good-looking strangers. Beez would surely have a bitch fit.

Beez had, in fact, been fairly nonchalant, popping his head around the door after the sorry incident and rolling his eyes.

"Oh God, oil spill," he cooed. "Come on you, bottle of water and chewing gum."

"Are you his friend?" Scott had asked. "Will you see him home?"

"Fuck no!" Beez was insulted. "You vom, you move on – the night's still young."

"Don't you think he needs to get into bed?"

"He'll be alright, just needs a breath of fresh air and a tequila. Do you know each other?"

"I guess. Well, not really. I mean, I met him in Rupert Street, tonight."

"I see," said Beez, taking Scott in from head to toe. "Well now you literally know our boy inside – and out," he nodded towards the vomit, "do you have his number?"

"Er, no. I don't think so."

Had I been fully functional, I would have been mortified. I tried to whimper words of objection before the sentences amalgamated into garbled nonsense.

"Oh God," Beez scoffed as he hoiked me up against his shoulder. "It sounds like Stephen Hawking's batteries have died. Look, I'm going to get this one sorted and then hopefully go to CXR. Join us in there in about half an hour? Hopefully by then his sanity bus may have reached somewhere approaching normal. Laters."

From there, I remember staggering down the road, firmly supported by Beez's arm round my shoulder.

"Oooh, bad move darling," Beez had whispered into my ear. "Now he knows you don't chew your sweetcorn."

*

After the aforementioned bottle of water, Beez had been right, I was starting to feel a bit more present, the road had stopped spinning and some of the horror of the previous hour had started to creep in.

"I vommed," I said in despair, close to pure vodka tears. "I fucking vommed."

"Oh darling, get over it," Beez was too busy sorting out our free entry passes into CXR. "You did it, he saw it, it's done. In suburbia, they shit in the street. At least your chunder missed his trainers. I mean, nice enough looking but trainers on a Friday?"

"He's a personal trainer."

"No excuse for shoddy footwear, darling. It's a basic rule. Anyway, we'll find out his worth later on if he turns up won't we?"

"I can't believe you gave him my bloody number!"

"It was a knee-jerk reaction. Your little performance was starting to generate a crowd. I got nervous."

"Okay, alright, let's just go in. Plonk me somewhere in a corner and let me sober up."

"That's the idea," Beez snorted.

*

The doormen at CXR looked like two gargoyles at the gates of hell: all beard, man tits and hands like gardening forks. Beez flashed the passes at them and pushed me straight through as they nodded in bewilderment. The whole thing had happened so fast that they hadn't realised we'd just got us in free with two Morrisons receipts.

48

CXR was a strange den, a natural habitat of that elusive breed: the lone male cruiser. They were exhibited here like a row of collectable figurines, in their variable shapes, sizes and colours, dressed mostly in tight jeans and big army boots with shaved heads and dark tattoos, and with more metal attached to various protruding body parts than the key cupboard of a Bangkok whorehouse.

They held their glasses like they might hold the hind leg of a disobedient Staffordshire Bull Terrier, and over the top of their pints they gave frantic eye signals to fellow prowlers in their focal range; *Here's one, tight hole, pierced cock, I'll take the goal end.*

They stalked through the smoky space, weaving in and out of their prey like big cats, waiting to ensnare a willing target and thrust them to submission with their hard, throbbing love sticks, so full of testosterone and spunk that they had tide marks inside their eyeballs.

The dance floor was half made up of these oversexed sexual predators, and half of men with average hormone levels. It was like the stage of some crazy social experiment, aiming to assess whether the predatory lot could behave themselves in a civilised environment. However, you're likely to see more restraint in the fox who was left in charge of a henhouse. As soon as the full twelve-inch cut of Donna Summers' "Love To Love You Baby" was spun by the DJ, all inhibition was thrown at the wall. Pervy perspiration levels shot up like rockets and while some of the cruisers simply spontaneously combusted on the spot, the less discreet were so overcome with desire they clambered over one another to stick their dick into the nearest available slot. And that's no good for the poor cigarette machine.

Tonight, the place was crawling with them, circling the dance floor, circling each other, just loitering long enough in one space to survey the area quickly for pieces of fresh meat to climb on and pummel, then moving on to

49

somewhere new if there was no one hopeless enough that they couldn't find a real date.

My first drinks here as a young twenty-year-old had been so petrifying that my testicles instantly climbed up into my body to seek refuge as soon as I walked through the door. I didn't want to be pounced upon immediately, gorged all over like a gnawed pencil and then left, deflowered with a rectum like a chewed fig. I remember that first walk around the perimeter of the dance floor, a thousand eyes watching me from the darkness like I was in some kind of African cannibal film from the seventies. I'd half expected someone to strike up a few chords of "Duelling Banjos" just to set the scene.

Nowadays, I barely regarded the cruisers. It was just the nature of the CXR beast. We had evolved into two packs, still able to co-exist in one space so long as one didn't steal the other pack's trade.

I made straight for the toilet again. If Scott did turn up, I wanted to make sure I at least attempted to look attractive under the circumstances. At present, I must look like shit on the proverbial shovel.

If the dance floor was cruise central then the toilets were semen HQ. The ambience was so seedy that I wouldn't be surprised if at least one filthy, underground porno flick had been filmed against these cold, hard tiles. You could consider yourself lucky if you found the one cubicle that hadn't got its own personal set of spy holes, created with care by a masonry drill brought especially from home. The hellish smell could make one's eyes water. It was the collective aroma of an unwashed floor, the blocked toilet bowls brimming with sour, brownish liquid and the cracked and grubby urinals that were covered in aggressive shreds of gaffer tape. It was an odour that rested somewhere between the rancid old meat of the Ridley Road Market litter bins and hell itself. I wondered how any porn "performer" could maintain an erection in such hideous conditions but I guess some people found it hard to fuck unless surrounded by the whiff of stale old piss and mildew. As far as dingy cottaging spots went, it probably only just trumped one of those French campsite toilets with a hole in the floor, littered with the acrid turds that just missed the bull's eye. And, to be honest, most of the upstairs customers were so rampant they would probably have signed up to get their jollies in the bathroom of 25 Cromwell Street if push came to shove.

It was the same story tonight. The queue for the cubicles was predictably long; possibly because nobody wanted their balls sized up by the over-zealous old pervert camped out by the hand-dryers. He was always there, waggling his member like someone shaking the last bit out of a Heinz ketchup bottle.

I moved up to the sink; the plughole was blocked with what looked like a substantial mix of gob and stagnant seawater. I peeked into the cracked mirror streaked with God only knows what bodily fluid. As I looked down, I noticed a familiar sight.

Why was it that, no matter what night you were in here, whatever time – busy or dead, there was always half a pint of flat, warm, stagnant lager perched next to the bowl?

Whose was it? What was it doing there? It was enough to put you off alcohol for good. And why was it that whenever I was at home, eating something delicate like eggs or aromatic fish, my mind would inevitably flash back to the image of that bloody lager and I would balk at the mere thought, unable to carry on.

Under the neon light and through the creamy streaks, I didn't look too bad. Obviously there was room for improvement, a light dust of powder and a bit of Carmex would have sorted it but, since I was void of these items, this would have to do. Besides, the bar upstairs was quite dark so hopefully

Scott wouldn't notice the state of the bedraggled old husk staring back at him through the dim flare of the CXR fridge lights. It was fortunate that Beez had insisted I buy a disposable toothbrush so I could, rather ostentatiously, brush my teeth with Evian water before we moved on. At least the smell was fresh, even if the look wasn't.

Sod it, if he wasn't interested in me like this then he wasn't worth bothering with anyway. Was it Marilyn Monroe who said, if you can't accept me at my worst, you don't deserve me at my best?

If I was going to be with anyone, it should be someone who could cope with me in all kinds of states because, God knows, they'd have to get used to it. And fuck *them* if they couldn't.

Elsewhere, Beez had found a seat in the upstairs bar, overlooking the dance floor below. Up here it looked as though it had been converted from an old church, with its uncomfortable pews and ecclesiastical-looking architecture. I'm sure that having thirty or so sodomites dancing to Madonna in an ex-House of the Lord would upset a few Christians if they ever found out. They're forsaking God in his own front room.

I had only asked for a cola but it tasted suspiciously boozy. I was pleased, in secret.

The music was heavy and I didn't really want to dance, but Beez and I made a pact that if the DJ played Rihanna then we would head straight to the floor, no questions.

"So, you think this guy will turn up?" Beez asked, using the two receipts that had got us in to brush the shit off the table onto the heavily stained, sticky carpet.

"I dunno, you saw him, I was too busy wiping the orange trail of goo from my mouth."

"Mate, if he was interested, he was interested. I don't think a bit of loose stomach lining will make any difference. You said yourself that you'd told him you were a bit fucked."

"I think I said something about him having a beautiful smile, oh God, kill me know."

"Oh man up! You're bound to get a recall darling. Look at you. You're gorgeous, talented and kind. You're a star. Stop being so bloody hard on yourself all the time."

I could feel an emotional five minutes coming on, Beez was starting to gurn and I could tell what was next: "I remember when we first started working together and you were this tiny, little nervous thing, forever dropping glasses, asking about regulated breaks, pronouncing Merlot with a T and Claret without. They all thought you were such a little prissy, brainless pretty boy – but I knew."

"Knew what?"

"That you were just a timid bird, with beautiful, elegant wings just waiting for the opportunity to outstretch, rise up and circle the heavens with your colourful plumage." He played with my hair as he talked. It was sweet.

"Fuck off Beez, that's the coke talking. I'm not a bird."

"Maybe it is the coke, but it's the truth. I love you man. You deserve to be happy. I want to see you happy before I go away." There was an eerie silence as he smiled a lopsided, half-daft grin. I eyed him with suspicion.

"Hold on, where are *you* going?" I held off panicking as Beez had been known to glorify the odd festival trip.

"Well, I wanted to tell you something tonight but I've been putting it off."

"Tell me what?"

"And then, with the whole sick drama..."

"Nathanial Beasley!" I only first-named him when I was serious.

"I wanted to tell you that... that I'm going to Australia for six months."

"WHAT?" This had come from absolutely nowhere.

"Yeah, I'm going to stay with an old uni friend who's just opened a surf school, he wants me to teach a bit out there."

"Teach what? You can't surf."

"I can! I tried it once down in Newquay. It wasn't massively successful since I fell off the board and landed face down in a rock pool. I had to have an anemone surgically removed from my eyebrow. It's how I got that scar." I was so taken aback that I couldn't even laugh at him thrusting his brow in my direction.

"But hey, he doesn't need to know that till I'm there and then he can't very well send me back, can he?"

"He could."

"He can't coz I've agreed to pay him back the air fare with the wages I make so he'll be out of pocket if he chucks me out. Anyway, I'm a quick learner, I'll pick it up. I'm good at picking things up."

"We're talking pretty niche skills, Beez, not twinks in Central Station."

"It'll be a scream. I've never been to Oz."

"But, you can't leave London, you'll miss us, we'll miss you."

"I'm not dying hon, it's only six months. I'm over London at the moment. It's the same old shit, the same old shags, week in, week out! Besides, the Aussie surfer dudes there are meant to be HOT!"

I felt like the wind had been knocked right out of me.

"What about me... you big arsehole?"

"Look, I would want you to join me more than anything in the world. It would be ace and I considered asking you a hundred times but, well, you've got your thing and that's cool. You have a commitment to something you love and that's totally inspired me to do something that I really want to do. By the time I've come back, you'll be nearly finished and we can get back to normal."

"What about the Boadicea?"

"Jason says he'll store my stuff in the office. He hasn't promised anything but he'll sort something out for when I come back."

I felt tears prick my eyes for the second time that night.

"But what if you don't come back? What if you love it out there and never want to leave. What if you get addicted to the bareback in the outback?"

"Aw silly Simon! It's just an extended holiday. I'd never leave my home, I could never leave you for good, I'd miss ya, you prick."

He stroked my arm.

"You're so busy at the moment; you won't even know I'm not there until it's time for me to come back." I noticed he didn't say "home".

"Oh for fuck's sake, Beez! I can't help being busy. Are you saying I'm driving you away?"

"Of course not, you know I do things for me."

"Well don't make out that I won't miss you and I won't think about you and wish that I was there with you coz I will. All of the above, even though I'm busy."

"Alright. Take it easy, don't get worked up. Your fancy man will be here in a moment and he doesn't want to see you with concealer running down your face like a half-creosoted fence."

"Oh, I don't care about that now."

"Well get your act together Ronseal, he's just walked in. Hey!"

Beez waved out to Scott who was squeezing his way past a very large, string-vested man who was balancing a pint on his beer belly.

"Hey!" Beez shouted. "He hasn't seen us, go and fetch him."

"No!" I snapped, wiping my eyes with the back of my hand. "Just keep waving, he'll see us."

I couldn't believe it, I couldn't even regurgitate my dinner to put this guy off, maybe it turned him on.

"Oh fuck this. HEY!" Beez cupped his hands over his mouth. Scott looked around to follow the voice, and when he eventually recognised us he smiled and began making for the foot of the stairs.

"Listen," Beez said, "I'm going out for a fag. I'll stay downstairs for a bit so if it's going well text me, er…*We Found Love* and I'll fuck off. If it's going bad text *SOS* and I'll come and rescue you. Alright? Good luck!" Our robust Rihanna song code always came in handy in situations where using the Queen's English was far too complicated.

He kissed me on the cheek and jumped over the chair, passing Scott on the first step.

"Yo," Beez said as he walked past Scott on his descent down the staircase.

Scott looked a little put out.

"Erm yo?" he mumbled back.

He caught my eye just as I stopped frantically finger-combing my fringe.

"Well hi there," Scott said warmly as he made his way over. I felt nervous. The fact that he'd followed us here was overwhelming enough and, if it weren't for the dim, grim lighting, I'm sure I would have been blushing an offensive purple by now. Scott sat far enough away to squeeze a small child between us but close enough that I could get another hit of Ralph Lauren. Was it slightly stronger than the last time?

"Feeling any better?"

I smiled and nodded. I was conscious that I might still smell of rancid old sick and, though the silence was making Scott a little uncomfortable, my mouth felt as though it were glued shut.

"Listen, unfortunately I've got a client early tomorrow and I'm already a bit fucked so I just came in to, well, get your number really. I'd really rather get to know you some other night when neither my work commitments nor... your digestive system can get in the way."

I was impressed, he'd managed a joke. I don't know whether it made me feel better or worse. I laughed along anyway, half expecting bats to fly out if I dared to open my mouth. He laughed too and I got another flash of that beautiful smile.

"So what do you reckon?" He was persistent.

"That sounds great to me." I found a voice, God knows where from. Scott pulled his phone out from his pocket and swung it round to me. Fortunately there was no ex-boyfriend type screensaver, just a safe picture of the London Marathon finish line. I typed in my mobile number. As I handed it back, Scott laughed.

"You must be worth it. £3.50 it cost me to get in here and now I have to leave."

"I only paid about £1.49...."

"Really, half price?"

"For some celeriac and dental floss." I passed over the receipts that had got us in earlier.

"My friend Beez's a bit jammy."

Scott laughed again; he was looking better and better. After a couple of flirtatious kisses on the cheek to say our goodbyes, he made his way back down the stairs towards the large guy in the vest, nearly knocking his pint off the protruding paunch. I saw him turn and laugh out loud under the blare of the music, giving a little wave as he trotted out of the front door. Suddenly my phone vibrated in my pocket, which made me jump. Surely he wasn't that quick off the draw when it came to texting. I fished it out and pressed the read button. It was from Beez: *Well?* I looked down. He was on the dance floor with a quizzical look on his face and the phone held up in the air. I cleared the screen and typed *Don't Stop The Music*. I pressed send just as Rihanna began to play.

And now my head was banging, because it didn't just stop at Rihanna. Once he'd lured us in, the DJ played a string of classics: Cheryl Cole, Kylie and that bloody infectious new Calvin Harris tune which we sang while jumping up and down, in a locked embrace. We drank vodka shots like prohibition was coming in at three and, finally, at four he played "Love Is A Losing Game" by Amy Winehouse. Although both Beez and I sung it to each other through vodka goggles, really I was singing it to Scott and Beez was singing it to some hunked-up surfer type from Australia whom he'd never even met. And that's when it was time to go home and spend some time alone.

*

"Are you getting up or what? There's a cup of tea waiting for you out here?"

There was a thump at the door, not that of a knuckle but more of a thick elbow. My flatmate Freya was obviously holding two cups of tea and unable to use her fists, though it could just as well have been her forehead. Freya was my best mate from university. We'd not clicked in the first months of the course but, after a year of bitching behind each other's backs, we bonded after a night on the poppers in the kitchen of some dreadful second year house party. We became firm friends ever since and moved in together the following year. Now, Freya and I shared the basement of a two-storey house, while Fiona, the landlady, dominated the top floor. We had only managed to break our flat-sharing marathon for one year, having been brought back together recently under respective nightmarish circumstances. Freya had split from a long-term boyfriend and I'd had a bad experience sharing in a student house where I had been continually dragooned into drinking yards of ale three nights a week (not ideal when trying to keep up a full-time job). Both Freya and I had managed to flee our pads at the same time and, not really wanting to leave the Hackney area, we begrudgingly agreed to share with a live-in landlady: bad idea. Not only was Fiona a mere four years older than both of us, but she thought that being a homeowner was some kind of status symbol and spent the whole time being a cranky old bitch who abhorred the idea of dividing her precious house with other people. She rarely bothered us, possibly because she despaired of our lifestyle and lack of responsibility. And so I affectionately named her Flowers, as in Flowers in the Attic.

I dragged myself out of my pit and wrenched open the heavy bedroom door which was always blocked by the fucking pile of the carpet on the other side. With each tug I felt more and more like an asthmatic opening a vault.

"Oh this bloody door," I moaned, another needle of pain shooting through my temples.

"Is she kidding with this?"

"Count yourself lucky, mine doesn't shut," Freya called back. "I could be lying there asleep, blissfully unaware of Flowers setting fire to my bed." Freya seemed to sense me cringing. "Don't worry, she's out. Out buying milk I expect. Though what she'll come back with this time remains a mystery. I don't think there's an animal left that hasn't had its tits squeezed over her grape nuts."

"No visual images, please, I feel gross."

"Oh," she sounded unsympathetic as she dunked a biscuit into her mug, "big night was it?" She didn't wait for a response. "Mine was; night out with the Walthamstow lot. Funny lot of buggers they are. All sodding maths teachers but when it's time to split the restaurant bill, they still have to get their calculators out."

I skulked over to the futon and picked up my tea, hoping it was sweet. Yes, it was. *Saturday Kitchen* played on the television; they were gutting a fish.

"Oh God, I can't watch that!"

"Were you out with Beez? How is he, I haven't seen him in ages."

Freya and Beez got on well, mainly because they were both so terribly middle class. But, in a non-middle-class way, she could easily drink him clean under the table, an accolade that she had always brought up at gatherings.

"Yeah, he's good, ended up going to CXR."

"Not that dump, what on earth for?"

Freya frequently referred to CXR as a dump even though she would never protest when she was being dragged there. I reckoned that she secretly held it in quite high regard. It wasn't so long ago that the three of us had spent a rainy Sunday afternoon there, downing tequila slammers and singing karaoke. And when Freya brought the house down with an unexpected rendition of Kate Bush's "Wuthering Heights" in its original key, Beez and I had joined the rest of the customers in being totally gobsmacked. She even managed a well-supported top C while simultaneously miming her (Cathy) crashing through his (Heathcliff's) bedroom window. After receiving rapturous applause, Freya staggered her way back to the table and slurred into my ear: "My sodding bra came undone halfway through that."

It seemed that even though her vocals were supported, her ample chest clearly wasn't.

"It was good actually, quite full."

"Look darling, why don't you lie on the sofa, take some paracetamol and we'll watch *Carry On Cleo*?"

"Mmm, that sounds good."

She got up and began to draw the curtains but I literally remembered two minutes of the opening credits before my eyes closed and I was back in a deep slumber.

I awoke only to the sound of my mobile phone ringing next to my head; the pumping sound of Salt n Pepa's "Push It" was so loud and aggressive that it had practically permeated my dream. I grimaced at my phone, wiping a trail of drool from the side of my face and groggily heaving myself up into a seated position. It must have been at least the two-hour length of the film since I had dropped off; the curtains were now half open, letting the winter sun spill over the big Freya-shaped indent in the sofa.

The phone was persistent but I needed at least twenty seconds to wake back up and, by that time, "Push It" had pushed it enough.

I let out a gorilla-like yawn and stretch before reaching over and checking the identity of the mystery caller. The number flashing at me on the illuminated screen wasn't recognised by my phone and I was hesitant to respond to those sorts of numbers but, shit, it could have been Scott!

What if he thought that I was ignoring his call? Or, worse, what if he worked on a one-call only basis and would banish me from his life forever if I didn't answer on the third ring.

The phone suddenly sprang to life in my hand; it was the same unidentified number which made me suddenly stupidly nervous. That first phone call was always as equally cursed as it was blessed. On one hand, the initial chase was exciting and it came with the added bonus that this Valentine's Day, I would be able to purchase a card for someone other than my mother. On the other, it was nerve shredding, as if one tiny wrong word and I'd blow it forever.

"Hello?" Dammit! I was aiming for cool but it had sounded more like I was bellowing down an empty corridor.

"Hey you." It may have been Scott, I couldn't really remember his voice to be honest. With each word he spoke, my brow furrowed further.

"Remember me from last night?"

Yes, it was definitely him.

In this situation, I had a nasty habit of mentally planning the wedding far too early. However, if my recollection of the guy was still a little sketchy, I'd just build up some mental image from memory; it was usually a grossly inaccurate one. They would be perhaps blonder, thicker haired, better groomed and with a much more defined physique than the eyesore I had *actually* exchanged numbers with under the influence of my alter ego: Miss Stella Artois.

More often than not, *my* creation had been so far removed from the gremlin sat opposite me that I had no choice than to fake my enthusiasm on the day and then casually erase their phone number from under the table while chatting.

With Scott, though, I was a touch more confident that I had made the right choice.

"Of course I remember you, Scott. I threw up all over you."

"Oh yeah, forgot about that," Scott snorted. He was either a good liar or I had just shot myself squarely in the ass.

"Oh, right. Well I'm sorry for that anyway. Too much weekend debauchery, it's not a regular thing. I'm not one of those guys." *I* was a good liar too!

"Glad to hear it. I wouldn't worry anyway, we've all been there."

"Have we?" Not quite the common ground I was after.

"Yeah, long story but I think I'll leave it to your imagination. Listen. I'm about today if you fancy meeting up properly."

Today? With this hangover, could I handle it? And would Scott be able to endure a drink with someone who looked and felt like something that had been dragged out of the Camden canal in a binbag?

"Erm, sure. Look, I just have to warn you, after you left, I got a bit pissed and I haven't had much sleep...."

"So another time then?"

"No, I didn't mean that, I meant I look a bit..." Did I really want to pull at this thread? "I mean, yeah that would be great." Ladies and gentlemen, I present Simon: taking a risk.

"Do you want me to come to you?" He was such a gentleman.

"Where do you live? Maybe we could meet halfway?"

"Okay, I'm in Stoke Newington."

"No way? I used to live there. I know it really well. Well, I'm in Hackney, five minutes on the train, I'll come to you." I was excited at the prospect of spending the afternoon in Stokey, having not been back to my old stamping ground for some weeks now.

"Cool yeah. How about The White Hart?"

"I love it."

"Great, there's something I've got to do in Abney Park cemetery first."

My heart suddenly plummeted. What could he possibly need to do in Hackney's most notorious gay al fresco cruising ground that was different from getting a quick gobble to warm him up for the main event? Who the HELL admits that? I knew he was a freak, I just knew it.

"Oh!" It was blatantly all over. Our wedding album was starting to dissipate before my very eyes.

"Hey, I'm just kidding!" Scott chuckled. The album reassembled itself in similar fashion.

"Oh God," I didn't want to seem like I couldn't take a joke. "Look, I'll see you at three yeah?"

"That's great."

"See ya babes." He hung up the phone. I couldn't seem to wipe the smile off my face. It was all so thrilling; the risqué jokes, the banter, the fact that I remembered him becoming sexier by the minute. I hadn't been this certain of anything for a long time, but I wouldn't start planning the honeymoon just yet.

I glanced at the clock on my phone: 1.15pm, I'd have to get going.

Well, maybe I'd jot down a mental list of my favourite holiday destinations on the way to the train...

*

The journey had to be one of the worst in history. Those five minutes seemed to last for hours; with every swerve of the tracks came a fresh wave of nausea. Every last shot of vodka that was poured down my neck in the last twenty-four hours had its own unique burning sensation in my gullet. Why

64

had I put on that facemask thing last minute, knowing full well I wasn't going to have time to let it work? I had to sacrifice fifteen minutes of jeans selection time in order to peel the bloody thing off. And when I eventually wrestled it free, I inevitably had a big burning circle on my face like the Japanese flag. Thankfully it had calmed somewhat since then.

My clothing choice had been fairly uninspired in the end: t-shirt, hooded top, jeans and an Arabic printed neck scarf. My hair was simply styled, shiny and freshly washed, smelling of a new coconut shampoo that might hopefully mask the scent of second-hand booze.

I hadn't put in quite as much effort as I normally would with a date, but I knew I could have done a lot worse. Besides, you don't normally get all dolled up for a Saturday afternoon drink in Stokey anyway do you? If I got too preened I might as well sit there with a badge on: *Unlucky single gay man: on another first date.*

As the train pulled into Rectory Road, I was grateful for the full five-minute walk in which to pull my nerves together before reaching The White Hart, one of my favourite east London haunts. If Scott had nothing else on this date, at least he'd chosen a good venue where I could quite happily relax, even on my own if the situation arose. As each shop passed on the way to the door, the butterflies circled my insides more frantically and, by the time I'd pushed the door open, I was rigid with nerves. Why did I always get myself in such a state? I was the same wreck when I stood next to Tony Blair's sister-in-law in the queue at Morrisons, three months ago.

As I glanced around, I could feel myself beginning to flush. There were so many things that could go wrong; he might have lost interest in me in the last few hours, he might be pissed, he might think that American tan moccasins with cream chinos turned up at the ankle are suitable for a casual date.

Or, I told myself, he could be amazing. That would be the most petrifying option: I could escape, unharmed from all the other possibilities, but it's harder to run away from something that might change your life for the better.

Well, he clearly wasn't here yet. The pub was huge but open plan so you could more or less see every possible hiding place from the front of the room. I began to walk through. *Please don't let me have to sit and order a drink on my own with the world dropping out of my arse every time the door goes*, I pleaded with whatever it was that was watching over me at times like this. But out in the back beer garden, I suddenly noticed that someone seemed to be in a similar state, wandering apprehensively up to the glass of the French window and examining the bar every few minutes, nervously flipping a cigarette between his two fingers with the tip of his thumb.

Here we go, I thought and waved to the figure who let out a puff of smoke in acknowledgement. Even from where I was standing, I could see his smile spread across his face and those pearly white teeth emerge from behind his soft, kissable lips. I smiled back as Scott, too, waved.

Phew! I thought, rolling my eyes to myself, this is tense, do I get a drink, go and see him, what? I decided that it was no good if I was going to keep spinning it out like this, I should just act upon my instincts. With that, I went to join my date for a nervous cigarette.

One drink in, we were both warming to each other. I had already learnt that Scott worked with clients in the St John's Wood area, even with a couple of minor celebrities whose names he couldn't possibly divulge. Bastard!

He also used to manage a high-profile club night called Club Bikai, a popular bangra gay night in Haringey and now, though he's no longer a manager, he can still get in free, drink for free and get people on the guest list whenever he wishes. Not a bastard!

I also learnt that he was born in Hackney and that he had one sister, Amanda, who was three years older than him, thirty-six, who lived in Spain with her boyfriend, Ice Cream (who was Italian, real name Chris).

I was really enjoying this and the glass of rosé was going down a treat, especially since I was topping up from last night's skinfull. There was a burst of impromptu winter sun that covered the deserted garden in a dewy glow. It was romantically twee and reminded me of the last few frames of the first *Kill Bill* film, obviously without Lucy Liu's massacred scalp rolling past our feet.

We were both smoking like troupers and often caught each other's eye momentarily, only to blush slightly and laugh it off after a few seconds. Those thrilling nuances of a great first date.

There was a bit of shameless flirting in the little quips, the innuendos and cruddy jokes. In short, it was fun, Scott was glowingly charismatic and I was getting such a great vibe that I was certain he was feeling it too. The shame and horror of vomit-gate was all but a distant memory.

"So, I know you work at this administration job in the City but that's obviously not what you want to be doing as a career since you, so obviously, hate it. You're not thinking of climbing up the ladder or anything?" he asked.

I hated it when people asked about my job. It was so far removed from what my calling was; it was mortifying to admit that I turned up to the office at all.

"No," I replied. "I have absolutely no desire to climb up anything there I'm afraid, it's just a means to an end."

Scott ran a hand over his short, clippered hair and wrinkled his thick eyebrows.

"What then, you've got something else lined up or…?"

I was going to have to say it. I was going to finally have to face the thing that Beez had not been allowed to broach for all of last night. And I wasn't holding back because I was ashamed of admitting it, in fact I usually announced it with pride. No, the only reason for my silence on the subject was that the dread that had been gnawing away at the back of my mind for the last two days like a starving gerbil might take over me and ruin this afternoon of pure pleasure.

Still, I had to say it now, I'd been set up.

"I'm actually studying at the moment." I looked down into the pink liquid swirling around my glass, hoping it was going to somehow get me out of this situation.

"Oh really?" Scott sounded genuinely impressed as he took another drag from his cigarette. "What, like an evening class or something?"

God, people could be so naïve! Why would I put myself through such physical, mental and emotional anguish for some poxy evening class? I'd rather not have this incredibly intense, life-changing experience shoehorned into the same bracket as Zumba.

"Well no," I corrected him, "it's actually a full-time course. It just happens to take place in the evening and at weekends, well Sundays and occasional Saturdays, or else I wouldn't be here."

"Shit, that's heavy. They sound like long hours, what are you studying?"

"Well," I said, "it's a drama school. I'm on an acting course."

Usually when I said this, the conversation immediately dried up. It was one thing being a student, totally another being a drama student. We were seen as show offs, performers and self-promoters and that was, apparently, extremely unattractive. That was one response at least. Scott's on the other hand was just as predictable:

"No kidding, that's really exciting. So you have to act like a tree and stuff?"

I had an answer all ready.

"Actually, I know it's a massive cliché and everything, but, in acting, when you think about how the body of a tree is similar to our trunk, the branches to our limbs and the roots to our—"

"Feet?"

"Well, our foundations really. Imagining yourself to be a tree is actually a very valuable , but basic, exercise in being centred and grounded before you open your mouth to speak." Shut up Simon, for fuck's sake!

I was met with a blank expression.

"But it's not like we 'act' like a tree. We're not wandering round, trying to channel a sycamore or anything."

"God, after last night I didn't think you could be sick anymore."

What he lacked in original humour, he made up for in timing. Scott flipped his cigarette butt onto the grass and rested back on his smile.

"Sorry, that was crap, but seriously, I think that's really cool. You're doing something challenging, something you really want to do and carrying on with full-time work as well. Phew, that can't be easy." I didn't expect this cool reaction. The words you could almost write, but his face held a look of genuine interest. I went on.

"You get used to it. The first term was a bitch, having to act in front of people you don't know but you get pretty familiar, pretty quick. Some people find the whole experience is too much and start to drop out; we've had several leave already."

"God, sounds intense. Which school are you at?"

"It's called the Old School and it's in Archway." Judging by the vacant expression on Scott's face, he'd clearly never heard of it. Not many people had. I certainly wasn't about to massage my own ego in front of Scott, by listing off the school's alumni; some of whom are quite successful soap actors.

"Yeah, it is intense." I steered us back on track, rambling on like some crazy person. "You can also find yourself feeling quite vulnerable too. Acting is a lot harder than people realise, you have to go to a few dark places mentally in order to understand some characters' motivations."

Where was this stuff coming from? I wasn't this up to speed with my own family members!

"What are your colleagues like, nice people?"

"They're all great." I smiled because it was the truth, I'd made some great friends. "We're all in the same boat, no one thinks they're better than anyone else. It's a very pleasant atmosphere."

"What about the tutors? Are they all cool?" Scott leaned forward. I took a deep breath.

"Yeah, they're all very nice..." Words failed me; I was a terrible liar so that would have to do. The fact that there was one specific person in that school, who filled me with ice-cold fear, who haunted my dreams and who tormented my very soul, was not really a subject for this glorious afternoon.

"Well, I think it's excellent. Well done you, I'm in awe."

I flushed a deep red, partly because his kind words embarrassed the hell out of me and partly because I was ill at ease with having to lie to such a sincere guy. Scott noticed my shift in comfort and reached out to put his hand over mine.

"I mean that," he said in a softer tone that sent my innards into a wild flutter. After a few electrifying seconds, caught in a locked gaze, I began to burn up from the face down.

"Phew." I forced myself to break this moment; my erection was itching to jump up and spoil everything. "I'm starting to feel quite hot." I moved my hand away and felt around for my jumper zip, pulled it down and threw open the two sides to let some air onto my oxygen-deprived torso. As I did so, Scott looked down and smirked. Confused, I traced the invisible line from his finger to the graphics on my t-shirt. But I recognised it immediately and looked down in dismay at the slogan; *Porn Star*. Perfect timing.

*

After the fourth drink, I decided it was time to get things moving in some direction and I didn't really care by what means as long as it was forward. I was enjoying Scott's company more than I'd enjoyed anyone's company in years and didn't want it to end just yet. In reality though, it was nearing seven o'clock and it was probably a better idea to go home and do some preparation for tomorrow. Sunday was a long day at school and there were many things I could devote some precious time to, the script for instance, or movement exercises, vocal alignment, the list was endless.

Scott suggested he walk me back to the station, maybe stopping off at his flat which was on the way, just off the High Street. It was so great that he suggested it and I agreed without questioning. Not only could I have a bit of sexy Saturday fun, but I could also check out the décor in his bedroom. I loved other people's houses.

We were both a little high-spirited after drinking so early in the afternoon and, bar a packet of shared Walkers, I'd had nothing to eat so my stomach had been making unattractive gurgling sounds for some time now. There was nothing in my system to soak up the alcohol; the alcohol that was now beginning to make me quite randy after ogling my gorgeous companion for well over four hours. It was time for my afternoon of hard work – batting my eyelashes in all the right places, inventing punchy one-liners on cue and laughing at everything he said as if I was in some terrible eighties chick-flick – to be wholeheartedly rewarded. Scott gestured for me to lead the way out of the pub; if he was going to act like the perennial gentleman, I could succumb to being a well-kept lady. Out into the chilly evening, we walked in a suspicious silence. He had a knowing smile on his face, which I chose to ignore.

"Do you love Stokey?" I asked, breaking the mood.

"Yeah, I've been here for so long now that it just feels like home, especially since my mum only lives over the other side of Victoria Park. I don't think I could ever leave Hackney."

"I fell in love with it once I'd moved here. It's got a great community spirit and I think it's superb the way that thy have their own patriotic merchandise. The Sunday mornings when the Nigerian ladies in their huge, brightly coloured plumes line the steps of the Baptist churches, Saturday nights when the grainy glow of neon on wet tarmac draws a faint line under the kebab house window, and summer in London Fields with the smell of freshly mown grass and fruity cider. It's like a rough diamond, Hackney." I was talking cods again.

Scott laughed a little. "You have such a poetic way of saying things."

"And you have a fucking beautiful smile." I hoped I sounded more convincing this time because I was nearly as pissed.

We got to Scott's house, through the front door and barely held off for two minutes before bursting into the bedroom, clawing at each other's buttons like a couple of ravenous squirrels might claw at an unmanned refuse sack. It happened so fast that I barely registered his room. Bar the walls being bright, I didn't remember much else.

Scott forced me against the wall and took my head in his hands; looking into my eyes for a split second before passionately pressing his soft pink lips to mine. At first he was tender but, as the momentum built, he began to gorge hungrily on my mouth. I allowed myself to be taken by Scott; embraced, fondled and licked, from the mouth, to the neck, to my earlobes. Everywhere. I felt his eager tongue brush passionately over my lips, as if desperate to be invited in. The pleas were pretty convincing, so I yielded and we kissed madly right there; vertical in his bedroom. I couldn't believe that I had become so loose in a stranger's home in the middle of the afternoon. Usually my mother's disapproving tut would resonate over my shoulder but there wasn't really time for all that now: I was drunk and I wanted him.

My left hand scrambled down onto the small of his back and into the seat of his jeans, manhandling and squeezing his firm buttocks, so hard that I must have left five perfect finger-shaped lines across his right cheek.

I kept my other hand on his face, willing him to carry on, running my fingers manically over his head and back down to his face. Scott moved his hands upwards, under my t-shirt and across the plane of my back, the rough skin from his searing, manly fingers grabbing at my flesh, grasping the back of my neck as he forced his lips down onto my throat, feasting on me as if I were a piece of ripe fruit. He pushed himself further into me, driving his groin into mine, forcing me harder against the wall. It was animalistic; the wild pant of breath, the strong, uncontrolled thrust and the manly saliva that dripped from his open mouth. This was an alpha male, staking his claim, and I was fucked if I was about to stop him. Jesus, he could have just pissed all over me and have done with it.

I could feel him rock solid against my hip and it was all I could do not to jam my hand down his jeans and start pumping immediately. I was miles ahead of him though, my pants were so wet; my cock was about to explode like a squashed cod liver oil capsule. I wanted Scott to just throw me down and climb on top of me, tear off my clothes with his hot and hungry hands and penetrate me, deeper until I was red raw, drained and defeated. I wanted to feel his skin on my skin, taste his sweat on my lips; feel his balls slap against me as he fucked me. But in a moment of sheer clarity, I took stock of the situation and pulled Scott's head away, gripping his temples between my palms. His mouth still kissed in the air, like a hungry baby being pulled from a lactating nipple. Scott's body froze momentarily but, as I could feel, his drive remained stiffly alert. Poor lamb looked as if he'd done something hideously wrong. I licked some moisture back onto my raw lips and flicked the fringe out of my eyes.

"I've really got to get home tonight," I whispered, I liked this sense of control. The exchange of power was as sexy as hell. "The truth is that I'm worried if I stay, I'll want to wake up here and I have to do some work for tomorrow or I'll be in the shit."

I felt Scott's muscles begin to relax; all but one lost tension. He pulled back slightly and panted with exhaustion. It had been hard work; I felt compelled to offer him a fag as a reward.

"Okay," he submitted. "I get it."

I slid about a metre back down the wall. God, he'd been holding me up! I caught his eye; within it was a touch of disappointment and rejection. I leaned forward, closed my eyes and kissed him again full on the lips.

"I really want to see you again," I said once I'd pulled away and rested my forehead on his, "because that was, and you were... amazing."

He smiled the best smile yet.

"Are you sure you weren't just acting?" Scott said.

"I may be in training," I grinned, putting my hand around to the back of his neck, "but I ain't that fucking good."

*

When I got home, I was filled with such an uncharacteristic energy I almost skipped through the French window without opening it. Freya had commandeered the sofa with a bucket of mini-poultry corpses and what looked like a league of cola. She was glued to a cookery programme she'd taped earlier. I plonked myself down next to her and she watched me grinning for a full minute. I purposefully gave her little attention.

"Okay, well this crazy behaviour is either because you've had a lunchtime shag or because you've seen Flowers swinging by the neck from her pretentious balcony outside," she quipped.

"Why do you say that?"

"Coz you're smiling like a gimp and it's Saturday evening. Normally you're dabbling in the black arts in an attempt to get you out of going back to school on Sunday. So who is he?"

"Just someone I met last night when I was out with Beez." I was still beaming.

"Some guy?" Freya pointed at me with half a ravaged chicken leg. "You haven't smiled that wide for ages. Gave you lockjaw did he?"

"No! Nothing like that happened, we just kissed."

"And I'm Miley Cyrus." She leaned back. "So, when is he coming over?"

"Coming over? Here? I can't invite him yet, I don't even know his surname."

75

It was true: I didn't. I barely knew anything about him. What was I thinking starting something now? The usual dread started to trickle in. I sighed. "I don't even know whether I've got time to get into anything anyway, what with school too..."

"I'm sure they can't stop you being in relationships. As long as this guy knows what the deal is from the off there shouldn't be a problem should there? You've told him haven't you?"

"Of course! Oh, I don't know, my life's not my fucking own at the moment." I stood up and dragged myself over to the door. "Which reminds me, I have to get through my Noel Coward play tonight; we've got a read-through tomorrow and, what with last night's vodka and this afternoon's boys, I've procrastinated long enough. I'll see you later."

Freya waved a chip in my direction and wiggled her little finger in adieu.

I flopped onto my bed where my copy of Noel Coward's *Hay Fever* was waiting for me, its bright yellow sleeve threatening to dominate my dreams forever more. I growled; the prospect of reading, absorbing and formulating a well-conceived proposal on how to play the character after four glasses of vino distructo was giving me an intense headache. Nonetheless, I grabbed the bloody thing and flicked to the relevant page. I started by immediately jumping to the back to see how many pages I would have to wade through before I could officially call the evening *productive*. Productive in this project at least; in all other ways the rest of the day had been productive. I flipped over onto my back and looked up at the flaking magnolia ceiling.

My God, when I thought of all the disastrous dates I'd been on before this afternoon, they all paled in comparison. The horrors of what I'd had to endure on previous occasions came back to haunt me. There was Yogi last year, the Asian guy who had seemed so forthright when I met him in the club. On date one, however, he was so nervous that I felt as if I were a member of the DSS interviewing him for benefit fraud. And at the end of the night, when a positively convulsing Yogi had bitten the bullet and moved in to kiss me, I had been so exasperated by his inability to pull himself together that I practically grimaced in his face. Needless to say, my acting skills had been put to good use when I immediately burst into crocodile tears and fabricated some bullshit that I was still in love with an old boyfriend and was sorry that I had wasted Yogi's time. I then waited for him to leave before I got another drink and pawed someone else.

Then there was Colin, the big burly estate agent who I'd met at the Boadicea's New Year's Eve party. I was dressed as Xanadu when he requested my number (I should have seen the warning signs then). We had gone out to an Italian in Swiss Cottage; a beautiful restaurant near to his work. He was such a frequent visitor that he was on first name terms with all the staff and took huge delight in explaining to me how they slid the pizza in and out of a big stone oven in the middle of the dining hall. Usually, I would feign interest but there was something about him. He ticked all the right boxes in chivalry: pulling out the seat for me to sit down and wooing me with talk of the sports programme he ran for underprivileged kids every weekend. He told me that he still lived at home as he tucked his napkin daintily into the neckline of his t-shirt. The t-shirt that was probably ironed with love by mother. Even that had seemed endearing at the time. I remembered staring at him with big, glassy eyes, well and truly smitten, picturing us stepping out of the church on the wedding day and through a tunnel of crossed pizza paddles. The romance continued right up until the second the food arrived. Upon being presented with vittles, Colin turned Neanderthal instantly. His tongue poked out from between his lips like a trapped eel and all the etiquette that he had walked in with disappeared somewhere into that pizza oven.

"Cor, fuck me, I'm starving," he bellowed, as if I was supposed to be impressed by the magnitude of his hunger.

I watched, my knife and fork still raised, as a once oh-so-mild-mannered Colin scooped up slice after slice of pizza and shovelled it into his open, passata-stained facial chasm. It was like watching someone throw a bag of fruit under a lawnmower. If this wasn't bad enough, he continued to talk, to no one in particular, as though his mouth wasn't rammed full of various Italian ingredients. I remained in a state of shock as I was showered with half-chewed pepperoni and shavings of parmesan cheese. I hadn't had the chance to even look at my food but I will never forget the image of my glass of red wine: full and untouched, save for a well-masticated piece of onion, calmly floating on the surface.

As if the nightmarish dining experience wasn't enough, Colin wiped his mouth with the back of his hands and offered me a lift home. I had to accept as I was in the middle of sodding nowhere. Nearly at our destination, he turned into a street that I didn't recognise, parked, turned off the ignition and rubbed his big, fat hands together while looking at my crotch and slobbering all over the gearstick! He then pounced upon me, clawing at my chest like a starving chicken might annihilate a lardy cake. Not only was the overwhelming stench of pancetta coming from his dinghy-sized lips enough to put me off meat for life, but the leech-like kiss with a tongue that flopped into my mouth like a newly dropped foal was too much to bear. The fact that he'd pulled over onto the kerb of a residential street and some little old dear walking her dog was gawping in at the window was the last straw. I managed to wrestle myself out from the clutch of his wandering hands and slam the door in his face. Colin lacked integrity, elegance, romance and wit. Who better to teach underprivileged kids than a big, gluttonous, inexperienced pig? I had since heard, on the Boadicea grapevine, that Colin had recently embarked on a long-term relationship. I hoped that it was with a cognitive behavioural therapist, or, even better, a fucking charm school.

None of those previous debacles could have possibly topped this afternoon. There had been more passion in those few minutes with Scott than I could imagine there would be in a lifetime with Colin, with his Nissan Micra and his mother's packed lunches. I let out a forlorn sigh big enough to ruffle the curtains at the other end of the room. What a great afternoon it had been, and what a terrible afternoon it would be tomorrow if I didn't get some of this play down! Once again, I scanned the first page, but it read like unconnected scrawl. Nothing was going in and it probably wouldn't tonight; I'd read the first sentence that many times that the words had lost all meaning. This is no good, I grumbled as I searched the walls of my bedroom, willing a distraction to occur. At that moment, my phone chirruped to life in my pocket. I pulled it out and looked at the screen.

"Luvly time spent wiv u 2day. Will be finkin of u all week now. Call me 2morrow Gorgus x"

I usually deplored text abbreviations with an unbridled passion; it was only meant for slack-jawed youths, lazy oiks or rude gals from Lewisham. In Scott's case, however, I'd make an exception. I pressed the phone theatrically to my chest, let out yet another laboured sigh and reached, once more, for the abandoned play.

Act 1. A room in the Bliss' House. There is a dining table and chairs and a large chaise longue where Simon and Sorel are sitting. Sorel is reading a book and Simon is drawing onto a pad.

No, it's no use, I thought, this means fuck all to me!

4

Good morning Starshine, the birds say hello.

My alarm call was intended to sweeten each early morning pill. Unfortunately it only worked for about ten seconds before grim reality seeped through the duvet cover like an oppressive sludge. I opened one eye and reached down for my phone which was letting out intense vibrations with every third beat. The alarm was getting louder and would have to be silenced. As I heeded my own direction, I noticed three things: one, I was still hungover; two, I was an hour late for school and three, I had numerous texts and missed calls from my schoolmates. Fuck!

This was the last thing I needed after a weekend of mucho distraction and nada preparation. I would be strung up.

I leapt out of bed and immediately almost fell back into it. I tried again and was successful in staying mobile under the weight of a gale force headache. With a little more caution, I fizzed through the usual morning routine, attempting double speed but really only managing speed and a half. I was meticulous when it came to my AM ritual as I held a firm belief that the neglect of a good standard of personal hygiene should be criminalised. Sometimes, however, the smell of a hangover could be unforgiving, no matter how much you spritzed yourself in oodles of Issey Miyake. Flossing, brushing, rinsing, hot showering, the application of strong moisturisers, eye cream and concealing fluid, deodorising and dressing, drying and sculpting my hair. It had to be in that order else I might miss something out and would run the risk of feeling incomplete and filthy for the rest of the day. Obsessive-compulsive didn't come close! With each part, I choked back a little boozy bile.

I typed a manic text to my classmate, Sophie, to put the feelers out that I was a little behind, though it didn't make that much of a difference. You weren't *allowed* to be late at the Old School. Tardiness was tantamount to the rape of a minor.

I glazed a dry piece of toast with strawberry jam and gripped it in my teeth while racing out of the front door. Pulling my jacket on at the same time, I hopped down the stairs and flew down the driveway. If I was going to get on the next bus, I would have to be nimble and, unfortunately, with yesterday's Vincent and Gallo working against me, I'd need to be sharper than this. I managed to jump onto the bus just as the doors were closing, much to the Nigerian bus driver lady's chagrin.

Archway was hardly the nicest place to spend your weekend. Upon first arrival, all those months ago, it had seemed so dismally shitty that I couldn't believe that I was going to drag myself here night after night. It certainly looked like the arse end of north London. However, after frequent nightly visits, I was starting to grow accustomed to the place. The drunks and drug dealers, who had once terrorised my long waits for the next available bus out of there, had now become somewhat familiar and were no longer a threat to my safety. I knew most of the local pub landlords. I was even on first name terms with the convenience store guy imprisoned behind bulletproof glass, yet protected by his large dog with slobbering jaws who threw itself at the counter door if anyone stepped within a two-metre radius. Surprisingly, when I enquired, the guard beast was actually a girl-satian.

The constant screech of the joyriders' cars coupled with the repeated chorus of ambulance and police car sirens had become ordinary background noise and I had grown used to the thick, smoggy cloud that descended upon me every time I stepped within a foot of the general area. The debris lining the streets, the piles of mouldy, stinking bread that was so discoloured and rancid that even the circus of pigeons that circled around it were turning up their mottled beaks in disdain. The chewing gum splattered pavement, the luminous sick trickling down the graffitied shop security curtain, the odd crumpled can of White Lightning swinging on its side in the wind like a small tin pendulum, made up the rest of the sorry backdrop.

The Old School, a building just off one of the side streets, blended perfectly into this macabre tableau. It was a small building, possibly built in the Art Deco period of the late twenties; its dull grey exterior and elaborate rooftop carvings made one think that, in its day, it may have been rather a spectacle. Now, however, it looked practically abandoned. In lieu of windows, two huge Perspex frames hung outside, advertising the training courses on glossy paper that had now been so weathered that all the blacks had turned to a glum green. The once smiling faces of the headshots underneath the plastic, now faded from years of neglect.

The name of the school was printed in large acrylic letters across the top of the building in a custardy yellow, currently covered in birdshit and mould. And this didn't look arty in a shabby chic sort of a way – it just looked crap. The door, virtually hanging off its own hinges from heroin-influenced vandalism and forced entry, gaped open like a demon's mouth; the entrance to hell itself.

To the left was a big, rusty black gate, padlocked and Chubb-locked; its bars towering over the street like a medieval gaol, casting evil shadows onto the grey pavement. The gate was shared with the café next door who used the area behind as a mini landfill site. It had subsequently become a rats' playground and a virtual hotbed of midnight prostitute activity. Many a time I had swung the contraption open, much to the surprise of some poor bedraggled trollop who was knelt behind it, giving someone a hand shandy in exchange for a bag of suspicious-looking powder. The gate screamed when dragged open, like a bag of drowning moggies and snapped back shut like the jaws of an angry, bloodthirsty crocodile. Jesus, I thought, next to this a week in a Dickensian workhouse might seem like paradise lost.

In truth, the school looked like the creepy old house at the end of your childhood street. A place designed to be framed by smog and dank, built on land where the sun never shines. A building long condemned to perpetual misery and decay.

Inside, there was more of the same. Chipped paintwork revealed grim plaster and leagues of gaffer tape-covered, unrepaired holes in the mucky walls and floors. Broken windows were stuffed back up with tights from old costumes and disguised by creased PVC gels. Cobwebs hung from the grubby ceilings where so many polystyrene panels were missing that you could see straight up into the razor-sharp jaws of the metal framing.

The green room was a concrete floor, scattered with discarded props from previous shows. A false leg, cracked mugs, a broken wooden sword, all like abandoned trophies – used, rejected and now thick with dust.

A few old moth-eaten chairs accompanied a huge gothic sofa which was held together only by its original varnish and pieces of duct tape. It sent out large, choking clouds of dust if anyone dared go near it, and had been the main catalyst of at least three pretty serious on-stage asthma attacks.

Old was definitely the word for this school. It was laughable that it was held in high regard by those in the industry. But there was little to laugh about when one had to dwell inside for hours on end, bracing the unbearable cold of winter or the unfathomable humidity of summer with no ventilation or heating. The smell of faeces grew ever stronger as the temperature rose and, in the harsh winds of autumn, the windows rattled like the bones of a thousand dancing skeletons.

The school, in a word, was a hole.

This proved to be a huge bone of contention with us students. When we thought of how each term's collective fees from all forty of us might have had a positive impact on the interior and exterior design of the place, it was laughable that it had remained so shambolic. The tutors had probably intended it to look like a Nazi war camp. That way, it might hammer home the fact that acting is not an easy game and there would be no tea and sympathy here for those unwilling to be berated into submission. And this is where I was about to spend my Sunday when I could have been spending it in bed with Scott, chewing on his nipples and being fucked like a buckaroo horse. Where was the justice?

I hared it up the main road, nearly getting hit twice by oncoming traffic – Sunday drivers were, any other day, road-ragers in this stretch of north London. I nearly knocked over a seemingly decrepit old lady who waved her stick at my back and shouted at the top of her voice, "Why don't you look where you're going, you fucking idiot."

Narrowly missing a fresh pile of dog pooh that sat proud, like a woolly mammoth's dump that had been deposited smack bang in the middle of the pavement, I reached the school door with a crash. The feeling of dread began to shroud me like a thick, velvet curtain. I knew I was in trouble. The tutors expected nothing less than one hundred per cent attendance on this course, the notion being that "the audience don't care if you're ill, have overslept or are in desperate need of a vital organ. They will have PAID to see you!"

I wasn't sure whether anyone *would* pay to see us at this current stage of our training except, possibly, if we all resigned and became lap dancers. This was the first time I'd ever been behind schedule and, since I was only about an hour late, I was secretly hoping that maybe they would be a bit lenient. I panted with exhaustion as I made my way through the dim corridor, lit only by a feeble orange light. It was like walking through the avenues of the Bates Motel.

I could hear the tinkle of piano music from the theatre door to my left, and the shrill tone of the dance tutor, Camilla, barking orders at my colleagues. Dance was my second lesson of the day and I dreaded it every Sunday, mainly because I had all the poise and allure of a lumbering Friesian. I exited the corridor into the grim foyer, where the photocopier and stacks of used A4 paper lay, collecting dust like documents in some Victorian bookshop. I tried to ignore the Head of the school's office door that stood to my immediate left. The last thing I wanted to do was to be found sneaking in late by him. Thankfully, the door was shut fast and there was no giant plume of smoke pouring out of the keyhole, which normally signified that the emperor was in attendance. Did this mean he could be out? If so, then that could mean that the trouble I was in could be halved.

The door in front loomed forever closer like the entrance to a Room 101, reaching out to me, an abnormally ethereal shade of white. I had no option; I had to push it.

It creaked open, letting out a piercing scream like someone being gruesomely tortured. The sound echoed around the walls, thus proving the worth of the excellent acoustics of the open space within. As I peered through the door, a sea of sympathetic grimaces appeared, all looking me squarely in the face. I could feel the redness creeping up my cheeks like multiplying bacteria. As I opened the door to its full extent, I saw the flatly unimpressed frown and folded arms of my voice tutor, Bea. The colour of her hair was every bit as fiery as her temper and, indeed it would appear, her current mood. I edged sheepishly forward and opened my mouth to plead my lame case.

"I'm..." I began but Bea beat me to the punch.

"You're late," she said, her expression remaining fixed. "Now fuck off out of my class."

I had no option but to remove myself from the building for half an hour for fear of being discovered by anyone else, least of all the Head who I prayed wouldn't get a full report of my unadulterated tardiness. A quick fag outside the shop two doors down and a proper rehearsal of my apology was how the time should be best spent.

The gloominess of the weather outside reflected my misery. Being disciplined by an adult is just as humiliating when you're in your thirties as it is when you're a kid, especially when it's over something as pointless as being one hour late for a bloody vocal class.

It was no use answering back to the tutors either; they'd been teaching here for years and were, no doubt, extensively trained in how to cope with any oncoming prima donna behaviour. Being a drama school, such theatrics may range from a fairly minor case of premenstrual tears to actually flopping your todger out and pissing on the *Complete Works of William Shakespeare* in protest. But I didn't want them to tar me with the same brush. I fought hard every day against the temptation to throw a diva strop. I strived to act as though I was fully appreciative of the life-changing experience I was being offered and respectful of those who were there to teach me. I was, however, starting to get mighty pissed off with it all. It only took a tiny bit of attention from an attractive potential boyfriend to remind me just how knee deep in the shit I was with study commitments.

I went through the usual rigmarole of planning my resignation speech, but I knew I'd never do it. Thousands of people auditioned for these places each year. I couldn't possibly discredit those who had left the audition room in tears the day I had been accepted by throwing it all away on a quick fumble with a personal trainer. I couldn't let my family and friends down either. Those who had been so proud of me when it had been announced that I'd got offered a place, having been so long out of the game since losing all my confidence in 2004: the year I had a rather minor nervous breakdown.

I thought of how my mother would say it: "Simon lost all his confidence in 2004 you know." In exactly the same way that others might say they'd lost their car keys.

My mother had always known that I'd end up at drama school, she boasted about it to any old Harris that would listen. She had already sent the ripple through my old drama college via the gossipy receptionist. She also managed to drop it into conversation with Peggy Downtheroad's window cleaner who probably only came in to steal a bucket of water. I couldn't disappoint her, especially since everyone within her circle of friends would be religiously tuning in to *EastEnders* to look out for the skinny dark-haired boy who "looks nothing like his father."

My parents had been divorced since I was seven and my father had remarried. It had been quite a messy divorce that had hit me and my sister, Martha, pretty bad. My parents had gone from not speaking to each other much to suddenly taking breakfasts in shifts and circling their favourite programmes in the *TV Times* with separate inks. I had been unaware of what was going on until I saw my dad's dark figure slumped on the sofa more than one night in a row.

Then the reality began to creep in; Dad was leaving.

He took me and my sister to meet some new lady who, I distinctively remembered, used to cut big notches into the sides of her carrots so that they looked like little wheels when they were sliced.
Martha, being two years older and fastidiously observant, had whispered in my ear, "That's Dad's new girlfriend."

This hadn't computed at first. Girlfriends were supposed to be young; they weren't supposed to own their own houses and have two goofy-looking children with dark-looking skin. They weren't supposed to have ex-husbands who would turn up in town in a leather jacket and start shouting at us across the square that we'd ruined his life, and they certainly weren't meant to make funny, high-pitched squealing noises after dark when the rest of the house had gone to bed.

It had all been a bit weird, especially when our mum had become depressed and was no longer able to take care of us two children. We were sent to live with our dad and the stepmother, who was awarded her "wicked" moniker as soon as she had her patchwork family in place. Her children had been given lovely warm beds, we had been given camping beds; her children were given money and affection, we were given the slipper. And it's not easy to watch your mother deteriorate while your father's spine becomes manipulated by some old witch and her fancy carrots.

Once my mum had begun to get better, it had seemed too late to renege on the agreement.

The witch had already made sure that papers had been signed and solicitors had been notified. My mum, however, did not go down without a fight and would often ring the house to speak to our dad, the witch listening on the other end, ready with a barrage of abuse.

Mum would often say: "Will you tell that troll of yours to simmer down, Stephen," which always hit the right nerve; the witch had found more than a match in my mother.

In hindsight, I knew that the witch must have been jealous of Mum; Mum had always been more attractive, more friendly and charismatic and, most of all, she had not been raised on one of the county's most infamous council estates with four other screaming girls who had all grown up to "shag anything that stands up to piss."

When I was fourteen, Martha left to return to Mum after an altercation with the witch's youngest girl and then, at sixteen, I followed suit, the life there becoming far too much to bear. Try as I might, I could never believe that I really had left the witch behind forever. She later ended up having another affair behind my dad's back and now he was single and enjoying life, free from ex-wives and the crossfire.

Mum had since grown in strength, but the struggle had made her cynical and she now strived for perfection. I couldn't tell her I was quitting, all I would get was a pained sigh and a "You're thirty-one years old and starting from square one? I suppose it's my fault..." etc.

It wasn't worth the hassle.

I stubbed my fag out and moseyed back on up to the school's front.

The music had stopped, the dance class was at an end and a few students were hanging around in pairs outside the building, nodding and waving greetings in my direction. It felt as though I was walking up to the parapet, ready to be beheaded by the guillotine of professional failure. I almost wanted to turn right around and march back out on the street, call Scott and ask if his penis would still be up for a bit of personal training of its own. Scott seemed a million miles away now, and there was nowhere that I'd rather be.

Two familiar figures appeared as shadows at the bottom of the corridor, making their way swiftly up to me. I knew instantly who it was as their faces appeared like two *Scream* masks; it was Lulu and Sophie.

"Mate," Sophie said, "what happened?"

Sophie had a wonderful knack of making everything sound far more devastating than it actually was. She lived in constant fear that someone close to her may get kicked off the course quite suddenly and, by the laws of elimination, she would somehow be next.

This terror was permanently etched all over her face, from her large, wide pleading eyes to her pale complexion, her downturned mouth and pained brow. And she had every right to be scared. The Head of the school liked to terminate students' places on the course like someone playing Call of Duty.

If you ever needed a chronological list of who had been culled so far, Sophie was your man. She knew dates, times, reasons; a calendar of broken dreams and aspirations. I found Sophie so endearing and funny; she'd been a firm friend since the first week. Although her attitude was almost entirely negative, her innocence and lack of ego coupled with her strange beauty was the talk of many of the male students who had been throwing themselves at her since the school year began. Sophie, however, had not been expecting such attention and it had added a little more than was comfortable to her current stress levels.

Accompanying her was Lulu who was wearing a similar expression of dismay only with slightly more slap. Lulu was a good mate too and the three of us stuck together like a little coven when outside of class.

Lulu was a real lady through and through and, in complete contrast to Sophie's timid, boyish good looks, she was sexy and enchanting in a more buxom way. She had voluptuous breasts which she forced into little corsets and wore sensational high heels with dramatically patterned smocks in bright colours festooned across her curvaceous frame.

"What? I overslept."

I really didn't want to get into this now, maybe after I'd been taken firmly up the banks by Bea, and that wasn't as good as it sounded.

"It's not like Simon, he's usually on time," Lulu said to Sophie, bypassing me completely. The words were so accusatory that I was beginning to doubt myself as well.

"Yeah," Sophie said and bit her bottom lip. "You're not going to leave are you?"

"No Soph, I'm not going to leave." I eased her tension by resting my hand on her shoulders, feeling them drop with relief. "I'm just going to talk to Bea and apologise. It should be cool, like you said; it's not like me is it? What was class like anyway?"

"Pretty shit." Sophie pulled her usual frown. "The boys were pissing about and Bea nearly sent one of them out. We played this long breathing game."

"It's called life isn't it?" I quipped. Lulu laughed, something I needed to lift my spirits a touch. Lulu had the most distinctive laugh I had ever heard, somewhere between a hyena and a squawking bird. It was so loud and high that whenever it was raised in a public area, you could see bemused pensioners rushing to duck and cover under whatever ledge was readily available for fear of a sudden seagull attack.

"Listen guys, I'll catch you in a bit, I can't rest until I've spoken to Bea." I moved towards the corridor.

"She's outside having a fag, all that breathing did her in I think." Lulu pulled Sophie towards the side door.

I walked tentatively through the building and into the green room where Bea was selecting a coffee from the new machine. She was scanning each option through her thin-framed, zany purple glasses that perched on the end of her slanty nose. Why she did this every day I had no idea. She knew exactly what all the options were, there were only five. And she selected a good, old reliable tea every time. Her sizeable posterior jutted out so far that some of the smaller students were struggling to squeeze through. Some were even assuming army-style tactics to help their friends past, never daring to ask politely whether she might not take up so much of a public thoroughfare.

"Bea," I said so feebly that she didn't even hear, or bother to respond. "Bea!"

She turned on her little flat shoes as the coffee machine jerked into life behind her. She had hair like Harry Potter, only hers was dyed an aggressive copper. Her thin lips were striped in bright fuchsia lipstick and she had big blue eyes that she fixed on me like an owl watching a juicy mouse. Her hardened expression immediately softened when she realised that it was me. I tried to look sorry; I was sorry.

Once again, before I could open my mouth, she jumped right in. Her tone was what I would call theatrically annoyed. Theatrical was a suitable prefix for every adjective used to describe anything in this school.

"Simon, I trust you have a good reason for missing my class and being LAAAAATE." She elongated the vowel and covered me with a fine mist of saliva.

"Not really, I just mistook the time." My excuse was as feeble as my little boy lost expression but it seemed to work.

"Look, I would normally hang a shoddy student from the rafters, but since it's you." She broke into a smile. The relief was palpable. Bea went on in schoolmistress mode: "However, you must appreciate that if you're going to live the life of an actor, you should be prepared for instant recasting if you don't turn up to rehearsals. It's one of the basics."

She stepped forward and threw one of her beefy arms round me with the same gusto that one might throw a large picnic rug around a cold orphan.

"Listen sweetheart," she gushed pleasantly into my ear. "You're just lucky that Rex isn't in this morning. I can't be held responsible if he hears from someone else but, providing you promise me that it never ever happens again, he won't be hearing it from me."

She raised a pencilled eyebrow and pursed her lips, waiting for my answer as her glasses dangled inches away from my face.

"I promise," I agreed through a mouthful of cleavage. Bea pulled away and laughed.

"Good boy. Run along now. Remember: in out, in out, that's what breathing's all about."

Thank God for that, I thought, promising myself that it would never happen again. Perhaps once or twice more, depending on whether Scott was into morning sex.

Dance class started shortly afterwards: I was determined to make a better go of this than I had of voice class. Even though I was useless, you couldn't help but enjoy the dance sessions. I did, however, resent having to wear the tights, a gripe I shared with at least half of my year. In every class since the term started, the hall was full of disgruntled-looking guys, fidgeting and pulling the Lycra tights free from their leg hair, adjusting their testicles and removing the inseam from their cracks with a perfectly hooked index finger. It looked like a routine in itself.

Camilla was the same as ever, her melamine white face expressionless, painted with autumnal rust-coloured lipstick and eyelids swept with a flash of green shimmer. She was swathed in an emerald pashmina that made her look like a cocoon with legs. On her unfathomably large feet she wore the kind of ballet shoes that made her look as though she had stuck her big flippers into two small pigs.

Her burnt-orange hair was scraped back into a tight bun and, in her hand, she gripped her trusty long stick of bamboo, which she would tap against the floor when agitated. Today it was tapping like the beak of a woodpecker.

She had partnered us up to perform a minuet that we'd practised earlier in the term, but when she went to remind us of the steps, all she was greeted with was a line of clueless expressions. This was not a dance school by any means, the elaborate positions I had "learned" thus far had all begun to seem the same. I had no idea what Position Five was. I'd only ever heard it on the Grand Prix before now. I'd always thought it was a relatively bad position to be in.

"Oh come on peeps, the minuet; one, pause, one, two, three, pause, one, pause." Her voice rang like a shrill metronome as she glided down the hall, her steps in perfect unison like an elegant bird of paradise. She looked hopelessly up at her company who were attempting to copy her steps but appeared to be not so much dancing as wading through a strong current. She let out a dainty sigh like a water balloon deflating, and tapped her stick on the cold, hard floor.

"Right." The crown was beginning to slip in her voice, though her face remained calm and unchanged. "Back to square one. Er, Liana what are those shoes?"

Liana, the youngest of the group, traced the invisible line from Camilla's long finger to her feet.

"Wha?" she said in her broad Essex drawl. "They're my character shoes."

"For goodness sake! Character shoes are plain and black. They're not slippers with Mickey fucking Mouse on them!"

At lunch, I accompanied Sophie and Lulu to the greasy spoon café for a bacon sandwich and a coffee. Once they had arrived I sat frantically pulling the fat off the family-sized slab of meat before me, haphazardly slapped between two slices of bread.

"Well?" Lulu had been fishing for information all morning. Even in dance class, from across a silent room she had been trying to communicate with me by using flag signals with two sleeves of notepaper.

"Well what?" I didn't want to appear to have my arm twisted so easily.

"Something must have happened last night and I'm guessing, since you're smiling, that you got some red-hot cock." Lulu licked the coffee froth off her spoon and plunged it back in for more.

"I might have." Another shriek from Lulu, she loved being right. Sophie smiled along, though it pained her to do so after my morning of truancy had left her emotionally drained.

"Thank God for that." Sophie's tension dropped a yard. "I thought you might be thinking of leaving."

"Who is he? What's he like?" Lulu's eagerness was adding to my thrill, I couldn't play cool any longer; I swung my body around like a thing possessed.

"Girls, he's fantastic," I began, dropping the bacon like a dead cat back onto the greasy roll. "His name's Scott. He's a personal trainer ... I know, and he also runs a club night. He's thirty-two, lives in Stoke Newington. He's an AMAZING kisser and he like, totally digs me."

Both girls looked as excited as I was.

"When can we meet him?" Sophie asked meekly.

"Oh God, Soph, not yet. I've only had a quick snog and felt his cock on my leg so far." I was trying to look nonchalant but the thought of Scott's cock on my leg made me want to wrap the bacon around my own and crack one out there and then.

"So, you've not planned the wedding yet?" Lulu's face was lit up like a bubble lamp.

"Don't be daft."

"You have, haven't ya?" she teased, poking my arm with her frothy spoon.

"No," I insisted, a smile breaking across my face, "but if I had, you're defo off the invitation list."

Our café table erupted into childish giggles. On our way back, Lulu was changing the topic.

"So, you were lucky that Rex wasn't in this morning. You'd have been boll-ocked!"

"Yeah," Sophie said, "apparently he's been in a foul mood all week. He's already got rid of two of the second years. Jeremy and Toby, Jeremy went first, then Toby."

"Really, why?" I began to share Sophie's curiosity and the accompanying fear.

"He just said he couldn't do anything more for them. He'd never really got on with Jeremy and Toby wasn't cutting it. The rest of the year are gutted but they've all been told in no uncertain terms that if anyone wants to complain, on their own heads be it."

She gulped as her eyes went like bowling balls, the stress seemed almost too much. "They've just paid for two terms' worth of fees which they won't get back, and now Rex has put them on some kind of industry blacklist. They'll never find work in acting now."

"That guy is such a cunt," Lulu spat. "I'm so glad I'm not in his play this term, I don't think I could handle it."

"Me neither," I agreed.

I'd only had the misfortune of running into Rex on a handful of occasions. Mostly he just stayed in his office, only deigning to come out when he had ample reason to put the shits up everybody. Rex Bamber, in case you hadn't already guessed, was the tyrannical, demon Head of the Old School. His most recent attack had been on Thursday, hence the reason why I had been so tense all of Friday and Saturday. Before the fumble with Scott, obvs.

Rex was a firm believer in commitment. If you ever missed a class then you would be juggling your place at the school with your hands tied behind your back.

So when Ricky Hellman, one of our cheeky chappy London classmates, had refused to attend one winter Monday night because his granddad was dying (he was in fact snorting ketamine till four in a back bedroom somewhere in Barnet), Rex had called us in en masse to "discuss" the matter.

Once we were all collected in the freezing cold rehearsal room and collectively confused as to why, Rex began to prowl the length of the room with his nose in the air, avoiding our gaze as he spoke. He was a relatively tall and slender man whose once-striking looks had aged rather badly. He was only approaching his late fifties but an overbearing addiction to nicotine had given his skin a faded yellowish tint. His hair, however, was always immaculate and remained perfectly coiffed into a darkish grey sweep on top of his long head. He wore rectangular glasses that perched on the end of his large Jewish nose and repeatedly pushed back up the bridge. He wore a knackered old cheesecloth blazer that stank of fags and a pair of blue Levi 501s that made Jeremy Clarkson look like Marc Jacobs. That day, he had held a long cigarette in his right hand that burnt a bright orange glow and threatened to burn us viciously if wheeled any lower. Rex did not pay any regard to the smoking ban. Any risk that puffing in enclosed spaces posed to asthmatics, students with weak lungs or those with an adverse attitude towards the filthy habit, was flatly ignored. ("Left wing parasites have no place under my roof" was his standard response.)

"We have a problem." Rex directed his voice up to the cracked ceiling, as if musing about something else rather than the matter in hand. His accent was posh and his words clipped. His thin lips were pursed as he stared. We huddled together on the floor to get warm as though we were waiting for the sky to fall.

"It seems Mr. Hellman has a penchant for breaking rules; the school rules, MY rules." Rex always quoted the three degrees of separation which, amazingly, ended up directly offending him every time. No matter how absurd. It was nigh-on impossible to escape the guilt. "Mr. Hellman probably feels that because he shares a name with the popular brand of condiments, he will be given special treatment while he masturbates all over MY RULES." The cool façade was beginning to thaw. I felt the fear tense every muscle in my body. "And just like his namesake is smeared across a cream cracker, I will smear that snivelling little toad across my boot as I'm kicking him out of the front fucking door!"

A girl in my year, Stella, immediately caught my attention. She was rigid: frozen and pale like a rabbit in the headlights, too scared to even breathe, her eyes like saucers.

"If anyone else would like to mirror Mr. Hellman's abhorrent arrogance by demonstrating to both me and the school that they are above the rules, I assure you that you are signing away your chance RIGHT now. Let me remind you that an obstinate actor will never find work in the industry. None of you have the talent or even the strength in the world out there. So you just think about that before you decide to piss me off before the end of this term."

He began to storm out but then spun round before he reached the door, a jet of smoke shooting out of his nose like the top of an old kettle; it razored through the air, scissoring straight towards my face. He was looking towards me and as he did his top lip curled into a disfigured sneer. As a final twist of the knife, he added, "Though, it is clear that some of you won't even make it that far."

It felt as though my heart had risen up to my throat and I struggled to gulp it back down. I felt nervous tears prick my eyes as Rex's gaze remained fixed upon me. His pupils didn't move; his evil grin remained unchanged. The man was a pillar of intimidation. From the top of his perfectly sculpted mane to the tips of his flat sandals, he was painfully firm, scornfully unapologetic and totally terrifying. In my opinion, someone like him, with such little regard for anyone's feelings or emotional wellbeing, was a complete danger to society. Cold of heart and impossible to impress, we were polar opposites. He waited until he saw a little of my spirit break, the flush, the fearful shudder, the quick downward flicker of my eyes. Then he turned, smiling that same cold, patronising smile he always did when he had exerted his power over us to cast fear into our souls.

"That's it," he threw to us, drifting out of the door and leaving a trail of curling white smoke in his wake.

I was sure I could feel a knot in one of my veins, cutting off the blood to my heart. It instead pounded like a bass drum in my ears. I was short of breath. Had Rex meant to say this to me? Was he not pleased with my work so far? I wasn't aware that he'd noticed me at all, let alone enough to pass judgement on any actual acting I had been doing. What was happening? With the questions came the mist of gloom that had shrouded me continuously over the last two days.

"Don't worry," Lulu had reassured me, "he plays games with you, he's testing your mettle. He meant to say it to all of us, not just you. He didn't sack Ricky in the end so just ignore it."

But it had been impossible to ignore. Being around Rex sometimes reminded me of how it felt being around the witch. There was almost no escape from people who hated you for no good reason and who thrived on being hated by you. But, unlike the witch, I couldn't help thinking that I'd voluntarily put myself in this situation with Rex. I had vowed, however, that if I could get through this course and still be standing strong, I would have won all rounds, hands down. With her, with him, the bullies at school: everyone.

Fortunately, Rex would only direct one play a term. If you were picked to be in that play, yes it was a golden opportunity but with it would also be a lingering curse. If you weren't, the only times you might ever come into contact with him were in the halls, or if something had gone awry and he was ready to bear down on all those present.

Rex's plays always included the cream of the school. They were made up of the actors who had impressed him in the first few weeks and, therefore, were instantly offered provisional places in his acting troupe and a six-month internship on a working show for good measure. But Rex was a very particular man and, once you had entered the lair of the Old School elite, you were expected to work like a theatrical dog. The standards were raised and you were immediately expected to demonstrate astounding levels of professionalism, commitment and talent for the course's entire two-year duration. This cemented your path to a successful acting career, but these places were hard to get.

People in the elite had trained themselves to live on three hours' sleep and to eat meals that enhanced their brain power at precisely the right time every day. They had given up their holidays and free time in favour of additional training to better themselves for the greater good of the group. They were immaculately preened, elegantly poised and mercilessly thick-skinned, having been tortured, berated and brow-beaten by Rex's stringent methods for hours and hours on end. In short, they had more or less sold their soul to Rex who, in turn, was able to give them the opportunity to go out into the world as well-trained predators. Most people were petrified of Rex, his towering frame and broad, masculine shoulders. His long, hooked nose atop which his small black shark-like eyes would scan every inch of your trembling figure, almost shattering his frameless spectacle glass with his penetrating, scrutinising glare. I would never want to be in that elite. Cowering under his tyranny for days at a time made me physically shudder at the thought.

Rex could sum an actor up with one look. It was as if the inside of his head housed a computer chip with everyone's vital statistics logged; complete with a grade mark for acting ability and ego. I was sure I would get a low D. Aside from the aforementioned incident, Rex never even looked my way in the communal areas, sweeping by me in a flash of cream and caramel. He was often heading straight for his office door that he would slam shut behind him. And it would remain shut while he was on the other side, wafts of white smoke billowing from underneath it.

Rex was an Olympic smoker and drinker and, rumour had it, a gambler and womaniser too. I knew that he was currently into his fourth marriage to our marionette esque dance tutor: Camilla and rumour had it that there was a baby on the way. We'd been informed of this last month by an ex-second year who had taken refuge in the doorway of the school, crowing about the woes she had suffered as a result of being thrown out the elite earlier that day. A small group of first years had formed around her and, since she had been drowning her sorrows in cheap brandy, she was giving away information from all angles.

"Once," she had slurred, "his third ex-wife, a former pupil, turned up on the doorstep with their two-year-old son. She was shrieking and screaming so loud that we abandoned our classes and filtered into the hallway. 'Since you're quite happy banging one of your students Rex,' she had cried, 'let's see how good she is at taking care of your son.' She just pushed the kid through the door and left. That student, my friend Angela, was discharged soon after and added to the blacklist. Now she works in..." She started to sob as she struggled to say the word out loud: "LIDL!"

At that moment, a stocky male student that Rex had sent out to resolve the situation interrupted the brandy-fuelled gossip peddler.

"Penny, you must leave now, else the police will be called." He extradited the defamed girl from the school doorway.

"No!" Penny had screamed, rather dramatically reaching her arm out behind her as she was dragged down the hall. "He can't do this to me. I was your favourite Rex. DO YOU HEAR ME? I was Lady Macbeth, I was Cressida. I was your MASHA for Christ's sake!" The door had swung shut as she was bundled through it, her protests echoing outside as she was escorted up the street.

We looked at each other in shock. She'd played Masha? Masha Sergeyevna from the Chekhov play *Three Sisters*? It was absolute common knowledge that Masha was Rex's favourite character ever conceived. Penny had been given the honour of playing her and NOW she had been tossed to the out-of-work actor knackers' yard?

Shit, none of us are safe in this place. Not even the good ones. I'd neglected to relay this information to Sophie, as I adored my friend and didn't want her to keel over with a premature heart attack.

We headed back to the school and walked through the dark hall to the green room at the rear of the building. As we passed the door to Rex's office, shut tight, we all shivered slightly as a globule of smoke dribbled out of the keyhole. The Master was in.

After lunch was another class that I had been dreading all week. I was supposed to have read the play thoroughly, in such detail that, if asked, I could chair a debate on any of the characters' motivations. I should also be able to dissect the twists and turns of the plot in relation to the playwright's style and period context. So far, I had managed two pages at home on my bed but the will to masturbate over Scott had been too strong to fight. I had very nearly mopped myself up with the book, but hadn't actually read much of it. I was surely screwed.

As luck would have it, the director for this particular play was Grant who was, thankfully, the most pleasant of all the school's directors. Grant managed to change the whole atmosphere of the place with his larger than life, camp wit. He was in his late forties, balding and rotund with a little pencil moustache and sausage-like fingers covered in old rings. Each ring had a story ("Said the actress to the bishop," he would quip) and although every one of them would compete with a two pound coin for size, and were decorated with flamboyant, elaborate jewels and engravings, they were all from ex-wives and NOT from old Marys languishing in dark bars. Grant was as dolly as tits but, quite unfathomably, was happily married to a woman and had, as rumour had it, three beautiful older children.

Although Grant was jolly and friendly, he did have the acerbic tongue of a scorned drag queen and the temper of a bull bison in mating season. You certainly would not want to get on the wrong side of Grant, not only for fear of disappointing such a truly great director, but also for fear of being publicly dressed down in every colour of the insult rainbow. In some respects, he was like Rex's busty mother. Before she had put her make-up and wig on.

"Who has read the play more than twice?" he asked when everyone had filed in, plays in hands and sitting in an apprehensive circle around him. Four of the eleven present put their hands confidently into the air. Grant looked around the circle, lips pursed and eyes alert.

"Twice?" he clucked. More hands shot up. I suddenly realised that I was one of two who were still sitting with their hands placed in their laps.

My partner in the duo of shame was Dominique; a twenty-seven-year-old former child model. Though mostly on the front of knitting patterns in the mid-eighties, she rose to instant fame when she appeared on the original Screwball Scramble board game box. It was an achievement that was lost on some of the more seasoned directors such as Grant. She seemed to want to retain that golden age and so continued to dress with long, billowing blonde curls in bunches, cascading down her orange tanned shoulders and onto a little tight gingham crop top. Her face was smothered in make-up, mainly bronzer and frosted pink lipstick that made her facial colour palette similar to that of one of those retro Fruit Salad sweets. Her nails were perfectly manicured and jewellery dangled from every available piece of flesh. Her bright blue eyes glanced over at me nervously.

"Fuck," she mouthed. She may have looked like a little princess but Dominique had the gob of a brickie. You could tell that in the past she had rebelled and probably had her daddy wrapped around her little finger more times than he would care to remember. Her glamorous looks and innocent nature made her a hit with the boys, but with the girls and the gays, she was a scream, uttering filthy comments, smoking like a Territorial Army junior and miming masturbation and fellatio behind tutors' heads when their backs were turned. She was also hysterically funny and shared my devilish sense of humour. Grant, however, was onto her from the off.

He slowed his pace: "Once?"

I sheepishly raised my hand, while simultaneously hanging my head. I expected to be publicly chastised, but, on the contrary, Grant was too involved with glancing down his spectacles at Dominique who was still sat there, hand placed firmly in lap, contorting uncomfortably under Grant's watchful eye with an apologetic, aggrieved look on her face.

"You see," she began, whining like a child who'd been caught stealing sweets from the sweetie jar, "I didn't really have time this weekend because I had to go out with my mother and then my friends were having a little gathering on Saturday which I couldn't get out of...." This little act clearly wasn't going to wash with old Mother Clap. Grant leaned forward.

"Listen sweetheart," he said, lifting up his hand to display the huge sapphire-encrusted golden disc decorating his index finger, "this ring may have been given to me by the mother of my darling boy, Hamish, and may have been used to pick the lock on Dame Maggie Smith's dressing room door in the Lyric Theatre some twenty-seven years ago, but it's not too old to take your bloody eye out!"

Once the onus had been taken off my shoulders, thanks to Dominique's winning script negligence, we ended up having quite a productive rehearsal. I managed, as the readings went on, to get a feel for which character I would like to play most. It was the bratty middle class, snooty brother with an attitude problem. Excellent, typecast again!

Dominique had been laid on the slab by Grant for most of the afternoon. Things had just got worse when she tried to inconspicuously search for a pen in her ginormous Hello Kitty bag and ended up completely upturning it. Last night's knickers came tumbling out and a rather large stick of lip gloss escaped and sped towards Grant's moccasins. He had merely raised one eyebrow in her direction as she apologised profusely, perspiring like a blind lesbian in Billingsgate Market. She was then asked to read alongside me as the sister of the piece. When she at last found the page and began to read a large excerpt from *Bridget Jones's Diary*, it was clear that the book she had been avoiding reading all weekend was not actually the right one after all. Grant didn't seem to be all that annoyed with her though; beneath his cold, unimpressed visage he was actually stifling the desire to burst out laughing. I could also see that he was placing a big black mark next to Dominique's name on the register, never a good sign in any capacity.

"Right, tomorrow night I will have cast it and then we will be reading through in the parts that have been given. DO go home and read the play, DON'T forget about it all evening and skim through before the lesson starts, and for God's sake get some sleep please, the lot of you. Half of you look more worn out than the original usherettes from Agatha Christie's *Mousetrap*. Now, off you go." He shooed us out with his hands to choruses of "Thanks Grant." I swept out before anyone could beat me to the one cubicle in the gents.

After I'd relieved myself of all the pent-up tension and a few bottles of water, I came out of the cubicle to find Grant standing before me at the urinal, his belly nearly touching the porcelain, his penis flopped in his hand. A stream of liquid shot from him as if he were hosing down cormorants after an oil tanker explosion. He didn't look up as I went to wash my hands but carried on urinating, bold as brass. I turned to leave when Grant called over my shoulder. "Good reading today my boy, I think you'll be pleased with your casting." It was awkward as hell but I managed a response.

"Thanks Grant."

I left the toilet smiling but shuddering slightly at the thought of Grant's flaccid penis dangling over the trough like a dead, hairless rat. I hoped I wouldn't remember this moment when I was looking down at Scott's, or, even worse, when I was eating a saveloy. Mmm, Scott. Although I had only felt his cock through our trousers, it had seemed well over average and definitely larger than mine.

My heart leapt, I was free. I could call Scott now and see what he was up to without the dread of starting school feasting away at the back of my mind. I glanced into the other room as I made my way out. The other group appeared to have gone home and, therefore, so had Lulu and Sophie. The third room, however, still seemed to be a hive of activity.

The elite were in there, training. They would be doing this until the early hours probably. I couldn't imagine Rex letting them away before ten or eleven; it was now just before six. Poor bastards, I thought, I had heard that they were performing a Joe Orton play with the fun taken out. That would be interesting – kind of like *The Jungle Book* without the jungle.

Dominique came sidling out of the ladies. "What a never ending joke today was," she whinged.

"I wouldn't worry, I don't think Grant took it all that seriously, at times he was trying to hide his amusement." I put an arm around her shoulder. "Besides, you wouldn't be you without a bit of blonde shoved in there somewhere." I affectionately played with her hair.

"I guess, thanks." She looked at the floor momentarily. "You want to go for a drink, everyone's down at the Glass Pig?"

I thought for a second. "I think I'll pass, I'm meeting someone and I can't really let them down." The truth was I had no idea whether Scott was even available, but I didn't want to make myself counteractively unavailable and I had a feeling that if I went boozing with the rest of the course then I'd stay there all night.

"Okay, I'll see you tomorrow?" Dominique made for the door.

"Oh, and Dom, don't forget to read the play tonight. You don't want to piss Grant off again tomorrow now do you?" I winked.

Dominique screwed her face up in protest. "Man, that guy is such a...." She held her clenched fist up to her mouth and violently simulated jerking an invisible cock onto her suspended tongue. At that precise moment, without missing a beat, the gents' door swung open and out Grant strode. He halted only because he was met with two horrified faces blocking his way, one with her hand placed suspiciously next to her open mouth. Dominique's quick reflexes kicked into gear and she took a deep breath, extending her hand out as if smoothing the air in front of her face.

"You are a fool, a blind, pitiable fool who has no desire or thought for others," she boomed, a line expertly lifted from *Hay Fever*. She looked back at our startled faces and gave a little smile. "I'm just getting in some practice for tomorrow, Grant." Grant shook his bemusement off through his hands and carried on walking.

"Well you'll have to give it more welly than that," he scoffed and barged his way through the door.

I left the building and pulled out my phone that had remained switched off for six long hours. In six hours, I could have been inundated with text messages and calls from my hunky squeeze! When I flipped my phone open, however, one lazy bleep to signify my mother had called was the only thing that rung out. My heart slipped a little when I thought of all the daydreaming I had done, imagining what the texts might have said. I even held off looking at my phone over lunch so that I could have something to look forward to at the end of the day. Glumly, I pulled my bag higher onto my shoulder and began to wade through the scattered leaves of newspaper that had collected at the door stoop. I slumped on into the miserable dark of the Archway evening. The weekend was coming to a close and in every house the length and breadth of the capital, people would be getting ready for an early night before their working week started again. I hated that. If there was one thing that working long hours had taught me, it's that you use your spare time wisely. My motto: when you have a spare second, fill it with a cocktail. It was the only way to keep sane. Beez thought the same.

Shit! I'd forgotten about Beez and the Australia business. I'd been too swept up with the Scott farrago, which I was slowly turning into a farce with all the mental chasing I seemed to be doing. Judging by the hostility of my empty phone box, the relationship already seemed like it would be an uphill struggle. I was clearly the one who would have to put all the legwork in. But then, wasn't I always?

I let out a relentless sigh. Things seemed to be changing so quickly; Beez was leaving, Scott was going off me already and I wasn't even going to start factoring Rex into the equation else I may just have to step out in front of a fast-moving bus. Maybe, I thought, just maybe a Solero would cheer me up. Into the shop I went. It didn't cheer me up, it set off my sensitive molars and the authentic orange flavouring made me wince. Life is so shit, I thought, and tossed the remaining ice cream into the nearest bin.

Suddenly, as if out of nowhere, my phone sprang to life. I fished it out of my pocket, dispersing various bits of lint across the pavement in my haste.

Scott's name flashed up at me from the small screen; I had thankfully resisted earlier temptation to give him a mobile pet name like Baby or Myboy1 (both previous entries for other quick flings). I would have to think up something more original if this really took off. I answered it, trying to sound as if I hadn't been drowning my sorrows in a hefty dose of E numbers. As a personal trainer, he would never approve.

"Hello?"

"Hey babe."

I loved the way Scott said babe, I didn't like it when Gok Wan said it, but with Scott it sounded effortlessly cool. I would just have to watch that it didn't extend to babe plural; that would be too much.

"Hey you." I flushed.

"All finished? I held off ringing earlier coz I knew you was at school." Scott's regional bad grammar was as sexy as it was charming.

"Yeah, all done, been a long day." I must learn how to practice formulating better structured sentences when embarrassed. It would surely be a weapon in my arsenal for future use.

"Ah babe listen, do you fancy a beer? Sounds like you deserve it. I had to pop and see a client this afternoon. Right fat fuck he was, he kept asking if we could stop and buy a Solero." I cringed and wiped a non-existent dribble of vanilla from my chin. "Anyway, I got back a bit ago and I haven't yet had a shower so... I'll hop in and meet you in town in, say, an hour?"

Too much info. I was now thinking about Scott in the shower, soaping himself down. The steam from the water rising and forming beads of sweat that dribbled down his perfect, pink, rock-hard nipples. My cock pulsated in my underpants.

"That sounds great, Scott. Oh, Great Scott!" I laughed. Oh God, I was laughing at my OWN shitty joke. Scott had the good grace to humour me. "Yeah." I composed myself. "It's just I've been at school all day in the same clothes and I'm a bit gross."

"I don't care babe, just come as you are. You can't go wrong if you just bring your gorgeous self,"

I laughed. It eased the corniness.

"You're a bit of an old charmer really aren't you."

"Me? Yeah, I'm afraid I am a bit, can't help it. Me mother brought me up right."

I loved his mother.

"Alright, where shall we meet?"

I wanted to see him, I wanted to look into his face, touch his rough skin, feel his stubble against me, squeeze his flesh and bite his neck.

"I tell you what, for old time's sake, let's go to the Wellington."

Oh. Sweet. Moses.

*

It was like returning to the scene of the crime. Fortunately all the evidence had been washed away and now, instead of bright-red vomit there was an unusually clean square foot of concrete. I pushed my way in. It was quite busy inside, full of men huddled in groups with cheesy house music on the sound system. A few stragglers loitered, eyeing up their fellow singletons. Standard Sunday fudge-packing fare. I felt a hand on my shoulder and spun round to see my white knight, resplendent in a plain t-shirt and grey hoodie beaming down at me from the extra foot he had on me.

"Hey babe." He smiled and I, without saying a word, stood on tiptoes and pushed my lips against his. It was totally forward but Scott seemed to like it, grabbing me around my shoulder blades and clutching me in further. I pulled back.

"Wow," said Scott mulling the kiss over his lips. "What a welcome."

"I felt I owed you something for last night." I had relaxed completely; it was like I was laying my cards on the table from the outset and now I could reap the rewards.

"You don't owe me anything!" Scott said playfully.

"Okay, but I can't take the kiss back now can I?"

"Don't take it back, keep them coming." He reached for his wallet. "Wine?"

I shouldn't be drinking at all, that would be two nights in a row and I would really have to read that bloody play. Oh well, maybe just one.

"Beer," I said after thought, "Tonight I'm going to be a man!"

Scott laughed. "Wicked, back in a sec."

But of course we didn't just stay for one. We talked and laughed and Scott had put his hand on mine. It was one of those fantastic drinks when you just talk utter rubbish but it's funny and it's comfortable, and you could sit there forever. And on the bus back to Stoke Newington we had been hardly able to keep one another's eyes off each other. People must have known what was going on because I was blushing like a schoolboy and Scott was being overly chivalrous.

Later on, after much kissing, exploring every part of each other's mouths with our tongues, Scott began to slide my top up and over my head and I literally ripped Scott's from his body. Our skin had touched for the first time, Scott's body burned into mine as he held me tightly; my chest rose and fell with the race of my heart rate. I traced my palm forcefully up and down Scott's back, examining every dip and outline of his defined muscles. I kissed his neck and chest and slid down his torso with my tongue. His smooth skin felt as soft as my earlier abandoned ice cream and tasted not of sour orange but instead of tangy sweat and cologne. I had then thrown Scott by pushing him up against the same wall that I too had been slammed into the steamy night before. I had pulled his thick, long shaft from inside his tight boxers and taken it between my lips, pleasuring and tickling every inch of it with my tongue. I inhaled its musty male odour and pushed it deeper and deeper into my mouth, sucking harder and harder each time. I looked up at Scott who was frantically playing with his nipples, eyes closed, enjoying each new sensation as it passed through his nervous system and back down into his rod. I fed ravenously on him, coaxing and teasing with every muscle in my mouth. Scott's body twitched more and more sporadically as the ecstasy reached its peak and then it had burst. Hot juice erupted over my tongue as Scott gripped the back of my head and groaned with release and relief. He flung me onto the bed and did the same. His touch was tender but his hunger was rough. I watched his spine ripple as he worked my cock, sucking and licking and beating it against his open mouth. It was passionate and dirty and after I climaxed, we lay on each other, exhausted and sweaty, nerves still tingling and breath hot and heavy. Scott scrambled up the bed to me and lay facing me, staring into my eyes.

"You're amazing," he panted, his voice soft and gravelly. We shared that long, lingering kiss again and I cupped his face in my hands. After we pulled away, I reached for a tissue to clean myself up; my jeans were still wound tight round my ankles, my socks dangling off my feet like an old man's scrotum. My penis was still raw, a sign that it was the most amazing blow job I had ever had in my entire modest sex life. I adoringly watched Scott wander naked around the room looking for his discarded clothes, his silver watch and neck chain glinting in the superficial light and his dick swinging between his legs like a rolled-up pink pancake. I thought about what excellent head he gave and had a startling revelation. His new phone nickname would forever be "Solero".

5

Sandra drummed one of her long, bejewelled talons on the desk as she flicked through the latest edition of *Coffee Break* magazine; the lime-green mohair jumper she was currently fashioning made her look a little like an out-of-season conker.

I had been rambling on about Scott for well over an hour and Sandra's concentration was beginning to wane. Her eyes involuntarily drifted back to the page even though I was looking directly at her while I was speaking. It was ten past nine and very few people were in the office at this time of the morning. The Project Managers didn't start surfacing until around half past nine, but Sandra and I (the two administrators) had to be in early doors to hold the fort. This involved mainly bitching about the rest of the workforce while drinking endless cups of tea.

We had to tea ourselves before the other staff members arrived so that we didn't get saddled with having to make a round for everyone else. People's hydration habits within an organisation such as Eco Scene were perplexing at best. I'd never dream of adding to my tea some of the strange ingredients that most of the Project Managers did. Raw mint, nettles, cloves. More often than not I would stand open-mouthed as I scanned the carton that they had given me, wondering which poor bastard's job it was to milk the hazelnuts that were poured into it.

Sandra had the same sentiments as me but her gripes were directed more at the arrival times of certain members of staff. She would suck her teeth and say, "Why do they think they can just roll in whenever they feel like it? In a minute, they'll be feeling my carbon footprint right across their big backsides!"

Of the main office, the admin department governed the front area. Sandra and I shared a break-out space with three other staff members. Carl, the IT and Outreach Manager whom I had helped to hire around six months ago, was a laugh, enjoyed a beer or two and was quite easy on the eye, plus he had turned up to the interview hungover, which I had found hilarious. Opposite me sat Pepe, the Company Secretary and my line manager. Though appointing him to manage any of us was an insult to our intelligence. Pepe was a short Spanish guy who suffered from a condition that I called Managerial Autism. He could sit for hours on end dicking around with Sage or waving annoying purple dockets in the air but he had zilcho people skills. If ever faced with a challenging situation in the office, he shifted and fidgeted in his seat, avoiding eye contact and flushing the same colour as the American Cherry Tan slip-ons he wore to the office every day but "Casual Friday".

English was obviously Pepe's second language and, although for the most part he was fluent, he could still gaffe his way through the simplest of sentences. Not that my Spanish was much better, mind you. He was also repellent to sarcasm.

Coming from a maths background, Pepe wasn't very clued up about environmental issues either. It was quite depressing to see him standing within a circle of board members at an important meeting, trying to tape together the titbits of information that he had picked up from watching *Countryfile* in an attempt to sound knowledgeable on the subject. I had no such desire to fit into this environment. If I didn't know anything about pesticides by now then I wasn't likely to, and I probably wouldn't want to learn about them either.

Last in our little club was Clarissa. Clarissa was the editor of Eco Scene's sister publication: *Coverage*. We had managed the production of the magazine in-house up until a few months ago, but with such growth in popularity as was brought on by the recycling boom of the nineties, *Coverage* was now run as its own business with its very own skeleton staff... of one, Clarissa.

Technically, though we shared an office with her, Clarissa only rented space from Eco Scene and, therefore, she wasn't *really* eligible for all the perks that she had when she was part of the organisation. This, however, did not stop her commandeering the best desk and plonking her arse down at it, helping herself to all the two-tiered cookies in the office biscuit barrel and charging the endless water filter cartridges and humidifier refills to the company, much to Sandra's chagrin.

Though an insufferable, and rather savvy, sponge, Clarissa was also an exceptionally clever and inspirational lady. She had read English at Cambridge, written many successful fringe plays, had millions of established contacts within the arts, much to my glee, and she played the trombone expertly. Grade eight no less. But being so creative had made Clarissa hypersensitive, to the point of excruciating irritation. Her worst habit was to miraculously develop the psychosomatic symptoms of any illness that was currently getting media exposure and creating unnecessary dramatics off the back of it. Although I shared an affiliation with Clarissa re the drama connection, I found her outbursts incredibly tiresome and so laboured that they almost always over-egged the theatrical pudding. It was also by strange coincidence that she always seemed to fall ill on the exact date that each new Terry Pratchett novel was released.

Another of Carissa's over-the-top claims was that she was able to tune in to animal psyche; a gift she'd had ever since she held a dying cat in her arms on the hard shoulder of a dual carriageway. She was forever showing us pictures of flea-bitten moggies she claimed to have healed through the power of meditative massage. I reckon that the real reason why cats found her so magnetic was because her clothes always had a slight scent of milk that was on the turn. But maybe that was just me being cynical. Clarissa was another one who would often saunter in late and faff about for the following half-hour which cut straight through Sandra like red-hot steel. I, for the most part, just tried to block it out.

Monday morning was our team meeting and I would have to feign interest and minute every pointless issue raised. I'd also inevitably have to sit there and try and mask my discombobulation as the Project Managers went cock-a-hoop at the good news that more chemicals were being banned from the production of all my favourite processed foods. It was tiring for me but then there was no motivation here. It wasn't an artsy or creative place to work. Miracles didn't happen and gossip was less about who shagged who at the Christmas party but more which fruit carries the most air miles.

I let out a sigh which blew the surface dust off my computer screen. This was a different world, I told myself, this world of sun salutations and washing apples before you ate them. It was their world and good luck to them. But I didn't belong here and soon I'd have to address that.

The door swung open.

With the reflexes to rival two young cheetahs, my Facebook page was covered with the company email Inbox screen and Sandra's *Coffee Break* was thrown swiftly under the desk and replaced with a copy of the much less interesting *Voluntary Sector* Magazine.

In walked Pepe in his little mac and terracotta scarf. His hair perfectly parted with a sizeable dollop of his wife's spittle. His do was so well structured, I sometimes wondered whether it was actually made of some kind of polyresin. However, not even Pepe's hard-wearing barnet could withstand an English February wind. Often, throughout the winter months, he would enter with a cow's lick at the front and with the parting humorously tousled. He had dark olive Brazilian skin, small eyes and a sloping nose atop wide, brown lips. His face was almost always set into a nervous smile from under which he often flashed a set of perfectly white teeth. Pepe was as tall as he was wide, which wasn't very much in either case. It always made me smile when I imagined how perfectly his diminutive, squarish frame would fit perfectly into a sideboard cupboard, if for some reason you ever needed to just lock him away.

"Morning," he chirruped. I hated it when he said that word; it was so painstakingly formal that it made me want to sever my own ears off. "How was your weekend?"

His tone was always the same. The Kray twins could have sat in our places, sharpening knives, and he would still have asked that question with unchanged intonation. I half groaned and nodded my head in response. Sandra tried to look as though he had broken her concentration. Unfortunately she was actually holding the magazine upside down. It instantly annoyed me that Pepe would never pick up on that even.

Day after day it was the same. Our blatant procrastination couldn't have gone unnoticed every time, yet Pepe refused to say anything about it, even as a joke. It was deplorable.

Sandra put down her magazine with the same relish that she might put down a Jackie Collins.

"Hi Pepe," she called over her green fuzzy shoulder, the fine wisps of cotton bending under her breath.

"Hi Sandra, was your weekend good?" He pulled off his little mac and scarf and hung them on the same side of the coat-stand that he always used. He pulled out his lunchbox and lined up his array of fruit in alphabetical order on the desk: an apple, banana and orange. The banality of it all drove me mad; I half wanted to get up and slap my knob down on his desk next to the banana, just to get a reaction.

Sandra examined one of her decorated nails and swung round on her chair to give everyone a good view of the retina-searing jumper. I could now see that it was teamed with a high-waisted pencil skirt and thick, gold elasticated cinch belt. Gold was definitely her colour of the month. In the style stakes, she'd give C3P0 a run for his money.

"Tally got food poisoning so I spent most of Friday night holding her hair back. Then Saturday I had to go down Leyton to get some trainers for Delvin coz the crappy little shop in the Angel don't do size elevens."

Delvin was Sandra's seventeen-year-old son who, if he was anything like his dad, was sure to be well on the way to becoming a hottie. Every time Sandra mentioned Delvin towering over the rest of the family, his size eleven feet or his wrestling singlet, an excited butterfly would escape from my tummy.

I was obviously so desperate nowadays that I was preying on the young. Yes, he was far too young for me now. But if the old adage was true, with size eleven feet he could be filed away for future reference.

"What about you?" He fell under her scrutinising glare. Here we go, I thought, another thrilling weekend at the house of Elverez.

"Well, on Saturday I had to change the lock on the front door because it was sticking and I couldn't figure out what the problem was."

Oh great.

"So I called the locksmith and he said that he would be a half-hour. So I went to Robert Dyas to pick out the lock. I didn't want it too shiny because it would not fit the rest of the door and not too heavy else the door would be breaking. I needed to find the perfect one in only half an hour."

Not too shiny? Not too heavy? Fuck me, it's Goldi-Locks!

"Then after he came I was wondering whether I should try and get the bees' nest from out of my garage. It has been there for many months now but I didn't want to disturb it because I know bees get angry and I don't like being stung. So I look up the best way to take away the nest on the internet and..."

I wondered how much more I could take of the lock and bee disaster before my head exploded and covered my Hewlett Packard 174D in shards of my cerebellum. How did I ever get in this position? There must be more to life than this!

As more people started to dribble through the door, the smell intensified. Why did everyone who worked here reek of that horrible odour that comes from leaving your washing in the machine for too long? I rolled my eyes. Every week I felt this way. I had to keep telling myself that it was just a means to an end. It would all be over when I'd finished my course and was set to walk straight into a glittering theatrical career. I doodled about on the computer for a bit, sidestepping any potential work that could and should have been done on Friday. By then it was around about half ten so I dragged my pad and pen from the desk in front of me and practically lolloped off my chair.

"Come on guys." Pepe was rubbing his hands together at the thought of running through the week's non-events. Why he got so pleased I just could not fathom, he never understood a bloody word that was said in there anyway.

His position in this organisation was held in the same regard as mine and Sandra's. We were just glorified manual labour. The only difference was that Sandra and I had accepted it while Pepe liked to pretend that he was otherwise.

Perhaps, if I had no other option but to remain in this job without any other outside career path, I might turn into Pepe. I shuddered. I couldn't ever imagine being that boring, or choosing to dress in the shades of brown that one might ordinarily associate with a dog's backside. We all filed into the little meeting room like Jews into Auschwitz. I often fantasised about digging my fingernails into the outer doorframe and wailing like an Iranian widow, in protest, to anyone walking by: "Don't make me go in there, I can't face it. PLLEEEAAASSSSEE!" but instead I painted a cynical smile across my face and made my way in regardless.

Cordelia was already there, pad and pen laid out, an acid smile burning its way across her thin lips. Cordelia was the Creative Director of Eco Scene: she definitely took the Cor out of the name Cordelia and the Cosy out of Eco Scene. Before she had taken over the previous January, Eco Scene had been spiralling towards closure. At the helm was a doddery old fool called Steadman, whom everyone had adored but who had been a total liability. In time, Steadman had begun to get a little senile and was giving the organisation's money away to nuns and *Big Issue* sellers in the street. As a result, he had had to "retire early" rather than be pushed off the proverbial plank. He was such a jolly old soul who used to have a big pot of sweets on his desk, like one of those loveable teachers you'd get at primary school. He'd also let us get away with murder because he always claimed to trust us, and this trust was only moderately abused. Coming from a time when environmental organisations were tiny rooms with four people in them, Steadman was distinctly old school and always wore a padded tweed jacket with comfortable, worn loafers.

It hadn't been like work back then. I would make personal calls at regular intervals, Sandra would read her Jackie Collins bold as you like, and the office had a much more welcoming and relaxed air to it. In short, it was a pleasant place to be, very different to how it was now. Once Steadman had left and they drafted in Cordelia to get the organisation back on its feet, all the fun had been taken out. She'd put a stop to unnecessary non-work-related calls with a monitoring system, banned all personal literature from the office and kept a watchful glare on her employees with those beady eyes behind those purple-winged glasses of hers. She reminded me of the penguin in Wallace & Gromit's *Wrong Trousers*, the one with the hidden agenda, as she sat there in her starched suit. Her hair was piled on top of her head like a blonde dog turd. The Kirby grips were soldered into place lest a stray hair did the unthinkable and tried to make a bid for freedom.

Cordelia was mentally scanning people as we entered the room like we were bar codes, grimly carried by the conveyor belt through her monstrous cash register. She hiccupped greetings to each in turn until we were all sitting down. Tim, the hot Senior Project Officer, was not in yet and Cordelia, no doubt, would be scribbling this onto her pad in a matter of moments. Tim was undoubtedly the office hunk. He was a bit rough round the edges and was the proud owner of a furry little belly that was susceptible to popping out of his t-shirt every once in a while. But the guy, for all his little imperfections, exuded sexual appeal. He wasn't married but had three beautiful little girls with a long-term girlfriend and, somehow, that made him sexier. Tim was the kind of guy who would suffer for his art; unafraid to get arrested outside Parliament for throwing eggs at politicians. He had tattoos on his biceps depicting fire and ice and wore flimsy, weathered shirts that draped around his torso, exposing tufts of manly chest hair sprouting up at the neck. He also had a way of speaking that had flirtation built right in; the smoothness of his voice and his suggestive intonation melted my groin with every syllable. He always took the boredom out of staff meetings, although I had to work hard to monitor my ogling in favour of actually listening and taking minutes. I entered the room and squeezed myself between Sandra and Carl. Cordelia raised her head and put her pen down.

"It has come to my attention," she began, no hello or welcome or anything, "that Eco Scene's flexible internet policy is once again being compromised and, I'm afraid, action will have to be taken."

People shifted awkwardly in their seats and wary glances were exchanged, none of which escaped Cordelia's attention. The truth was that we were all guilty, but one was going to have to take the bullet. I couldn't help but assume that she was referring to me as my desk was the only one visible from the front door and, therefore, I was exposed to the entire office. I was going to have to confess. I opened my mouth to whimper when suddenly the door swung open and the scent of Golden Virginia and motorbike fuel filled the room. Cordelia's neck shot left and her nose wrinkled up as though an incontinent bird had just shat on her shoulder.

Tim stood there; Biker God. He had a helmet under one arm, a filthy leather jacket wrapped around him and ripped jeans exposing dark hair on olive-skinned thighs. I felt a female shudder ripple round the table like a Mexican wave.

"Sorry I'm late," Tim said breathily as the team members nearest the door shifted a seat round to let him sit. "Bloody bike nearly went over. What did I miss?"

"Nice of you to join us, Timothy." She always called him Timothy, even though he was never known as anything other than Tim to anyone else. She went on, looking at him as though he had pissed all over her shoes and then had the audacity to ask her to pop it back in and zip him up. "I was just saying about the office internet usage. It's being abused and I have no choice but to deal with the offender, offenders or with the office as a whole."

Tim feigned shock and plopped himself down.

"Well, how can you tell who it is? Surely the internet is monitored via a single server." He wasn't bothered by her, he was much more of a bring-it-on kind of guy.

"I have the list of websites." She pulled out a leaf of paper, seemingly from nowhere. Fourteen arseholes banged shut.

"Make-your-own-cleaning-products," she read from her script, peering up and scanning the room. Oh fuck! I realised that she had my whole internet life history there, immortalised in Times New Roman. I prickled.

"Yeah, that was me." Tim shrugged.

Cordelia looked as flummoxed as I did.

"You?!" she spat.

Both she and I knew that she could never beat Tim to the punch. She didn't have the guts or the intelligence to outsmart this man.

"Yeah, I was doing a piece for a magazine on ethical cleaning. What's next?"

This was like a game to him. I could see it in the way he leant forward and rubbed his hands together. I continued to watch this exchange in utter disbelief.

"Okay." She furiously scanned the page in front of her. "Aha! Pin-the-tail-on-the-donkey.com?" She raised an eyebrow.

"Yep, me again." Tim leant back, effortlessly cool. "I was looking for ideas on how to make our website more appealing to kids."

"Right." Cordelia was more furious than she thought she was letting on. "Aha! Beer-in-the-evening.com." She knew she had him now; there was no way he could spin this to look as though it was beneficial to the organisation, he was bound to buckle under the pressure. Her glare was razor sharp. Tim's shoulders dropped.

"Aaah, you've got me there, Cordy," he said. She smiled with sadistic pleasure. "I was looking for somewhere to take you out this weekend."

Game, set and match.

Cordelia's face went puce, she couldn't argue with that. Tim leaned back in his seat and placed his hands behind his head, glancing quickly around the room. My hero took the bullet for me, I thought as I struggled to catch Tim's roving eye. Just when I thought it wouldn't come, I got a wink and a smile.

The rest of the meeting was pure comedy. Cordelia's face never did pale back to its usual alabaster white and she continued to glow a healthy cerise throughout the whole ninety minutes. A couple of times she stumbled with her words and when one of her papers wriggled free and floated down to the carpet, dodging her grip with every swoop, I had to stifle a giggle.

It would have been less chaotic to have asked Coco the Clown to chair the meeting. It was highly amusing to see her squirm so much; it made her human, which she had to be deep down. Usually, the woman was so anal that her skirts had a permanent suction mark woven into the fabric. Now she had lost a little control, she was as imperfect and clumsy as the rest of us.

After a fairly uncomfortable Any Other Business when she brought up the same point twice, everyone began sloping off back to their seats. Tim remained in the meeting room, Mr Cool and Relaxed waiting for his chat with Ms Uptight, the original odd couple.

Cordelia removed herself from the office for a bit to regain composure before she re-entered the room. She had probably gone to hoik the daft silk petticoat out of her bottom before attempting to discipline the office rebel. Sandra and I were in pieces.

"Lord, that was fun-ny!" Sandra giggled.

Pepe was less than amused. For some reason, he had a kind of sick fascination with Cordelia. She was everything he wasn't: business-minded, organised, composed (if you disregarded the last hour) and she appeared to know what she was doing even if it was clear to everyone else that she obviously didn't. She slotted into the over-inflated manager's role like a hand in a glove.

Pepe, on the other hand, was clunky, shy and avoided confrontation at all costs. He was like a piece of jigsaw puzzle that you hammered in even though it didn't fit and, as a result, the whole of the top left corner just didn't look right.

Cordelia was somewhat of an inspiration to poor, insecure Pepe and I found that to be the most depressing thing ever. I often wondered whether they might be secretly having an affair since he spent so much time ogling her from afar. Considering he was about four-foot nothing and she towered over him like Godzilla in a court shoe, the walk down any sort of wedding aisle would be comical in itself. The last time they were unified in such a fashion was particularly cringe-worthy. A couple of months ago it had been Cordelia's birthday. Pepe, not really knowing how best to offer her congratulations on arrival had visibly panicked. Instead of greeting her with the obligatory birthday wish, he had inadvertently puckered up his lips to give her a kiss on the cheek. She wasn't expecting it, he wasn't expecting to do it and yet they were in full view of the office and had to go through with it.

I watched in horror as he literally stood on tiptoes to meet her on bended knee just for one clumsy birthday smacker. Jesus, I'd thought, even their kisses are formal. If they were to ever conceive children, she'd probably choose to dip her Tampax in his sperm rather than have any sort of contact. And, to be honest, I wouldn't blame her.

I went back to staring at a blank computer screen. Yes, I had emails to plough through and phone messages to check, but I wasn't really in the mood. I'd much rather ponder on how ugly the spawn of Cordelia's eggs and Pepe's smeg would be. And then I couldn't get the theme tune to *Fraggle Rock* out of my head.

There was a clatter of marble on wood and the office door burst open. A jumble of bags, crushed velvet and Body Shop cocoa butter waddled through the door. It was Clarissa, her hair a cacophony of autumnal colours and her thick glasses magnifying her eyes so much they looked like two huge tax discs stuck to her face. The bags went down with a crunch as her huge, billowing wax jacket was ripped from her body and thrown with gay abandon onto the coat-stand. Miraculously, it hung quite straight.

Clarissa didn't make eye contact with anyone though everyone was staring; playing right into her hands. Her sage green and purple velveteen dress coupled with the braid dangling from her frizzy wig gave her a look of Maid Marian sitting on an electric fence. She sighed as she dropped into her computer chair, grimacing down at her brown, organic turn shoes that looked practically edible. If I didn't know any better I'd have thought it was the Sealed Knot re-enactment day. She sighed again, this time a fraction more audibly and a dollop more crestfallen. I had to go over.

"What's up, Clarissa?" I trod carefully so as not to appear like I was buying into her performance.

"It's Hecate!" She swung round in her chair; she sounded like an irritating child who wanted an ice cream. Sandra rolled her eyes and swivelled back round in her chair. I, on the other hand, was genuinely confused.

"What, the Greek Goddess? What's she..."

"No, not the Greek Goddess; my blasted neighbour's cat! I'm cat-sitting for my neighbour."

I remembered. I also remembered that I hated cats. I was continually at odds as to why anybody would want to own one themselves, let alone look after someone else's riddled little flea buffet. Unfortunately, Eco Scene was cat central; a veritable honeypot of feline lovers from across London. The kind who made stupid baby noises when they spotted an abhorrent picture of a tabby in a fishbowl on the front of a greetings card. The very thought of which sent spurts of bile up from my innards.

"Darling little puss puss," she went on, not resisting the temptation to mimic a baby voice one bit, " is obviously not used to Auntie Clarry and has scratched her all over. I think she needs space to breathe. She's missing her mummy and she needs to have time to pine on her own."

Pine on her own? She'd be offering the creature cognitive behavioural therapy next! The only thing worse than people loving cats, in my opinion, was when they felt the need to personify them.
Clarissa needed to be told that her neighbour was not, in fact, Hecate's "mummy" at all. The only maternal presence in Hecate's life had probably eaten her brothers and sisters.

Clarissa tugged a velvet sleeve halfway up her arm to expose the battle scars underneath. Three long, aggressive-looking marks stretching from wrist to near enough elbow stared back at me. It almost looked as if her arm was trying to burst out of its own skin. I winced in pain but Clarissa remained comparatively nonchalant. Clearly, when you are a cat lover, you take the rough with the smooth.

"I'd leave her alone," I agreed. "Those scratches are vicious, you don't want her tearing you apart like Sandra does with the TK Maxx sale rail. There'll be nothing of you left."

Clarissa looked up from her wounded flesh. "I can't give up on them just because they're a little challenging, where would that get me?"

I shrugged, not really knowing how to respond.

She fished around in her indigo and claret mirrored bag and produced a small packet of what appeared to be plant seeds with a dodgy etching of a ginger cat scrawled across the front.

"So I've bought her this..." *Jolly Pussy for Feline Harmony* the label read. My eyes immediately widened. "My friend Sukee from the Cats Commission at Wye makes these amazing powders. They are designed to relax and calm your troubled tabby. You just sprinkle a little into the litter tray which generates a homeopathic vapour that penetrates their senses while they excrete. It has an immediate positive effect on their emotional well-being."

Now I had seen everything. Cat mood-altering powders? Wasn't that really a thinly veiled way of playing God? Didn't Nurse Ratched do the same with Jack Nicholson at the end of *One Flew over the Cuckoo's Nest*?

And why put it in the litter tray? Surely the only part of a cat that makes direct contact with that place would be the privates and the anus. If that was where the engine room of a cat's personality was located then maybe I should try sprinkling a little on Cordelia's chair. With her anal retentiveness, it would disappear like frozen peas up a Hoover nozzle. Maybe then she would cut me some fucking slack.

I looked over at Sandra, but she had stopped listening a long while ago. The theatrics of Clarissa pushing her cat cocaine was certainly of no interest to *Coffee Break* magazine and, therefore, of no interest to Sandra. I glanced over at Carl who looked as if he'd just been given an extremely difficult sum to do, mouth agog with a frown stuck to his face like a Mr Potato Head. These kinds of conversations may seem absolutely ludicrous but they were also perfectly normal to those who had been in the office longer than the couple of months that Carl had worked there.

Clarissa swung round on her chair and began pulling her day's equipment out of the flimsy cotton bag. This included a strange liquid that swirled around conspicuously from inside a cylindrical Tupperware. It was green but practically luminous, the kind you might see in a witch's cauldron in a children's book or dripping down the walls of a low-rent European bar. She rested the potion on the table like an apothecary and continued to pull the rest of her things out of her many other satchels.

I needed to get out of here! I was feeling oppressed already and I'd only been in for two hours. The tension from other people's neuroses lay heavy on me like a wet cloak. I disguised a quick fag break by pretending to rush to the loo when really I changed direction and charged down the stairs and out of the front door. I flashed a little smile to the sweet female receptionist who beamed from behind her desk.

Pulling the packet out of my pocket, I stuck a cigarette between my heavy, pouting lips. This was miserable. Six long hours before four long hours before I could see or even ring Scott; the shining beacon at the end of the long, treacherous road. At least I had familiarised myself enough with the play that I may have put myself back on easy street for tonight's rehearsal. I took a long drag on my cigarette and breathed right back into my chest.

"Guilty conscience?" a gravelly voice whispered into my ear. As per my actions from a few nights before, the smoke came back out of my mouth; not in a pile of vomit but in splutters and coughs like someone with acute bronchitis. Tim stood behind me, leaning over my shoulder, his lips centimetres from my earlobe.

"I don't know what you mean!" I pushed the words out, careful not to cover Tim's face with whatever was clinging to my epiglottis.

"The websites." Tim drew on his own cigarette, slinking around me to get within eyesight. "There were more you know. I had to explain how I came to be searching in gay magazines and bar listings too!"

"Oh Tim, I'm sorry, I didn't know she'd pull a stunt like that did I?" I was sure that I was burning from the outside in. Tim remained cool.

"How did you cover it up?"

"Potential hospitality venues for partners. I told her that meeting with the more male-orientated groups of the charity sector was gayer than working in the cloakroom at Madame Jojo's. She didn't argue with that."

I blushed. "You're a star, thank you, you saved me." I stopped myself before I began to sound any more like some harpy. Tim smiled a little at the corner of his mouth. "How are your gorgeous little girls?" I asked, desperately trying to find some leverage to hook me out of this uncomfortable silence. It seemed wrong to be shamelessly flirting while talking about his children. Any children in fact.

"Oh, they're great. Tilly is having to be surgically removed from her favourite blanket, Molly is losing all her teeth and Jossie is learning how to spell out swear words with Alphabetti Spaghetti. So creative."

I laughed at the thought.

"So... why *did* you take the rap for me earlier?"

I was eager to know but I didn't want him to massage my ego. I suddenly realised that I was wearing a doughy-eyed expression. The same face that Hecate might pull as her arse comes into contact with the doctored litter tray.

"Well, I didn't want to see you going down." He drew on his cigarette and stopped, momentarily pensive. We both sensed the innuendo but neither said anything.

"Well that's very good, I owe you one." I threw my stub to the floor and performed the awkward "I don't fancy you really" dance around him to get to the front door.

"Just buy me a beer sometime."

The words that Tim merely tossed to my left sent shivers up my spine. Was this a potential date scenario here? Couldn't be! He was spoken for, and had three beautiful little girls. I squeaked in acknowledgement and hared up the stairs. Well, if he was game then I certainly wouldn't kick him out of bed for farting.

Lunch came and went. I treated myself to an Italian chicken cob from the sandwich shop down the road. Clarissa seemed to be munching on floor tiles when I got back. I later discovered from the packet that they were actually charcoal biscuits.

"Good for indigestion," she snapped as I stood, gawping at the little black discs. I wondered how she developed a taste for charcoal. Probably the only vegetarian option at a friend's barbeque.

Another four hours and the first part of the day would be over. The scent of Pepe's gargantuan blood orange came drifting over the partition. I had held off combing the internet all day for fear of Cordelia's retinas boring two perfectly rounded holes into the back of my skull.

Once I had completed my handful of meagre daily tasks, that was me done for the next seven hours. I was reluctant to ask for more work because I didn't care enough to complete it. On the other hand, if they thought I was underworked they may take the necessary action and get rid of my post altogether. Then I'd be left with no job and no money to pay for school fees. My predecessor had suffered a similar plight. The story was now an Eco Scene legend.

The girl had had so much free time on her hands while she was supposed to be working that she'd managed to write a full-scale operetta on company time. It wasn't picked up until a project officer caught the review of *A Shoal of Imbeciles* in the *Metro* one morning and came to the conclusion that it was mainly autobiographical. Once the story had been leaked to Cordelia, her contract had not been renewed and the role had been made obsolete. Since then, all administration roles had been under fire and, thus, I had been promoted from office junior to sole administrator for the whole organisation. My main duties were to handle mail, electronic and postal, and order and audit office supplies. The office supplies, however, had to coincide with the Environmental Policy. A policy that made *War and Peace* look like a greetings card. Biodegradable plastics, organic paper, ink made from vegetable extracts, it was all highly expensive but it did mean that if you weren't happy with your first draft of anything you could literally eat the evidence.

The afternoon brought about much more procrastination. Pepe was peppering the hours with more facile questions about the membership finances that I was meant to be managing. He followed each answer with a frown and a grimace, making me feel like I was speaking to him in Klingon.

Oh for Christ's sake! I had wanted to shout, I didn't sign any cocking invoice, get it through your skull you incompetent little prick. I instead shook my head and said, "It wasn't me Pepe" for the umpteenth time. I could see Sandra's lime shoulders shudder as she silently chuckled away. Cow! She'd cleverly managed to keep out of Pepe's space all day and, consequently, had avoided being questioned continuously. Normally I wouldn't care, but Pepe had a knack of making me feel incredibly stupid by being doubly stupid himself.

Five o'clock dragged and, even though I had the same dread that I always felt at this time every day, it was slightly less heavy than the prospect of having to stay in the office for another four hours listening to Pepe's mind-numbingly dull account of when he tried to get into the wrong car in Morrisons car park. I wrestled my enormous bag up over my shoulder and turned my monitor off.

"Right," I puffed, as if I'd just finished an extremely long and important project, "that's me done." Sandra merely wiggled her fingers my way and carried on burying her head in a mountain of paperwork. Pepe tore his eyes away from his Excel spreadsheet long enough to smile half-arsedly in my direction.

I turned round, Carl winked and Clarissa wasn't even there, but the crumbs of charcoal left on her chair didn't seem to be all that bothered that I was leaving either.

I was blue. Surely at work you were meant to have a gaggle of mates who you went out for a beer with when the office closed, ones who you bitched about the managers to. But not this lot. They were so demotivated by their sorry little jobs that it was a life-altering decision for them just to order a pint of Guinness. And who could blame them when the only examples to take a lead from were Little Miss Anally Retentive and Mr Perpetually Repulsive?

How much longer could I take of this? It was getting me down and, therefore, must surely be affecting my overall mental state with knock-on effects on my acting stamina. I felt like rummaging in Clarissa's bag and racking up a line of that cat powder. Or, I thought, I could plan an evening of escape for this Friday with my buddy, Beez. It had only been two days but I already felt that I hadn't seen him in weeks. While I'd been sorting through articles on which organic farmer had the tastiest plums, Beez was probably carrying out a similar assessment with a couple of Hampsteadian twinks.

As I descended the main stairway, I pulled another cigarette out of its silver packet and shoved it between my lips. Once out of the building, I sparked it up and drew a long breath through the filter.

Life was shit.

If I didn't have to pay the astronomical school fees out of my own pocket then I wouldn't have to waste the rest of my time in this stupid office, sorting through post for stupid people who have no grip on reality.

How did I wind up in a bloody environmental organisation? I had no interest in saving the world. It was such an unachievable goal now anyway with the food crisis looming, oil reserves running out and climate change just around the corner (well what do you know, I had learned a few things). Nowadays it was more appropriate to save yourself from the world.

And if I didn't have this job I could stop being so miserable every day, and I certainly wouldn't need to go slaving away every night like a hooker with one leg and a mortgage. I could go and teach kids freelance or something like I did when I was sixteen. Mind you, since the paedophilia panic of the noughties it was no longer appropriate to leave your kids with a man for eight hours every day. This world I was meant to be saving seemed to be too far gone to save and I was fast becoming a victim of the whole sorry situation.

Thank God for fags and friends, and Scott. While my big love (drama) and my big hate (my job) collided, at least I would have these three friends. That is until Beez moves away, Scott cheats on me and the fags give me cancer. Oh well, I sighed, by then I reckon it will be my time to shuffle off this mortal coil anyway.

I half ran, half limped my way to the 205 bus, nearly choking from tobacco indigestion. I had literally swallowed that last cigarette and it was now playing havoc with my chest. I slumped into a seat next to a rather large lady who smelled of Shreddies; all I needed now was for Clarissa to board the bus with her sour milk aroma and we would have breakfast. The lady could obviously smell the scent of freshly consumed smoke and shifted her bosom to the right, sucking her teeth. I couldn't be arsed with her attitude so I got up to board the stairs, battling with my script which seemed to want to stay within the vice-like grip of my big bag.

"For Christ's sake," I cursed as the script broke free and scattered various bits and pieces across the filthy bus floor. As I scrambled around, trying to retrieve different paraphernalia from in between people's feet, I noticed the two items that had furtively rolled away together. My dance tights and my watermelon Body Shop lip balm had landed neatly at the polished lace ups of an attractive and snappily dressed businessman. I snatched them both up and wove the tights around my hand in embarrassment while the man looked at me with a condescending glare.

"Oh I'm a fucking drama student," I barked, thrusting the runaway articles back into my bag, "get the hell over it."

6

Just three more hours, I thought, and I can go home and watch telly with a glass of wine and a big hard-on. I'd been thinking about Scott all rehearsal. Scott's muscles... Scott's olive skin... Scott's erect, pink penis and then, as if by some strange coincidence, my own crackled into life.

The rehearsal had started off bad and was slowly descending into Armageddon. Fortunately I was not actually due to be on stage for another five pages so I was kicking back my heels and trying not to wince as others got berated for Grant's pure pleasure. Right now, Liana and Bobby were trying to peg-leg their way through the first scene. It was not going well considering that the play was set in the age of *The Great Gatsby* and these two were playing it like the great unwashed. Grant was playing with metaphors like a child might play with its own snot, throwing them around the room and watching them stick to any available wall space.

At the moment he was laying into Liana who was trying her best but coming off less Eliza Doolittle and more *Debbie does Dallas*.

"For God's sake, NO!" Grant sat forward and shot a beady glare at his targets: "If Coward had wanted the play to be set in Walthamstow, he would have given YOU a Staffordshire Bull Terrier and YOU a bottle of methadone. AND AGAIN!"

Liana attempted to pull off an RP accent, but it wasn't very convincing.

"Ra-TH-er Simon, I fink we should tell our mo-TH-er before it's too lite."

With every TH a spray of saliva covered the open page.

"Oh Jesus Christ, you sound like R2-fucking-D2 now! You must talk to each other." Grant was bordering a queenie fit.

"Me and Bobs do talk to each over," Liana protested. "He's a bredren innit?"

She gestured towards Bobby who nodded in slack-jawed agreement.

"Not you two, you donkeys, the characters." He prodded his book. "The characters in the bloody play are talking to each other. Ring any bells? It must play like a real scenario else the audience won't believe in you. They won't be sold on your relationship and, more importantly, they won't follow the bloody story!" He clutched his head in mock desperation. "I'm losing more patience than Harold Shipman here. Right, everyone take five minutes while I get my head together. You two, I suggest, have a serious 'fink' about your characters, else I may not be able to justify what I do with this Parker pen and the holes in your arses!"

He slammed down the heavy, leather-bound book with such vigour that a plume of invisible dust seemed to escape its pages. As Grant swept out of the room, the group communally exhaled. I pulled out a cigarette and made a beeline for Liana. The perplexed look on her face had not altered for well over an hour now.

"Hey mate." I swung my arm around her petite shoulders. She was considerably shorter than me and I kind of looked like an orang-utan hugging a tree stump.

"Alright mate." Liana returned the favour with a tender squeeze of my tummy. "I'm tryin', I just don't know what he wants."

"Call me a fool," I said, dragging her over to the outside door, "but I reckon he just wants a little bit of acting."

"That what I'm doin' vo bruv." She was small, she was white, but she sounded like one of the large Nigerian ladies I frequently saw outside the hair salons in Hackney.

"I don't mean it like that, I mean that you're going to have to stop being so self-conscious about your accent because the nerves are holding you back. You need to just dive in." I looked down but she just frowned back at me. "Ya get me?" I growled.

"Safe cous, safe," she nodded and her golden-hooped earrings swung like giant pendulums against her shiny black ponytail. "I can do dat. Nah, give us a toke on ya fag."

*

The rehearsal failed to pick up speed after our short break. I watched Grant jump from person to person, digging his talons in at every given opportunity. He'd given up on Liana and Bobby and had moved onto Dominique. However, her over-the-top gesticulations and sing-song voice forced him to grimace each time she was required to hold the action up for more than thirty seconds.

They had not even got to my part, which I had suspected we might not after the farcical playout of the last two hours. In fact, Grant had given up altogether by half past nine, thirty minutes before we were due to end. He had sashayed off to the nearest cavernous wine bar to take stock over a glass of Galliano and lemonade, leaving a sea of miserable faces behind him.

I arranged to join a few of my colleagues in the Glass Pig to drown our sorrows in a cheap pint. But I thought it was probably best to sign up for a tutorial with Bea first, as an extended olive branch for my previous lateness. I walked into the grey corridor that separated the two rehearsal rooms, where the noticeboard hung. I stood and perused the board for the signup sheet with my back towards the door to Rex's smoky office. If I was quick, I might just make a speedy getaway before Rex came out to lock up. The possibility of bumping into him inadvertently and either having to feel his icy glare upon me as I awkwardly stepped aside or, even worse, being forced to instigate some polite apologetic small talk just to fill the painful silence was almost too much to bear.

I shivered and tentatively scanned the area. The door was shut. I appeared to be safe. Just as I located the tutorial list and decided on a necessary time slot that would not impinge on my hours at Eco Scene or, indeed, my hours out boozing with Beez, I heard the heavy door behind me begin to creep open. The hairs on the back of my neck stood up with each creak of hinge. With every inhalation, the musty smell of Benson and Hedges crept further up each of my nostrils. I could feel my breath catch in my throat at the mere squeal of the doorknob turning. I didn't dare look behind me in case I was faced with my innermost fear. My concentration shifted into entirely focusing on any following tell-tale signs, but there was no extra sound.

So far, so good.

The door could only have opened a centimetre, two at most. Maybe it was caused by an airlock from the closing of his office window, or maybe it was a result of the school roof caving in? I could handle that. The prospect of being crushed dead by six tons of timber seemed far more attractive at present than having to face that monster.

Silence.

I slowly pulled a pen out of my bag, careful not to scratch it on the inside of the lining and give myself away; the frightened deer within eyeshot of the bloodthirsty wolf.

I scribbled my name on the sheet of paper and was just about to turn around and flee when another document caught my eye to the left. It was on the other noticeboard, the one that was of a much better quality than ours.

Ours looked as though it had been used as a battering ram in the London riots and then hammered, lopsided, into the grey wall.

This noticeboard, however, was immaculately polished, with a plastic cover and memos pinned up in perfect symmetry, typed in Times New Roman and printed on expensive ivory paper. This was Rex's Elite noticeboard. Usually it wasn't worth even looking at. I'd rather not read of the privileges that the Elite group was offered, it would only make me envious and sad. Exclusive character study outings to Europe were the most likely to be advertised. Play readings in exquisite halls in London with unlimited tea and scones, prearranged meet-and-greets with industry professionals. All we ever had on ours was a few hand-scribbled Post-It notes telling us we were all shit and, therefore, needed to come in for the whole of the Easter bank holiday weekend. This time, however, something on his board grabbed my attention.

Next term, readings will take place for casting on the second day of term. Peter Shaffer's Equus. *Only Rex's group need attend.*

The deceptive curly font did not detract from the biting directness of tone. *Equus*, one of my favourite plays and they were doing it here... this year.

I loved that play so much. I remembered reading it in secondary school after it was recommended to me by my old drama tutor. At only eleven years old, he told me with absolute sincerity that it was the principal character, Alan, that I was born to play. Ever since, I had been obsessed with it. Alan was a troubled boy whose mental torment was exacerbated by uncontrollable teenage sexual urges battling against the stringent views of his overbearing Christian mother. The play was infamous for its shocking climax when Alan reaches breaking point and takes to his favourite horse's eyeballs with an ice pick.

Maybe my drama teacher had noticed how I had shrunk into the corners as a teenager, only to emerge when fully immersed in the safety of a drama class where I could be anyone else but myself for an hour. Maybe he had known about my struggles with the witch in my home life and seen it reflected in Alan's predicament. I don't know the reason. But I had always thanked him for bringing this fantastic character to my attention. Oh how I wished, now I was old enough to understand Alan, that I might be given the opportunity to bring his character to life.

If only.

I was so lost in part dream, part exasperation that I barely noticed the creak of the door behind me beginning again and the sound of slow footsteps emerging from within. Suddenly, that oh-so-familiar odour of expensive aftershave mixed with dirty fags protruded closer and closer towards the back of my head. I found that I was cowering in the shadow of the very person I had been trying to avoid. I could feel his presence like a dragon behind me. I could also practically hear his eyeballs rotating in their sockets as he took in the unbelievable sight of someone as pitiable as me, deigning to cast my feeble eyes over his scribed words.

I closed one eye, nailed to the spot and rigid with fear. With the other I saw a shadow silhouetted against the wall before me, the lips parting to speak, a thin ribbon of smoke escaping from the space between and twisting its way up towards the ceiling. It was like a horrible shadow puppet growing and shifting into a sinister black avatar. I heard the purr of the words before they were spoken, as if some demon on my shoulder was preparing me for the sentence. I pulled the small amount of oxygen that I held in for the last thirty seconds even tighter.

"I presume," the shadow began, "that you are only looking left because you are bored of looking right. I say this because there is no way, in an abject fiery hell, that you would ever THINK that you would be castable in this."

A finger shot out from behind me and jabbed its way towards the paper that I had been reading. A well-manicured but ever-so slightly yellow fingernail covered the Eeeek of *Equus*. The cuticle flushed from pink to white with the pure force of pressure. The finger did not move and neither, it seemed, did the figure. In a vain attempt to respond, I half shook my head, trying to look as casual and nonchalant as was humanly possible. Instead, I seemed to achieve the complete opposite. The finger relaxed and the colour began to flood back into the tip.

"Oh good." The growl was half as soft but twice as menacing. "Because *Equus* happens to be one of my favourite contemporary plays."

As his tone softened, so too did my shoulders. Maybe he was about to share my sentiments. Maybe he too, felt an affinity with Alan. Maybe this was my way in; a great opportunity to establish some kind of mutual empathy with Rex and, therefore, some kind of connection. A kind of unity that you were *supposed* to share with your tutors. Maybe this is just what I had needed. I felt this may be a good time to turn round and start gushing on about my feelings on *Equus*, when his sharp intake of breath indicated that Rex hadn't yet finished. It kept me rooted to the spot.

"And so, as you may be aware, with all my favourite plays," his words were slow, controlled and without urgency, "I wouldn't allow shit, worthless acting to befoul any of them."

He began to march slowly away from me towards his office door. My heart felt as though it were made of glass and teetering on the edge of an extremely high shelf.

"Shit, worthless acting," he said, stopping for a moment, "such as yours."

The words hung in the air for just long enough to push my heart to the stone floor where it shattered into a million pieces. And then he calmly closed the door.

*

"He really is a holy shit bag," I thought as the hard wind blew in my face. I had walked the length of the Archway Road away from the school, feeling emotionally bruised and battered. Rex's treatment of us innocent actors was not only demoralising, rude and degrading, it was also painfully unnecessary. What had I ever done wrong but try my best? Why was I being chastised for giving it a shot? What kind of arrogant arsehole made people feel as if they were unworthy of even being under the same roof as them? Especially when we were paying for the privilege.

Besides, we were only actors. It was not like we were running world economies or saving lives. Why did Rex feel the need to drill me into the ground just because I wasn't a convincing Shylock or couldn't emulate "crestfallen" at the drop of a hat? And why did he enrol people just to make their lives hell?

I thought back to my audition. There were twenty petrified faces in the holding area, called into the lion's den one by one. And one by one, they ran out of the rehearsal room in tatters as they were told in no uncertain terms that they "couldn't act their way out of a lump of shit." Every time the door opened and another hopeful was shown the exit in floods of tears, I sank lower into my chair. When it was my turn to enter the cripplingly intimate space, bare, save for a panel of hard-faced judges, I had barely even

144

noticed Rex and his all-encompassing presence. I had just rattled off my pieces at breakneck speed, fully expecting to get laughed out of the building. After I was done, Rex, however, had been positively beaming. Far from the man I knew and loathed now.

"Good," he'd said after the last squeak of my modern monologue. "Good." He pondered for a moment while he regarded his notes. "You come from Hereford. Is that right?"

"Er, yes Mr Bamber, that is right." I was expecting questions about my acting, not my hometown. I tried to sound aloof, as if Hereford was the Mecca for all successful actors currently treading the boards in London. If you counted Nell Gwynne and David Garrick, it probably was... once upon a time.

"I remember Hereford well from my old childhood days. We used to go on long loganberry walks with my great Uncle Hester." He didn't seem to be speaking to anyone in particular, certainly not casting an eye over the reddening mess that stood before him, twitching with discomfort as each agonising second passed.

"Used to holiday in Leominster. Do you know it?"

For a second, I was so embroiled in my self-deprecating inner train of thought that I hadn't even registered the question. He looked up from the paper he was examining.

"Sorry?"

"Leeeeominster," he cooed. "Do you know it?"

The two students that made up the rest of the panel, perched either side of him, eyeballed me like statuesque Dobermans.

"Er, yes. My grandfather is a former Mayor of Leominster, Mr Bamber."

His focus shifted again, almost as if there was something else in the room, darting across the floor. I turned to look.

"Rex," he corrected me. To call the situation strange would be like calling a Room 101 an irritating bind. "I liked your pieces, Stephen."

"Simon."

"My brother-in-law's name is Simon. Charming fellow. Paints boats." The information was baffling but all these tenuous links seemed to be gaining me brownie points that I hadn't earned. I uttered some inaudible sound to feign interest.

"Your Shakespeare was interesting. You did Shakespeare without doing Shakespeare by choosing Flute playing Thisbe. It was canny, I liked it." He paused, never looking down at his notes. "Your second piece was less favourable but there was something in your eyes that didn't quite make me want to stab myself continuously with a blunt object. (Pinteresque pause.) I didn't... I didn't hate it... We'd like to offer you a place."

My mouth hung open for a few moments as my heart dropped and wriggled out of my cock.

"Really?"

"Yes, we'll send a letter of confirmation to your home address upon which we expect to get a deposit of five hundred pounds before August and we'll see you on the second of October. Pick up a list."

An ivory piece of paper was thrust into my face by one of the Dobermans to his left, missing my nose by millimetres.

"If by any chance you change your mind, and I recommend that you don't if you are serious about getting into the industry, then you need to let us know at least four weeks before the date in order to think about getting your deposit back. Otherwise you can fuck off."

My elation was too much to stifle.

"Thank you, Mr Rex, I mean Rex. Thanks," I blurted out in a mad frenzy, grabbing the piece of paper and smacking myself in the face at the same time.

"No need to thank me, you did it." His smile was genuine. His warmth radiant. I just wanted to dive over the table and give him a hug. He seemed to sense this apparent air of incipient camaraderie and put a sudden stop to it. "Yes, thank you, Simon. You can actually piss off now."

I came back to earth with a thud, clutching my piece of paper in one hand and my comfortable audition shoes in the other.

Out on the street, every emotion imaginable rushed through my head. The disbelief, the excitement, the slight bewilderment about what had actually just happened. Without really thinking, I had wandered into McDonald's and ordered nine chicken nuggets, a usual act of impulse, and telephoned my mother. I was barely able to squeak down the phone to her that I had been accepted onto the course.

I remembered thinking that my life was about to begin. No more rubbish administration jobs (ha!), no more feeling like a failure (ha, ha!). I had always dreamed of being an actor and now it was becoming a reality, and Rex Bamber agreed with me.

Rex Bamber. I had impressed the man who was impossible to impress. Maybe we would grow to be good friends, maybe his wrath would change me for the better, bring me out of myself a bit more. Maybe I would be one of those prime students who would be invited round to his for dinner long after the course had finished.

"Oh do finish the Pinot Grigio, Simon and tell me about reviving *Hamlet* under the direction of Peter Hall. How is the old crone?"

"He's still taking an empty space and making a bare theatre. A haw haw haw!"

I smiled as I stuffed the dry, synthetic chicken into my mouth, picturing my autobiography on the shelves in Waterstones: *Life, Camera, Action!* with a foreword by Derek Jacobi.

The reality of the situation couldn't be further from that rather sickening preconception, seen through what appeared to be rose-tinted double-glazed French windows. This wasn't fun, or exciting. This experience wasn't changing me, unless you called the metamorphosis from sprightly individual to quivering wreck a major professional leap forward. And as for Rex's and my long-standing partnership... I do think that a firmly grounded relationship should contain more exchange than a few heart-breaking personal insults and some indecipherable whinnies in response.

I sighed; I seemed to be doing a lot of that recently. Bloody school, bloody Rex. Why was this so hard? Why couldn't I just believe in myself enough to disregard his treatment of me and exploit this amazing opportunity for all its worth? Why? I realised, in my glum little mood, that I had autopiloted all the way onto the Tube platform and was inadvertently staring down as the little mice scurried in and out of the deep rail tracks. How long had I been chasing this dream now? Eight years. Eight long years and I was no better off now than the day I arrived. Still watching the vermin escape through the tunnels of our underground capital and still feeling sorry for myself. How depressing.

Once, on my own at Hampstead station after a shift at the Boadicea, one of the little rodents had actually dared to run up the platform towards me. I must have been sitting still for such a long time that it had bravely set out to examine what was cohabiting its home. I was so flabbergasted at this rare occurrence that I stopped and stared. David coming to challenge Goliath. It was at that moment that I realised that it was in control of me. Even a tiny mouse on a huge platform in massive central London wasn't too scared to take an opportunity if it thought it might benefit from it. But I was a zillion times bigger than that mouse and I couldn't be half as assertive, I didn't know how to be.

The train arrived but I seemed to look straight through it. Not even the 10:34 to Angel could penetrate my misery. The weight of the world lying heavy on my Topman-styled shoulders.

I was halfway down a page of the play, which was being read but by no means absorbed, and the ping of the doors signified that I was still at least four stops away. The patronising woman purred over the Tannoy: "*This* is Camden Town" in such a way that made one think that Camden Town was the station they had been waiting for all of their lives. A scurry of people got on. For no reason at all, I looked up. Beyond the neon prints and skinny jeans of the rabble boarding my carriage, two guys stepped onto the train. One looked strangely familiar. I shot my book up to shield my face, I didn't really want to cut some rug with anyone at the moment; I was one sigh away from theatrically dropping down to my knees and banging the train floor with my fist. Who was it? My beady eyes peered over the book. Whoever they were, they were holding hands and laughing. Something about the smile just gave it away seconds before the realisation crept in.

It was Scott.

No, correction, it was Scott hand in hand with another man. An attractive man. A man who was much older, taller and far more stylish that I could ever be. A man who carried off designer stubble without having an uneven spread or copious amounts of tender in-growing hairs. A man who looked far more Scott's type than I did. I was surprised that neither of them noticed my eyes boring into them with enough electricity to power half of the Northern Peninsula all by itself as these furious thoughts raged through my head.

Scott is seeing someone else. Scott is seeing someone else.

Their hands were clasped together as they shared what appeared to be an endless joke. Obviously this guy was HILARIOUS. They surely couldn't be laughing about anything that came out of Scott's mouth; it was always so insipid. The bitterness was instant. I glanced down at the held hand; Scott was now massaging this guy's wrist, probably checking for a pulse. Anyone who would want to cheat on others behind their backs in broad daylight must surely be missing one. They both had those pointless rubber matching bracelets on. The kind that, when thrown out will pollute the earth and strangle unsuspecting curious wild fowl. It was easily the third minute before I regained composure and stopped staring with my mouth hung open like a carrier-bag filled with water. I had to get off this train, NOW! I couldn't share a transportation carriage with Brad and Angelina, carrying on with Jennifer Aniston a mere stone's throw away. I would get off at the next stop. I would just have to wait for the announcement

"This is ..."

I wrenched my book back up over my face and grabbed desperately at the handle of my bag, managing to smack the side of the seat so clumsily that I was sure I would have generated some interest from my fellow Tube dwellers. I didn't care, I had to get off. Tears began to prick my eyes, I could feel my face hot and burning and my heart had risen up and was lodged firmly in my throat. The small space between my seat and the door seemed like miles away – I might not make it!

I did make it.

I jumped through the door and practically fell to a squat on the platform in a move reminiscent of the end of *Platoon*. I certainly felt like I had just escaped some kind of war. My bag followed a split second behind and crashed into my back, knocking me a little off-balance and onto the floor. The train had sped away now and so I was free to look up. I dropped the book down and realised that I was crying; real, slow and heavy salty tears came rolling down my face, it was too late to stop myself. I began audibly sobbing, opening my mouth and letting the sound come out. It was almost animalistic – I had nothing to lose anymore, I felt I'd lost everything. The book dropped to my side as I wiped at the tears with the back of my hand; many had run into my nose. The crying stopped, as though a wave of pain had subsided. But I put my arms around myself and stayed for a few minutes, splayed on the platform as the legs of other passengers passed by, untroubled and uninterested.

7

"So what's the matter with you then?" Sandra seemed genuinely interested but I couldn't be doing with her cruel-to-be-kind approach this morning.

"It's nothing, I'm having an off day," I barked. To be fair to her, she did know when to stop with the interrogation. She shrugged and went back to her magazine, the fringing on her golden shoulder pads followed suit, swinging in the wake of the movement.

I kept punching away at my computer keyboard, ordering stationery by typing in the words with such ferocity that it was a miracle that the keyboard didn't shatter underneath my fingers. Carl also knew better than to question; I had practically snarled at him when he asked if I wanted a coffee this morning and he wasn't about to get his head bitten off twice. Clarissa was yet to come in but I was sure that when she did she would feel the brunt of my wrath in full force. I couldn't be bothered with any of her New Age methods for getting over a thunderous mood. If she had her way, I'd be sitting naked and burning coriander halfway up the fire escape. And I bloody hate coriander. She flounced in at ten and picked up on the aura of the room before she even said hello.

"Dear me, there's a bad energy in here." She walked about, pinching the air. "I don't like this at all, it should be needled."

"So should your bloody armpits," I scolded under my breath.

"What's happened?" She plonked her bag down and the mirrors embroidered onto it rattled with force. She was about to sweep her way over to me but I cut her off mid-dive.

"It's fine Clarissa, I'm just having an off day. I don't need tea or sympathy or anything in powder form to ward off residual forces, I just need a bit of time to myself."

I don't think I had ever been this forthright with her. She pursed her lips and gave an overly empathetic head nod. Even though I went back to my computer screen, I could feel her over my shoulder, watching and waiting for me to buckle under the strain and dissolve into tears on her dusty shoulder. After five minutes of being painfully unable to concentrate on the Hennes online sale, I snapped. I swivelled round, so fast the accompanying gust of wind tousled Clarissa's fringe ever-so slightly.

"For God's sake, WHAT?" The look on her face was one of pseudo-considerate understanding, it was infuriating. "For the love of all that is holy, would you just leave me alone! I can't stand it much more."

I'd created quite a furore now and I could see, after the cold shoulder I'd given Sandra earlier, she had eloped to the opposing side.

"I'm sorry guys." I turned. "I'm sorry, Sandra. It's been a shit weekend, I've had the wind knocked a little out of my sails and..."

I felt the tears coming. So did Clarissa as her bosom moved a little further in my direction. I caved. My cheek went full pelt into her chest and the tears came thick and fast. She patted the top of my head, as though she were stroking that mangy old alley cat of hers. But it was tender and her touch was soft. The smell of sour milk was slightly overbearing, but mixed with a hint of dusty old books it was also quite comforting. I raised my head, I could feel that my eyes were puffy and I had left a rather sizeable pool of drool on Clarissa's rustic cardigan. She cupped my head in her hands; so much so that my cheeks rose up into my eyeballs. And then she blew, softly on my sore, red eyes. Her breath was sweet; like strawberries mixed with sweet tea.

"*Aragon*," she said. I tried not to look surprised as she held my face and traced every inch of it with her pupils. "*Lllw myth wafadas, llan fadr mygwr. Kall dras mychgr langmarchann.*"

Oh-my-God. She was speaking to me in elvish. Although I couldn't see them, I knew exactly what my other colleague's faces behind me were doing; they were as stupefied as I was.

"You should be at peace now," Clarissa said calmly and slowly released her vice-like grip. As she turned back to her bag, I couldn't help but feel that those words had been more calming to her than to me, but when I looked back, everyone seemed to have been transfixed by them. Certainly Sandra, who remained agog for a good five minutes.

"So I'm guessing," Sandra dared to brace the topic after a morning of nigh-on total silence, "you've been jilted."

Clarissa's earlier bizarre recital of Tolkien had thawed any previous frost between us.

"Well not so much jilted, as totally shat on. That bastard. Prick-teasing, emotionally starved bastard..."

Behind me, Clarissa tutted in scorn. I turned full circle.

"Flax seed caught in your teeth?" I spat. She retracted her head back into her neck with surprise and hurried back to her filing.

"I saw him on the Tube with another guy." I couldn't look Sandra in the eye. I was crazy mad. She paused.

"That's it? The other guy could have been anyone. It could have been his brother."

"Sandra, they were the same age and they were holding hands. You don't hold hands with your fully grown, attractive brother in broad daylight. Maybe in parts of the Forest of Dean they do but certainly not here." I buckled. "He's seeing someone else. He's been dating me and seeing someone else."

"Well were you *officially* together?"

"I don't know! Do we need to define it? Doesn't the fact that we've been intimate award me with some sort of fidelity?"

"Well, people are all different. Sometimes you have to have that awkward conversation else the other party gets the wrong idea. Maybe you need to ask him not to see other people."

"I'm not asking him anything, I'm never seeing him again."

"Is that what you want?"

"Sandra, I can't be involved with someone who is into multiple dating, that just isn't me. Who knows where else he's been sticking it."

"Yes, but does *he* know that just isn't you. Maybe, since you haven't addressed it, you need to mention exclusivity before you write him off as a cheat. I mean, it's only been a week."

"Well, I know it's only been a week but... Oh, I'm not talking about this anymore. Just drop it. I'm never dating again. All men are bastards."

More tutting came from over my right shoulder.

*

The afternoon plodded on like a bag of wet cement being dragged across a dual carriageway. Every time I thought something was going well, stupid bloody Scott and his stupid bloody smile entered my mind. Every smell reminded me of him in some way. Even the sour air pulsing through the ventilators on my way to school seemed to remind me of him: his hot breath on my cheek, the faint sweaty smell as he pushed his moist skin up against me. Well fuck him, and his skin and his breath! Fuck it all!

I barely noticed rehearsal slip by. I just sat there, my head buried in my book, watching as Grant tore yet another strip off a clueless Liana.

"For Christ's sake girl, how many more times? Coward is the name of the playwright, it's not a directorial criticism."

I didn't really speak to anyone. I thought that if I did I might expunge all my negative thoughts by crying inconsolably on their shoulders. I might start weeping salty tears into the otherwise dry and unstained t-shirt of someone who had only squeezed past me to use the neighbouring urinal. Sophie and Lulu were in the other group and when we were all divided like this, you barely got to see anyone outside of your cast. You felt as if civilisation was a million miles away. And, for the following three hours, it was. Grant managed to stop the action, once again at my bit and not continue any further, so I pleaded to be let off early, feigning a bout of tummy sickness.

"Oh very well Simon," Grant scoffed. "To be honest, unless this girl pulls her finger out pretty soon, we'll be doing the Marcel Marceau version to save time."

Miserably, I made my way back home. I didn't even want to call Beez. Not even his witty chat, peppered with saucy innuendo, would lift my spirits. It was ridiculous! How long had I known this guy, Scott? Five minutes? And I was acting as though terminating our partnership would cost me three children and the Volkswagen estate. I think it was a mixture of allowing myself to actually trust someone and them *still* letting me down that hurt the most. It was almost as if I'd fucked myself. And I was pissed off that I had actually cared enough to be hurt by it. This hurt, after such a short time. Horrible feelings over a horrible man.

The opening bars of Lady Gaga broke my attention and I pulled my phone out of my pocket. This horrible man was actually calling me right now. This second.

The words Scott flashed on and off the screen, each letter assaulting me with its unashamed boldness. I could answer, but I would only be vile; never actually broaching the topic but spitting venom at him through the phone for no apparent reason. No, I didn't want that. We never talked about exclusivity, I was just being too sensitive and childish, and that was my stupid fault, not his.

The phone seemed to ring for an age. Each second that passed brought a new internal struggle. And then it stopped, the last bar of the ringtone reverberating through the deafening silence, the last hostile note of our relationship. No following bing bong, no message left. Gutted. The drab anti-climax seeped into my bones like a dead weight. I was truly miserable now and the after-effects of that minute-long adrenaline rush only deepened the trench.

When I got home, I took myself to bed, pretending not to hear Freya, pretending not to care.

*

The next three days slumped on with little motivation or hope. I was stuck in a stupid rut of my own creation. I don't think I cared about Scott particularly anymore, but the whole situation had shoved a big cracked mirror into my life's face and I didn't like what I had seen. Beez was moving away, Scott had lied and cheated on me and I was in a dead-end job so that I could pay to do something that I didn't even know if I was any good at. And if Rex was to be believed, I was almost certainly wasting my time on that score.

The only silver lining was that Tim had noticed my misery and took it as a green flag to toy with me. He had purposefully knocked into me in the office corridor and playfully winked.

"Okay there?" he'd asked with that irresistible lopsided smile.

"Yeah," I lied, "just thinking about things, you know?"

"God, don't think about things in here with the thought police around." He nodded towards Cordelia's office. "They'll ram raid your flat looking for any corroborative evidence that you have been using company airwaves for personal reasons." I managed a half-arsed snort of acknowledgement. "Whatever it is," he said, leaning in and speaking softly, his smoky breath tingling my ear once more, "sort it out, you're no good to us miserable."

And with that, he left me, feeling a little better but ultimately more annoyed. How could someone so gorgeous and who seemed to have genuine affection for me not only be in a serious relationship, with three daughters, but also not even be of the same sexual orientation? He should have *wrong tree* stamped across his forehead.

Clarissa was decidedly "heads down" for a good portion of the day. She clearly didn't appreciate the grim charcoal aura that was surrounding me at the moment. And no amount of goatweed and/or any of the lesser-known fresh herbs that she was prone to harp on about could cure this ailment. I managed to contribute a little to Sandra's witty banter but, more often than not, I just grunted in her direction and pretended to be busy, though both of us knew that I wasn't fooling anyone. She did, however, have the good grace to leave me be and let me get on with it.

At lunchtimes, I ploughed my energy into learning my lines for this part. Somehow the tormented, bitter soul of the Simon in the play was connecting fiercely with the Simon reading it. I seemed to empathise more with his turmoil as he held Myra, an attractive older debutante, in his arms and professed his undying love for her. His anger towards his sister in the first few scenes matched totally with the anger I felt towards everything going on in my life at the moment. As such, I managed to channel a few of my frustrations into his and somehow breathed life into his words rather than mine.

This managed to transpose particularly well onto the stage.

When we finally managed to get to standing my part up in rehearsal, Grant, who seemed to be missing a certain amount of hair atop each ear from pulling it out in a mad rage over Liana's continuing grapple with method acting, seemed practically absorbed in my performance.

"That's really working Simon," he said after the first evening's run-through had gone exceedingly quickly. "You're bringing a certain dimension to the character that I have not noticed before."

Personally, I didn't really care whether it was working or not. Nothing was going right elsewhere in my life, so I was more than prepared for this to come crashing down around my ears as well.

On the second night, my scene with the actress playing Simon's sister, Carmen, who I believed to be really rather easy to work with since she put in the effort to learn the lines and deliver with the necessary conviction, went by without a hitch.

"Well Simon," Grant thoughtfully ran one of his myriad glistening jewelled rings over his top lip, "you're succeeding rather magnificently. And because you are not playing for laughs and giving the character substance, it is becoming a devilishly amusing performance. Kudos!"

The positive response garnered much support from my fellow colleagues and, as a result, everyone else subliminally started to up their game. Even Liana, who had now been demoted from one of the principal characters to an understudy maid, had pushed her own troubles to one side to congratulate me. Throwing her arms around me after the second night's triumph, she uttered the words: "Boi, you is killin' it man."

Not knowing how to respond in the correct fashion, I threw her a handgun gesture and excused myself from the situation.

By the third night, my grey cloud began to brighten a little. The first act ends in a hysterical ensemble comedy scene where each member of the Bliss family, each having invited a significant other down to their house for the weekend, are so embroiled in their inter-family arguments that each invitee gets completely ignored and left desolately hanging around the tea table. I played it with the same bitter underlying tone – one that I had been used to playing. Suddenly I was finding my namesake to be an easy character to slip into. He seemed to be an exaggerated version of me with a few alterations, such as being posh and fancying women.

After that evening's rehearsal, Grant leapt out of his seat to walk me to the door. As I pulled my coat on, he ushered me to one side by the front door.

"I must admit," he confessed, "you've always been hiding in a corner to me, never really sure what to make of you. But my dear fellow, one might say you have arrived."

His compliments made me uncomfortable and I squirmed as I tried to burrow myself further into my jacket.

"Now I don't know what it is that you have managed to connect with, but keep it up. You have made my job very easy. Your colleagues should be kissing your feet. But, of course, you didn't hear that from me."

"Thanks Grant." I flushed. In ordinary circumstances I wouldn't have believed someone who talked about me with such high praise, but I respected and trusted his professional opinion and couldn't help but feel a little overwhelmed by his words.

"Right, one more rehearsal before the big day on Monday, so keep it up. Now fuck off and do some more line learning." Grant shooed me out of the door with a golden encrusted hand and so I followed his direction. But as I turned back, I noticed that he hadn't gone. He stood watching, a little smile tickling the corners of his mouth. The kind you see on a father's face as he watches his child ride off down the street for the first time on a bike without stabilisers. He seemed to be watching his pupil with a quiet pride. And suddenly the dark cloud that hung over me lifted.

8

"I'm telling you, you've got to get back in the game!" Sandra bleated as she filed an expertly painted nail, this time resembling a miniature pineapple atop what looked like a mountain. Some might say an abuse of artistic licence on behalf of the nail technician.

"The game? Sandra, I'm not Peter bloody Stringfellow! I'm thirty-one, I shouldn't be chasing after boys like some over-zealous scoutmaster, they should be coming to me."

We were supposed to be stuffing envelopes together for the Eco Scene annual lecture but it was becoming increasingly obvious as the morning wore on that I was doing most of the stuffing.

"All's I know is that when a bloke lets you down, the best way to get over him is to get under someone else." She seemed fairly confident in this theory.

"Where did you read that?" I joked. "The Big Book of STD Nursery Rhymes? Besides, he didn't let me down; I let myself down. I thought too much into it, let myself wander into a territory that we hadn't actually discussed. He hadn't promised me anything or committed to anything. I was too presumptuous. He should be able to do what he wants."

She sucked her teeth in disgust. I was fairly certain that if any man had attempted such a thing with Sandra in whatever part of the dating to relationship process, she would have had to be held back from cutting his genitals off with the first available blunt object that she could lay her claws on.

"I know it's a bit unorthodox but we're in the 2010s now. Relationships are more open, men are more metrosexual. Romance is dying and the rules of monogamy don't really apply anymore. You've got to be a little more available, a little less rigid in your thinking."

I tried to sound aloof through the stack of envelopes towering between me and my colleague.

"But you're not like that." She had me there.

"Well, I'm a bit more traditional." I didn't look up for fear that my burning hot face would set the invitations alight. "But, you know, I'm learning."

"Well.... let me give you a hand." She swung round, tossing the nail file onto her desk.

"Oh, great." I reached over for the pile of address stickers that I had purposely been avoiding tackling alone.

"Not with that, with this." She was scribbling what appeared to be a website address on a piece of paper. She handed it over, the fringing from her candyfloss pink pleather jacket tickled my arm as she did so.

"What is it?" I was curious.

"A better dating website than whatever you're on, not a lot of people know about it because, well, it's an untapped resource. It's a bit underground."

An underground dating website? Gollum sprang instantly to mind. Pepe and Cordelia had been in a meeting for over an hour now and so we were carefully monitoring our volume in case one of them popped up unawares as they had so many times before. I looked at the paper: www.madeinheaven.com. I shrugged in confusion.

"Well, you know when my sister lost her partner two years ago?" she said quietly.

I vaguely remembered Sandra telling me once that her sister had lost a boyfriend to a terrible motorcycle accident on the North Circular the year before last. I nodded but I didn't really like where this was going. The link between this website and Sandra's brother-in-law's untimely passing was starting to throw up images of some kind of séance group. She wasn't suggesting I find love via an Ouija board, was she? I wasn't that desperate.

"She was a bit embarrassed about looking for love at her age and in her situation. She wanted to start dating again but didn't really want to go through the normal channels. So a friend gave her this web address."

"And what is it exactly? For those who are unlucky in love and full of shame? This isn't doing a lot for my self-esteem Sandra."

"Not necessarily; it's for those people who are not the 'dating website' kind. You know, those who have suffered a loss, or those who are divorced. Some disabled, some young offenders."

Was she serious? I was actually lost for words, I was so shocked.

"Are you saying that I should apply the same principles in my quest for a relationship that I might to finding work in a halfway house?"

"Of course not! What I'm saying is that the people on this site are not the kind that would want to advertise publicly. They're not looking for casual sex or meaningless flings. They're searching for something with more gravity, more purpose. Besides, there are some real finds on there. My sister dated a number of really nice men before she found her Keith."

"What, she found her current boyfriend on here?" I gestured towards the paper. "The very cute Jamaican guy with the big guns and the soft lilting accent?"

"The very same."

"And what was wrong with him then? He's not wearing a bionic leg under those khaki trousers is he?"

"No! He was a divorcee, but not in the messed-up kind of way. He married young, it didn't work out, back on the market, didn't want anyone from his past to see him on an internet site." She was so matter of fact about it that I couldn't help but be a little intrigued. I turned the paper over in my hand.

"But hey, if you want to go back to your way, don't let me stop you." She picked her nail file back up. "Because your way is really working out at the moment, isn't it?"

I pursed my lips in reluctant defeat.

"Okay," I said. "I'll have a look. Now would you please help me sticker these envelopes before the postman leaves?"

She thrust her nails in my face, nearly plucking out an eyeball.

"Thirty quid each hand I paid for these," she spat. "I ain't stickin' them fuckin' things for no one."

And that was that.

A couple of hours later and I was nursing far too many paper cuts so Sandra was forced to take over. Pepe had not yet emerged from his meeting with Cordelia so I grasped the opportunity to capitalise on the absence of senior management and give Sandra's sister's website a go. I must admit that I did hold out a small amount of faith in it, even though I wasn't sure I wanted a partner who harboured any of the unfortunate ailments as stipulated by Sandra in her earlier sales pitch.

I typed the address into the browser.

Made In Heaven: it was catchy but it made me think of *Highway to Heaven* and Michael Landon descending the white staircase, trying not to wince through the snugness of his alabaster slacks. Well, first I had to sign up for an account, that bit was easy enough; just copy and paste the info from one of the myriad other websites that held my personal details.

I might have to change my picture though. Let's face facts, if I was going to find a man properly the pot plant headshot had to go! Maybe when I got some attractive acting headshots done, I could include one of those; all sultry and serious and leaning against exposed brick somewhere in Dulwich. Oh sod it, the other one would have to do, maybe I'd score myself an attractive horticulturalist! So far so good. Now, what category did I fall into?

Well I'm not crippled, divorced or agoraphobic so I guess **Looking For Something More** was the most appropriate for me. Although **something more** should be a bit better defined. I mean I'm not looking for a cheap tanning salon or a second-hand piano am I? And I'm pretty sure Gary Glitter was "looking for something more" when he was busted in Cambodia.

Right, I was in. Now, where was the browsing facility? I clicked on **Categories**.

What did I want in a man? Well, I definitely didn't want Reformed Offenders, that's for sure. I mean, I'd watched a few porno movies set in prisons but I didn't really want to transpose that fantasy into my own bedroom. Dating someone with a background of arson and petty theft wasn't really my idea of a dream partnership. You couldn't spend an evening in bed, in constant fear that you might wake up with all your silver fillings pilfered. So "no" to reformed offenders!

Widowers? Hmm, widowers. Not sure I could date a widow. In my limited experience, they were usually men whose untimely loss had suddenly jolted them into living life "to the full". They were the most irritating men of all.

Besides, I didn't want to live life to the full; I was quite happy with my mediocre existence staggering along as it was. And I had absolutely no desire to paraglide, abseil or watch the sun rise over Glastonbury Tor at three in the morning, so that adage would be lost on me anyway.

I was fairly sure that someone who had lost their partner so suddenly and tragically wouldn't want to be shacked up with me. Me, who bitched and moaned about life continually and used the phrase "I wish I was dead" over and over when I was so hungover that I couldn't function. God, this wasn't going well.

I searched the page for a Miscellaneous category. There was no such thing, but there was a Phobia category, which might work. As long as they weren't homophobic, I was fairly open to accepting most phobias. I'd seen an episode of *Trisha* once where a woman had been petrified of buttons. It was a bit weird but I suppose I could live with such a person. I'd always felt that I'd never realised the full potential of Velcro in my wardrobe, so perhaps now was as good a time as any to make a start.

Of course, the website didn't go into too many details as that would be discriminatory against those with fragile constitutions and a major breach of equal opportunities laws, so I had to do my best guessing work. There were only three guys on there anyway, and judging by the looks of them all I would say one had a fear of mirrors, one a definite fear of sharp objects, like a razor for instance, and the last, an abject and serious phobia of good dress sense.

Okay, Men of Stature, I bet this one had a massive prospective browser surge. I expected some of the candidates to have double-barrelled names, but in reality the only things that were double-barrelled were their chins. I guessed I would have to seek solace in my own pen: the Looking for Something More category. Two pages, eight per page. Good volume of clientele. The men weren't too bad either.

Tom, thirty: Investment Banker looked fairly normal, albeit a little hard-faced. The kind of guy who always pulled out too quickly for fear of getting shafted himself. Not a good sign.

Marius, twenty-nine: Web Designer was very handsome. I didn't have a lot of common ground with web designers though. I'd barely completed the first bit of The Legend of Zelda before giving up and going back to the far less-complex Solitaire on Windows.

Other than that, this category was looking pretty good. Of course, they'd put my goofy red face at the top of page two so I was practically selling the words Looking For Something More single-handedly via the tool of product placement. Hopefully, I'd slip a bit further down the page once more people with the same surname initial as me cottoned on to the wonder that was MadeInHeaven.com.

Suddenly the squeak of Cordelia's office door jerked my reflexes into action and I quickly clicked onto the staff database to pretend that I was carrying on with a spot of housekeeping. There was some insipid small talk going on behind me as Cordelia and Pepe shared a corporate joke. I rolled my eyes at Sandra as they both crowed like a couple of old harridans. Pepe then came waddling back over to his desk.

"Oh," he sighed. "That was an interesting meeting about the organic cotton project going on in Dhaka."

"Hmm," I agreed, pretending to be so bowed down with work that I barely had time to listen.

"Yes, apparently the use of Paraquat on…" his words faded into insignificance. A para-twat talking about Paraquat. "So how is this invitations ready to go?" Pepe's managerial supervision knew no bounds, he was actually gesticulating towards a stack of takeaway menus.

"Worked off my feet to get them done, Pepe," Sandra said. I could see she was frantically trying to mop up a puddle of nail polish remover with the sleeve of her blouse, from where she'd knocked the bottle over in haste.

"And I helped," I whinged.

But Pepe wasn't interested. He'd managed two and a half minutes of social interaction with his team today. He was done.

Fortunately for us, the earlier meeting between the two Titans of Titworld had been in preparation for their long meeting in central London this afternoon. They had both left together, Cordelia loitering around my computer screen while waiting for Pepe to zip up his windbreaker. Then began the eternal struggle with the hat-stand so he could retrieve his flat cap that was a little higher up than his twiddling fingers and tippy-toes could reach on their own. Cordelia was like Inspector Gadget; her neck extended to its full length as she tried to catch me out on the internet. Fortunately the organisation database page was mostly a dark sage green so I could see her head bobbing around like a frustrated peacock, reflected in my screen. When Pepe eventually stumbled upon the revolutionary idea of pulling the hat-stand down to reach his aforementioned hat, they were off, leaving the ring of their painfully uncomfortable, empty banter echoing up the stairs. Pepe, once again, was chuckling as if some kind of creature had crawled into his throat and dragged the laughter out itself. The internal battle of the invertebrate who was longing so for an unrequited love; one of the true "pin-ups" of the Third Sector. How could anyone find that woman attractive? She had all the allure of a dead springbok.

Right, back on the net again. The rustle of paper over the partition told me that Sandra had plunged back into her magazine. I typed the web address back into the browser and went back into my account. My heart jumped slightly as *1 Unread Message* appeared in a very attractive blue box.

Ooooh, that was quick. Perhaps my face being placed atop page two wasn't all that bad after all. I made a mental note not to get too excited; he could, after all, be a sex offender. Mind you, any sex at all would be a bonus. I clicked the message and up popped my suitor's category in big bold letters: Gay and Jewish.

Okay, I could live with that. Although, was that really an ailment worthy of constraining yourself to a secret website? Everyone knew that on a Friday night in Soho, half the punters in The Pussyklub were made up of former members of the Israeli army.

His name was Greg, he was thirty-one, he lived in north London, and he was an estate agent who still lived with his family. Oh God, not another fully grown male who still lived at home: I'd had such trouble with the last one. Although, to be fair, he might actually *need* to still be living at home. Like if he was saving money to invest in a global housing project for Nigerian orphans or if he needed to care for one of the family members who was seriously ill. God, how I hoped one of his family members was seriously ill.

In his picture, he appeared to be on some sort of night out as he was cradling a bottle of Corona. That was a thumbs-up; that he wasn't adverse to going out and getting bladdered. That kind of attribute would always tip the scales in someone's favour with me. The picture was quite blurred so I couldn't really get a good grip on the dimensions of his face. I could tell though that everything seemed to be in the right place and he didn't have any unwelcome facial additions that I would be hard pushed to tear my eyes from as the date wore on. I couldn't really judge his height but he had a shock of blonde hair and a tanned complexion. All in all, he had the look of an Antipodean cutie. I didn't really have this down as a particularly Jewish look: I was a little relieved. Not being discriminatory at all but, had he been too orthodox, I didn't know if I could have done the big furry hat and curly sideburns thing. I searched for the personal message that Greg had left.

Hey Simon, great pic. (Oh God! Potted plant head strikes again) *Hope ur well. Want to meet up sometime for a drink? Greg*

Short, succinct, to the point. There were a couple of texting abbreviations that might start to grate but I could cope with that for now; he

170

was an estate agent, he was used to using shortened lingo. I looked around as if I might be put off messaging him back purely by something going on behind me. I started to type.

Greg. Thanks for the message. Would love to meet up (nope, too desperate). *Would be up for a drink sometime. This weekend perhaps? Simon*

I proofread it. Yep, I was batting back with the identical amount of indifference. It was all ready to send. So send it I did.

Then came the waiting game; the painful stretch between messages. Every five minutes, I checked that Inbox. Greg certainly wasn't as forthcoming with the RSVPs as he was with the invites. He'd probably changed his mind. Desperate guys like me who answered a come-hither minutes after it was sent are not exactly the kind of guys you can enjoy any kind of chase with and so, what's the point? He was probably laughing at old yucca plant head with all his mates around the water cooler: "Simon? What kind of common name is that? A haw haw haw."

Men were such shits! I busied myself with an extra-long game of solitaire to pass the afternoon. Sandra and I had a mini-gossip about Katie Price's new stripper hubby over a couple of Hobnobs. Before I knew it, it was time to go to school. I barely had a chance to check the page, but I did so anyway, just out of curiosity.

My heart jumped again. *1 Unread Message*, my new favourite phrase in the whole world, was flashing at the top of the page.

This was getting a bit exciting. I was beginning to think Sandra's proverb was right about jumping straight under another man's trunk if you find yourself jilted and miserable. Or at least jumping onto his dating profile.

I clicked. Greg's photo appeared back on my screen – I'm sure he looked more devastatingly attractive this time round; almost as if he were looking at me personally.

Simon. Great stuff! This weekend is good. Busy Saturday day. Dinner in the evening? Let me know if you're free. Greg

And then he left his mobile number. It was like getting a set of keys to his goddamn door.

My message from the elusive Greg had me leaving the office in high spirits. I practically skipped down the street a la Fraulein Maria, Joni Mitchell plucking sweet music into my ears through my iPod headphones. It was a good evening to be alive.

I mentally scanned Greg's photo through my memory bank, the pixelated face appeared clearer and clearer the more I recalled it. So much so that he could look like a totally different person in the flesh, and probably would.

I was doing it again, getting too involved too quickly. I'd never even met the guy and yet I was still visualising Greg and I sitting up in bed reading property details together and snuggling up on the sofa, watching *Location, Location, Location* and criticising. Only two fairly banal messages from him and already I was dreaming up a make-believe perfect relationship, blindly stumbling into the trap of my own fantasy. No real person, however, could ever be as exciting as your imagination would have you believe. If they were, you clearly had a shit imagination.

I bartered with myself not to think about Greg for a whole evening of school and, if I managed it, as a reward, I could have thirty minutes of blissful time in bed supposing what it would be like to have him sleep next to me. I stopped. Hadn't I done this with Scott and all the others before Scott? And hadn't they all ended in misery, denial and self-doubt? Was I somehow addicted to the rejection? I bit my lip all the way to school.

I entered the gloomy doors of 373 Snaresbrook Road for another evening of high dramatics, over-enunciation and crippling dread. I walked down the bleak corridor with its mismatched colours (Rex's attempts to cut corners were mirrored in the colour scheme, borrowed from the paint leftover from the recent Archway Underground refurb). The chipped board on the floor, the painted-over but never quite covered etchings of past students' initials on the doorframe all seemed to be designed specifically to depict the claustrophobic panic of someone unable to escape their own fear. After which Rex's door at the end was the only thing to look forward to. It was either jammed shut with a wisp of smoke curling through the keyhole or left slightly ajar; the nicotine-stained walls within, teasing the curiosity of the brave soul whose resolve would only let him approach so far before blind terror froze his steps.

Devastatingly, it was the former; shut with the oh-so-familiar smoke snaking through the gap under the uneven door. The office could actually be on fire for all I knew. Well, if it were, it would take all my strength not to wedge a chair under the door handle and ignore the terrifying pleas from within. Given the amount of alcohol continuously circulating through Rex's veins, he would scream up a treat only to be found hours later, a charred skeleton, still gripping onto the Jack Daniel's bottle, his hundreds of Chekhovian manuscripts in little piles of ash all around him. Anyone who had that much kindling in such a small space deserved to perish. I smiled a devilish smile that one could only muster up when considering something truly wicked. But it was Rex's fault, he had driven me to this, fantasising about his agonising death and feeling no guilt at all.

Lulu chatted as she knitted. I think it was meant to be a scarf but looked more like something snagged on the barbed-wire fence of the Yorkshire Moors. Lulu had a habit of bringing old-fashioned fads back into the public's consciousness. She was a one-woman movement in personally rebranding such things as the kilt and the Arran jumper and I presumed the knitted tea-cosy bobble hat wouldn't be too far behind.

"So I said, and Sophie can vouch for this," she said to no one in particular. Sophie cradled a cup of dark coffee, her wide eyes fully attentive, confirming every detail with a timid nod of the head. "That although he did say my arse looked nice in my skinny jeans, he meant it in a truly complimentary fashion and that what he meant to say was that he'd really like to see it again."

"And this is the romantic bit?" I was puzzled.

I had been promised a Mills and Boon-style version of the events leading up to the meeting of her new boyfriend, of all of five days I might add, but it seemed to be more *Remington Steele* than Danielle Steele. The mere fact that Sophie had been present for the whole length of this outrageously sexually charged encounter between the two was a little disturbing in itself.

"So I let him buy me a drink," she went on, unfazed by my cynicism. "And I told him in no uncertain terms that there was no way I would be going home with him because I never do that on a first date."

"So you waited until the second date? Which was actually the first date because the first date wasn't actually a date, it was a conversation in the corridor of the Big Chill Bar."

I raised my eyebrows, I just couldn't let this one slip through unnoticed.

"And now we're together and we're going for a trip to Kew this weekend." Her eyes barely left the needles.

"But you hate gardens. You thought a hydrangea was someone who was afraid of water."

"Well, I've changed."

174

"In five days?" I turned to Sophie. "And you let this happen? How could you?"

She shrugged.

Sophie nodded. "I must admit, it was embarrassing when they started kissing, I didn't know where to look, especially when he startled fiddling with your bra."

"Fondling in front of your friend?" I turned back to Lulu. "Shame on you!"

People around started to get up and collect their belongings, there was a collective surge of activity, it must be six thirty and, therefore, time to go to voice class. The lesser of many evils.

*

Bea stood straight, eyeing us students as we filed in like cattle, each trying to escape her beady eye for fear that she would pick on one of us first. Her ample bosom heaved with each breath, purple glasses balanced perfectly on the end of her nose. She was resplendent in a grape jumper and dark blue jeans. I shuffled in and caught her eye, her gaze softened and she smiled back. I hadn't seen Bea since that fateful day when she excused me for my tardiness. It was clear, however, that that rather terse altercation was all forgotten. The last student sneaked in and Bea strode over to the door, flinging it shut.

"Right." She rolled the first consonant, partly to warm up and partly to show off her own vocal range which had been extensively trained since her days as an actress. Days when she was continually working and at least three stone lighter.

"Warm up." She clapped her hands and, without a sound, there was a communal groan. This was the hardest bit of the evening. After spending all day in an office you were now required to tap into some sort of reserve energy and make these next four hours matter. Once you had reached a certain peak, you could then plateau and actually last much longer than you expected, but the first hurdle was always the most difficult.

I knew what the warm-up would be; it hadn't changed since the mid-eighties. Follow My Leader.

The mainstay game devised to serve two purposes only: to entertain little children at birthday parties and to humiliate fully grown adults enrolled on drama courses. Not that I objected to the game as such, it just had no suspense factor; no thrill. It didn't so much warm up as prod a bit with a limp twig. The first few rounds at the beginning of the course had been the worst, especially for the shyer students of the group who hadn't yet managed to settle into the whole improvisation thing with much comfort.

One crucifying incident involved a fragile mature student called Cass. She'd had doubts about her acting ability from the start, which had been picked up on early, and so Cass had been berated unmercifully by Rex who had treated the whole business like some kind of blood sport. Finally, after months of trying to appear strong, but actually appearing desperately unhinged, Cass had snapped while carrying out the role of The Leader. And having your nervous breakdown reflected in the actions of twenty other classmates can't have been easy to deal with first-hand. It was only when we began to realise that she had been crying and pummelling the floor with her fists for a little longer than was humanly comfortable that Bea stepped in and escorted her out of the room; a shrieking and snivelling wreck. Cass was never heard of again; dumped on the ex-student slagheap like so many other unfortunates. Their only legacy was to be etched on Sophie's memory list,

176

their names quoted at regular intervals for the next two years like fallen soldiers on the battlefields of the First World War.

Bea's eyes scanned the room once again, but it was obvious to both me and her who would get chosen.

"Ah, there could only ever be one Leader today," she sounded positively excited. "Step up Simon."

That bitch hadn't forgotten at all.

*

It was while I was lying on my back and inhaling through my nose that I snatched my first thought of Greg and his blurry picture. I'd managed a full half-hour without thinking about him, which was undoubtedly a personal record.

In the last five minutes I had managed to string together a few original ways of flailing my arms like a maniac to make Follow My Leader interesting and varied enough for all those taking part. It was only now, in the calm of a breathing exercise, that I could stop being on show and find a sliver of inner peace. This was the only moment of a typical school evening that I could actually get some time to myself. We were meant to be tensing then relaxing every single muscle in turn from our toes to our faces. This was an attempt to build a tunnel through our respiratory system for the breath to travel from our bellies, through the lungs and out of our mouths without any tension. Lying on that disgusting floor, where a rodent could dart from any of the gaping holes in the crumbling walls and skydive into your open mouth at any second, was hardly the perfect environment in which to find your inner utopia, but you just had to get on with it. The school itself was never going to change, what had to shift was your attitude towards it.

After we had achieved this clean flow of uninterrupted breath, we would bring ourselves up to stand and try to keep the same smooth channel, this time putting noise on the breath without the support of the floor against our backs. To do this, we let out the sound: "MAAAAAAAA." The theory being that if we discovered how to support our voices without the need for a solid back support then all our lines would be delivered clear, loud and strong. That was all well and good but once the whole room had got the sound going, it played like a recording of a traffic jam on the M1 at midnight on Christmas Eve.

The exercise had sounded unusual at first but there appeared to be some logic to it after you'd got over the initial bizarreness. Drama school itself was bizarre, like a mythical place that nobody in their right mind would understand unless they had experienced it first-hand themselves.

Bea would circuit the room, breathing with us, calmly repeating the instruction with her sing-song delivery, and touching our bellies with her warm palm. She went about, lifting our arms to check that we were relaxed, and jerked our heads back on our necks to ease out the steady flow of breath. What we must have looked like to the untrained eye: a gaggle of stationary geese, honking in protest at one another.

It was true that there was nowt so strange as drama folk.

For the most part the vocal training was monotonous, but to master it would prove invaluable when put into practice onstage. It did, however, only ever serve as foreplay to the final game of the class or the usually informative Shakespeare monologue section.

More often than not Bea would select a favourite soliloquy from one of the Richards or Henrys (they were all the same to me) and we would act out every word, beating out the rhythm and performing it in various formats and pitches. Depending on how you were feeling that day you could either feel inspired or ridiculous, in equal measure. Tonight, I was nonplussed. I think Bea sensed this as she picked on me for every single demonstration.

*

Between voice and movement classes, we had a fifteen-minute lull. Lulu skipped off to the newsagents across the road to furnish herself with the appropriate amount of Lucozade and chocolate. "It's sugar, for all the moving."

I, instead, decided to loiter around the photocopier and go through some of the less well-learned lines for *Hay Fever*. Hopefully in this spot, I might not suffer the usual interruptions that I would had I hung out in the dank common room with my excitable peers. The downside was that the photocopier was situated at the adjacent wall to Rex's office but, if I was savvy enough, I could get away with a few readings out loud without disturbing the dragon inside. No doubt it was poised to emerge from its lair, bubbling over with white-hot rage and smoking at the nostrils.

Thankfully, when I got there the office door was slightly ajar. This most certainly meant that he had popped out for a mid-evening scotch, a little flutter in William Hill or perhaps just onto the street to bunny punch homeless people and the elderly. Something I'm sure he did for fun when there was no one to abuse in the immediate vicinity. With the coast clear, I fished my well-thumbed edition of the play out of my bag and started to read out loud.

I went back over each sentence, frantically attempting to tune deeper into the character and zone more out of myself. I was beginning to see Simon's mouth saying the words instead of mine, taking Simon's expressions on instead of mine. I was feeling the tenderness of the character I was becoming; the tormented, childish boy tainted by his own pretentiousness and emotional stiltedness. My speech got louder with every repeat, the words took on their own hardness and frustration. I could let the turmoil shape his voice; he was crying out for something he wanted, something he couldn't have the way he wished he could, if only he could verbalise the anguish and strain.

It all seemed to be making sense now. I was believing. I was seeing. The walls around me melted away and my vision blurred at the corners, as if someone or something else was trying to see through my eyes. I was no longer succumbing to my own train of thought, but trying to take on somebody else's.

My voice broke and tears pricked my eyes.

The sounds that followed were soft, deflated. That Simon had been defeated and this Simon understood. A strange sensation made me turn, almost as if I felt a rush of wind behind me, only slightly colder than the surrounding temperature.

At once, I froze in horror. Rex stood over me. There he was, his figure tall, erect. A pillar of dark shadow towering over my feeble shape, ready to crush me at my most vulnerable. A lit cigarette in one hand; the smoke curling upward like the trunk of a slithery eel, the other hand on his hip, the perfect position to catapult from with an accusatory leer and a pointed finger. I stopped dead, just like I had when my mother caught me wanking over pictures of David Ginola at the age of fifteen. But, on Rex's face there was no hard look, no flared nostrils or tight lips. There was more of an air of... well, serenity.

His carriage was not tense with frustration, his fingers were not stiff and rigid, a fire did not burn in his eyes like two gas central heating boiler pilot lights. He was not looking at me, but looking into the distance, beyond the woodchipped wall. The expression he carried when listening, truly listening to a performance that he "did not detest".

Only about three seconds of silence passed, yet it felt like three lifetimes. With each second the situation grew more and more awkward and my face burned a fresh shade of cranberry. His arm dropped, he moved slightly to his right and continued on into his office. The quiet was deafening, it was like the world had stopped for a few seconds; the squeak of the cogs grinding to a halt was forever reverberating through the eternity of total nothingness.

With the slam of his door, it started again. The colour seemed to flood back to the room, I was able to breathe normally and my muscles released themselves from the vice-like grip of terror. What the hell just happened? Why had Rex not said or done anything? Surely a snide comment, a scoff or a sneer should have been thrown at me like a wet rag, but, nothing?

Maybe, just maybe I had witnessed a positive reaction, something rarely seen by the minions outside of the Old School Elite. Maybe I had just witnessed approval.

*

Movement class flew by. I tried not to broadcast my earlier run-in with Rex as I didn't want to set myself up for a dramatic fall from grace. Rex had a way of building you up to knock you down and I didn't want the others to think that I was unaware of this. I also reckoned that if I divulged any sort of meek hope to my comrades that I may have cracked Rex's surface crust, there would surely be one bastard willing to bring me crashing back down to earth with a cold dose of reality.

"Yeah well, remember what happened to Dean? One minute Rex chirruped on about his Basanio, the next his Torvald went down like a fainting sumo wrestler."

On my way home, I glanced at my phone. I don't know what I was expecting to see. Maybe a text from Scott, a missed call, or even a subliminal message from Greg since he didn't yet know my number. Instead, I decided to speak to someone that I hadn't seen or heard from in days. I keyed in the name and let it ring.

"Well hello stranger," Beez answered in his usual chipper way. "It's been like a fucking light-year! Don't tell me you've been neglecting your bosom buddy just because you're having hot sex now. That's so shit babes."

"No way." I shrugged off the disappointment that came hand in hand with any thought or mention of the disaster with Scott. "That's over I'm afraid. Fucker! So much to tell but not over the phone hey? How about Saturday night? I'm busy up till then."

"Hey sure, gutted about the boy. All men are shit anyway. You're better off doing what I do: oil them up, climb on top and then leave them out with the recycling. Any more than that and you just end up with tissues and issues, so not worth it."

"Well what about you, any action this week?"

"Nothing to report. Thought about getting a bit of head on the Heath the other night but I know them all now, no fresh blood. You can't have an anonymous fuck with someone if you already know what their spooge tastes like. De-pressing!"

"Hmmm." I couldn't really contribute to this conversation. "Well I'm sure there's something I'm meant to be doing on Friday. I should be about quite early on Saturday."

182

"Well Friday, I'm doing MDMA with my good friend Sammy so if you wanna meet up on Saturday, you'll be doing all the talking. I'll call you. Laters."

"Yeah, laters."

A tell-tale click. My plans for Saturday cemented.

Freya had long gone to bed by the time I made it home, leaving an empty packet of Monster Munch in her wake. I just crawled into bed and a warm feeling washed over me. I lay on my back, face up, staring at the little spots on the white ceiling. I'd have to report that in case the landlady went bananas. Her hating me didn't help. She was more likely to assume that I'd been balancing on the top rung of a step ladder with a black marker pen just to piss her off.

I turned to the empty pillow to my left. Perennially empty, but maybe not for long. Oh, it was stupid I know, I'd only had one silly little exchange with Greg this afternoon but I just had a feeling in my waters that this one might be a keeper. He seemed so keen, so succinct, so grown up – unlike that stupid tosser Scott, hand in hand with some pecker on the Tube.

I imagined Greg's face next to mine on the bed, pixilated but still gorgeous. I would kiss him tenderly on the lips before I turned out the light and then I would roll over and feel his manly chest against my back, move with him as he breathed in and out, clutch his arm to my chest as we drifted into slumber. I began to ache for him; some dude I had never even met. But in reality, I think I was just pining for the intimacy that never came.

The next day I received the best news ever via my mobile phone. I'd woken up thinking of Greg, although I'd totally forgotten what he looked like so I think it was more Jake Shears with Greg's name. Sophie had texted me super early – she'd obviously had another sleepless night of foreboding that someone else might be kicked out of the school while she dared to rest her eyes.

S. No school 2nite. Camilla's ill. Yippee!! See you tomorrow. Have a great night off! Xx

Amazing: time off!

I suddenly felt inspired to do a million different things: tonight I could categorise my CD collection, clean out that junk drawer I've been meaning to do for ages, cook a nice dinner or ... meet my future husband...

9

I hadn't been in this bar for about three years, not because its location was somewhat off the beaten track but out of choice. Kudos was notorious for its clientele of fat cat, sweaty despo perverts and their Filipino buy-a-boyfriends. All sauntering around with a certain arrogance as if they owned the joint and I was an illegal alien. Yuk! It was like a frigging meat market here. It looked like some kind of prostitute turf that you might see in those old films about the Vietnam War. In fact, I was sure the phrase "Sucky sucky, five dollar" had been mentioned at least once tonight from the rancid cubicles in the toilets downstairs. Why on earth had he wanted to meet here?

I had given Greg the benefit of the doubt – he didn't sound like he knew London all that well, which was confusing since he said he lived in Kilburn. Maybe he wasn't "scene". Okay, that could be a problem. I think I needed someone who was scene, especially if I was going to introduce them to Beez. I couldn't possibly enjoy a night dancing to Atomic Kitten in front of the video wall in GAY with someone who was going to be judging me all night. I'd spent an evening with a self-proclaimed "non-scene" date before: as pure as the driven snow to my face but as soon as my back was turned he was rubbing his own cock and then sniffing his fingers.

Greg had already texted that he'd promised his friend that he'd have an early drink with him and his mother (!) and that he'd definitely hook up with me later. *Hook up* was my expression, his response had been slightly more Dickensian than that. In truth, his appeal was beginning to wane. I couldn't leave now though, cold feet or not. I had to get the whole Scott debacle out of my mind and replace him with something else, even if it was another disaster.

I surveyed the room; the razor-sharp looks from some of the Asian beauty queens were enough to slice the head off the Venus De Milo but I kept walking, feigning nonchalance. He wasn't here, unless he had turned fat or foreign in the last two hours. I slid up to the bar.

What are you wearing? Greg had emailed. *How will I know it's you?*

I had decided on debuting a new fuchsia-pink jumper that I'd bought from the Illustrated People sale on Brick Lane over Christmas. It was made of lovely soft wool and had prints of doves and guns across it: a unique find that I had been saving for a special occasion. Apart from those stolen dates with Scott, my social calendar between now and then had been drier than a Gandhi's flip flop so I thought if I don't get it out tonight then I never will.

I looked at my phone – he was ten minutes late, nearly fifteen. I hated it when a date was late, it was so unchivalrous. How dare he leave me standing in a bar of his choice while he sat drinking with some mate and his old lady. I glanced again at those around the room. Maybe I had missed him, you do look over things when you're nervous, and the bar was about three people deep. I could have walked straight past him. I walked gingerly up to the bar, looking over the heads of the Filipino boys, trying to get a glimpse of those on the front row. Oh-my-God! There he was! He was holding up the bar; waiting.   Our path was blocked by two gossipy old queens. Gosh, he was tall! Much taller than I'd imagined – though his picture had only been a headshot and you couldn't really tell his height from the ambiguous grey background. He was also breathtakingly handsome; sunkissed with a strong jaw and a mop of blonde hair atop a chiselled and symmetrical face. I thought about confidently striding over to him but panic rooted me to the spot. He was far too fit for little old me. Surely he'd take one look up, one look down, throw his vodka down his neck and make his polite excuses. I'd had that many times before; hell, I'd done it *myself* so many times before. Once with

186

the guy who wore the American tanned slip-ons. Again with the pissed-up supermarket cashier with his dad's suit on. And not forgetting the time I ran from the Australian beefcake who had fewer teeth than I remembered when I was tonguing him in the dim light of the back bar in Islington.

Oh God! I couldn't handle the rejection from someone so beautiful. I already knew I was out of his league, I didn't really want it proved and broadcasted for all the punters of Kudos to see. My mouth went uncomfortably dry. I had to do something, I couldn't stand him up. I'm sure I was overreacting. He was probably *looking* for someone a little more at the riff-raff end of the scale: a welcome break from all the models and table dancers he was used to, kind of like when Jennifer Aniston went out with that plumber from Essex. As I made the decision to stride on over, I noticed that Greg seemed to have a drink already. He didn't seem to be ordering at the bar and, at the same time, didn't appear to be waiting for anyone or watching the door for someone to enter. He just seemed like a regular lad, having a drink. In fact, come to think of it, he didn't much look like his profile picture. I doubted whether that was him at all.

At that moment and right on cue, I heard the squeak of the door hinges behind me as the front door of the bar swung open. I turned round to catch a glimpse of who was making such a racket, as did the rest of the place. What can only be described as something from Middle Earth bungled its way through the arch, wielding an umbrella that was nearly as big as its owner, even though the night remained dry. The figure stopped and stood, both hands on the small of its back, rocking back and forth on its feet and inhaling deep lungsful of air. I recognised the face, albeit much more aged than the one currently swimming around in my memory.

Mother of Mercy, I thought. That's him.

Greg was about five-foot nothing and wore a dark blue cagoule that looked as though it had been ironed flat. From under this expanse of waterproof fabric hung a pair of ill-fitting jeans which had been turned up that many times they could have held about three cups of rainwater. The shoes were sensible hiking boots, the kind that irritating couples wear on Sunday afternoon walks, and his hair was not so much short and neat than shit and naff.

Okay, I was judging him on first appearance and I was wrong to do that but I had to be honest, I had limits and this guy was about three miles away from them, having a potted meat sandwich in a clapped-out old caravan. Without even speaking to him, I knew instantly that we were totally incompatible. I was far enough away from him; surely I could sidestep around the perimeter of the room and slip out of the front door with little drama. If I ran I could be out in seconds and put the whole sorry business behind me. It would, however, look slightly suspicious if I started doing a *Mission Impossible*-style stalk across the dance floor, especially since I was standing underneath the fucking mirrorball. I may as well have had a t-shirt on that read "I'm right here, Daddy-O".

While I wrestled with my conscience, Greg was having a similar fight with his waterproofs, cagoules not being made of the most flexible fabric and this particular one, wrapped around quite a large trunk, was proving to be the least flexible of all. Once he'd jerked the zip up and down a few times and pulled the thing over his head, I caught the full extent of what I was dealing with. The waistband of the aforementioned jeans had been pulled up to near enough nipple height, and the tight chequered shirt that Greg had chosen did little to mask the two droopy moobs that were now flopping over the top of his belt, hanging south like two deflated whoopee cushions. A belt that, no less, had a Swiss Army knife pouch dangling from it like a pair of dog's bollocks. Well, at least if I wanted to slit my own wrists tonight, I'd be able to lay my hands on a suitable weapon. He was folding the coat back up as I started to make my way into the darkness and into what I thought was a convenient shaded booth where I could, at least, gather my thoughts and make my planned getaway. As I moved backwards I bumped into someone else in the dark. Oh please God, no!

"Sorry," I pleaded.

At that moment, out of nowhere, ear-splitting disco music erupted from behind me and lights exploded into my face. "AAAAAAAAAH, FREAK OUT!"

It was the start of the crappy disco. I'd just bumped into the lighting rack. My beautiful pink jumper, displayed in all its glory by the glare of the traffic lights twinkling in various sequences over my head. I was the only person on the dance floor and, it seemed, the only person in the whole place who was wearing pink. In short, I was fucked! Greg looked up. A wonky smile spread across his little face and he began to stroll over like Gizmo as styled by Roger Whittaker. I let out a sigh that was so low it practically dropped out of my bottom.

"Ah, Simon, is it?" he held out his hand. His voice was snooty and grating, like how I imagined Walter the Sissy to sound from all those *Beano* comics I read as a kid. "I knew it was you, instantly."

Why did you say "is it" then?

"Really?" I said, not bothering to introduce myself. "What on earth gave me away?"

"Well, at first it was the pink jumper, but then, I haven't been downstairs yet. The place could be awash with pink jumpers for all I knew."

Oh God, could you just STOP TALKING!

He pointed. "No, it was more, that." He could have been pointing into the stratosphere behind me, he was so short. He was actually pointing to ear level behind my head where a shelf hung with a group of various potted fake shrubbery displayed on top of it.

"They looked like they were growing out of your head," he pointed out, "just like in your picture."

Great.

I didn't have the heart to do a runner, I decided after a bit of thought – I managed to drift off while Greg was droning on about some pointless altercation with a bus conductor on the way over. I realised that I wasn't really that kind of guy. I too had had disastrous dates with people who clearly didn't fancy me. It was more courteous to just humour the other person for one, maybe even two drinks and then make your excuses. I couldn't possibly be so heartless as to... Oh for fuck's sake, was he still talking?

The first ten minutes had been devastating. Poor Greg had been so nervous he'd said all the wrong things. After hearing that I was an actor he'd said, "But you're too old aren't you?" I'd known that he hadn't meant it like that, but after the realisation had set in he'd been so adamant in pleading his innocence that he just kept on digging a larger hole for himself. I'd told him repeatedly to forget it and not to worry but he'd ploughed on. I was not far off from telling him that I couldn't be offended because I didn't care enough, but I just nodded and smiled. My mother would have approved. Now he was launching into his bag of anecdotes, all of them mundane and not in the least bit amusing. Acting amused when you're not at all is totally exhausting. After just the one story I felt like I'd been violently raped for half an hour.

"So," I bellowed over him, just so I could get a word in, "How long have you been dating then, Greg?" He looked at his hands, bashful and a little reserved.

"You'll probably think me a bit sad and pathetic," he whimpered.

"I assure you that my opinion of you is unlikely to change." I wasn't lying.

"I've been doing this now for fifteen years." I was genuinely surprised and a little crushed. Greg was no different to me really. We were both looking for a bit of romantic attention. What was it Fay Weldon wrote? *Something to do and someone to love, that's what everybody wants.* At least he's shown up for all those dates. Even tonight, it wasn't his fault that he wasn't my type; I should treat him with a bit more respect.

"Fifteen years? Wow, and you've never found the right guy?" My voice was more sympathetic than I'd intended.

"Well, let's not pooh pooh tonight just yet," he laughed. The look that followed was one of hope. I felt a bit sick.

"No fucking chance," I whispered.

"I've met a million *right guys*, but for some reason I can't find the one."

"Maybe the right one will find you and not the other way around. I mean, you are very sweet."

He blushed.

"Musicals!" He blurted out for no apparent reason. "Do you like musicals?"

Okay, hopefully this would be a good bit of common ground for us. We were only halfway down the bottle of red. Maybe this would see us through to the end and I could scuttle off, banished to his memory bank forever.

"I love musicals Greg, I'm an actor! Of course I love musicals."

"Oh great, I've just been to see *Wicked*. Have you seen it?"

"Er, no, I haven't. Not yet anyway."

"Oh, we should go," he beamed. "I've seen it about ten times. I want "Defying Gravity" played at my funeral. Have you heard it?"

Before I could even knit the words *defying* and *gravity* together in my head, he'd whipped out his iPhone and started frantically searching through his music library. Once found he pressed play so that the loud music played to a fairly unimpressed audience. Worse still, he was miming the words. Halfway through the first verse, I put my foot down.

"Okay, I got it." He seemed a bit deflated. "It sounds good. I don't really need to hear anymore."

He put his iPhone back into his pocket like a reprimanded schoolboy might pocket his catapult. The whole act was beginning to grate. Why would you want a song called "Defying Gravity" at your funeral anyway? It would be a bit inappropriate to suggest that you might levitate yourself back out of the coffin.

"Are there any other musicals you like?" I asked, trying to lighten the mood and sound like I gave a shit.

"Oh I love ALL the Lloyd-Webber ones," he cooed. "Anything with Sarah Brightman. She really is the goddess of the West End stage.

"I remember her when she did a play called *Song & Dance*; a reworking of *Sunday In The Park With George*."

I was no Andrew Lloyd-Webber superfan but I was pretty sure from the programme of some terrible musical review I had watched at drama school that the play *Song & Dance* had been a reworking of *Tell Me On A Sunday*. So, like a bitch, I cut him short.

"I think you'll find it was *Tell Me On A Sunday*, but don't worry, it's an easy mistake to make." I couldn't resist being a touch smug.

"No, no, no" he debated. "I have the CD of the original with Sarah Brightman and Wayne Sleep. I can assure you that it was *Sunday In The Park*

With George. I have a recording of the opening production back in 1982 from The Palace Theatre."

He seemed to be getting a bit upset at the thought that someone might be questioning his Sarah Brightman knowledge, or that he might possibly be, oh I don't know, WRONG. He began to frantically start searching for someone he thought might be able to help him out. I was over it. I was about to say as much when he lifted up his hand.

"Excuse me!" he shouted over to the barman who was now collecting drinks glasses. "HEY! Excuse me!"

The urgency in his voice made the barman rush over, oblivious to the pointless and trivial question that was about to be pressed upon him.

"Yes mate?" The barman was about my age and fairly easy on the eye.

"Well Sir." Oh God! He was going to do it. "Me and my date here…"

For fuck's sake, he didn't have to say that. I found myself sinking further into my barstool.

"We were just discussing Andrew Lloyd-Webber and…"

"I'm just going to stop you there buddy." He held out his palm. "I can't stand any of that musical shite so I really can't help you."

This. Was. A. Nightmare. I didn't look up: I felt I would be staring failure straight in the face. Fortunately, the barman moved away.

"Greg, I really don't think…"

"There must be SOMEONE who can confirm this." He was agitated now. Getting all hot and sweaty for no reason. I thought he might cry.

It seemed he'd spotted someone outside. "Ah, he looks about my age."

He slid off his stool, spilling his drink in his haste and haring for the door.

"Excuse me," I heard him shout as the door swung shut behind him, "my date in there…"

This was my moment. I quickly sunk the rest of my glass of red and jumped off my seat. It was my golden opportunity to make a sharp getaway. I was just going to run, there was no point in being polite anymore, I'd done that for nearly an hour and I had nothing left to give. I grabbed my coat and made way to the door. In my rush, I locked eyes with the barman for a split second. He smiled a lopsided grin.

"Good luck," he called.

"Blind date." I gave him a pleading look, hoping that he understood. Though, what did it matter? At least I could leave this shithole; he was stuck here!

Once out, I walked quickly away down the street as tiny spots of rain began to fall on my skin. A narrow escape indeed, I told myself as I heard yet another person protesting against poor Sir Lloyd-Webber somewhere behind me, through the spitting rain.

*

The journey home had been long; the quicker I got home and scrubbed the remnants of the last two hours off my skin, the better. I half expected frantic texts from Greg on my way, questioning my whereabouts and lambasting me for doing a runner on the first date, but there came none. To be honest, I probably deserved it if there were any. If anyone had done the same to me, I'd have hidden under the duvet for a week. Not even the lure of a bacon sandwich and a *Judge Judy* marathon would coax me out. I decided to switch my phone off; I couldn't be doing with a dressing-down, least of all one that was carefully constructed for maximum impact via the medium of text from someone I couldn't stand. Once I got home, the suspense was killing me: I had to get a flavour of whatever drama Greg was trying to pull me into.

Right on cue, my phone beeped twice.

Twice? Oh dear. I was expecting nothing less than a two-page rant on what a complete bastard I was, probably in some sort of Wildean phraseology.

I glanced down.

Fuck! I recognised that number.

Hey babes, where have you been? I've been thinking about you. Give me a call. Scott. Xx

Was he serious? I mean, I know he didn't see me on the train the day when he was linking arms with some raddled old arse-bandit, but that wasn't the point. He was still seeing someone and continuing to string me along, eking out the pain, willing me on to make a fool of myself. How rude is that? So he's still prepared to make a prize mug out of me even though I'd politely given him the opportunity to back out? What had I done to him to warrant that? Why couldn't he just let me be? Was it not enough of a hint that I hadn't called? All men were such...

But wait, hadn't I heard two beeps? Maybe there was more to this tale. Perhaps he was texting more lies, or even an explanation. There must be some reasoning behind this; sending the first message on its own was simply unfathomable... unless it really *had* been a relative, but then, you don't ogle relatives like he did that guy on the train.

I scrolled through to the next message, prepared to read more scandalous rubbish, perhaps even an apology.

No such luck, it was actually from Greg:

Like the squirrel said to the acorn tree: nuts to you!

Classic! I thought. Then I deleted them both.

10

"I'm telling you, Sand, it's pointless." I glumly trawled through the dating website again like someone might flick through the Argos catalogue.

"You had a bad experience man." I could barely hear her over the jangle of her earrings against her sailor-topped shoulders. Today's jacket looked less designer and more like something you'd drape over the windshield when it was frosty. "You gotta keep going. You of all people should know that."

"I'm losing the will to live. I cannot go on anymore bad dates – they're wearing me out!"

I took two showers to wash that date off. My skin felt so dry, I had to open my mouth every five minutes to make sure I wasn't dead. I would persevere, I just wanted it known that Sandra's sister's offerings had been no more forthcoming than my own. The smart arse.

Pepe emerged from behind me, a spectre. I could hear the squeak of his slip ons before I smelt the Old Spice – and I didn't mean Cordelia.

"So," he said, "there's a buzz in everyone about tonight." I was barely listening. "We are very excitable at this time." His attempt to start a conversation with either of us was futile. Only Carl nodded in agreement. I didn't know what the hell they were all on about so I just grunted.

In the photocopy room, I'd managed to get accosted by Tim again as he gave me a cheeky wink. After last night's disaster, it was all I could do to not get down on my knees and feast on Tim's cock like a starving Alsatian. Something, anything to feel a man against me, his hot scent in my nostrils.

"So, tonight's the night, eh?" He threw me a heartbreakingly gorgeous smile and sashayed out; the smell of old nicotine on his Greenpeace t-shirt followed behind.

What the hell was everyone on about tonight? Even Clarissa was lining up her wheatgerm tablets and taking them at irregular intervals just in case she forgot *tonight*. All I knew about tonight was that I had another night off. It had been agreed that we would all be called in to do a full day's rehearsal on Saturday, bearing in mind that the showing of *Hay Fever* was on the following Monday. I was planning to have a couple of beers indoors and a night in front of the TV. Clearly I was missing some amazing social gathering that everybody here was attending to-*bloody*-night. Whatever it was. I searched my memory for any kind of note to self. There was something missing but I wasn't sure what.

I sat back at my desk and waited for Pepe to be absent before calling over to Sandra.

"Sand, what the hell is everyone going on about tonight for, have I missed something?"

"You're kidding right?" She shot me an awkward glance.

"Nope, I'm racking my brains..."

"The Eco Scene staff party? The one you're organising. That's tonight." She turned around, shaking her head at my stupidity.

Fuckshitbollockscraparsefuckwillycrap!

I was a week behind! With all the dating and drama nonsense, I had completely forgotten! I was meant to find a venue, book a table. Since last Friday it had totally fallen out of my head. Oh shit, this was serious. Everyone in the office would surely have been ploughing on about this for weeks. Had I been tuned into my work at all and not to devious men and Noel Coward, I would have noticed. The whole thing had just clean passed me by.

"Oh yeah." I tried to act casual but sounded distant and robotic. "It's so under control I barely remembered it was on."

I wasn't fooling anyone, least of all Sandra, but she was kind enough not to interrogate. I coolly slipped my phone into my bag.

"In fact, I really should go and make sure everything is okay at the venue. Don't want any hiccups at the main event." I got up. "Can you tell Pepe that I've just popped out to the venue and…"

"I'll tell him, run along now." She waved me out of the door with a bank statement. "Good luck."

I turned and made for the exit. I was going to have to do some serious work here. This had to be a good night else it would go down in history as my total balls up 2012. To go with the 2011 and 2010 editions. I didn't want that on my conscience with Monday looming, and I didn't want to give Cordelia any further ammunition to put me on the chopping block. I swear that woman carried round an emergency copy of my P45 in her handbag, ready to serve at any moment.

*

"What do you mean you're fully booked up?" This was my last stab at getting somewhere remotely eco-friendly. But the fuchsia-haired Bristolian girl behind the desk at the Paint Your Wagon organic juice bar was being particularly eco unfriendly.

"I'm not being funny, Sir." She was right, she wasn't being funny. "But I'm afraid it's Friday night. We're booked up every Friday night for about two months."

What was it about the Bristolian accent that made me so weary? Upon first listen it sounds dumb country bumpkin but there is always an underlying current of knowing menace. The Bristolians, I feared, may eventually take over the world. I sighed, hoping my puppy dog look might change her mind. It didn't.

"Listen, there's a bar over to the left, further down Leonard Street. Me and my mate went there last weekend for a drink, it was practically empty. Maybe they'll be able to sort you out."

"Really?" There was a God.

"Oh yeah, it's uber trendy. So cool it doesn't even have a name." Her eyes widened.

"Erm," I didn't like the sound of this. To our lot, the word *cool* only applied when joined with minty and fresh in the adjectives on a bottle of mouthwash. "I don't know."

"Otherwise, it's a bottle of cider on the kerb, up to you." She wasn't stupid. I eyed her, but I couldn't deny that I was defeated.

"Okay."

"It's next to the coffee bar. Have a lovely evening."

I smiled my most acidic smile and turned away, heading in the direction of her description. Over the road, sure enough, was Underground Coffee Bar and, next to it, a door where a shifty-looking, beefy foreigner in a filthy vest was standing, sparking up a cigarette. I pushed past him for the door. I shoved it but it didn't give way.

"Ees closed," the guy said without looking up.

"Oh, do you work here?" I didn't want to assume that he was blue collar, just because he looked it.

"Yes, but ees closed. Open later." His third failed match was flung into the road.

"Cool. I'm looking for a venue to host a party tonight."

His dark eyes lit up and his gravelly, stubbled chin spread into a leery smile, showing his nicotine-stained, stubby teeth that razored towards me like the top of a severed tin can.

"Go on."

"Well, not so much a party, just drinks, but there'll be about fifteen of us so..."

"We do it," he said, with all the enthusiasm of a teenage girl at a Justin Bieber concert.

"Okay, can you accommodate us on such a busy night?"

"Yes, we do it." His sinister smile was etched across his face like a Quentin Blake character.

I had no choice.

"Er, okay then, around 6pm?"

"Perfect."

"We're from Eco Scene. Over the road."

"Ees good!"

"Okay, well see you then."

"Okay."

"By the way, what's the bar called?"

"Lekh."

"Lech?"

"No. Lekh. Ees a Polish word."

"Okay, great."

And that was that.

I swaggered back into work, slightly overdoing the smug act. Sandra smelled a rat.

"So either you managed to find somewhere suitably dull for this evening's event, or you got some on the stairs." Her smile was cheekily lopsided.

"I'll have you know I'm as dry now as I was when I left." Nice!

"Right, so where are we going?"

"Well, it's a little... erm... rustic haunt just down the road from here. It's so cool that it doesn't even have a name."

"You've never been there before have you?"

"No, but I have it on good authority that it's a charming little watering hole."

"You've probably got the hole bit right."

Turns out that Sandra was absolutely correct. After opening the mystical door with so much force that my molars still ached, we descended the stairs into the mouth of hell. As I surveyed the cavernous space within, my heart sank deep into the pit of my stomach. Sandra and I had left the office a little bit early to get a heads-up on what we were to expect from the venue. My Polish friend was nowhere to be seen but his equally putrid inbred cousin was behind the bar, seemingly polishing glasses with a filthy rag. In fact, the glasses had looked cleaner before he assaulted them with said cloth. An East German poster hung limply on the wall, one corner lingering desperately close to the candle that had been forced decoratively into an empty soy sauce bottle.

Sandra's face looked like the cover star of *Trout Monthly*, mouth open and bottom lip bobbing up and down. She was frightened for me.

The place certainly was dead, in fact I expect most of its regulars were probably dead and buried underneath the dodgy floorboards. That girl in Paint Your Wagon had done this on purpose, the cow! I hoped she choked on one of her own sesame seed and carrot muffins. I needed a well-deserved beer before the rest arrived; anything to ease the pain of what was sure to be a monumental let-down for all involved. I sidled up to the bar but didn't recognise one of the beers on display. In fact, I would probably need my tongue ripped out to be able to pronounce even one of them. I had never seen so many V's and Y's on such a small surface area. My sigh was so heavy that it blew out two candles to my left.

"Look," Sandra sounded positive, "just act as though everything's okay. It'll be fine. They might even like the ambience of the place."

"Sand, there's more ambience in Brompton cemetery." I was nervous.

"If anyone says anything, just say you wanted to try something different, no one else offered to organise it so I'm sure they won't argue." She patted my tense shoulder.

At that precise second I heard the trip-trap of footsteps down the stairs. I sprang into action, hastily clicking my fingers at the barman.

"Right, Sir. Er, could you put some music on or something?" He jumped to my aid, dropping his stained cloth and fiddling underneath the counter where, presumably, the gramophone was kept. Nondescript European pop filled the space. It was like the *Eurovision* meets Armageddon.

Tim was the first in, followed by Pepe, resplendent in blue jumper, blue corduroys and shoes. He looked like a yard of fabric. Cordelia was next, looking like someone had smeared dog shit under her nose. She wrapped her poppy-red pashmina tighter around her as if it might shield her from the potential disease dripping down the nicotine-stained walls. She wore her hair in a sort of cottage loaf bun that wobbled with every jerk of her neck, which was in overdrive now she was so far out of her comfort zone. Clarissa and Carl brought up the rear, her clinging onto him as though she were being forced to enter a stinking Victorian gaol against her wishes. A few waifs and strays filed in behind them. Everyone stopped and looked around them. I held my breath waiting for the air to break. Nobody looked in the least bit impressed. Tim was the first to speak.

"Simon, what the hell is this place?" He looked squarely at me, confused and perplexed.

I looked at Sand, a turbo fake smile plastered over her face like a circus clown.

"Well I..." I couldn't lie. A confession was about to come steaming out of my mouth.

"It's bloody fantastic!" He outstretched his arms, walking over to me and enveloping me in a tight hug. The smell of leather and musty fags only slightly relieved me. He moved from me and walked around, holding court. The rest of the party looked less than convinced.

"I mean, look at it. No pretention, no idiotic suited prats, no crazy capitalist marketing crap on the walls. It's like drinking in an old commies' pub in pre-war Russia. I love it!" I fell in love on the spot. His speech was so impressive that the group instantly warmed.

"I mean *War and Peace*, eat your heart out! How did I not know this was even here?" He sauntered over to the bar. Rather bizarrely, we all watched him as though at some kind of promenade theatre event. "Hi mate." The barman sneered back. "Bottle of strong lager please."

As the group began to venture further in, the barman presented Tim with an aggressive-looking dusty bottle containing some undisclosed liquid.

"Two pounds please." He proffered his hand.

"Two quid?" Tim laughed. "The beer is the cheapest in London. Brilliant find. Good show old man."

Normally I wouldn't have been happy with that moniker, but Tim, well, he could call me what he fucking well liked.

After a few cheaper than cheap drinks, the party seemed to be going well. Even crabby-arsed Cordelia had let her hair down and had an ultra-watered-down white wine spritzer. The last time she had consumed such a drink, Blue Nun had been the tipple du jour, so she looked slightly taken aback when offered a Chilean white. Tim had been sinking giant bottles of Polish hooch since his entrance and was tipsy, but in that sexy controlled way that mentally stable men are: charming, funny and affectionate. Not like me; one too many and I'd flail my arms about to Gina G and start expletive-ridden rants with the nearest available coat-rack. Eventually the staff had dusted off some old Motown CD and we all had a boogie to Freda Payne's "Band of Gold". Pepe had done the old classic shifting from foot to foot. Considering he was from South America, the home of the hip wiggle, a fur-trimmed ottoman had more rhythm. Even Cordelia was starting to sway from the seat she was firmly glued to. Her movement was painfully subtle, in the same way that high rise council blocks are designed to slightly sway in heavy wind so they don't break in the middle. She even managed to temporarily break her usual habit of judging me. I was being good. Well, not so much good as unable to drink anymore of the firewater that was masquerading as European beer. It was far too strong. Sandra had discovered Polish rum and was in full swing, tossing her feathered earrings over her bejewelled shoulder-pads like Alexis Carrington. Clarissa had been nursing a glass of tepid water all evening, mainly because of her allergies, but she too got into the spirit. In fact, I saw her in a different light. I imagined her being quite the party girl in her heyday. She clearly enjoyed the atmosphere, even if she couldn't partake in the hedonism.

After a good hour, Cordelia had had enough. She called the meeting to order. The crown had slipped slightly and she was starting to slur her speech.

"Just before I depart, I must just tell you that we are having a new addition to our team on Monday."

Oh God, I thought, is this her way of shoehorning me out? Taking on someone else and gradually making me obsolete.

"My nephew, Craig, will be joining us for a couple of weeks. He's been studying organic cotton farming in Nicaragua for the last two years and has decided to stay in London, with me... on my sofa. So don't be surprised if you see an attractive young man walking around the office. He's with me!" She laughed at her own joke; we tittered out of politeness.

She got onto wobbly feet and swung her pashmina around her so violently that it actually covered her head. How many had she had?

"Have fun," she threw over her shoulder as she attempted to mount the stairs, her red cloak draped over her head, squashing that lovely do. From the back it was just like *Don't Look Now*.

We couldn't help but giggle when we found out that what she had thought was Chilean chardonnay was actually strong vodka from Krakow.

Once a few people started to drift away, I knew the night here was officially over, but I didn't want to stop.

Tim eventually staggered over to me and draped a limp arm round my shoulders, His breath smelt of nicotine and beer – bliss!

"Great night boy, you did a great job." He gave me a stubbly, moist kiss on my cheek. "I'm off now so don't have too much fun without me."

Still reeling from that surprise public display of affection, I watched him ascend the stairs, probably going home to nail his girlfriend. Lucky, lucky bitch. That was it; I needed to get laid... tonight.

Sand came up behind me. I could smell her perfume a mile off, she was wearing enough to stun at least three robust ostriches.

"Oh Si," she giggled. She was another one who turned into a funny drunk. A party girl through and through. "I don't want this to end."

"Me neither." I spun round. "Fancy a nightcap in town?"

"Umm."

"Oh go on! Just one, I promise." I was pleading a little more than I wanted to. Sand looked around, Carl had left and Clarissa was admiring a poster with cats on while simultaneously wrestling with her knitted scarf.

"Yeah, go on then." She flung an arm around me. "See," she said, "everything you touch turns to gold man, you just don't see it."

I'd never taken a compliment before and I wasn't about to start now.

"Get a move on will you? Let's hope this walk sobers you up a bit."

*

Without her even noticing, I had steered Sandra in the direction of Old Compton Street. She'd been half in a daze anyway, sambaing to some Caribbean music that wasn't even there, practically hot-stepping the length and breadth of Charing Cross Road. We passed Kudos on the way and I let out a little shudder, the other night's date still fresh in my memory. I wondered where Greg might be now. Probably painting his World of Warcraft characters while sticking pins in a voodoo doll with my printed-out profile pic attached to it; pot plant and all.

It was easy to get Sandra into GAY; the lure of Jennifer Lopez playing inside was all I needed. I thanked the Lord that she had sampled the lambada in her latest tune, otherwise Sandra would probably be at a bus stop now after refusing point blank to dance to "that Gaga crap."

After that, it was plain sailing. We kept furnishing each other with large rum-and-cokes, topping up on the already consumed strong Polish booze. I liked GAY but I wasn't so sure about the clientele. It was full of scene queens all looking to upstage each other, even though they all looked exactly the same. Oversized glasses, super-tight skinny jeans and cool white vests, olive tan, perfectly sculpted facial hair and uber-cool tatts. So far removed from my sort of person – the grooming is so fastidious that they don't look like real people. I mean, who decides what these guys wear? Just because it's featured in *GQ* magazine are we automatically supposed to like it? I had tried to keep up with fashion many times but had never looked right. I don't care how amazing you think you are, *everyone* looks remedial in double denim. I scanned the room for a potential snog, if nothing else. Sure I caught the sight of a few lurkers, but I wasn't that desperate. Most of the guys in here were already partnered and stood, deigning to make a few subtle movements to the music next to their vacuous boyfriends who were dressed in exactly the same clothes. I didn't even know why I was here. It was beginning to anger me. After a good twenty minutes of attempting to make flirty eyes at a couple of boys who couldn't have been less interested, I visibly harrumphed myself. Sandra had wandered into a group of lesbians on a fortieth birthday party and was having a great time, swinging her large African necklace through the air like a gold-plated lasso. I had visions of her stumbling and accidentally decapitating the over-zealous bull dyke who was standing a touch too close for comfort. I would steal swiftly to the toilet and return quickly enough that Sandra wouldn't notice I'd disappeared. I headed for the door, leaving the collective whoop as Madonna's "Vogue" burst out of the speakers behind me. The stairwell was cold, a fierce breeze from the fire exit had followed me in and I shivered as I made my journey up. The sudden drop in temperature reacted immediately with the alcohol and I instantly felt pissed. I had to hug the wall just to help me ascend the stairs. I must have looked like some kind of starfish, gripped to the hull of a big gay boat.

Jesus, I thought, I really am quite well oiled. By the time I reached the top, I was smashed and barely able to unzip my fly to separate my cock from the crotch of my pants. The guy on the door noticed my inebriation and raised his eyebrows. You can fuck off, I said to myself, I may be hammered but I'm still able to work a liquid soap bottle myself so I'm not giving you a pound. I smiled, impressed that I'd managed a fairly aggressive flow of piss without any landing on my jeans and/or shoes. I then began the eternal struggle of putting the thing back in my trousers. Turning around, I noticed that a queue had formed behind me. I was now thankful that I hadn't let a cheeky fart slip out. I stumbled to the sink and splashed water over my hands, grasping the sink to stabilise myself and keep from falling headfirst into the array of cologne bottles. If I did, that was sure to cost me more than a pound. Making a quick getaway before the doorman could accost me with a fistful of kitchen roll I was on my way down.

"Simon?" a voice bellowed behind me. They couldn't want me; it must be some other Simon.

"Hey, Simon!"

Oh shit, that was me. I spun around so fast that I nearly fell down the next step.

Holy shitballs. It was Scott. He was too close for me to run; I stood gawping at him like a drunk deer in the adultery headlights.

"Simon." He reached me and went to put a hand out.

"Hey," I protested, swinging my arm away from his two-timing claw.

"I've been trying to call you." He smiled. Damn that smile, damn those teeth. They weren't mine anymore. I couldn't even look at him.

"Right," I agreed. "You did try to call."

"But you didn't answer. Are you... angry with me for some reason?" He looked genuinely confused. Was he for real? Did he really want to hurt me even more? Was he really that selfish?

"No, I'm not angry," I said, angrily.

"Then, why haven't you answered my calls? I thought..." he dropped his voice. "I thought you were into me."

"Oh please!" I scoffed. A few splashes of undignified saliva escaped from my lips. "The only person who is into you, Scott, is you!"

He looked angry.

"What the fuck are you talking about? What's the matter with you?"

"There is nothing the matter with me... at all."

"Right, well I'm out with my mates and I don't really need this so I guess I'll see you around." He was not the kind of guy to stick around for a drama and I wouldn't blame him, but he created it so he'd have to bear the consequences. How dare he walk away from me!

"Do you know what, Scott..." I spat. "You could have been amazing, you could have been someone who changed my life. You could have been the one man who I really loved. You had to ruin it all, had to ruin it with your little friend!"

"What little friend?"

"Don't play the innocent with me." Oh God, this was getting worse.

"Simon, I'm not listening to anymore of this, it's ridiculous. You're drunk," he sneered.

"Yeah, I'm drunk. But you're a TWAT.... and I'll be sober tomorrow."

Ace!

"Fuck off" was the best response he could come up with. He left and I cried. Cried so hard and for so long that I couldn't even remember what I was crying about. No one came to help. And when I was done I went downstairs. Sandra had already gone, leaving a text on my phone to say as much. I gathered my belongings together and glumly left the building, leaving Scott partying somewhere inside.

*

Oh. My. God. The first thing I noticed were that my eyes were crusted with dried tears. I had to use all the muscles in my face to wrench them open. Then I noticed that there appeared to be a woodpecker in my head, hammering its beak against my temples. I had to force back the urge to throw up there and then. I felt truly awful, one of the worst hangovers of my life. I skimmed through last night's events, from what I could piece together over the battleground that was my brain. There was dancing, copious amounts of rum and something that didn't feel quite right. Had I argued with someone? Had I cried? Oh God, no! Had I done both? I couldn't think about it now, my brain would surely explode.

My phone sprang into action. Somewhere in the genius of my conscience last night I had managed to set myself an alarm to remind me that we had an emergency rehearsal today. I had received a late-night text on my way home from an unknown source, now discovered that it was actually Liana on some random phone. She never had credit – it was understandable. Now I had to get myself into gear and haul my ass into school; whatever state I was in would have to pass. If there's one thing Grant hated more than bad acting, it was bad acting at the hands of the demon drink. That was utterly unforgivable.

After nearly falling asleep twice while dragging a pair of jeans up my apparently dumb legs, I managed to locate the front door and lurch out onto the street. I nearly threw up twice on the Tube, fighting the window open to be immediately sobered up with the force of the gust of wind swirling round between the carriages. Eventually, I got to school. The smell of booze emanating from my pores was almost too much to bear and Dominique, sucking on a Lucozade bottle, visibly swooned when I wished her a good morning. Everybody gathered in a tight circle as Grant strode into the room, clutching his notebook like Moses with the stone tablets.

"Well people," he looked like he was controlling the urge to dry hump something, "I'm happy to say that I think the standard of your work this term has, thus far, been of an extraordinarily high calibre. But we must not get complacent. The play is in two days and I am hoping that we can straighten out some of the creases this morning. You will, of course, be free to leave when I am satisfied that you are ready to show the work in front of my colleagues. If that means we stay till three in the morning then so be it."

Grant sneaked a quick smile in my direction. I pulled my face back together, having gormlessly zoned out slightly while trying to piece last night back into sequence.

"You are very fortunate that you have had a shining beacon of hope in the class. Someone who shall remain nameless."

God, I couldn't stand all this ego-massaging when sober, hungover was even worse. I smiled a cock-eyed leer and prayed that the two Pro Plus I'd boshed outside would start to kick in soon.

Luckily, I wasn't in the first scene so I managed to pull myself back into consciousness by the time I entered the stage. The tablets coupled with the booze had given me a new lease of energy and I breezed through the first scene, high on a happy vibe. It was a little louder and over-zealous than my previous efforts. Grant didn't look impressed.

"Down a notch please, Simon." Grant barked from the sidelines. "This isn't Prozac night on the gibberish ward. Remember the sincerity."

"Sorry." I made the cardinal error of explaining myself. "I was just trying something."

He gave me the warning look over his glasses, the one that told me in no uncertain terms to cut the prima donna bullshit.

"Simon," he shot, "you can try it in the desert with a fucking tea towel on your head for all I care, as long as you pay it for real. And again…"

I stumbled through the next scene and took the break opportunity to rush to the gents and splash some water on my puce-shaded cheeks. I heard the door swing behind me. Finishing up, I turned around to come face to face with our director, his big face serious. I whimpered pathetically.

"What are you doing?" he demanded.

"I'm just washing my…"

"Not in here, out there." He pointed a sausage finger in the direction of the theatre. "Your performance is decidedly below par today, Simon."

"I'm sorry. I can't get it right every time." I regretted the words instantly.

"Well you're in the wrong fucking industry then, dear."

"Sorry Grant, I don't mean to sound uppity. I'm just having an off day."

"Yes, well. You better pull your socks up, Simon. I'm not one to dole out unnecessary praise so soon before a showing, it's never productive, but I meant what I said. And you of all people should be wary about how you look on Monday."

"Me?" I was genuinely perplexed. "What do you mean?"

"Let's just say that someone has let it be known that he'll be keeping an eye on you." Grant's eyes were fixed dead onto mine.

"Oh great." Now I felt sick. Obviously he was talking about Rex. I'd clearly upset him with my performance the other night. How naïve to think I could have done anything less. "You mean my head's on the chopping block?"

Grant said nothing.

"Just do better," he said. Then he pushed past me and fumbled with his fly. "Else I'll be forced to slip into your trousers and play the bloody part myself."

Rather than catch another glimpse of his hairless, gerbil-like penis for a second time, I made a quick exit.

I grabbed a coffee with Dominique at lunch.

"Babes, you're doing fine." Bless her for trying to make me feel better.

"I'm not, Grant knows I'm hungover. It's written all over my face. He's giving me such a hard time."

"Oh Jesus, Simon, I spent virtually the whole of last term high on coke and no one even noticed," She was half looking at me, half zooshing up her hair in a compact mirror. The mirror, no less, with encrusted cocaine embedded in each scratch.

"No," I said. "We knew."

"Oh whatever. I'm screwed anyway. I'm only here because I'm not intelligent enough to be a hairdresser." She scrambled around in her handbag for that ever-elusive frosted pink lip liner.

"But you, babes, you could go dead far. You're a natural."

I'm not sure I was that convinced of praise coming from someone who wasn't blessed with enough smarts to open a bottle of TRESemmé. But any praise was good, right?

"So, what are you aiming to do at the end of all this? I mean, if you truly believe you don't belong here."

"Really?" She lowered the gloopy slop wand from her pouting lips.

"Really."

"I want to sleep with Rex, get pregnant and inherit the school." She was deadly serious.

"That's... ambitious." I felt as though my hands were tied.

"Isn't it?" She went back to her mirror.

I strode back on stage with a new confidence, somehow knowing I wasn't as ruthless as Dominique was comforting, I knew at least that I had some talent and was not getting by on my sexual allure alone. But then I didn't have Dominique's tits, or so little inhibition that I could let men into my vagina like shoppers on the opening day of the Next Blue Cross sale. If there was anything I'd learnt from this morning, it was to keep my emotions within, to internalise the character's expressions and keep the thoughts modest and in moderation. It worked. Grant's expression went from outward exasperation to inward exhilaration. By the end of the rehearsal, he had gone from frantically scribbling notes, to actually watching and enjoying the performance. Suddenly, the highly comedic piece was all the more humorous because we were playing it totally straight, which became a huge learning curve for us all. We finished a little later than expected after a case of mild hysteria when one of Liana's breasts popped out of the low-cut chiffon blouse she'd borrowed to play the maid.

"Luckily," Grant chuckled at the end, "the only tit in the performance was one that isn't included in the programme. Might I suggest you wear a brassiere to tomorrow's run-through Liana. This isn't a front window of an Amsterdam whorehouse."

"I didn't think maids could afford them," she argued. Grant rolled his eyes.

"Of course they did," he snapped, "else their nipples would be forever hovering over the scones."

As I left, Grant winked at me. "Better," he mouthed. I wasn't quite out of the doghouse yet and, if Rex had his way, I would probably never even get to the doghouse. I'd be shot in the back and left to decompose somewhere on the crazy paving.

I made a decision to not go straight to bed but to sharpen up on lines when I got home, and in no circumstance was alcohol to pass my lips for at least the next two days, until the play was over. As it happened, I fell asleep with the play opened over my face; a lovely pool of spittle saturating my monologue on page eight.

11

I was up in much better spirits the next day, remembering Grant's words about complacency. I was determined to do better today. I had been so preoccupied yesterday, I had barely enough time to fret over the previous night's altercation with Scott: the devastating words, the tears, the vitriol – block it out, block it out, block it out. I had to do a good job today, this was the last chance to perfect my interpretation of the character, to make sure I was doing everything right. I couldn't give Rex the satisfaction of crucifying me in front of the whole room. If I was going down, I was going down fighting.

My last scene was with Maeve. It was a kissing scene that we had held off rehearsing in detail so that we could devote real time to it on its own. It had been slightly glossed over yesterday which I was thankful for. Had Maeve got close enough to me for anything, the toxic fumes on my breath would surely have taken a layer of skin off her eyelids. Luckily, Maeve was a ballsy actress, unafraid and willing to experiment on the stage in front of others. She also had a pair of bosoms that could not only bounce you off after you threw yourself at them, but could lift you back off the floor and pat your head in comfort at the same time.

When I arrived at school, Maeve had looked well up for it.

"Ready tiger?" she slurred.

"Well, I've always said *darling*, that if there was any girl I'd jump on..."

"Oh stop, anymore and I'll have to change my tights."

In all honesty, I was a bit nervous. No one ever tells you how to play a kiss just right. Hollywood would have us believe that we all do it with our mouths closed; that we stiffly position our necks and keep our lips firmly pursed while simultaneously leaning into the light. How far were you meant to go with smooching on stage?

I wasn't used to kissing girls; was I meant to do something different? I mean, how is a lifelong vegetarian meant to cope with a tough old husk of rump steak? I recalled a hideous moment at college. We were doing some dreadful Spanish play and I was grossly miscast as the Don Juan of the piece. And of course, being the lothario, the script required that I kiss the female lead repeatedly. Being so nervous I practically lampooned my poor co-star on the first try. As I pulled away and she wiped my drool from her mouth with the first available patch of her poncho, I remember her looking decidedly defiled. Trying, unsuccessfully, to not appear disgusted, she graciously handed me back one of the bands that had separated itself from my train-track braces and stuck itself to the top of her palette. I didn't want another similar nightmare, so I apprehensively waited to hear from Grant how I was meant to play it. His silence was terribly unhelpful.

"So," I said to Maeve before Grant yelled the obligatory starting signal. I was trying not to sound as though we were nearing the end of the date and it was left to me to determine whether we would go back to mine for a shag.

"So." She leant in closer. Oh great; she was a sexual predator. As was her character in the play.

"I'm guessing that Simon is nervous about kissing Myra. I mean, he doesn't strike me as someone who has had that much experience in this area. He still lives with his parents for God's sake."

"Oh I don't know." She fingered her script. "I think he has the same urges as every other mucky little boy. He probably cracks one off night after night thinking about Myra. I mean, she's the one who's playing it cool. She's probably more likely to be taken aback. She's not used to real passion from men who love her. Probably more from men who see her as a sexual object, not as a vessel of unbridled romance."

Well put. My penis began its slow journey inverting into my balls.

"Right," Grant honked, "shall we begin this scene then? Remember, I'm looking for reality. I don't want anything phoned in."

"Good luck," Maeve whispered before launching full pelt into her first line and thrusting her breasts forward so fast I half expected her nipples to boing out on comedy cartoon springs.

Live it, I told myself, make it real. Visualise, believe. Suddenly, as if transported into another world, at my most vulnerable, with the whole class' eyes on me, I felt naked and ashamed. The whole of the other night's drama came flooding back to me. Scott's lost face, my hurt, my pain, my desperation. I had acted like such a prize fool, goading him. I suddenly felt the urge to want to speak to him, just tell him I was sorry, kiss him, ruffle his hair. Go back to that stolen Saturday afternoon at his flat. Now it was all gone.

"I mean, what do you have to say to me, Simon?" Maeve as Myra looked at me, one eyebrow up, lips pursed. I studied her hard for a second and began to visualise Scott's face: sad, confused, helpless. I took his face in both my hands, felt the softness of his skin beneath my fingers and traced the outline of his lips with my thumb. He looked surprised, like he hadn't expected this to happen. I searched his eyes, looked for a trace of recognition; I wanted to speak to him through my eyes, tell him that I was sorry and that I still cared for him but I couldn't speak. My voice was tied to the back of my throat. I went to talk but the words were dry.

"I can't do this anymore. I love you too much." I felt a hot tear escape from my eye and trickle down my cheek. He placed his hand on my hand, took it in his. His hand felt warm, comforting. I had to kiss him, maybe just once. It might be the last kiss we ever had. I had to make it count. I leant over the table and placed my lips on his; softly, tenderly. I wanted him to know that it was the kiss of true sincerity and not something he might be used to in the dark corners of some Vauxhall dive. It was full of meaning. I closed my eyes. At least if he never felt his lips on mine again, he would know that this last kiss was real and had meant something. A gift from me to him. I shut my eyes, and when the kiss was over and our mouths had ceased their contact, I looked at my hands in his. If this was ever going to stop then I would need to break the chain. So I pulled my hand free and kept it in my lap. A beat passed before I looked up.

At first I was confused to see all my classmates staring at me, some open-mouthed, some dabbing at their eyes with withered bits of tissue paper. Seeing Grant snapped me back into reality. He looked a little watery-eyed himself.

"That," he said, choking back a tear, "was really rather good."

I turned to look at Scott, who had magically morphed back into a very attractive actress once more. An actress whose sexual allure I was no longer afraid of. She smiled.

"I think," Grant said, "that we are ready to kick arse tomorrow. And let's show those other fuckers what we can do."

*

"Mate, that was stunning. What the fuck is going on? You're knocking them out of the park bruv." Liana was the last in a long string of compliments currently circling around the beer garden.

"I don't know, I guess I'm just learning how to channel real things into the staged." I was beginning to sound a little big for my boots. The reality was that I didn't know the secret to my current success. It had just, sort of, happened. Ever since I started to feel something real in life, real things had happened on stage. It wasn't rocket science, it all made perfect sense actually.

Liana looked at me with a certain confidence, a hint of admiration.

"Liana, I'm just inspired by the rest of the cast. We're all as good as each other. It's an ensemble piece, no one of us is any better than the other."

"That's horseshit and you know it." Lulu had sauntered up behind Liana and was bobbing up and down like she was sitting on the back of some gypsy wagon going over a cobbled path.

"Hey!" I hadn't seen her in nearly a week. Sophie was in hot pursuit. I wrapped my arms around the pair of them; I hadn't realised just how much I missed them.

"For fuck's sake, Simon, your performance is all round the school. What's this about puckering up this afternoon? By all accounts you're smashing it." Lulu hugged me even tighter.

"There's no WAY you'll be leaving tomorrow." Sophie immediately relaxed in my grip.

"Oh, that's old news." I shrugged it off. "I want to hear what's happening in YOUR plays."

"It's alright," Lulu shrugged too. "I play a dim nurse who takes her clothes off at the drop of a hat so I'm finding it all a little impossible to get wrong. It's mildly enjoyable."

"And I have barely two lines. *What time is the show starting?* And *He's on at nine Mabel.* I'm trying them in a variety of different ways but there's very little motivation behind either of them," Sophie added.

"But enough about our morbid tales of dramatic failures. How would YOU like to come with US to the performance of the century? You know

Charlie who got dumped by that girl in the elite who got kicked out because she had a stroke in the night and woke up with a Chinese accent?"

"Victim number twenty-nine," Sophie added.

"She's only gone and got herself a part in a new musical based on the *Seven Samurai*. It's called: *Kimono!* And it's on tonight."

"Sure." I checked my phone again. "Oh shit no! I can't, I'm meeting Beez tonight. I've been so busy recently I've neglected him completely. He'll never forgive me if I bail."

"Oh no worries." Lulu waved a limp hand at me. "Now you're a big star, I expect you'll drop us all like flies."

"Don't be silly," I laughed.

"It's true," Sophie agreed.

"For pity's sake girls, I've had some minor success in one play. May I remind you, I've got one more whole year to fuck everything up."

"Well I think you're being modest, aim for the top darling." Lulu smiled.

"Not too high though, it's a long way down." Sophie nodded.

Lulu scoffed. "Are you here to piss on everyone's cornflakes or what?"

*

The Boadicea was fairly lively for a Sunday. I couldn't wait to give Beez the good news. He was, however, totally preoccupied in training a new, young and devastatingly attractive member of staff in the workings of the glass washer when I arrived on the scene. He had the poor boy bent so far into the machine that I was certain he would re-emerge with the lemon washer freshener dangling off his perfectly styled Gok Wan glasses. As I

222

walked up to the bar, I noticed that Giles, hand on half a pint of stagnant ale, was looking decidedly glum. Although I was by no means attracted to Giles' personality, there was something about those doleful eyes that made me want to take both of his cheeks in my hands and squeeze his face together until he looked like a chubby, little Chinese boy. He sighed so forcefully that the collar ruffled on the silk shirt of the woman sitting with her back to him. I winked at Graham and Freddie who were perched in their usual spot, patiently watching Beez's and the new boy's bottoms, poking out of the dishwasher and wiggling in perfect unison.

I tentatively walked up to Giles. I could tell that I would have to choose my words carefully else I could be on the sorry end of a long, moaning outburst.

"Evening."

"Oh, hi Simon. How are you?"

"I'm well, Giles. Yourself?"

"Not too good, to be blunt."

"You're never too good darling." His grey eyes dropped a little further. "What on earth's the matter?"

"It's Gary." I scanned my memory for any recognition of the name.

"I don't know who that is."

"You know, Gary, my new fella." I hated the word "fella", it was right up there with "bird" and "wifey".

I still had no idea who he was talking about.

"It may surprise you darling, but I don't follow your love life." I liked to be acerbic with Giles. I'd never quite got over my obsession with him all those years ago. Now I was totally over it, I liked to revel in that fact. He cottoned onto this a while ago, however, and always looked as though he could never be bothered to argue.

223

"Anyway, what about him?" I remained nonplussed.

"Well, you know he has two dogs."

"Giles, I just said I didn't know him, throw two shih tzus into the mix and now I'm totally lost."

As it happened, I could vaguely remember seeing Giles one Sunday lunch in here, with his arm around some beefcake in a waterproof jacket and hiking boots, chained to the necks of two infested-looking mutts.

"Well we're thinking of going away to Sitges, one week at Easter, and he's insisting he bring Sylvester and Tweetie."

Bloody Sitges. It seemed that anyone who was someone in gay London was running away there every summer. The gay capital of Spain apparently. If you hadn't been then you were clearly not living as a proper poof. From the stories I'd heard, people had returned to the UK with so many STDs they were having to declare them at customs.

I wasn't in the mood to start offering Giles advice on who he could palm his pets off on while he went abroad to get buttfucked continuously for two weeks, stopping only to twist the lid off a bottle of lube with his bare teeth.

"Can he not get some kind of dog-sitter?" I was only mildly aware that such a thing existed.

"He won't, says they won't recognise anyone else, they'll just pine for him and he wouldn't be able to enjoy himself knowing that they're sat there watching the back door for a fortnight."

I imagined that he'd have no objections to two slobbering bitches manning his back door in a four-star hotel in Spain but I kept my mouth shut.

"Look Giles, I can't help I'm afraid, but I'm sure you'll sort something out. I mean, it's only a holiday. Can't you just go somewhere else? Go somewhere in the UK where you could take the dogs. There are loads of places."

It dawned on me that dogs seemed to be the topic of choice in this place at the moment.

"I guess, thanks for the ear." He took a sip of his pint. "How are things with you? How's your drama thingy?"

"What, school?" I hated the way people asked me as if it was some kind of hobby that I took up on the weekends. Like at the end of the course I'd have a nice certificate that I could put in a nasty frame next to a cross-stitch and a memorial plate of the Queen.

"It's fine." I didn't want to go in any more detail. If he didn't know how important drama school was to me by this point, he clearly wasn't interested in my extracurricular activities. His knowledge on the subject then *should* be minimal.

"Babe." Beez had come up for air and was beaming at me, eyes twinkling like two fog lights.

"Daaaaaahling," I cooed. "How's tricks?"

"Very fucking good," he said, wiping his hands on his trousers. 'Just showing the new boy, Gianni, the ropes.'

Gianni emerged, his glasses all steamed up and beads of sweat trickled down his rosy red cheeks.

"*Buongiorno.*"

"Er, *buongiorno!*"

"Yeah, so once you've pulled that thing out of there, you give it a rinse, pop it back in and you're done." Beez finished off the dishwasher cleaning instructions and took a sip from a long glass of lemonade.

"Okay," Gianni tripped off in the direction of the sink. Both Freddie's and Graham's eyebrows raised so high, they were practically tickling the ceiling. Ten minutes of live free porn for them.

"Oh for Christ's sake guys. Eyes back in their sockets please." Beez threw a towel onto the bar in front of them. "Right, a break I think. Come on you, let's get upstairs. I've got an hour."

I followed him up the stairs and into his room where he fumbled in the top drawer of his bedside cabinet, desperately trying to locate a wrap of coke.

"Oh Jesus, I know it's in here somewhere. I had it out last night."

"You went out last night?" I was jealous, even though the night before had been enough of a night out to swear me off them for another month.

"No, stayed in. Sat on Gianni's face."

"WHAT?"

"Yeah babe amazing, rock-hard Italian cock. Fucked for two hours then used his mouth as a pillow for another hour. Absolutely incredible. But I know we didn't use all the coke coz he had some GBH."

I couldn't believe I was hearing this.

"How did you manage to sleep with the new guy before he even started his first shift?"

"Oh no, didn't know that then. Turns out he kept that quiet. Pure coincidence that he was actually working here. That way, as it happened, he didn't have to worry about getting to work on time."

"Oh-my-God."

"Oh don't be such a prude. He only had to peel the condom off his sticky face this morning, and he was already at work." He laughed and high-fived me. I was so in awe of Beez's confidence. Had I done that, that shift

226

would have been purgatory. A lot of nervous shuffling, my big red face and a healthy dollop of intense paranoia. Beez just got on with it. Life goes on.

"Got it." He lifted the wrap up to the light as though he'd pulled Excalibur from the stone. "Now pass me that Blockbuster card."

By the time I had handed over said card and moved a heap of junk to find a suitable place to sit, I had a line thrust in my face.

"Erm, I shouldn't really." I was aware of the responsibility I owed the play tomorrow. I didn't trust myself to just stop at one.

"Oh, COME ON!" he pleaded.

"I've got this bloody play tomorrow," I sighed. "After that, I'm a free agent."

Beez did his best reluctant acceptance face.

"Oh, okay. Just this once," he said. It didn't stop him from hoovering a line up like an industrial vacuum cleaner.

"Well, I have some news." There was a slight apprehension in his voice.

"Is it bad?" I sat up.

"Yes and no."

"What does that mean?"

"Well, the good news is that I know my flights for Australia."

"That's not good news," I grimaced.

"Oh right, well the bad news is going to be devastating," Beez said.

"Why." I eyed him carefully.

"It's next week."

"NEXT WEEK? What the fuck?"

"Well, I managed to find a super last-minute deal. John was okay with me leaving soon and there's no point in leaving it too long if I can knock a hundred off the initial flight is there?"

"But you weren't meant to be going for another month, I was meant to have longer than a WEEK to get used to the idea. What the hell am I going to do?"

"Darling, you know I love you." He put his arm around me but I stiffened. "And I hate to say it, but this isn't about you."

I held that thought for a moment. He was right and I hated it when he was right. He was always right. I took a deep breath.

"Okay, Beez. Okay." I tried to stop myself from tearing up. I would miss him so, so much. But in honesty, school had stood between us for some time now. If I was truthful, I probably wouldn't have *time* to miss him all that much. I didn't dare tell him that though.

"This is really good news for me; the best. And it means that the sooner I go, the sooner I get back."

"Well there is THAT I suppose." I didn't want to thaw just yet.

"So you forgive me?" His puppy dog eyes were back. They made me think immediately of Giles.

"Yes.... Fuck!"

"What?"

"Well, you better pass that fucking line over now, I'm going to bloody well need it."

12

Another Monday morning at Eco Scene. Another week over, a new one beginning, all leading to somewhere but who knows where? I was still at this bloody office, I was still single, Beez was leaving and I only had a fraction of hope that I was any good at this acting business. I know that there was a buzz surrounding my recent performance, but honestly, I was still pretty much in the dark. All these mixed messages kept rearing their ugly heads about whether Rex was putting my neck onto the chopping block or not. Some people were hearing good things, Grant was telling me bad things. This whole situation was a brain fuck. I was half tempted to give it all up and go and join the Amish, cut my hair round a basin, purchase some Restoration buckled shoes and start calling myself Brother Jeremiah. Anything, yes anything, was better than harbouring some crazy ambition to be successful in the dramatic arts. I was a crazy fool to ever think I could handle it.

I pushed the office door open in such misery that I almost forgot to let go of the handle.

I saw Sandra's hair before I saw her; piled on top of her head with what looked like the Bayeux Tapestry wrapped around it, keeping it from flying loose. The oversized bolero did little to mask the bottle-green silk shirt beneath it, which hovered over a delightful pair of black stonewash jeggings. She looked like Billy Idol meets Floella Benjamin meets Edwina Currie. If such an incarnation were ever to exist.

"Morning." She spun full circle which, somehow, managed to make *me* feel dizzy. "Good weekend?"

"Yes, fabulous thanks, yourself?" I lurched over to my desk and flung my bag down. Same thing: day in, day out.

"Yes, it was great. Leon's swimming gala on Saturday afternoon."

I know it was wrong but the mental image of Leon's tall, eighteen-year-old frame in speedos set a ping-pong ball off in my trousers.

"Did he win anything?"

"Nah, I said to the woman: the only way that boy'll swim is if you reel a fiver on a fishing line in from the other end of the pool."

I blurted out a snorty laugh and, as I did so, I looked up. Someone I did not recognise was coming out of the post room. Someone young and male. We hadn't had new blood in this office since the guy had come to fix the photocopier two weeks ago. And from the back he'd been a potential dilf, but when he turned around he'd looked like he'd trapped his bottom lip in the paper tray for a good four hours.

"Who is that?" I craned my neck so far forward I must have looked like some kind of seabird.

Sandra sucked her teeth.

"Child, you don't remember?"

I searched my brain for yet another piece of vital information that I may or may not have forgotten which may or may not mean that I was losing my job.

"Er, no. I don't think so."

"Cordelia said on Friday night. You know, before you left me in that club. It's her nephew innit? Chris or Charles or something."

I kind of remembered something before I hit the bottle in a big way.

"Oh yeah."

He loitered for a second, not noticing my eyes boring into him. He was average; shaved head, chin dimple, blue eyes. Shit, he was looking right at me. I put my head down and pretended to sift through make-believe papers. Tentatively, I looked up again. He was still looking; he smiled quickly and moved away behind the bookshelf. The smile had been slightly uncomfortable, almost forced. He was almost definitely straight. If I thought that from the beginning, it saved me a lot of trouble in the end.

The same old Monday routine continued. Pepe entered the office, all smiles and malapropisms, regaling us with pointless stories of some boat race he watched over the weekend. Clarissa flounced in not long after, a cacophony of various materials, looking all sorry for herself and brandishing her latest battle scar from the feline Satan she was currently sitting.

"The calming powder not doing the trick then?" I asked. She knew I was winding her up.

"She just needs to get used to me, used to my habits, used to my smell. It's not her fault." Was she breastfeeding this cat? I rolled my eyes at Sandra who shrugged her shoulders.

"Well you wouldn't know," Clarissa spat. "Neither of you are animal lovers."

"I love animals." Sandra faced off. "Especially between two slices of bread."

And then it was time for the weekly meeting. Sandra and I rushed to be the first ones in and sat down; somehow we believed that the earlier we were there, the earlier it would finish. It never occurred to us that the meeting began when everyone was present, not just us. I continued signing my name in various styles in my notebook, just to pass the time. Cordelia came in; she looked awful, as if she'd been up all night retching into the mop bucket. She was dressed in a suit that was unpressed and far too small. The sleeve was practically up to the elbow and the trousers looked like a pair of pedal pushers. Honestly, didn't this woman ever watch *Dynasty*? Did she not know how to power-dress in a way that befits someone in her position? And did one of her peers not think to slide a *Grazia* magazine her way once in a while? I tried not to let it bother me. Pepe normally sat to her right but today the seat was saved for the nephew. Pepe would surely be seething with jealousy; the pomade from his perfectly sculpted fringe would be melting and leaving greasy droplet tracks down his silly face.

"Now," Cordelia said, just as the nephew arrived and levered himself into his seat. I could tell that underneath the crisp Gap shirt was probably quite a nice bod. He smiled at me again; there was no chemistry there. I had to snap out of this train of thought when I realised I was frowning at him for no good reason.

"I'd like to welcome my nephew, Craig Scholes." Cordelia's voice was raspy. She'd clearly spent most of the morning making friends with the toilet seat. "If you'll forgive my sluggishness; I'm not quite well."

Not quite well? It was a line lifted straight from a Jane Austen novel. I wanted to tell her that the only cure was to perambulate around the environs.

"What is wrong?" Pepe was doing a poor job of looking concerned. It was like some scene from a terrible amateur dramatic play.

"While I am not wanting to undermine the organisation of Friday night's event, which, I'm sure you can all agree was... above average, I do seem to have felt troubled since I left. I have had a particularly turbulent weekend I'm afraid." A backhanded compliment, followed by a spiteful swipe.

"Oh dear," Pepe couldn't really answer that. Across the table, Tim was looking fairly chipper for a Monday morning. He'd probably been offered a healthy slice of morning sex before he came to work, lucky shit.

"Well I thought it was bloody marvellous. Bravo Simon." He clapped a couple of times and I blushed. Why did I keep defaulting back to her bloody nephew? He wasn't even looking at me anymore.

"Anyway, Craig has been out in Nicaragua, supporting a group of young farm workers who are attempting to start farming cotton without using pesticides…"

My brain automatically shut off. I continued to sign my name on the paper, putting a heart in the dot of the I, curling the S a little bit further under the other letters, adding Scholes at the end.

When the meeting was over, I spent a full ten minutes, staring at my computer screen before I realised I had nothing to do. When I had started this job, everything had been a mess: the filing systems had been appalling; there were stacks of publications and periodicals collecting dust in various piles around the office. I had set about making the space more organised, updating the electronic filing and maintaining the in-house database. Wanting to create a good impression, I had managed to turn the office around in a matter of weeks. Now, of course, having been so efficient so early, there was nowhere else to go. I drummed my fingers on the desktop. I daren't mention my lack of duties to Pepe, lest he find more tedious filing for me to do. I was bored but I wasn't that fucking bored. As I drummed, I cast my eye over to my little personal pinboard. There, as if backlit with a hundred-watt bulb was Sandra's little slip of paper: madeinheaven.com.

Should I? Was it too risky? Pepe was sitting right there and, judging by the fact that I was never busy, he might get suspicious if I started typing ferociously and looked all excited. Cordelia was probably not going to stay long. Halfway through the meeting, she had turned the same colour as a breezeblock and had nearly chundered into one of the spider plants. I wanted to stand up and say: Jesus woman, pull yourself together. Didn't you ever do Aftershock at university?

Probably the only thing she had downed in her university days was some boring old hill on the Pennines on the saddle of a Brompton foldable bike. First gear all the way.

Why not have another little look? Even though I had sworn myself off dates altogether forever more, it couldn't hurt to be tempted back into the fold just once, should a handsome young man take my fancy. I checked around me. Clarissa had her earphones in; no doubt listening to some baroque music while she fannied endlessly about with her bloody Gift Aid declarations, Carl too was busy with another project. Even Sandra looked immersed in work, though from here I suspected that *Coffee Break* was due another tall tale about one of her sister's many unfortunate ailments. I typed in the first few letters and was slightly mortified to discover that the address was already saved in my browser history. The history of my days at Eco Scene that read like a roll call of procrastination and desperation.... Right, I thought, just for fun. Let's look in the offenders' pen. I had to admit that, although I would class myself as a law-abiding citizen, I didn't necessarily have to partner up with another goody two shoes. Didn't they always say opposites attract? Perhaps dating an offender would be a bit more interesting: endless tales from a chequered past, a really rich and meaty story to tell – this made me think of gravy, which wasn't very sexy at all. There was always something fascinating about being somebody else's rescue, perhaps finding me might be the catalyst to get them back on the straight and narrow. Wouldn't that be far more rewarding than dating someone "just because you both watch *TOWIE*"? I tentatively hovered my mouse over the bold words and clicked.

It was practically a smorgasbord of hard-nosed, rough-looking porn fodder. The kind who called their Staffordshire Bull Terriers names like Razor and wore jeans that were spattered with emulsion paint. Something in my trousers jumped. Their usernames were standard fare: Fitboi82, scallylad4u. I just knew that what I was really looking at was a grab bag of Dwaynes, Shanes and Damiens (no doubt spelt phonetically). Half of the profile pictures were just duplicated mugshots. Not one of them looked impressed with having their photo taken. Possibly because it had not been that long before when the officer taking the snap had busted them, puffing on green on the hard shoulder of the M25 in an unmarked Ford Fiesta. This was not really me; I couldn't go out with this sort of person. Me, the guy who returned all the mail for the previous occupants of my flat back to the sender. Or maybe it was? I wasn't finding any luck anywhere else.

I made a bargain with myself to pick the least suspicious-looking and just send a casual hello, thus placing the ball firmly in his court. That way, if he thought I looked a little too vanilla for him and his renegade ways then it was up to him not to persevere. This website could, of course, be serving as some sort of pen-pal scheme. Meaning they answered the mating call of any poor desperate bastard who was willing to part their lips and make it! Before I knew it, I'd be gulping down my Frankie and Benny's date waffles, just so he could get home as the electronic tag started to beep. After a short scan, I decided upon a still quite hot young man by the name of Joel (Joel? I mean, you couldn't make it up!). Of course it didn't say what Joel was found not guilty of. He was certainly guilty of rocking the dusky pink polo shirt with the collar up look without any hint of irony. I chastised myself for picking the most stereotypical of them all, but praised myself for the guts I had to find to do it. Double click and I was in. The message box in front of me looked intimidatingly large. What was I actually going to say? I'd never spoken to a felon before... Were you supposed to talk normally, or in some sort of street lingo?

Oh Jesus Christ, Simon, I scolded myself, the guy isn't on Death Row, he probably just pilfered an Aero from a local Costcutter.

"Hi," I started. In one word, I'd already managed to sound painfully pathetic. Still, it was better than "yo!"

I had to stop and think. Trying not to sound generic took some preparation. I scanned his profile quickly. It said that he was into film, cinema, pubs, clubs. So far we had two things in common: I wasn't much into my films. My attention span never let me commit to staring at a large television screen for longer than forty-five minutes.

"So, seen any good films recently?" It was the kind of patter you might uncomfortably ask someone you were stuck in a lift with, but I had nothing else. I went with it.

"Like your profile pic, btw." The acronym saved me from sounding too past it. I pressed send before my inner cynic forbade it. It was done. Now, I just had to wait. I smiled to myself: I had officially jumped over a new hurdle. Now only time would tell whether it was in vain. At that moment, I felt a presence behind me. I spun round. There, in all his glory, was Craig, patiently waiting with my post in his hand and a smirk on his face. Holy shit, I was totally busted.

"Your post," he said, proffering a couple of limp envelopes. I could feel that I was blushing a previously undiscovered shade of red that Dulux would bite my hand off for.

"Er... thanks." My embarrassment made me incredibly hostile. I snatched the paper from his hand.

"No worries. Simon is it?" He appeared unmoved. I was a hot mess.

"Yes, Simon. That it is, I mean that it is. I just said that." I was dancing on one syllable words with wobbly legs.

"Cool. I'm Craig. Nice to meet you."

Without thinking, I stretched my hand out to him in some awkward formal gesture that humiliated us both. I could feel every eye in the office fixated on me. He snorted slightly and shook my hand. His hands were warm, his handshake confident. I felt as if I were turning into a pillar of salt before his very eyes.

I suddenly became conscious of the screen behind me, displaying the scene of my crime in all its glory.

"I was just…" My nerves meant that I felt the need to try and explain.

"Hey, none of my business." He had a certain cock-eyed assurance that was automatically attractive. I let out a painfully strained exhalation of breath.

"Cool."

Then, in a move that took me totally by surprise, he leant into me and whispered close to my ear.

"Good choice, he is well fucking hot. Though personally Simon, I think you could do better."

And with that Craig, the guy I thought was straight, the guy whose coolness was currently crushing my very being, the boss's nephew, presented me with a lopsided smile and turned to walk away before leaving me with a devastating parting shot.

I practically wet my seat.

*

The rest of the afternoon played like some crazy dream. Had I imagined the whole business? It was like the guy went from zero to hero in my affections and it was all I could do not to start following him into the copier room and start dry-humping the Laserjet 3000. I kept feeling my insides surge with a rush of adrenaline every time the door swung open. Unfortunately my glee-filled eyes were only met with those of one of the fat, sweaty science boffins that worked for us, rather than the office hottie. It was only on my lunch break at my desk that he caught me by surprise, creeping up behind me while I took a big slurp of Lilt.

"Afternoon," he purred. I was so stunned that a big swig began to seep down my nose. Let's just say that the totally tropical taste is lost on the senses within the nasal passage. I thought I would be vomiting pineapple and coconut-flavoured bile for the next two hours.

"Jesus," I blurted. "You scared me."

"Not still flicking through some hot boy catalogue are you?" His lopsided smile had a knowing air.

"Look, about that..."

"Oh God, I'm not going to tell darling Aunty Cordelia. I've already had the Gettysburg Address on the evils of Facebook." He turned and propped himself up against my desk.

"Okay, thanks. I don't really want to admit that I'm a sad single AND lose my job all on the same day."

"So you ARE single?"

"So you AREN'T perceptive?"

He snorted.

"Well okay, I'll make you a deal. I won't tell Aunty C that you're using a charitable organisation's resources to cruise the net looking for your next horizontal friend, if you do me the honour of accompanying me for a dark drink somewhere tonight."

Was he seriously asking me out on a date, in my place of work? In front of everyone? I could practically hear the muscles in Sandra's neck straining to hear us over the partition. If it were any other situation I would have jumped up and done some kind of Charleston dance right there in front of him, singing the words: you asked me on a date, you asked me on a date! I don't think I'd been offered a date since some oblivious girl in primary school asked me to the summer dance. I obliged and we held hands all night, bobbing up and down to "Donald Where's Your Troosers". Little did we both know.

"I'm so sorry," I said through firmly gritted teeth. "If it were any other night I'd jump at the chance. I really would, but I can't tonight."

He stuck his bottom lip out, which slightly irked me.

"So who or what are you standing me up for?"

"Well, you see I'm actually studying at the moment and I have a, kind of, assignment to do." I didn't really want to go into it.

"Right, what are you studying?"

"It's a media course." My response was a little too quick. It even clipped the end of his sentence.

"Okay. Cool. So you'll join me another night?"

"Are you asking me out on a date?"

"I guess so." He winked. That irked me as well but I kept it under wraps. Was this guy over-confident or was I a little under-confident?

"Well, I guess if it's a date then I would be rude to turn it down."

"I will be personally offended."

He was cocky, I'll give him that. Luckily, he didn't wait for a response. He just gave me a little wink and sauntered off in the direction of the photocopy room. I smiled after him but was intrigued to know more. Was it like a flirtatious game of cat and mouse or was he really a precocious little boy who thought he could get what he wanted, including me? If he was anything like his Ice Queen Aunty then the latter was pretty damn likely. For now it was going to have to wait, I had more pressing things on my mind. In particular, knocking the Noel Coward ball right out of the park ranked pretty high on my to do list. Stuffing my things into my bag, I gave my colleagues a strained goodbye as I left the office and tripped off down the stairs. The nerves had suddenly descended on me and I wasn't sure that I could do much about them. Tutors had always said that you are meant to use your nerves in a positive way: channel them correctly and interweave them into your performance, using nervous energy to drive the action forward. But I was a nervous guy I'm afraid. Asking me to channel my nerves into a performance was like asking a rapist to channel his sexual desire into polishing a table: the one just didn't go with the other.

All the way on the bus, I frantically thumbed through my script. The other passengers must have thought I was mental. I kept saying random words aloud, getting them wrong, ripping the pages open and then audibly correcting myself. If anyone thought that I could channel this psychotic behaviour into something more positive they were clearly deluded.

It seemed like seconds before I was walking up the school's steps, littered with my friends and colleagues acting in exactly the same way. Many were warming up, trying to look like they were relaxing but barely able to stop themselves rushing to the toilet every five minutes. It was like Lourdes out here. Dominique was parked outside the ladies' toilets. She had managed to find a beautiful fifties-inspired dress to match a rather ostentatious hat that she had borrowed for the occasion. It didn't seem right to mention that the play was actually set in the thirties, it would just throw her off-kilter.

Grant, on the other hand, looked as cool as a cucumber. I don't know whether this was quiet confidence or whether he was putting a brave face on everything. He walked past me while I glided through the corridor. I was hoping to be invisible but he did give me a secret wink so I knew that I was very much here.

Rex's office door was shut with its obligatory trim of smoke hanging to the floor. No doubt he was in there, rubbing his hands together at the thought of all the ammunition he would be gathering this evening. Tonight it was our stage, but tomorrow it would be his. Crits (critiques) night always followed performance night. Crits was like a forum whereby each student's performance would be criticised (or praised) by the tutors one by one. It was like a horrible circus ring where Rex was the master and would delight in recounting our acting in the most minute detail, picking the worst bits out and using them as knives to pierce our fabric and shred our hopes like scraps upon the dressmaker's floor. He could remember a wrong look, a misjudged step, a bum note, a tense limb, a botched line as if they were his children's birthdays. He would delight at acting them out in various dramatically embellished ways so that you couldn't help but feel disembowelled and humiliated by his clownish imitations of your idiocy. Crits night, in some cases, was worse than performance night. At least on performance night, once the words were spoken there was no taking them back, there was nothing you could do about it. On Crits night, Rex's critique of you would be remembered forever, like a black mark against your name. And I hadn't had bad crits all the time. In fact, my first ever had been practically glowing, although I was sure that Rex was just setting me up to knock me down.

The next few had got worse and worse until my last – a crit for a singing showing that I had performed an excerpt from *Into the Woods* in – I had been told that my recital had been like "a deplorable Marks and Spencer's employees' amateur Christmas show". Luckily, that night, I had prepared for the worst and sunk a couple of cans of Stella so I really didn't care what old arse face had to say. It was the first time that I had looked practically carefree. Rex had retaliated by glaring at me like I was the customary fungus growing on his toenail before dropping the subject altogether and moving on to the next sorry victim.

The rehearsal room was full of people strolling around in makeshift costumes, speaking their lines to themselves and gesticulating with a modest fervour. It was like mufti day at Broadmoor. Lulu was the only one who was unfazed. She sat casually, mouth smeared with bright-red lipstick and wearing a garish polka-dot dress. She was finishing her eye make-up and rolling her eyes at those who were going into it slightly more than everyone else. I sidled over.

"Evening, you look calm."

"What's to stress about?" she said, vigorously sliding the mascara wand in and out of the bottle like she was masturbating a rodent. "No one can change anything. We've done all the work we can, we should just enjoy it." She grimaced and began to reapply said mascara.

"There's nothing wrong with a few healthy nerves," I said, my voice shaking violently. I was surprised that a bit of sick didn't come out.

"I don't get nervous, it's a disease."

"Where's Sophie?"

"Throwing up in a dustbin somewhere. I don't know why she's so nervous. She's only got two lines and they're probably as wooden as hell."

It was plain that Lulu was nervous. She was never this bitchy in ordinary circumstances.

I found a few spare seconds to rummage around in the disgusting costume cupboard for some reasonable attire for my namesake. I managed to find a passable white (if you ignored a few stains) shirt and some smart trousers. I didn't have time to run an iron over them, they would have to do. How anyone could describe the bedlam of that room as a "costume cupboard" was beyond me. Clothes were flung in there and the door jammed shut. The garments then, somehow, managed to tangle themselves up even further so that, once you entered the room to retrieve something, you were met with a ball of fabric, with sporadic limbs jutting out of it hither and thither. It would have been quicker to build a time machine and travel back to the period where the costume was from than to paw around endlessly on your hands and knees, trying to find a suitable pair of breeches and some buckled character shoes that hadn't been pissed on by the rats that lived within.

I had a quick read of my script once more, but the words danced on the page. The rollercoaster of emotions of the last few days had been such that I had no other option than to pull it together for the show.

Sophie emerged from the back room, looking worryingly green. She said that she was alright but I didn't have the heart to tell her that she looked like a gooseberry with a wig on.

The hour drew near and, as the five-minute call sounded, Bea strode in dressed in a low-cut yellow top. Not everyone can carry off the colour yellow; Bea was one of those people.

"Right students," she boomed, her jangly silver necklace rattling against her voice box. "You have five minutes now before the first play goes up. As you know, when the other students are performing you will stand AT THE BACK and watch. You need to leave enough space for the second years and, of course, Rex's group who will be sitting at the front. Order of the day is..." She pushed her glasses further up her nose and read from a dog-eared piece of paper that was to act as the playbill. No doubt the ancient photocopier had mangled yet another batch. "Group One: *Hay Fever* by Coward, Group Two: *What The Butler Saw* by Orton and Group Three: *Augustus Does His Bit* by Bernard Shaw. Got that?"

We nodded in reluctant agreement. I think half the class was hoping that she'd come out and say that the day had been cancelled as Rex was dead.

"Okay, so Group One, if you could take your positions backstage, we will begin in a few minutes."

As she bounded out of the room, we inmates of Group One, as if shackled together, made our pained journey to the back area of the stage. As I was on first, I needed to be closest to the entrance – the worst place to be if you weren't counting on watching the audience members take their seats one by one. As I gathered myself together and defiantly strode to take my place, I caught Lulu's eye from the opposite side of the room. She mouthed something that looked like good luck but it could just as well have been goulash. I nodded: a stiff smile on my lips. I needed a second to steel myself and get into the moment.

At that precise second, the doors swung wide and in walked a sea of excited second years, excited presumably because they knew that it wasn't them that had to perform this afternoon. They could relax. There was Donatella, the old slapper whose real name was just Donna. She sat with a few of the others from the year above, who thought they were better than everyone else. They seemed to spend the whole time at the school, brushing their manes, sharpening their talons and looking down their beaks at all those below, ignoring the fact that they had been in exactly the same boat at this time last year. Compassion seemed to have totally passed them by. There were a few of the cocky boys who were just there to eye up the first year talent and then the poor gay guys who looked worn out from a year's worth of berating from both their peers and from Rex. These were just the second-rate second years; the elite had yet to arrive.

I turned my head away and tried to bite back the onslaught of panic that was threatening to take over my whole being. Then I looked back – and caught an even more terrifying sight. Members of the Old School Elite had surfaced and were now making their way into the room. Even through the slit

244

of light through the door, I could see them gliding in, with the poise of a line of swans, their noses held high and the gait of a row of perfectly preened ballet dancers. The room fell silent as they made their way to the front row, some second years scrambling to pull their bags out of the paths of the chosen ones. There were only about eight but they commanded the room: four perfect boys, four perfect girls. They were so far removed from the rest of us that I didn't know their names and knew them only from brief recognition. They looked like the kind of people who would stand next to you on a bus, waiting for you to automatically give up your seat and dust it down for them before they plonked their faultless buttocks down. The boys were beautiful, without being sexy. Their faces like porcelain, their lips arched like the bow of Cupid himself. Oh God! I could feel about three spots uproot themselves through my skin almost instantly. The last one in, Rex, strode over to his chair in the middle of the throng. The room was so silent you could practically hear the dust shifting on the filthy floor. Every squeak from his shoes echoed through the sombre hall. He opened his mouth to speak:

"What you are about to see is a collection of shorts from the *Comedy of Manners* genre." His whole persona changed with the utterance of these few words. He went from calculated demon to authoritarian dictator in a matter of seconds. Hitler had nothing on this bastard.

"The humour of which is both subtle, razor-sharp, caustic, relevant and erudite. One laughs because the whimsy is not conspicuous; it lives within the words that the characters do not say. The tricks are not there on the plate for you to feast upon; they are in suggestion; between the lines, interwoven in the pauses, beats and breaks. They are in the pace, in the breath, in the energy that the actors bring to the floor. The material will not carry the weight of a maladroit performance. We shall see today whether our students have what it takes to bring these pieces to life."

He turned and placed his cheeks on the royal chair. As he did so he nearly caught my eye but I turned away just in time. There were a few agonising seconds before the next three words were spoken. The three words that had signified the beginning of every show since the school began in the mid-eighties. Three words that were meant to revive the theatrical surroundings in the absence of theatrical surroundings. The three words that Rex had made famous.

"In black... AND..."

I had no time to take a breath; I pushed the door open and stepped onto the stage.

13

The courtyard of the Mohitos Tapas Bar was packed. After every showing we would inevitably end up here, relieved that yet another show was over and we could have at least one guilt-free drink before the horrendous death rattle of tomorrow night. The tutors would be back at the school now, preparing the obituary of our acting talent with sharpened tools. I would rather be here downing a pint. The vibe was positive. *Hay Fever* had been a success I think. There was certainly praise from the majority of my peers who said that the ensemble had worked amazingly well, but on the side said that I had been doing most of the working. Many guys had come over to shake my hand, congratulating me on a job well done. In truth, there had been some exceptional performances this afternoon. Colm, an Irish guy who had been so nervous in previous shows that his teeth chattering together from backstage had practically drowned out those speaking aloud, had really nailed his interpretation of Dr Prentice in *What The Butler Saw*. And even Liana, who had managed to keep her breasts in her shirt while pushing a wobbly-wheeled tea trolley, pulled off an understated, and incredibly funny, turn. Luckily, she had aced the task of holding two sets of rattling cups and saucers while simultaneously delivering the lines with gusto.

In a complete reversal of fortune, Sophie had triumphed in her recital, projecting her lines with such enthusiasm that both carried weighty laughs where, on paper, it seemed there were none. Lulu, on the other hand, got sudden stage fright that was palpable and uncomfortable to watch. Her limbs were like sticks of rhubarb and, at one point, she walked into the scene with so much tension in her trunk she could have easily been mistaken for the Tin Man. She was now being consoled by Sophie over a glass of Pina Colada – it was cocktail happy hour and Sophie had thought this might cheer her up a bit. Unfortunately the river of black mascara that flowed from Lulu's eyes, all the way down to her chin, somewhat made a mockery of the curly pink straw and wedge of real pineapple.

"I mean, I don't know what happened," she shrieked. "I knew it, I knew the lines, the blocking, I knew all of it. It's just not fair."

As much as I loved Lulu, I wasn't about to pander to her. In the acting game, I was fast learning, it was every man for himself. This was a sure-fire lesson that one should never be too complacent too early on.

Dominique had also been astonishingly competent; it seemed that the Comedy of Manners suited her, even if the costume was about twenty years ahead of its time.

After a round of well dones and raking over each presentation in turn, I was a little overwhelmed and felt that I needed my bed more than anything else. I waved a few goodbyes to those who caught my eye and downed my Woo Woo. I didn't want to make a grand exit, so I just slinked off into the background. Lulu would never have forgiven me if I'd stolen the thunder from the best drama that she had performed all afternoon.

While on the bus I stared out of the window as we sped past the school, I saw Rex pulling his coat around him on the outside steps. He appeared to be muttering something to himself while removing a cigarette out of his pocket. I had no idea what he was saying but I caught myself in the window, gurning forward to get a better look at him. If he were to look up, that would be my life over. I hurriedly looked in my bag for my phone, to distract myself. There it was, tangled in my headphones. I pulled it out and looked at the message that flashed on the screen. New email. Hmmmm. I clicked. It was from madeinheaven. Apparently I had a new message that I hadn't checked for over twenty-four hours so they were notifying me before they deleted it. With it being a discreet website and all.

New email from Joel, it read, *Hey dude, like loads of different movies but, in particular La Haine, Kill Bill and anything by Mike Leigh. Like your profile too. Fancy a beer?*

Then he actually left me his number. He was a fast mover, I liked it. And even though I had never heard of *La Haine* (I didn't speak French), I absolutely loved *Kill Bill* (the first one, at least) and adored Mike Leigh films (*Secrets and Lies* was my favourite film ever). I wasted no time in copying the number and messaging.

Hi Joel, Simon here. Film choices are a perfect match! This is my number. Meet this week?

It was succinct without being too emotionally attached. I think all my emotion, plus my reserve stash, had been used up this afternoon.

Now came the agonising wait for a reply.

*

Monday: the day of truth. Not only was I gearing myself up to be dragged face down over emotional hot coals this afternoon, but everyone else seemed to be in the truth-telling game today. I wore a shirt that had hung in my wardrobe for well over two weeks now. I had bought it in the White Stuff and I NEVER buy things from the White Stuff. Possibly because I resent ever having to pay over the odds for something you could pick up much cheaper (and better fitted) elsewhere, but also because more often than not the clientele of the White Stuff were the dad-type men of my age. Those who tend to veer in the direction of said shop to search for something uncharacteristically casual for a Sunday afternoon "bring your own kids" barbeque where other similarly styled dads stand about talking about lawnmowers. I, therefore, bypassed the place altogether in favour of searching Topshop for some women's skinnies. On the rare occasion that I did pop in there (three weeks ago), thinking that I should relent and start dressing in a way that befits my age and gender, I spotted a checked number among the yards of fabric that I would actually WEAR. This being an utter miracle, I tried it on and purchased immediately, honouring the shirt with the best coat hanger in my wardrobe (a thick wooden one) and vowing to wear it on a very special occasion. Since no such occasion had presented itself recently, I decided to wear it today. I was in a good mood. The play had gone well, I had experienced a rare bout of self-belief and reassurance and (if I'm honest) I was hoping to impress Craig. I even splashed a sizeable amount of my new Tom Ford aftershave on. I looked ready to have a couple of pints down Soho rather than a couple of green teas at work. I checked myself in the mirror. I looked and felt pretty good.

When I entered the office, Sandra wasn't so complimentary.

"Morning." She took in my measure. "New shirt?"

I did a clumsy gesture as if flicking my hair off my shoulders. I wasn't very discreet when it came to showing off – I just wasn't used to doing it sober.

"Yes," I sat down in my seat as if I was sliding into the passenger seat of a marine yacht.

"Makes you look your age," she said. This coming from a woman who was wearing a navy anchored bandana and a waterfall cardigan that was the same colour as a whale's dorsal fin. I felt like telling her that she looked like she'd modelled herself on an Oyster card but it wasn't worth the hassle.

"Thanks," I said, my balloon deflating a little. "Good weekend?"

"Nah," she carried on eating a Special K bar without turning round. I could see from here that she was on a celebrity gossip website.

"Oh really, why?"

"Sammi and Ronnie have fallen out again, I don't see why they can't just make it up. It's devastating for the rest of the family."

I searched my brain for any mention of these two names from Sandra's family circle. They didn't sound familiar.

"I'm sorry to hear that. I'm sure they'll work something out. Are there kids involved?" I wanted to show Sandra that I was a caring friend, even if my fashion sense was a little off (according to her).

"No, no kids. Not yet anyway. I reckon they'll get back together, they always do."

"Well there you are then." I turned on my computer and stopped for a second. "Sorry Sand, who are they?"

"Sammi and Ronnie? *Jersey Shore*. It was back-to-back on MTV this weekend."

Christ.

Clarissa swept in after the usual mob had settled. Pepe seemed to have an existential crisis at half nine when he couldn't decide whether to sit down or go straight to Cordelia's desk first thing. The squeaking of his shoes grew louder and quieter the more he clip-clopped up and down the office. With every squeak, my stomach tensed a little more. I was beginning to feel as though God had not meant for me to feel at ease and calm today. I'd clearly missed the memo. There were so many things testing my resolve, especially this imbecile who needed to WD40 his footwear before he slipped his ridiculous feet into them. I was not about to give into my fury; I put my headphones on to drown out the rodent chorus.

I decided that I would give Clarissa some attention. Maybe she could zen me out again like she did the other day. No such luck. When she arrived, a bedraggled swirl of purple and violet, she all but threw her vitamin pills down her neck and swigged a huge glug of crazy juice from that filthy canister that she carried around. She was just about ready to get herself all in a flap and so concentrated on very little else other than her computer screen. After an hour, she slammed an open hand onto the table. I half expected one of her mood rings to involuntarily snap and catapult across the carpet.

"I mean, HONESTLY," she growled. "How can they expect me to type? They know about my ailment. I'm finding it too much of a struggle."

This was obviously a leading question. Carl shrunk away. He was a straight man; he was not equipped to deal with the incessant ramblings of someone whose tantrums were sponsored by the estate of JRR Tolkien. She started a mock whimper that was really a whine. I turned around, ever the carer.

"Clarissa, what's wrong?"

"It's this BLESSED computer. Cordelia told me that she was going to look into buying the dragon thing for me and it's not been done and I don't know how much longer I can go on."

It was all a bit over the top, especially for a Monday. I contemplated continuing with this conversation, it was only going to end in my tears or Clarissa's frustration, or tears of frustration from both parties.

"Dragon thing, what dragon thing?" Inside I was laughing, imagining Clarissa drawing up a proposal to have a fire-breathing cryptic sat on her desk. Cordelia would go mad and her hairstyle would be leaping up and down on her head like it was on a piece of elastic. I half wanted to follow it up with a request to have Pegasus help with distributing the team minutes.

"It's computer software. Voice-activated word processing," Carl piped up. I hadn't heard him speak for about three weeks. "We're onto it Clarissa. It's just an expenditure that we have to have authorised by the board."

"Oh really?" She was so furious that her glasses practically steamed up. "And does your board know that, without it, the magazine will be published in double the time? And does the board know that I have repetitive strain injury in my wrists from years of playing the cor anglais to INTERNATIONAL ORCHESTRAL STANDARD?"

"Erm." Carl looked genuinely frightened. Sandra had completely stopped what she was doing and had turned her chair around to see what was going on. Pepe normally stepped in at times like this but, like Carl, he was a heterosexual man who couldn't bear the wrath of a menstruating woman with woodwind instrument-influenced ailments. He suddenly found an abandoned empty filing cabinet extremely fascinating.

"Clarissa." My voice was calm, almost patronising. "Nothing can be done about it at the moment. I suggest we all calm down."

"I AM CALM," she seethed. "I am NOT hysterical, I am TRYING to work, but since THAT is impossible then I am merely VENTING my frustration."

"But it is not doing anyone any good." This was not going very well. I didn't really want to see this side of Clarissa, let alone be involved in it.

She rose out of her seat like something out of a swamp, her hair appeared to have a life of its own, and the various layers of scarves and cheesecloth enveloped around her like the roots of a tree.

"I do NOT need lectures on working from someone who spends most of his time looking for RAPSCALLIONS to take for DRINKS on the INTERNET!" She spat each word out; rolling her r's like some Shakespearian grand dame. After that, she swept out of the room.

I really hoped that by some miracle of nature, Pepe's ears had rejected the last comment. I don't think they had but he had the good sense not to get involved. I was bright red and pissed off. I had only tried to help and once again, had been cut down with a slice. Sandra was the first to speak.

"You better go after her Pepe," she said. He squirmed a bit, wishing he were back in his mother's front room in Argentina rather than in this room, right now. It was probably best to let her get a bit of air. Silly cow. How dare she fly at me like that! I'm not responsible for her period; I didn't plant that seed in her and make it bleed every month. What the hell is she having a go at me for?

I stood up to go to the bathroom myself and caught a glimpse of Cordelia in the gangway. She'd heard everything. A little knowing smile glimmered in the corner of her mouth as she turned around and headed back to her desk. Ha ha, it seemed to read: I've got you now.

After lunch, Clarissa had come back in, much calmer and slightly sheepish. I hadn't seen so much badly disguised sniffing since waiting in the toilets at Heaven. She apologised to everyone in turn, but I was so furious that I didn't even look at her. I was annoyed that she'd ruined one of the only days this year that I had come into the office in a good mood. If she wanted redemption now, she was going to have to beg for it. Sandra, Pepe and Carl had all kept their heads down, out of the line of fire, which was wise. It would only take one ill-advised comment from anyone, and they'd be collecting their teeth back up off of the hessian rug. I decided to do a spot of database housekeeping, but was typing so furiously that I was sure that my fingers would go through the keyboard. You could have cut the tension with a pair of Crayola scissors. I felt Craig drift by a couple more times than was normal. He was hovering at one point but I had lost interest. Noticing him would have meant turning to face him, which may have meant catching Clarissa's eyes, which would have meant having to thaw and I wasn't quite ready. I would let the stupid old bism stew for a bit.

Eventually he made his way over, brandishing an envelope like it was a box of chocolates.

"Hey," he said. I swivelled slightly round so as not to expose myself too much to the people behind.

"Hi."

"How's it going?" He sounded cool, like he had heard what had happened. I smiled but it was far too tight-lipped to be a smile, it was more of a sneer. "Okay, I get it." He sounded like he wasn't taking it personally, which was good.

He leant in closer, I could smell CK One on his neck. It was delicious.

"Look, I just came over to see whether you were free tonight? I like to act quickly just in case either of us goes off the boil."

I can't remember telling him anything about being "on the boil". The fact that I was simmering at present was neither here nor there.

"Sorry," I winced, I genuinely was sorry. I didn't like blowing people out on two nights consecutively.

"Okay, I get the hint." He didn't even to pretend to show his disappointment which made me feel bad.

"No, it's not that. It's just...." I didn't want to give too much away straight away. "Look, I had a kind of exam yesterday and I have to pick up the results. It's complicated but the process takes a while. So I'd rather not commit to you tonight if I'm not sure whether I can actually make it."

"Oh right. What's the exam for?"

"Why don't I fill you in over a drink some other time?" The argument with Clarissa had given me some kind of adrenaline-infused confidence. I was never this forward in person, only to those whose faces were mugshots on a computer screen. That reminded me, I must email Joel.

"Well now, I've been knocked back twice in a row. They say third time lucky but I can't handle that much rejection. Why don't you let me know when you're free?" He had a twinkle in his eye. He was obviously the naturally flirtatious kind. I'd never be able to pull of this kind of magnetism without constructing a script and having a large shot of absinthe. Again, I didn't want to be too hasty so I just smiled and nodded. He dropped the post on my desk and slid away. Just as he moved, Clarissa drifted into view, pouting and doing her little lost dog routine. She opened her mouth to speak but I was having none of it.

"Save it," I spat and whisked back round to face my computer.

After I capitalised on my new-found hobby of actually doing some work for the rest of the afternoon, five rolled around quite quickly and I was back at the school steps before I knew it. Crits night had descended upon us once again and I, for once, was feeling moderately self-assured. Still, it was a well-known strategy of Rex's to set you up only to knock you down. He was known to get tutors to cast problem people in the starring roles, just to humiliate them for a week and then fire them on the spot. Something he did without the opportunity for reproach. He would gleefully slam the door in the face of the unfortunate soul whose dream he'd just thrown against the grotty wall. On the very rare occasion that Rex's plan backfired and the unfortunate soul had completely pulled it out of the bag, he would still have no option but to make an exhibition of them and fire them anyway. He would then give us a warning speech that made the Foreign Legion sound lenient and shapeshift the whole mood of the place from one of progress into one of doom.

The crit style was already laid out: a set of chairs that lined the walls of the cold rehearsal room; four out front for Bea, Camilla, Grant and His Royal Highness of Douche Land. His chair was nearest the door so that he could somehow manage to not breach the smoking ban laws by merely sticking his head out of the door if any official-looking people were to stop by.

One by one, students began to file in, some looking suitably glum, others more chipper. Some had built up a resilience to Crit night and flounced in, got annihilated and walked back out, unscathed, unscarred and ready to fight another day. I envied these few like no other. Lulu looked like she'd had a bad night and a bad day rolled into one. Her eyes were puffy and her hair looked as if it had been dropped on her head by some kind of clumsy seagull. I wrapped my arm around her shoulder.

"Come on Lu, it's only one performance. You can't get it right every time." She looked daggers at me, as if I'd told her that I'd murdered her family and kept their uvulas as souvenirs. She shrugged my arm off her shoulder, wrapped her pashmina a little tighter around herself and chose a seat that was totally in the opposite direction to where I was headed. There were only a few remaining seats left so I was forced to wedge myself into the nearest available one. I turned to notice that I had actually plonked myself next to Che, a tall American student who I ordinarily would try to avoid. Che wasn't a bad guy, he just had the ability to bore me into nigh-on paralysis with his drawn-out anecdotes about things that were far too highbrow for casual small talk. Politics, classical music, architecture. All subjects that were well out of my immediate grasp.

Che was young and impressionable, therefore Rex seemed to despise him less than any of us so he always got the easy deal, even if Che was, in the grand scheme of things, ultimately forgettable.

As was common practice on Crit nights, the person next to you had to write your critique down as the tutors were saying it. This was so that you could take the notes away with you and also had nothing to hide behind while you were being defiled in front of everyone. I guess it was also so that you didn't suddenly feel compelled to wield the Parker pen you had in your hand you and plunge it deep into Rex's jugular.

"Shall we do each other?" Che asked without any sense if irony. I didn't have the energy to point out the obvious either. Having been brushed off twice in one day by both Clarissa and Lulu for no apparent good reason, the sheen of my positive mental attitude was beginning to wear off.

The tutors began to walk in. It was a sombre affair, a bit like a cremation service. Even Grant, Camilla and Bea, who were all perfectly pleasant on any other day, were forced to look overbearing and morose. They all looked as if they were about to tell us that the end of the world was nigh and there was sod all we could do about it. As ever, Rex was last in. He marched in softly, as if critiquing us was the last thing on his mind: a cunning trick.

When the dust had settled and forty or so rectums had suctioned themselves to the hard-bottomed chairs, it was time to begin.

"Right," Rex spoke with a jovial yet calm tone. He had a knack of luring us into a false sense of security by initially appearing friendly and congratulatory. Baiting the hook to catch the fish. The act was so convincing that you could almost mistake him for a caring and kindly man. It was in this moment of sheer relief that the rush of euphoria made you want to run out and throw your arms around him. We all, however, felt tied to our chairs.

"Normally, we run through the plays as per their running order on the day. However, I propose that we do the plays in a different order. Bernard Shaw will be first, Orton second and Coward last. Any objections?"

It was not a question so nobody responded. Members of our group, however, began to frantically eyeball each other in desperation. Liana mouthed WTF in my direction. She was right. What the actual fuck? Why was he doing this? It could mean that Rex thought that our play had been so good that he wanted to end on a high. It could, of course, mean quite the opposite. This was purgatory but we couldn't reveal our discomfort. I tried to trace Grant's face for any tell-tale signs. He just sat stock still, staring forward. He obviously knew that this was going to happen but whether he agreed with Rex or not would not be an option. After a few moments, Rex began to speak again.

"Good. Bea, since your debacle is first on the list, then please do proceed."

Bea uncomfortably picked through her notes while Rex took longer than necessary to roll a cigarette. You could have cut the atmosphere with a plastic machete. As Bea gave her notes to one student, I watched Rex look over the top of his rimmed spectacles at her, then back to his long fingers as he separated strands of free tobacco from their packeted brothers, nimbly rolling the cigarette into a perfect cylindrical shape and then bringing it to his lips to moisten. I was poised, waiting for a forked tongue to shoot out and coat the paper but, to my chagrin, the tongue that protruded looked relatively normal.

All three other tutors had finished grilling the now squirming student and were sat waiting for Rex to finish dicking about with his fag and throw his two-penn'orth in. He had not yet sparked it up and was not about to hurry himself up on the account of anyone else. We all just sat: silent. The student's face grew more contorted in badly masked agony. Rex took one long drag and jumped to his feet.

"Yes, it was a comedy and, yes, you had a reasonable amount of humour in there. However, as you entered the stage, you looked as though you didn't know how to walk into a room." Rex was a ball of energy, clowning from one side of the room to the other while he illustrated his point. "The tension, the anxiety was like a cancer in your joints and your legs flailed about as if separate from your body."

The student nodded along, trying to take in the criticism without bursting into tears. She didn't know whether to feel complimented or unsexed. Rex carried on without ever mentioning her name once, as if she didn't deserve the acknowledgement. I was certain that he didn't even know what her name was.

"To say I was moved was a slight over-exaggeration. I didn't feel the need to ejaculate over your performance but it was not abhorrent. All in all, a teetering around average."

He stopped to draw a long suck on his cigarette before breaking his vigour and looking over the rim of his specs.

"Though some might argue that average is worse than bad."

He delivered the last line with a smile that was both devastating and terrifying. He then sat himself down and folded one leg over the other, satisfied that his summary had had a beginning, a middle and an end and that it was neither positive, negative or indifferent. It was a puzzle that the poor student would have to work out for herself. For that was the game, apparently. He rolled his cigarette round his fingers and took a sharp breath to indicate that he was done.

"And on!" he said, a phrase that he would repeat no less than forty times this evening.

And on we went; every student dissected, some derailed, some praised. Those who were glorified, however, were always dealt a cold blow to accompany the compliment:

"A satisfactory performance, that you will struggle to live up to."

"You seem promising as an actor, it's as a human being that you toil."

Lulu in particular was dealt a fate worse than death: barely even a sentence, more of an utterance. "Ugh. And on."

Sophie, on the other hand, was practically applauded.

"From such an opaque actress, a voice suddenly escapes. I think you will have to work a hundred times as hard to match that composure and poise in the future. But I wish you luck."

Slowly but surely, it was our group's turn. Rex had been less than impressed with either of the first two groups' work, branding them both as "pleasant enough background entertainment" but nothing to "moisten the head."

Hopefully, the Coward play would be the best of a mediocre bunch.

They started by order of the cast list, which meant I was about halfway down. Liana was first.

"If we can ignore your pitiful attempt at Received Pronunciation that was about as convincing as a leper in a beauty pageant, then it was a rather balanced performance."

I mouthed a well done to her while Rex's gaze was diverted. Dominique then got "rather charmless but there was room for charm to be invited in, if you weren't such uncomfortable bedfellows." I wasn't so sure that it was a rave review, but she seemed happy with it.

I was next. I gave Che the obligatory nod to begin scribbling, which he did, thankfully. Grant was first.

"Simon, you managed to achieve what seemed unachievable at the beginning. After a slightly wobbly start, you believed the words. You thought through Simon's mind, your blood travelled through Simon's arteries and your heart beat in his chest." Grant maintained a fixed composure in front of his boss.

261

"Now, I'm not saying that the performance was definitive, but it was fresh and you were extremely easy to work with. At times, you carried your peers with you." I wanted to cry but instead I gave Grant a nod of thanks and looked to Bea who was next in line.

"I agree," she smiled. Her pink lipstick made her mouth looked like a huge slice of watermelon. "There was a real timbre to your voice which smoothed out the camp that is in your natural speech. The breath was easy and supported which meant that even when you were barely a whisper, you were audible. Again I wouldn't say that the performance was fully realised, but your potential development, with a little more time and concentration, will be exciting to see."

I was flushing a dark red now. I could feel the tears of relief threatening to burst their banks. Camilla leaned forward.

"The movement, again, was natural. You had a slight bit of tension at the beginning, but then you were first on stage so that is understandable. You must remember to warm up fully so that you enter with an energy that will carry you through to the end. It was a well-rounded and clever performance."

I could see Che's pen darting around the page. My heart was beating so fast in my chest I felt compelled to hold it lest it fly out and shoot across the floor. My eyes moved along the line. Rex had rolled at least five cigarettes throughout the evening and he now sat looking at number five that he flicked between his fingers. He didn't look at me, but I had to look at him. I felt unable to tear my eyes away. After what seemed like an hour, he took a sharp intake of breath. I clenched my butt cheeks together in case anything popped out.

You could have heard a pin drop in the silent auditorium. "I didn't hate it."

He didn't take his eyes off the cigarette. Che's pen stopped, my ears seemed to block with imaginary cotton wool. I could feel my pulse in my temples. After a few seconds, I swallowed, which I was sure everyone could hear like a foghorn. Rex seemed to sense my torture and looked back at Grant.

"And on," he said for the thirty-fifth time.

Five more to go.

*

I was so bowled over by the amazing crits that the first drink slipped down my neck without even touching the sides. Liana was celebrating, as was Dominique. Lulu had gone home to sulk. She was the ultimate diva when she wanted to be. I thought she was only making the situation worse for herself but she wouldn't listen. Sophie was relieved that nobody had been made to leave. In short, the term was over and we were all extremely excited, therefore the booze was flowing and spirits were high. Ricky Hellman, one of the students who had been repeatedly reprimanded for tardy time management but who had more lives than a lemming and a cat put together, staggered his way up to me. I liked Ricky, he was the kind of person who wouldn't have looked twice at me in secondary school, but now that those shackles had been cast away, we were quite good friends. Ricky was attractive, buff, a total womaniser and coke addict but made no apologies for being any of the above. He was a charmer, a cheeky chappy and never ever let me pay for a line of charlie. Drugs which he offered at will on the understanding that if he got so wankered that he couldn't stand up, then he could crash on my sofa.

"Hey! Simone!" His arm was outstretched and his beer was sloshing everywhere. He had a county drawl that was either Essex, Surrey or Buckinghamshire. I couldn't quite pinpoint the exact locality.

"Hi Ricky, good work today my friend." I was always a little more butch when I spoke to Ricky, but we were both aware of this charade.

"Well old boy, you know I do try my best." I giggled. It wasn't so long ago that Rex had described one of Ricky's earlier performances as so glib that he stood a good chance of being upstaged by a turd in a wig.

"What about you though chap?" He maintained a vice-like grip on my neck which was beginning to chafe. One of the main reasons why I could never be straight: because I couldn't endure all the brotherly roughhousing and horseplay. I bruise like a peach.

"You did a stellar job, mate."

"Oh, I don't know about that." I attempted to wriggle free.

"Well, I reckon your performance was ace. Gave a few of these prick ticklers a run for their money. I think even His Nibs enjoyed it. Usually he sits there like a bulldog licking piss off a thistle but I was watching him throughout your bit. He was loving it."

"Really?" It hadn't even occurred to me to ask someone to watch Rex while I was onstage. That plan was genius.

"Look, me and a couple of the lads are gonna jump this place in a bit and go somewhere a bit more, you know, exciting. You in?"

Inwardly, I groaned. As much as I enjoyed his company, Ricky simply couldn't reciprocate unless he had a little chemical help. It wasn't personal; he was an addict, though he'd never admit it to himself. The Twelve Steps to him were those metal things you climbed to board an Easyjet flight to Ibiza.

"Where?"

"A little wine bar on Old Street. The Pony."

I knew it because it was near work. I remembered it from a few months ago when I had been stood outside waiting for Ricky to score, hoping that none of my colleagues happened to live nearby and might be out walking their dogs at such an ungodly hour. Funny really, seeing as we'd only popped out for a quiet drink. I had to admit though, that if I was to get rotten then tonight would be the night. We had a whole week off until our next class and I could just about cope with the office on hangover day. I nodded.

"Excellent news me old mucker. I'll gather the troops and let you know."

"Okay buddy." I managed to fight my way out of his arm and he winked and sloped off. I thought I'd run up quickly and congratulate Sophie who was in a gaggle of girls. I pulled her free.

"I just wanted to say well done you," I said after kissing her on either cheek.

"Oh, you're so sweet. I feel really bad for Lulu though. She's so upset, she said she might leave the school." Those big eyes of concern came back to haunt her.

"Oh, look, no one's going anywhere. She just needs a week to get herself back on track. She'll be right as rain before you know it."

From behind Sophie, I could see Ricky and his mates, Dan and Ben, getting ready to bounce. Ricky motioned for me to make a getaway.

"Look Soph, I'm going to go. I need some sleep." I didn't want Sophie knowing that I could be partaking in anything less legal than a pint of lager. She wouldn't understand.

"I'll see you in a week, if not before." I gave her a quick hug.

"Okay, Simon. Take care and well done," she smiled.

I smiled back. She was a good friend; she deserved a break.

The boys followed me out.

Ben, Dan, Ricky and I proved to be quite a team. Of course, Ricky had already bought the stuff so there was no chance of my waiting around for him again, pulling my cardigan tighter around me like some two-bit hooker. There was a fair bit of banter going on and Dan, a notorious drinker, had a bottle of whisky concealed within his inside pocket so we were getting pretty annihilated before we'd even set foot in a bar. If Ricky was the Artful Dodger of the group, then Dan was the Fagin. He was what one might call a rogue – an exceptionally good actor, a well-spoken and handsome gent but an utter scoundrel in drink and infidelity. Ben then must be the Oliver; a quiet, softly spoken guy with a good sense of humour and an infectious laugh. I guess, then, I was the Nancy.

We'd stopped by another pub on the way, purely because we knew that they had a big enough toilet to accommodate our naughty nocturnal habits. Unfortunately, we were getting so many suspicious looks that I never got around to having a line of coke. I, instead, had to more or less babysit the other three as they ricocheted off each other, fell over and nearly walked into the path of at least three speeding cars. Once off the Tube (which was a mission in itself) surprisingly we were let into the Pony. Ricky was quite trolleyed by this point and he ushered the other two off to get us all a drink.

"Listen Simon," Ricky slurred into my ear, his warm alcohol breath on my neck. "Since we've already done a fat one, why don't you go and sort yourself out in the toilets."

He pushed a little paper parcel into my palm which I immediately transferred to my pocket.

"We'll get some drinks."

I was totally going to enjoy this. Todd Terry's classic anthem, "Weekend", had just started playing and I was about to go and cut myself a king-sized line as a reward for putting up with these three roustabouts for the best part of twenty minutes. Into the toilet I went, checking for any signs of suspicion. Seeing as it was Monday, there was no one on patrol, so I holed myself in the nearest cubicle. The lights were neon so that you couldn't see where to cut a line but, luckily, the package that Ricky had handed me was dark so I would just use a corner of that, two if I had time. I opened it up and started haphazardly forming a jagged line with my Blockbuster video card. I needed to hurry up as I'd been busted like this once before and it's not a pleasant experience. Neither is having to turn out your pockets in front of a bunch of strangers on a packed Saturday night in Vauxhall while three Muscle Marys next to you tutted and whispered "amateur".

I quickly rolled-up a five-pound note and snorted: one up one nostril and one up the other. Suddenly, I heard the outside door open, a shuffling of feet and the squeak of a tap turning. I figured it was probably a good idea to flush and get the hell out of there. I wiped my nose and stuffed all the paraphernalia back into my pocket, flushing the toilet with my other hand. As if that medley of sounds was going to be fooling anybody.

Swinging the door open, I was relieved to see no one was waiting for me outside. I stumbled over to the sink and continued my charade by washing my hands. I didn't stop to look at the figure next to me at the communal sink but instead looked straight in the mirror. Had I even checked myself in the last hour? My hair was a bit windswept and I was beginning to look my age.

"Well, well, well," a voice that wasn't instantly recognisable came from my left.

"Excuse me?" I turned to face whoever it was who was repeating their words in threes.

"I thought you were busy tonight..." It was Craig, the boss' nephew. I slipped in shock and nearly landed flat on my bottom. I saved myself by gripping onto the sink.

"Holy shit!" I steadied myself on the basin. "You scared me!"

"Well I should hope so too. You deserve nothing less for standing me up and then lying about it." He shot me a flirtatious smile. Outside of the confines of Eco Scene, he looked quite handsome. His hairline was slightly receding, but that was okay. He was dressed in a simple polo shirt and jeans with brown smart shoes. Not half bad for someone I wouldn't look twice at if I could have the pick of anybody. Lucky, then, that I couldn't.

"Ha! I've literally just finished. Well, about an hour ago."

"And how were your results?"

"They were good. Exceptionally good. That's why I'm here, we're celebrating." I was trying to look like I wasn't on coke, the irony being that when it kicked in, I wouldn't care if I looked like it or not.

"I see." He paused. The air was thick with sexual tension. "Well, do I get that drink now?"

I was in a difficult position. I wasn't really in the date zone and I didn't know him well enough to introduce to the Old School lot as anything other than a brief acquaintance. On the plus side, meeting the boyish trio might quash the old luvvie drama queen stereotype. Perhaps this was the best way to find out. The coke was starting to kick in and I was beginning to not care.

"Sure," I said. "Why the hell not?"

It turned out that Craig had popped in for a drink after meeting some girlfriends. He had not been ready to go home just yet and, seeing as he was staying with Aunty Cordy in Kings Cross, Old Street wasn't that far to stagger back from. Ricky, Ben and Dan had welcomed him with open arms. Ricky in particular had play-punched and tousled his hair like they'd been old friends for years. Then he decided to play the matchmaker role and began talking me up and listing my credentials like I was a pearl necklace on one of the shopping channels. Unfortunately his drunken emotional gambit rang more true of an old sea captain describing his faithful old dog. Craig saw the funny side and laughed along. We must have looked like a Punch and Judy show with our wooden jaws and glacial eyes. Thankfully the lighting was dim. After a couple of drinks, Craig and I drifted away from the throng.

"I like your friends," he said. "I didn't realise you were at drama school. Interesting take on a media course!"

"Well, we've never really talked long enough for me to tell you. But you know now."

"I do, so how long have you been working at the office?"

"Oh, about two years now."

"But I guess the dream is to do something a bit more..."

"Exciting."

"Exciting, yes." He smiled.

"What about you? I mean, I hear you're part of the organic project or something?"

"I'm not interested in any of that shit. I'm into filmmaking. I did a three-year-long degree, was bumming around for a couple of years and wanted to try my hand at doing independent documentary films. Getting them out there, you know. Aunt Cordelia happened to be chatting to my dad and saying that she'd put me up here if I wanted to assist her with the organic cotton project and publicise some of their work through film."

"It's a great idea. I've got to be honest, I never get involved with anything at work because I don't know anything about it, and so I just get on with the menial stuff."

"But you're making things ten times harder. If you let down your guard, I don't think anyone's going to chastise you for opening yourself up to new things and experiences."

"I guess." He was so easy to talk to that he was making me consider getting more involved at Eco Scene. Like that was ever going to happen.

"And how do you find London?" I realised that I was chewing my own lip, like those high school girls do in American movies set in the fifties.

"Well, it's a big change coming from Devon, but I like it, it's so full of life and art and people. It's kind of hard not to like it."

"I guess. I think it takes a lot of stamina to live here. You have to put up with those people every day. And they're loud, and smelly, and get in the way."

"It's an exercise in strengthening your communication with people. They must think about you in the same way."

"But I'm not any of those things."

He laughed. "No, you certainly are not."

Then I did something I almost never do. It wasn't the coke; hiding the first two lines from Craig had been absolute purgatory so I opted out of the following two. It wasn't the booze, as I was drinking slower now that I was ensconced in conversation. It might just have been the chutzpah brought on by my recent run of success. I leaned very slightly in and turned my face to meet his lips. Ever-so carefully, I touched mine lightly on his. He kissed me back, opening his mouth and letting his tongue tenderly explore mine. It was slow and intense. I pulled away and licked my lips. He looked down and grinned.

"That was.... nice" was the best I could come up with. I didn't want to seem like an over-excited whore.

"Yes, yes it was."

We leaned in for another, and another, gradually moving our hands to the backs of each other's head and neck as we let our desire take over. We pulled away and laughed and proceeded to get exceedingly drunk while my hedonistic friends behind me partied away in their own little worlds.

14

Of course, I hadn't prepared myself for the possibility of an awkward office romance. We hadn't discussed how we were going to play it around the workplace, whether he would come up to me and start inadvertently rubbing my shoulders as everyone else gazed on in shock. While riding the night bus home (alone, thank goodness) with a stupid smile plastered across my face, the thought never crossed my mind that at some point it was going to be weird. Would he tell my boss? What would she think when he came home at all hours and she was waiting in a flammable nightie and sponge rollers wrapped in a chiffon scarf with a map of Kenya printed onto it? Him smelling of booze and regret with my hair on his collar and my DNA on his lips. Oh God.

It was a crisp March morning. The top deck of the bus was steamed up and smelled of the morning breath of a dozen commuters. There was an eerie silence, permeated only by an isolated cough here and there, or the muffled cry of a baby downstairs. And as the bus rattled down the Hackney Road, and the nice announcement lady kindly informed us of each stop in turn, my previous night's joy turned to sudden dread. I tried to immerse myself in the *Dragon Tattoo* book that I had started to read about a hundred times since the Old School had begun. I never managed to get past page twenty-one before another play was thrown at us to read immediately. Trying to do any recreational pastime such as reading while at drama school was inevitably an attempt in vain. At times I wanted to cave in and watch the bloody film, but I could never ignore the fact that the book would inevitably be richer in quality than the film. Plus, I always made up the characters in my head. It ruined the illusion when I saw that Daniel Craig had been cast as Blomkvist in the *Dragon Tattoo* movie. My version of said character was slightly portly and bespectacled, so that was that shot to shit. I folded the book back and stuffed it into my bag; it was at home there, and it had been for the last six months. I couldn't read when my mind was plagued with thoughts of the other night with Craig.

My stop came and I missed it on purpose, just so I could walk a bit in the cold morning air and get my head together. Could you get fired for pashing off with the boss's nephew? I'm sure it wasn't really a sackable offence, but then Cordelia had been itching to read me the riot act for a good few weeks now. Anything she had on me, she'd use. The walk spun by, mainly because I wasn't thinking about anything other than my current plight. As I ascended the stairs, my nerve and resolve went in the other direction. I peeked around the door. Nothing had changed. Except that I was a little early. Sandra would surely notice. She did, and said as much.

"Yes, I – have – work – to – do."

"Oh come on, you can do better than that!" She had me. I knew better than to mess with the master of bullshit.

"Okay." I sat down and stuffed my bag under my seat. "But if I tell you, you can't tell anyone. I mean anyone!"

I could see that Sandra was sitting with a pen and paper, writing another sad mag tale. If I wasn't careful, not only would my secret be broadcast to the office, it would also be immortalised in glossy print for all the readers of *Coffee Break* magazine to read while they emptied their colostomy bags.

"Go on," she said, the tassels on her mock military jacket quivering as she spoke.

"I have a problem," I said gingerly.

"Oh, got it. But if it's anything like Leon's then you just need to scrape the worst of it off and dab with a warm sponge."

I wondered what on earth could have been wrong with Leon, but I didn't have the time to argue the toss – if you'll excuse the pun.

"No, nothing like... whatever that was. I bumped into Craig last night."

"The guy from Stoke Newington?"

"No, God, not him. Major old news. No, Craig, you know Cordelia's nephew."

She looked pensive before the penny finally dropped.

"Oh yes, I know. The one who delivers the post. Well, not THE post, your post."

"Yes, well he delivered something a bit more than that last night, if you catch my drift."

She was shocked.

"Serious?"

"Yep, we kissed. A lot." I couldn't believe I was saying it.

"That is crazy."

"I know, but you're the only one I'm telling because I don't know how he's going to be. It could be really awkward. It might not. I'm freaking out."

"Look, don't freak out." She held out a reassuring hand which I grabbed. "Do you see it going anywhere?"

"I don't know."

At that moment, as if he'd been waiting for his cue in the wings, the door opened and in walked Craig. He looked a little tired and his t-shirt was crumpled. He looked adorable. My heart fell out of my arse. As if he sensed my pain, he turned.

"Morning," he said. The words lingered in the air for a minute before he shot me a glance. He mouthed the word *tiger*. Oh God. I needed to speak to him, and it had to be now. I jumped up and gave Sandra a knowing wink as I followed Craig down the hall.

"Psst," I hissed and he swung around, surprised, "in here."

I motioned him into the photocopy room and half closed the door.

"Hi," he said, slightly bemused.

"Hi." I was all out of puff. "Sorry, didn't mean to pounce on you as you've just got through the door but I needed to check something with you."

"Pounce away!"

"I just need to check that, last night..."

"Do you regret it?" He looked a little crestfallen.

"God no! I just need to make sure that it won't be ... awkward between us. I mean, we're in the office together, we kissed, you know..." I was so red that I'm sure if I stood next to the window, lotharios and perverts would begin to queue up at the door.

"Of course not! It was only a kiss, we're not, like, boyfriends or anything."

"Sure," I realised now how much I'd been overreacting. It *had* only been a kiss. Maybe my reaction was a subliminal signal that I wanted something more. There was one other pressing issue that I was reluctant to address.

"I have to make sure that you're not going to tell Cordelia, or anyone here."

He raised an eyebrow.

"It's not that I'm ashamed or anything, I just want to keep my professional life and my private life separate." I was pleading which was really unattractive and borderline pathetic.

"Then why the hell did you mingle the two?"

"Because… I'm human." He nodded in agreement and we left the room. I don't know where we had ended up, but I had made my point clear and I hoped that it had been well received.

I winked at Sandra as I sat down. Pepe was just coming through the door with Clarissa in hot pursuit. She was clutching some kind of box in her claw which she tentatively popped on my desk.

"I just wanted to apologise for my er… little outburst yesterday."

I went to speak.

"Don't say anything, just please accept my gift and we'll say no more about it." I thought it was quite rich that she was telling me how I should react when it was in fact me who was the victim. Yet, rather than get into any battles, I nodded and opened the little box. It was full of what looked like a bunch of big toes – some brown, dodgy-looking gloop with an almond stuck in the top of each one. No doubt the result of the real chocolate-making course she had been harping on about a few weeks hence. With a nod and a wink, it was all over. I'd wait till I got home before throwing them in the bin.

*

At lunch, I found myself with a little spare time on my hands so I thought I'd better check my emails to see if there was any news yet on the ASOS Spring Sale. I suddenly realised that I hadn't even responded to the top one yet from the delectable rogue that was Joel. Should I, now that things seemed to be kicking off with Craig? Was it fair to do that? Oh hell, like Craig said himself, it was only a kiss, we weren't boyfriends or anything. Now, where was his last response? I did a bit of searching to get on the correct screen. I would have to be quick, Clarissa's comments yesterday had made me hypersensitive on the *it's behind you* front.

Joel, sounds like we share similar interests. Fancy chatting more over a beer?

I typed in my number and pressed send. I was getting all bumptious now that I was fanciable and a promising actor. About bloody time too. I heard the dropping of envelopes on the space of desk behind me and turned to see Craig smiling over me. Shit! I really hoped he hadn't witnessed my adultery.

"Good afternoon," he said, managing to sound aloof and devastating at the same time.

"Hi," I was finding it difficult not to concentrate on covering my screen.

"So what you up to?"

"Er, working, eating lunch. The two main activities that go with a day at the office."

"Oh, you're a comedian? Well, I was wondering whether you wanted to join me for a drink after work on Friday? That is, of course, if it doesn't interrupt your exciting day of working and eating lunch?"

To be honest, I just wanted him to get away from my desk in case he raised any further suspicion. Sandra seemed to have an antenna growing out of her head. I swallowed hard. I wasn't sure whether all this paranoia was worth it. Maybe I should just stick with Joel. Okay, he was likely to steal from me and cost me thousands in personal insurance but at least we didn't work together.

"Yes." The word escaped before I could stop it.

"Excellent, I'll see you at the bottom of the stairs on Friday." He winked and moved away.

I swivelled back round to my screen. Luckily I had been quick enough to click back to my Gmail page before Craig had arrived to interrogate me. I breathed a sigh of relief. The top email flashed unread. Surely Joel hadn't responded already? I looked closer. That wasn't Joel, it was, in fact, an address that I didn't recognise, yet a name that I did: rexbamber@oldschool.org.uk

My blood ran cold.

Rex Bamber? The same Rex Bamber? What the hell did he want? It could be a round robin, informing us all that we were going to be kicked out of the school. It had happened before, a few years ago. Though it could have been an Old School urban legend. There were many of those flying around. One that instantly sprang to mind was the tale of John Hill, the student who met an unfortunate end. Apparently John Hill had perished in a building blaze that took place in the late eighties. An electrical fault had set alight to the costume cupboard, where John was said to have passed out drunk. Now, rather tactlessly, John Hill was the code word we used to alert each other if we had seen a fire in the building. The aim was not to alarm the audience by blurting out FIRE and getting everyone in a fuss. Instead one should calmly say "John Hill is in the building" and the technical staff would usher patrons out in a collected and efficient manner.

Yet, one fateful night, Liana was put on Front of House duties when one of Rex's unextinguished cigarettes burned a hole in the carpet of a rehearsal room while a play was in session. Surrounded by smoke and not knowing what to do for the best, she burst through the door, all in a flap, and screamed at the top of her lungs to a stunned audience and cast: "Fuckin hell guys! John Hill is on fire!"

I stared at the words in front of me. The only thing to do was to open the email and read whatever fate was written within. My heart pumping in my chest, I clicked on the text.

Simon, I need to see you. 6pm, my office. Rex

Again, it wasn't a question, it was an order. What on earth could he want to see me for? Had I done something wrong? Oh God, this was too much to handle. Tonight's plan of catching up with Freya was shot to shit now; my evening would now be taken up with fashioning a noose out of my old bed linen. I had to respond, so I typed something equally direct.

Rex, I'll be there. Simon

It was 2pm now. I had four agonising hours before I could find out what this all meant. Sandra could see the frustration on my face and mouthed the words: *Okay?*

I think so was my response.

*

The dark doors of 373 Snaresbrook Road were even more intimidating when not littered with students. It somehow seemed less of a thriving educational monument but more like one for the criminally and mentally insane. That was ironic as the last four hours had been such torture that I thought I'd end up getting sectioned way before our little meeting. I must have looked so tormented while I stormed around the office that Pepe and Carl had practically dived under their desks to get out of my way. Clarissa had been wisely silent, she was obviously eager to find out whether I had enjoyed the homemade chocolates but she dared not ask. I would have to practice feigning delight at home ready for a critique tomorrow. It would be very difficult to dream up since they were probably now languishing in landfill somewhere.

The front door was slightly ajar which was less "come hither" and more "meet your fate". I pushed it open and the piercing creak echoed around the empty corridor. It was such a haunted old house stereotype that I couldn't help but roll my eyes. I half expected Rex to be sitting in his office in a crushed velvet smoking jacket, licking virginal blood off an open razor blade.

I made my way up the hall to the infamous shut door to the lair of hell. Surprisingly, the door was open. This was my moment, I could run away and never come back or I could venture in and see what was awaiting; the motivation behind the mystery email. Rex seemed to sense my anguish.

"Simon?" He remembered my name.

"Er, yes Rex, it's me." I answered, trying to sound familiar but sounding more like I was trying to bring someone out of a coma.

"Well come in, don't loiter in the doorway, man!"

I went in. The room was so nicotine-stained that it looked like the inside of a rabbit warren. The walls were adorned with posters of past shows; some were old, peeling at the corners and curling off the plaster. There were shelves of books from one corner of the office to the other. Leagues of bottles of Cabernet Sauvignon decorated the desk and poked their emerald heads out of the crammed litter bin. As I walked the metre to his desk, the soles of my trainers made an audible suction sound. I passed no less than four ashtrays that overflowed with cigarette butts and mountains of grey ash. I dropped into the battered and what appeared to be gnawed chair opposite his. A desk separated us, thank God. I couldn't have coped with him actually witnessing me physically shaking. He didn't look up; he was too busy studying his computer screen. He sat in silence for a few agonising minutes. I knew that he would talk when he felt it was necessary and not because it was polite or anything to acknowledge when you have company. I admired one of the posters. It was a hand-drawn sketch of three sisters in profile. It was a rather magnificent portrait, etched with charcoal.

"Done by my daughter," he said without looking up. "Before the digital age, she hand-drew all of the school's promotional material. Do you like it?"

There was only one answer.

"It's awesome."

"Awesome?" He looked at me over his glasses and I chilled to the bone.

"She is a rather famous artist now, with exhibits in the Saatchi gallery alongside a couple in New York and one in Milan. But I will be sure to let her know, when she asks me, that you think her earlier work was 'awesome'."

He had succeeded in making me look stupid. I squirmed in my chair. He was loving it.

"Simon, I'll cut to the chase, I can see that you're all... unnecessary. I think your work is appalling." He won first prize for an inspiring opening line. I bit my lip and nodded. "So you agree?"

Catch twenty-two must seem like heaven compared with this.

"I don't really know Rex, how do you want me to respond to that?"

"I expect you to fight your corner. Well, I'd expect that of someone with balls so that rules you out, I suppose. Forgive me for such an obvious mistake." I wanted to run out. "That is to say I *thought* your work was appalling." He took a sharp breath and crossed his legs. "Something on Sunday shifted my opinion. There was a truth in your performance, there was ... something."

In a strange way, being complimented by Rex was worse than being berated. With a compliment there was always a chance that you might play along with a bluff and make a prize idiot of yourself. At least when he was being nasty, you knew it was real.

He looked at me. His pallor was grey with age and his skin was like an old piece of chamois leather. His eyes were bloodshot and tired. It looked like this game was wearing him out, slowly killing him. I kept breathing; it seemed like the hardest thing in the world to do at present.

"Do you have anything to say?"

I thought for a minute. I guessed I should thank him for saying something nice.

"Thank you?"

He scoffed.

This was surreal. It was almost like I had him in a different arena, a different plane. I was so terrified that I could get away with being slightly cocksure since I had nothing to lose.

"Listen, we are doing open rehearsals for *Equus* on Friday. Don't put on some pantomime phantom surprise. I saw you checking out the noticeboard so I know that you're aware that we are doing it this term."

He had me there.

"I would like you to audition."

"Sorry?"

"Oh, you heard me. The auditions are at 11am. I will expect you to have read the play and have gained some kind of insight and interpretation of the characters. Particularly Alan. He's a little younger than you but, since we're strapped for younger actors, I think you could manage it. You can play younger anyway."

I thought immediately of work. Would Cordelia seriously let me take the morning off to further my career prospects in something else that had nothing to do with the thing she was paying and investing in me to do? Rex must have read my mind.

"If you aren't interested then I must assume that you are not committed to your cause and, therefore, there will be absolutely no reason for you to continue pursuing it. I cannot waste time and energy on someone who is happy to fade into the background, regardless of how *happy* it makes him."

This was unbelievable. All I had done was give a sustained performance once in my whole time at the school and this cunt was issuing me with an ultimatum. The offer could be life-changing, the break that I had been striving so hard for, how could I turn it down? Cordelia would simply have to suck my dick.

"I will be there," I said feebly.

Rex smiled.

"Then our meeting is over." He reached under his desk and produced a full carrier-bag that jangled as he presented it to me. Maybe it was a bag full of the last remaining shards of my dignity.

"Be a good chap and pop this into the skip on your way out." I took the bag and stood up. It was clearly full of empty bottles from the previous night's boozing. He pushed it into my open hand as I backed out of his office and made my way down the hall, leaving the sound of the lighter flint and the click of a computer mouse in my wake.

I believe that in no less than ten minutes, I had signed my soul to the devil, and it felt neither bad nor particularly good.

15

I sat at my office desk, in a sort of fog. Sandra had phoned in with barely a croak. She had been struck down with something that was too contagious to be introduced to the rest of the office and was spending the day, no doubt, shrouded in a leopard-print blanket and watching Jeremy Kyle for research and inspiration. I was gutted; she was the one and only person I wanted to share my news with. I couldn't call anyone at the school for fear of being perceived as a gloater. I didn't really have any ideas on how I was going to handle this situation just yet. It was too crazy to comprehend let alone share.

I stared at Sandra's empty chair; I'd never missed her more. There was always Beez, but I just felt that his recent plans had driven a wedge between us. I couldn't help but take it personally. It was ridiculous I know, but that's how I felt. I was out of his scheme at the moment and it hurt. Suddenly a figure appeared and made its way over to the abandoned seat.

"Morning." It was Craig. I'd barely given him another thought.

"Morning."

"Turns out we'll be sharing a department. Since this desk is free for the day, I'll be sitting here." He held a pad to his chest.

I smiled. I didn't really care but he didn't cotton on. He just busied himself with arranging his various wares around him. I kept looking at a blank computer screen, yesterday's events swimming around my head. A few hours later, after answering a couple of insignificant emails, a new one popped up. It was from Craig sat directly in front of me. If I strained, I could read it over his shoulder as he typed it if I wanted.

Cheer up, what's up?

Even though I didn't feel like it, I thought I should answer back seeing as he'd made the effort to feign concern for my general wellbeing.

Nothing, I typed back. *Had some interesting news from school.*

Oh, anything serious?

Quite. The Head wants me to audition for a part that it is quite a, er... challenge.

Cool, what are you wearing?

You can see what I'm wearing.

No, for the play you dummy, THE PLAY!

I thought awhile. It was a long time since I had seen *Equus* but I was sure that in the last West End revival, the lead had been starkers.

Well actually, since you come to mention it, I don't think the part requires me to wear clothes.

You're f**king kidding me! When do the tickets go on sale? I'll have front row every night.

Even though I hated the expression, I did actually LOL at that.

It suddenly occurred to me that it was Wednesday and my audition was on Friday, a mere two days off. Shit, I needed to read the play and, more importantly, I had to get Friday off. There was a certain amount of brown-nosing that I would be required to do before Aunty Cordy would even consider allowing me the time away, I wasn't exactly in her good books at the moment. What excuse could I come up with? Well, Sandra had the monopoly on illness at the moment and I couldn't run the risk of crying wolf on the day. Noel Coward I could do, Chekhov I could do, even Shakespeare I could do, but pulling a sickie from work had to be one of the hardest acting jobs in the profession. No, I had to be honest with her; Lord knows, it would be a first. She might even appreciate it!

Be back in a bit.

I vacated my seat and walked the green mile up to Cordelia's desk. The air seemed to alter as I walked. The Project Officers watched me as I casually strode up to the back of the office, as if it was the rarest sight they had ever seen. Half of them looked frightened for me; I could see the panic in their eyes. I kept walking, undeterred, until I approached Cordelia's desk. She had her head down, signing cheques with a pen, holding it like it was a quill and she was the Madam De Smug.

"Cordelia," I said but the words were raspy, the density of the air had robbed me of my voice. She chose not to hear. "CORDELIA."

"Goodness Simon." She jumped and, as she did, the white cottage loaf on her head rode side-saddle.

"Sorry," I inched into the chair in front of her, "may I have a word?"

She eyed me for a second. She didn't say as much but she knew I wanted a favour. It was the second time in as many days that I was having an uncomfortable interview with someone who held too much power in a rather inconsequential institution.

"Of course," she said, her words like shards of ice. "You know my door is always open."

That was ridiculous for a start; she didn't have a door, it was an open plan office.

I composed myself, which was hard to do under such scrutiny. I could hear the starched linen of her oversized jacket, creaking as she leaned forward.

"It's just that I need to ask if I can have Friday off. Please."

"Oh, you mean THIS Friday?" Not, GOOD Friday.

"Yes, this Friday, as in tomorrow."

"Well that is short notice, Simon. I mean, who will cover the phones?" She looked back at her cheques, as if the conversation was over. The next line came from nowhere.

"Craig!" I shouted.

She looked up.

"I beg your pardon?"

"Craig said he'd do it." I'm sure he'd agree if I haggled with him over date number two, which was kind of a form of prostitution. So be it. I'd whored myself out for Rex, I might as well go for broke.

"Oh, well I guess if he's making friends and doing people's jobs for them then I suppose one can't argue with that. Might I ask WHY you want tomorrow off? Will this be a regular occurrence or will you be employing Craig to cover you part-time?"

What the hell was her problem? That she hadn't been laid since the Berlin Wall came down was certainly not my fault.

"Well, it's school. I have a rather important commitment at school."

"I see." She took her glasses off. Her eyes were actually quite big out of those gigantic frames... and slightly boggled.

"Simon, I understand that you are studying at the moment and we at Eco Scene want to support that, we really do. It is of paramount importance that our staff have a life outside of the office and aspire to move up in the world, whatever world that may be. However, as stated in your interview, anything that proves to be detrimental to the organisation, whether it be from a staff member's performance, punctuality, even their appearance, then we may have to consider other staffing options."

She was riling me now. She had me on a spit and she was enjoying turning it slowly. I couldn't lose this job, it was paying for half my fees and I simply didn't have time to look for anything else while school was taking up so much of it. I wanted to argue with her, I wanted to tell her that if there was room up that bony arse of hers then she could take this job and stuff it up there with her own talons. I didn't though. I couldn't.

"Cordelia, you have my word that this is a one-off. And I will make up the hours. Whenever you want." I was defeated.

"Oh wonderful. There is a board meeting next week in the basement. It's about Rachel Carson, the scientist who discovered the use of pesticides in modern-day agriculture."

My heart sank.

"Since I can't go, you won't mind covering will you? It's only two hours or so."

It wasn't *only* two hours, it was super boredom personified.

"Okay," I said through tight lips, inwardly praying that this commitment didn't conflict with any plan that Rex had for my life from this moment on.

"And you also won't mind that I've banned the viewing of any non-environmental-based websites to be allowed on the server at all times including lunch breaks. But then, you'll be too busy making up the hours you've missed to be upset about that." Her gaze went back to her papers. I wanted to grab the ball of withered old wool from the top of her stupid head and pull and pull until her face slid off her skull. Miserable old bitch.

"Okay." I nodded slowly in agreement.

"Great. Thanks for taking the time to come and see me, I'm really glad we had this chat."

I stood up and pushed the chair back with such force, I swear there were four perfect trenches worn into the carpet. I looked down on her before I turned. *I'll get you, you bitch*, I thought as if passing the message through to her telekinetically. *I'm just biding my time.*

And with that I made my way back to my desk.

I sat down and typed a message quickly.

Please, please, please do me a favour. If you cover for me tomorrow morning then I will buy you a huge drink tomorrow night. Pretty please...

I looked over the partition but only saw the back of Craig's head.

The response seemed to take forever. Then it came.

You're on! Just let me know what I have to do.

You're a f**king star!

*

I had been in this rehearsal room a million times before. I was familiar with its smelly brown carpet and dilapidated old chairs that spilled old foam out of every fabric wound. I knew of its filthy windows and the horrendous false ceiling with half of the blocks missing that looked like a horizontal, square version of the Connect Four brackets. But for some reason, today on audition day, it looked totally different. Perhaps it was the fact that I was here at ten in the morning rather than ten at night: the air seemed to be slightly cleaner and the whole atmosphere, when not filled with the collective dread of several students, had shifted into something... changed.

I had arrived an hour early to get some final reading and practice in, but I was so nervous that the words were just swimming on the page. I had been up all night reading the play. I managed one skim read, one in more depth and then selected my chosen passage and ran through it over and over. The text was extremely dark and heavy. The character, Alan Strang, is probably one of the most twisted and troubled characters in contemporary English theatre. To say I was nervous about giving him justice was an understatement. I was shitting it. As I read on under the dim light of my bedroom lamp, I was shocked at the brutality of the climax of the piece. Alan, who is both sexually repressed and morally oppressed by the strict religious views of his mother, lashes out in the most violent way, by taking a pick to the eyes of the only creatures that he feels close to and safe with: his horses.

It would take some skill to pull this character off. Alan himself was going to take a lot of energy and insight to play but the more I read, the more I related. Not that I had ever run at any kind of equine beast with a pair of pinking shears, but I'd certainly had experience of an overbearing parent, especially when grappling with my own sexuality under the scrutiny of my peers.

I had decided that, in picking the specific piece of prose that I had, it would be a gross misjudgement to play anything too obvious. The inner turmoil needed to be subtle: of someone keeping something in, rather than hitting out. When we are frightened, an immediate reaction is to pretend that we are not. That was going to be my attempt today. To play him normal but preoccupied. Preoccupied with something that he was an expert at hiding. Of course this only scratched the surface, but it was a good starting point.

Surely Rex couldn't expect me to be right on the money with such little time to prepare, but then with Rex you couldn't expect anything.

The door opening broke my concentration. It was Aaron, the resident stage manager. A beefy-looking second year who rarely spoke to you unless there was something worth speaking about.

"Oh!" he exclaimed. "You're here, you're very early."

"Yep, just wanted to get some last-minute read-throughs in."

I didn't have the guts to tell him that the only thing I had been reading for the last few minutes was the unidentified brown stain that had trickled and dried down the back wall.

"Got you," he disappeared and the door slammed behind him. I was once again alone in the silence; I could hear the comforting hum of traffic in the distance. The thought that there was, indeed, a world that I could go back to when this was all over was reassuring in itself. Just when I had started to regulate my breathing back from its panic-stricken speed, the door opened again and my heart jolted.

"Simon, Rex is prepared to see you now if you're ready," Aaron said.

My stomach flipped. It was like I was being led to the castration table.

"Er, I don't know." The nerves had revved from being a slightly unwelcome annoyance to an out-and-out condition.

"Mate, if you want my advice, just do it. If you don't know it now, another hour in this room will make no difference. No point in prolonging the agony." How could he be so calm? My stomach was trying to crawl back up my oesophagus so it could find a safe place to hide.

"Um, okay, I guess." Oh God...

"Okay, I'll tell him." He disappeared again and what seemed like an age passed before he popped his head back around the door.

"Right then Simon, let's go."

I picked up my bag and walked the steps to the door, my head bowed as if in mourning. Kudos to Rex for beefing up the drama. I had a feeling that once I opened the door and walked through, there would be absolutely no going back.

Walking back out of the main doors after the audition, I felt numb. There was nothing to feel particularly happy about, I was just glad that it was over. Tripping over at the very beginning hadn't helped matters, especially since it wasn't a little stumble, but more a comedy plummet that seemed to go on forever. My bag handle had got caught on the outside handle of the door as I walked through and had pulled me back out of the room as if I had been lassoed by a shepherd's crook.

Then, when I wrestled it free, the door behind slammed shut with such a bang that I practically leapt ten feet in the air with an almighty "WAAAAAH" and landed on all fours like a cat. I should have just landed face down in a custard pie and have done with it. Rex, Aaron and somebody I had never seen before waited patiently as I did a wonky growth dance to get up on my feet again. Well, at least I'd managed to do a physical and vocal warm-up in the space of thirty humiliating seconds. And all the commotion had taken my mind off the bloody play for the first time in two days, so that was something.

Once the charade was over, I sat waiting for the first word from Rex. He paused while he tried to register what had just happened and then calmly introduced Aaron and the stranger, whose name was actually Philippe. Philippe was an extremely lean, tall, copper-haired and alabaster-complexioned guy whose wrist was limper than a stick of boiled celery.

"Perhaps you should take a minute to compose yourself," Rex said from behind his desk. I concentrated on my breathing. "Just let us know when you are ready."

He was soft today, serene. Almost as if he was willing me to do well. I felt ready and nodded.

He raised his hand.

"In black... AND..."

The speech had gone relatively well, but you could never really tell with Rex in the room. I think, in hindsight, that I had gone halfway there with the character. I don't know whether it was a definitive performance but it was certainly the best I could do in the circumstances. I had visualised, retraced old steps through painful emotions that I had only really half-considered given the time that I'd had to prepare. And I remembered Rex saying that the character, Alan, was a lot younger than me so I played it with a slight knowing edge, as if I believed that I was more knowledgeable than I actually acted. All in all, it was an uneven performance with lots of elements that hadn't been fully executed, much like Alan's state. Hopefully there was room for improvement. I had no idea what Rex thought. When I finished, he just looked at me, chewing his pen. Aaron was unmoved and Philippe had smothered his face with a lascivious smile. I didn't know whether this was a good or bad thing. After a moment or two, Rex broke the silence.

"Right, thank you. And on."

That was my cue to not let the door hit me in the backside on the way out. Or at least not let it hit me in the backside... again.

And so there I was, walking out onto Snaresbrook Road after the event: cold and confused but hopeful.

When I got back, Craig had not burnt the office down, thank goodness. He had, in fact, said that the morning had been very quiet. Sandra was still unwell and Clarissa was away. Pepe was in a meeting and Carl was busying himself with work.

"Thanks for helping me out," I said as we exchanged places next to my desk. "I really appreciate it."

"It's cool. So, you gonna tell me what it was for?"

"The part is for a play called *Equus*. It's a very dark, moving, spiritual piece. In short, it's a fucking dream part. But the director is... how can I put it? Challenging. He will be very difficult to impress."

"I see." Craig looked concerned. "Do you think you did impress?"

"God, I don't know. You never know with these things do you? I hope so."

"Well you can certainly try your impressive skills with me tonight."

"You know what Craig, another night would be..."

"Nah ah ah, you promised."

"But I've had such a long..."

"I know but you sound like you're in need of a drink and I think you should make good on your word."

"Okay," I said, "I'll buy you a drink. Where do you want to go."

Turns out he was quite happy drinking around here. There were a few bars around, but none compared to the Underbelly in Hoxton, a brilliant bar with a rustic Southern American interior and decent lager on draught. As usual for a Friday, it was rammed, but we managed to get a semi-decent spot away from the speakers, enough that we didn't have to shout like there was a double-glazing pane between us.

"So tell me more about your independent films then," I asked, cradling an ice-cold Stella in my hand.

"What do you want to know?"

"What were they about?

"Well the first one I made was about growing GM food and its impact on the economy of global corporations."

I pretended to yawn.

"Oh ha ha," he joked. "The superstar actor is taking the piss out of the lowly amateur film director."

I laughed it off, but his words stung a little.

"I'm just teasing, go on."

"No, I'm not now, you've ruined it."

"I haven't."

"It's always the same with you actors, you think you're the most interesting ones in the room."

"Hey, back up buddy, a guy could get offended!"

"Oh, I don't mean you," he scoffed, "but I have worked with certain actors who spend their whole lives searching for affirmation, desperate to be loved, defined by their peers. And half the time, they're not even as good as they think they are. Most of the people I've worked with have been fairly mediocre."

I couldn't believe I was hearing this: I mean, I was sitting right here.

"You know what I mean though, don't you? You must meet these kind of people all the time."

"Actually I don't," I fought my corner on behalf of all performers everywhere. "It's actually an incredibly difficult decision to pursue something that is perceived to have no academic credibility. It takes immense strength, faith and courage to go for it in the industry and I take my hat off to anyone who puts it out there and perseveres with it. Often you have to go it alone with very little support and with zero income. Criticism left and right all the time, told you're too fat, too short, too gay! So therefore, I DON'T think that wanting a bit of attention once in a while is too much to ask. Often it is how we survive. If you'll excuse me."

I got up and headed to the toilet. What a douchebag. It was so rude of him to start defaming my friends, my peers and my world to my face, especially when he didn't know what the hell he was on about.

The toilets in the bar were covered in cracked mirrors. I stood in front of one and looked at my reflection for a second. This whole drama school thing. I wasn't wasting my time, was I? Was I just kidding myself that I was going to make money out of selling a skill that wasn't especially unique? Maybe I should jack it all in and become something else, something that didn't fit me and made me wish that I'd really gone for something that did. I was over thirty now. Maybe I was too far gone. My phone beeped in my pocket and I fished it out. A number was ringing that I didn't recognise. It was a landline. I pressed the button.

"Hello?" I could only just hear a mangled voice over the voices, glasses and music outside. "Sorry, you'll have to repeat that, I'm in a bar... Who?"

"Mate, it's Aaron."

"Oh, Aaron. Hi. You okay?"

"I'm good mate. Listen. You did it. You got the part."

The world stopped for a moment.

"Sorry, say that again."

"You got the part mate. Rex will give you a call over the weekend. Well fucking done!"

I was unable to speak. I garbled a thanks and hung up. Was this for real?

I pushed open the toilet door, walked straight up to our table, picked up my glass and drank thirstily. Dribbles of beer spilled over the top of my glass and trickled down my chin.

"Whoa," said Craig looking up as I wiped my face with the back of my hand, "what's got into you?"

"Nothing, I just think we're a little slow. I want to speed up." The truth was, I wanted to celebrate, and if I was going to endure this droning fool for the entire evening then I was going to have to get absolutely rotten.

"Okay," Craig started to drink but it was clear that he wasn't adept at downing pints of lager like someone from Hereford could. He coughed and spluttered.

"I don't think I can do that," he said.

"Okay, then let's get some shots." I pulled out my debit card. "On me."

Craig didn't object, and neither did he put up a fight when I dragged him into no less than five bars and ordered a pint of Stella with a tequila chaser in each one. Or when I pulled him into an empty shop doorway and forced myself upon him, pushing my hungry tongue into his mouth and sliding my hands down his slim, soft tummy and into the top of his jeans. My hands were threatening to move all the way down and I continued to tongue him while I tugged at his cock in a public London alleyway. But suddenly he pulled back.

"Let's go back to mine," he panted while I kissed him between words.

"Are you serious? Back to my boss's home?" As drunk as I was, I still knew it wasn't a good idea.

"She's out," he said. "She always goes to see her boyfriend on a Friday in Suffolk."

"She has a boyfriend?" I thought that the only thing Cordelia made friends with on a Friday night was a big slab of tofu. I had no idea that she was getting frigged in a box room somewhere near Lowestoft.

"I don't know. My place is twenty minutes..."

"I could molest you in your boss's bed."

And that is how I came to be on my back on organic cotton cream sheets with my ankles in my hands, and a tongue in my arse, looking up at a picture of my boss at Eco Scene accepting an award from some guy in a kaftan. An award for, oh I don't know, Most Hideous Outfit Ever To Be Made From Natural Resources.

I then had my head held on the very pillow where she rests her spider-web ball of hair every night, having my mouth abused with the piston motion of her nephew's love shaft.

Finally, as the smutty dénouement, I was clinging onto the bedstead where she hangs her canvas satchel handbag every morning, being buggered like there was gold in my stomach and you had to dig deep to find it. And when Craig pulled himself out of me, I thought I had actually shit myself on my boss's duvet cover, which was a step too far even for me. It was in fact the condom coming out last. It had been filthy, furious, drunk, clumsy and quick. The popcorn equivalent of meaningful sex. No real mechanics or skills, just an overwhelming desire to fuck or be fucked.

As Craig went to the bathroom to get something to clean ourselves up with, I couldn't help but think of Cornelia's smug face as she signed those cheques the other day, and I still didn't feel satisfied that I had got my own back. What could I do? Set fire to her dreamcatcher? Smash her wind-chimes? Throw a Molotov cocktail into her laundry basket? All too obvious. It was then that I spotted it. A chord shining like a golden thread, spilling out of her bedside drawer. And when Craig came back in with a toilet roll and began to, rather chivalrously, wipe his juice from my stomach, he smiled and I smiled.

"What?" he said cheekily.

"Nothing," I was still pissed and slurring, "come here."

I pulled him to me and gave him a lingering kiss. He kissed me back, blissfully unaware that Aunty Cordy's camera had a new photo on it: me, naked, sucking her nephew off my fingers, in her precious fucking bed.

16

The walk of shame through Kings Cross wasn't so bad considering that at least half of the population on a Saturday morning were in a similar state. The guy who stood next to me at the bus stop was still wired. So much so that he was practically licking his own eyeballs.

I smacked my lips together. My mouth tasted like I'd slept chewing on a dead man's ball-sack. I had searched for water but there was none, and rather than search Cordelia's fridge for a glug of lukewarm soya milk, I opted to buy some from a shop. Heaven knows I must smell like a brewery, they'd probably throw bottles at me just to get me out of the shop. Craig stirred slightly but had not woken from his drunken slumber. Fortunately we'd had the good sense to dispose of the used condom and wank rag in a sensible way before we'd licked each other's tongues for a final time and passed out on opposite sides of the bed.

As I danced round the room, collecting discarded items of clothing while trying not to wake him up, I had found a two pound coin on the floor which would buy me a bit of breakfast that, technically, he owed me. Once I found all the necessary garments and performed the tricky "descent of stairs and dress yourself too" manoeuvre, all I would need was for Cordelia to arrive home early to really let the cat out of the bag. Thankfully there was no click of a court shoe on breezeblock, or the tinkle of a bicycle bell to divert me to the back door. I slipped my shoes on, listening out for any tell-tale noises from upstairs, got the door open and power-walked to the nearest safe spot. The spot which meant that I could, quite feasibly, have been merely visiting the area if Cordelia happened to ride on by.

As I tottered to the nearest shop, my phone began to ring in my pocket. Shit! What if it was Rex wanting me to come in today? I couldn't, I just couldn't! It was Beez.

"Daaaaaaaarling," he cooed. "You know how a telephone works, that's reassuring."

"Ooooh, not so loud Beez, my head's falling off my shoulders." I winced.

"Oh-my-God! Pissed last night without me. I'll never forgive you... Oh alright, I accept your apology! Good night?"

"I think so, my arse feels like I've had an entire Sylvanian family inserted into it. You know, the rabbit family with the sticking out ears. Each of them. One by one."

"Oh that's amazing! Drink and a shag. I'm so jealous. Did the earth move?"

"Well at least my bowels didn't so that's enough for me."

"You must fill me in ... no pun intended. Any chance you can come over tonight and help me pack?"

"Pack what? You have no stuff."

"Okay then, help me sink a gram and go through all our old pictures. It is my last official night after all."

Oh shit! Really? It had come around so quick; I thought we had at least one more week. I'd been so self-absorbed, the time had sped by without me even noticing.

"Of course I can and of course I will. Shall I bring anything?"

"Just your divine self, and a bottle of vodka, and any spare boxes. And leave your sore arse at home please."

"I can but try."

"Laters."

I turned my phone off and swept into the shop on Pentonville Road. The one I just knew would let me buy booze at nine o'clock in the morning.

*

"Oh Christ, look at us!"

We had downed a couple of vodkas and were now giggling over a terrible old picture of us at some Halloween theme night in 2001. I had long hair and was wearing a pair of angel wings and Beez was wearing nothing but a pair of leather pants and a smile. I also had my nose pierced, something that I thought was really cool at the time but was actually very prone to infection more often than not. It was also always getting caught in my face-towel, flying out and being replaced with one of Freya's small hooped earrings. For that reason she was constantly referring to me as "the prize bullock".

"I look so young there," I moaned. "I've aged so much. So much even in the last few days."

"Well I'm not surprised." Beez grinned. "You sound like you've had an emotional rollercoaster that would put Rita: Queen of Speed to shame. First you get the part, then you get the boy. And last time we went out you were convinced that you wouldn't get either. I mean, well done you."

"Yay me!"

"Let's have another line to celebrate." He didn't wait for me to answer before he started racking them up and I didn't argue when he offered me the rolled-up tenner.

"Such young little princesses with such big dreams," Beez said, followed by a couple of horrendous wet sniffs and a few hacking sounds.

"I know, whatever happened to those dreams?" I looked out to an invisible sea.

"We're living them babes, you and me. Maybe not together but we're certainly making a go of what we have individually. You've done great. You're going to be a superstar. Totally on the right track." He stuck a cigarette in his mouth and attempted to light it with the bottom of the lighter.

"And what about you?" I'd snorted my line and a trickle of heinous-tasting liquid was making its way down the back of my throat. Cocaine mixed with mucus. A disgusting process really, why did we do it to ourselves?

"Me? Why I'm a drifter baby." He put his foot up on the table, mimicking John Wayne... or was it Cher? I couldn't be sure. "All I need's my gee-tar and my dawg and my man. Then I follow the sun to wherever I's gotta go."

I laughed. It was a lazy laugh. My facial muscles were beginning to fail me.

"You're a good guy, Beasley. And good things happen to good people."

He jumped down off the bed and met me nose to nose.

"Well then, I guess you'll be getting yours reeeeeal soon, pretty man."

I looked into his deep blue eyes. I don't know whether it was the coke or the fact that he looked so beautiful at this very moment that moved me. I kissed him. Once. On the lips. Not a deep kiss but a lingering romantic kiss. Beez and I had kissed each other a couple of times before. Once absolutely caned off our heads in Heaven. The DJ had played "U Sure Do" in among a drone of generic house music and it came as such a total surprise that we had both had simultaneous out of body experiences and found ourselves on each other's lips. It was no biggie, we just carried on dancing.

The second time was a moment like this, at Christmas time. In front of the Christmas tree in Covent Garden. We had been shopping, had a glass of mulled wine, held hands down Oxford Street and, in front of that big old pine, twinkling and winking with festive cheer – it just felt right. And now. Third time a charm.

"What was that for?" Beez asked after a couple of seconds, his breath on my cheek.

"I dunno." I leant back. "Call it a parting gift." I took the cigarette from his mouth, laughed and popped it in mine.

"To see you on your way, little lady."

That night after a little farewell drink downstairs with the others, I stayed over. We slept in each other's arms but we didn't kiss again. Any further action would have tarnished the beauty of what happened before. We didn't want to have sex with each other, that wasn't what it was about, I just loved him and that kind of love is rare. When you love someone like that, there is no explanation for your actions and the other person doesn't need explaining to.

We held hands on the Tube all the way up to Heathrow. He had his huge backpack with things dangling off here and there: a pillow, a bedroll, a colander for some strange reason. If someone had attached a harmonica to the front of it he'd have looked like a one-man band.

Beez asked me to join him because he didn't like goodbyes and he didn't want an entourage. I actually suspected something I'd not seen in my friend for quite some time; he was nervous. He kept checking his money, his passport, his first aid kit. I was calm. In a non-malicious way, I kind of liked being the grown-up for once. I hated airports because I hated the moment when that person disappears from view, seemingly forever. I likened it to a coffin disappearing through a curtain in a crematorium; you know the body is still there but there is no way you can get to it. No changing your mind. You can't ask them to wheel it back out and say that you'll bury it behind your herbaceous border after all. I made sure that he had a *Bella* magazine for the journey.

"But it's full of rubbish," he protested.

"Well wipe your arse with it if you get caught short in the bush." I pushed it into his hand. We had coffee; neither of us was able to hold much of a conversation. You never can in these situations. There's nothing really to do in airports except talk about flying and neither of us wanted to broach that topic. After meandering around Boots for the umpteenth time I'd had enough.

"Beez, I'm going to have to go. And it will have to be here outside Boots because I don't like goodbyes. Least of all ones where you gradually fade into the background as the security queue gets shorter and shorter. Besides, the shopping is better on the other side." I could feel myself beginning to well up. Typical. I hadn't seen the guy in weeks and not even broken a sweat but now I knew I couldn't see him for six months, I was depressed.

"Okay." He made an optimistic sigh. "I guess the journey begins here... for both of us."

"I guess it does." I kissed him on the cheek. "Bye then, big man, call or text when you get there."

I turned to go for fear of flinging myself at his feet in despair. Just as I went to step away, he grabbed my hand.

"Spiders," he said. I looked at him and his face crumpled. "I don't know why I said that."

I did. I nodded and mouthed the word *bye* and started to walk quickly away, not looking back. The tears were slow at first, but then came thick and fast. I cried for Beez and his frightened little face. I cried for myself and the guilt of not making more of an effort with him on his last week in London. I cried for all the times that Rex had nearly driven me to it but I had never let him see me in tears. I cried for all the rejection and pain I felt every day for not thinking I was good enough to be an actor, or administrator, or even a human being. I cried for ignoring Clarissa and throwing her chocolates away without even tasting them and, last of all, I cried for Craig. Craig who would wake up and find me not there; naked, confused and alone.

*

When I got home, I sat up with Freya and watched some baking thing on TV. The cow upstairs had stopped crashing and banging to let us know that she was home.

"Does she not know we get it?" Freya said without taking her eyes off the screen.

"She could of course be hanging herself."

Neither of us moved: a testament to our concern.

"It will be okay you know," Freya said. "He'll be back before you know it, and it sounds like you won't have time to even notice he's gone. Throw yourself into school and think about what you do have and not what you don't."

That's why I love Freya. Okay, she wasn't very tactile, but she was a long-standing and loyal friend who I cared for very much. Her sage words of wisdom stuck with me as I climbed into bed early, my copy of *Equus* gripped in hand.

I suddenly realised that I hadn't checked my phone all day. I had no idea what was going on in the outside world. I wrestled it out of my pocket.

First of all there were three missed calls: two from Craig and one from a, now-familiar, landline. Second there was a text from Beez.

I called my answerphone. One new message.

'Simon, it's Rex. I'm not going to bother myself with following up on this call, if you don't respond or get this message then it's your tough shit I'm afraid.'

His ice-cold tone froze my blood. Aaron had told me that he was going to call this weekend, why hadn't I answered? Because I was on the Tube to bloody Heathrow for half the sodding day! Was it too late to call now?

'Just to let you know that rehearsals for Equus will begin on Tuesday at six. I do not expect you to be off script but I do expect you to bring at least double the insight that you brought on Friday's audition. More even.'

Tuesday? That was quicker than I expected. I thought I'd get at least a week. There was more.

'You do not have to attend regular classes on Monday now, for this term you will be working exclusively within my group and you will not be joining your old sessions. And, Simon, a word of warning...'

It was like a curse bestowed on me from a gypsy.

'I would forget you ever had friends at the school. You are part of something else now and they will not understand that. You should be in it for one person and one person only. I will let you decide who that is. Until Tuesday.'

Click.

Who was that one person? Me? Him? I was clueless and shell-shocked. Give up my friends? I could never call time on my friendships with Lulu, Sophie and, to a lesser extent, Liana. Perhaps that might be one of his rules, but it certainly wasn't mine. A new dread manifested itself in the pit of my stomach. It was so palpable that it fed straight to my groin and made me feel like I was going to throw up. The whole idea of starting the school again, meeting a new set of people – ten little Rexes in their own right – was almost too much to bear. What if I didn't want this now, what if I opted out, would I be spared? Or would that be the end of my acting career before it had begun. And not just from acting jobs but also to be blacklisted from every arts centre and theatre bar in the land for all eternity. I told myself I was being dramatic but that's the very bloody thing that started this whole mess in the first place. I was too anxious to read the play now, so I just pulled the covers over my head. Not even Beez's farewell text had cheered me up: *Spiders? LOL xx*

*

Monday morning, I woke up in a foul mood. Beez had gone, the play just wasn't going in and I was anxious about tomorrow. I couldn't seem to get myself in the right frame of mind. Why oh why did I have to go into that stupid shitting Eco Scene and pretend like I wanted to be there? We all knew that I was running out the clock until something better came along, why didn't we just admit it and stop dancing around the obvious? I hated it, and it hated me.

The bag handle threatened to wrap itself around the door handle again and nearly garrotte me for the second time this week. I wrenched it off with such force that I nearly ripped the whole thing apart. Sandra was back. She was dressed in a simple nautical top and navy trousers. She looked positively fashionable. When I saw her face, however, it looked like a clock designed by Dali, practically dripping down her front. She looked like hell.

"Mording."

"Christ Sandra, what are you doing here? You look like you need another day in bed."

"Oh, don't send me back there," she whinged. "Next door are having an extension done and I can't cope with all the drilling. I'm here so I can get some p and q."

I didn't have the heart to tell her that her outfit was more P&O.

"Well, I'll stop talking then and let you get back to normality."

The truth was I couldn't see Sandra getting anywhere near normality until she'd shaken whatever it was off. I couldn't afford to get ill before rehearsals so I tried to steer clear. I'd fill her in on my eventful weekend when she was able to react with all the necessary theatrics without coughing her guts up.

The door swung open and in walked Craig. I'd forgotten all about him. What with Beez's departure and the whole *Equus* hoopla, our evening of rampant bumming had jumped clean out of my mind. There was probably good reason too. He didn't stop, he didn't wave. In fact, he practically stuck his nose up in the air as he shot past. I wasn't having this! If there was any good time to vent my frustration, it was most definitely now.

I waited a second before I heard him go into the photocopy room. Why was it that all my dramas seemed to play out in that room? It was ironic then that, without me, the room itself was used for photocopying, which required no drama at all. I jumped up and followed him.

"Morning," I said upon my entrance. It was fraught with meaning. No reply. "Are you okay?" I was goading him to respond. I genuinely couldn't think of what I had done that was so bad.

"I'm fine." His reply was tight-lipped and there was no eye contact.

"You don't seem fine."

"I tried to call you yesterday after you left me on my own." He shot daggers at me.

"I had to go, I was late for something." I was shocked. "Jeez, would you just calm down?"

"Don't tell me to calm down. I nearly got caught in Aunty Cordelia's bed. I had to run around, tidying up all the mess."

"Look, I'm sorry. Like I said, I was late for something. Did you expect me to get the Dyson out and clean my half of the room?"

"You're not funny and you've got absolutely no manners either," he hissed. He really was mad.

"Oh for God's sake, Craig. I have enough drama queens at school without another one casually thrown in for good measure." I made for the door.

"You could have answered your phone, you just ignored me and I hate being ignored."

I turned back.

"Well you're going to hate me for the rest of the day then!"

Game, set and match.

*

Five o'clock couldn't come soon enough. I grabbed my bag and escorted Sandra out of the building.

"I really think you should get a cab, you'll never survive the bus."

"I'll be okay. You off to school?" she asked, pulling her cerise jacket further around her shoulders. I didn't have the time to explain that tonight I was spared. I was no longer part of the school as she knew it. I just nodded.

"Go home and treat yourself to a Cup-a-Soup," I said.

She hunched over in the direction of the bus as I scooted off in the opposite direction towards home.

At seven, the texts began.

The first was from Lulu:

'Dude, where are you? School's about to start! Ding, ding, ding!'

The next was from Sophie.

'Simon, put my mind at rest and tell me you're okay.'

I didn't know what to do. I couldn't explain it all in a text; I should have gone in to see them.

Ricky texted: *'Mate? Everything tickerty?'*

And then another from Lulu half an hour later.

'Mate, FFS, answer me!'

Everyone's concern should have made me feel special, but instead I felt harassed. I was trying to read the play and I couldn't because of the constant questions. The last straw came when Sophie texted for a second time. I didn't even wait to read it properly. I typed frantically.

'For goodness sake, I'm ill, now bugger off would you!'

I felt a pang of guilt for being so direct, especially with Sophie who wouldn't say boo to a goose. I didn't hear another peep all evening, which upset me more, but I choked it back and carried on reading. Perhaps being unkind to them was a better way of shedding my old friends. Did I say better? I meant easier.

*

After a fairly restless night, I knew that today was the Day of Judgement. Tuesday had arrived. Last night, I felt like I'd got a much firmer grip on the play but its dark nature had created a sort of black fog around my head. Like when you watch a disturbing horror movie and you just can't get the image of someone being beaten to death with their own severed arm out of your mind for a couple of days. I practically snarled at a woman who got in my way on the bus, I stormed up the street, nearly knocking a suited man flying. I just didn't give a shit about any of these people anymore, I had a purpose to fulfil and that moment was slowly descending on me. I didn't have time for other people's sorry little lives.

Sandra was slowly getting back on form. She was keeping herself to herself, but I could tell she was observing me from the way she kept silent as I slammed my things down on the desk. I was imagining what I might do to him if Pepe started banging on. I'm sure his tiny little limbs would look excellent on a skewer and slowly roasted if he pushed me too far today. But he didn't. No one was biting, which drove me more insane. Eventually Clarissa jolted forward in the race to piss me off.

"Oh!" she exclaimed, wrinkling up her nose. "There's a dark aura in here today."

I rolled my eyes so fully, I swear you could hear them turning in their sockets from outside. She started tutting.

"It's really off-putting actually. I don't know if I can work with such a fug in the air."

"I don't know whether you can work at all," I said, just loud enough. "Perhaps your dragon can come down and rescue you?"

"I can hear you, Simon," she said over her shoulder.

"Well I'm talking loud!" I snapped.

"There's no need to poke fun, I'm merely speaking of what I find in this room. It's oppressive."

"Do you know what's really oppressive?" I swung myself around to face her full throttle.

312

"The fact that you come in here, day after day, wielding your potions and banal anecdotes and throwing them at us like we're meant to swallow them up. That is oppressive. The air is constantly thick with your drama, I've never known anything like it. AND I GO TO DRAMA SCHOOL!"

With that, I turned, not bothering to follow my scathing words with a look of disdain. I'd had it with her, she was a snivelling mess and I couldn't cope with it any longer. I was not a babysitter and I was certainly not going to massage her ego. It felt good to get that out. I smiled to myself. I was getting sick of everyone leeching things out of me and never getting a thing in return, it was utterly exhausting and I wasn't having any of it.

I could feel a change upon me. It seemed that Sandra could too as she spent most of the day avoiding me. I didn't care, I wasn't about to apologise for being honest. No one had a right to tell me how to behave. From now on, I was going to do what I wanted, when I wanted and fuck them if they couldn't handle it. I guess I was moving onto a new way of thinking: perfect for my first night as an Old School Elitist.

As I made my way, once again, up the steps to the main doorway, it was as if the other students were parting to let me through. Some whispered, some students' gazes followed me all the way up and through the doors. The news had obviously got out that I was headed somewhere that wasn't mentioned in the school brochure. Most would question whether Rex had made the right decision; many would act spitefully out of jealousy since they hadn't shown similar potential or flair.

I had arrived purposefully punctual so that I wouldn't have to greet any of my former comrades. I'm not sure that they would want to converse with me now that I had been invited to join the other side: it was their loss. The door to the elite room was slightly ajar. I could tell from the hum of voices inside that the group was already there, waiting to meet their new arrival. I had a choice: I could run and never know what it was like to be somebody, a force to be reckoned with in drama circles, one of the rare few who were given a golden ticket into the industry, a real expert at something that wasn't boring, monotonous or mundane, or I could walk through those doors and accept that I was worthy of this truly indescribable opportunity. I craned my neck slightly. Rex's door was open and the light was off. He must already be in there, briefing the others before I arrived. I swallowed hard, it was now or never.

The door opened easily as I pushed it and a white light seemed to consume me from within. Inside was a sea of faces. I smiled, albeit nervously, and as the door swung shut slowly behind me, a curl of cigarette smoke escaped just in time to snake its way up the empty corridor.

End of Book One

BOOK TWO

1

I smiled back at the group, fifty per cent of which seemed wholly unimpressed. This was mainly the girls. The boys were the only ones who beamed back at me, moderately pleased that I was here at all.

"Ah, Simon." Rex jumped up. My immediate reaction was to flinch; however, the more he spoke the more it became evident that I was dealing with a totally different person. He appeared insouciant, pleasant, maybe even a little excited. I'd seen him act like this once before when he was pissed and chatting to a group of attractive young ladies after a graduating show. He placed the tips of his fingers on my shoulders as he made his way around me from left to right.

"I don't know whether you've seen Simon around the school," he gushed, continuing to circle and perform a kind of jerky dance around me like the fool in a Shakespearean comedy. I felt ridiculous and in the spotlight. It didn't occur to me to actually enjoy and revel in the praise I was being given. I wasn't used to it in this place.

Some of the girls looked me up and down as I turned and watched Rex hop and skip from foot to foot in his bizarre routine. One lad who towered above the rest, and whom I had never seen before, was upright like a grandfather clock, a big beam on his face like a Cheshire cat. He seemed very pleased that I had joined the group and nodded in all the right places. I recognised Philippe, the flame-haired, porcelain-faced, flamboyant guy from my audition. In his rehearsal clothes of tracksuit bottoms and loose-fitting t-shirt, he looked effortlessly cool and attractive. He gave me a sexy, knowing smile and his eyes glittered like the two sapphires that adorned the sausage fingers of my previous director Grant. Three girls sat together, each looking as

317

bored as the other. One in particular looked like she wanted to be anywhere but here; my demeanour was an offence to her retinas.

"And it is THAT performance," spat Rex, "that got him where he is today." Suddenly, realising where he was for a moment, Rex regained his composure. One of the curls from his perfectly coiffed hair had escaped in the whirl of his superlative-peppered speech and he smoothed it back into place as he fished yet another cigarette from his jacket pocket.

As he sat down, I realised that I was the only one standing and immediately felt vulnerable and exposed.

"Perhaps," Rex said, after a few agonising seconds of silence as I was scrutinised and he worked out why his upside-down lighter wouldn't light his fag, "you would like to introduce yourselves and say a little about your background. It might put Simon at ease."

As he said this, he peered over his glasses. He must have spotted that I was so rigid with fear that I was leaning forward at a considerable gradient.

Another long pause. I wanted to grab my bag, thank everyone for their time and run down the corridor to the safety of the outside world. The air in the room was so thick that I could barely breathe. Philippe jumped to my aid; I'd not heard him speak yet. All the conversations we'd had thus far had been with our eyes rather than our mouths.

"I'll start, I'm Philippe." He sounded remarkably un-French for someone with a name like that. His words were clipped and his voice was clear and slightly effeminate. As he talked, he kept his arms crossed as if I would have to earn the right to see him with his arms uncrossed. I instantly fancied him, but his body language was so hostile I wasn't really sure which part of him I fancied. He continued.

"I've been in the group for two months. I was Henry Wotton in *Dorian Gray* and I'll be in the chorus in this production. I can't WAIT to see

318

what YOU bring to the role." His cadence at the end of that speech suggested that he had been my competition. It was fraught with insincerity.

Next was a fairly dumpy-looking girl with a strange hairstyle that looked like a bowler hat with a broken rim. A longer flap of hair hung over her face like the flimsy tongue of an old boot fished out of a canal. If she had bothered to style it as the hairdresser had when it was cut, then it might look like it was supposed to. I could tell from the way she was glancing at some of the more stylish female members of the group that she was struggling to keep up with their styling.

"I'm Hilary," she said. Her accent was wobbly as if she was trying to brush a posh coat over a fairly thick regional base. "I was Anfisa in *Three Sisters*. I'll be playing Alan's mother in this."

Some of the other girls smirked. It was clear that the only reason Hilary was in the group was that she was adept at playing older, matronly women.

Next up was the tall, simple-looking lad whose hundred-watt smile had now faded to a still impressive sixty watts.

"Hi," he said. His accent was thick Yorkshire. It was the kind of accent that Hovis had made famous. You could imagine him walking along cobbled streets, pushing a bike and doffing his cap to the townsfolk.

"I'm Brian. I played Dafydd in *Chorus of Disapproval* and I'll be playing Alan's father in this. Nice to have you here."

I nodded in thanks. It was strange that Rex had chosen this couple of misfits to join his team. They must be bloody good actors because they looked and sounded ridiculous. Next came the three girls, Isabella, Kerry and Sharron. She pronounced it Shah-ron, which smacked of someone who was trying to make a rather common name sound interesting. They barely looked at me as they spoke; fortunately, they were all in the chorus so I didn't have much to worry about. It suddenly occurred to me that all this hostility could be the result of intense jealousy that someone so new had managed to bag the best part in the play. The thought didn't make me feel any better.

Next was a sweet-looking, softly-spoken guy with strawberry blonde hair and long, feminine fingers. When he spoke, I noticed a north-eastern accent.

"Hi, I'm Lisle. I've not really performed in anything yet. My last performance didn't reflect my best work." He didn't look at Rex, but I had a fair idea where that critique had come from. "My performance as Bassanio in *The Merchant of Venice* got me here though and I'm playing Dysart in this."

That was interesting casting on Rex's part. I would have imagined that given the masculine and strong cerebral presence of the psychiatrist who interviews Alan throughout the play, the part would have been better going to the big tall dufus. Rex had his reasons I'm sure.

Another chorus member, Patrick, a lad with a broad Northern Irish accent, was next to introduce himself, and last but not least was the girl on the end, who looked at me as if she had just discovered a pile of sick in her handbag. She was diminutive but perfectly formed, with limbs that seemed to naturally point at the end. I remembered her waltzing in and sitting on the front row during my performance in *Hay Fever*. I remembered gazing at her elegance. She had long, golden curls that fell down her back and big, wing-like eyelashes that, if they were fake, they weren't the kind you buy in Claire's Accessories. She wore sweats but still managed to look a million dollars in them, and she held her book as if it was an extension of her hand. The one saving grace was that she had terrible skin and tiny breasts, so I mentally chalked one up for myself. She pursed her lips and opened her mouth to speak. I was temporarily transfixed as I watched her lips part and the words bubble out of it.

"I am Cecelia," she was Australian, I hadn't expected that, "otherwise known as Lady Bracknell, Nora Helmer and, of course, Masha Sergeyevna." She let out a giggle at this and nodded at Rex. This bitch had played some hard hitters and, unlike the drunk girl in the hall, she had succeeded in performing as Masha, Rex's notorious favourite character. She inhaled audibly to signify that she must now be listened to again. "And from today, I will be known as Jill."

Shit! I knew it! She was playing Alan's love interest. This was going to be a challenge in every way. How was I going to stand being judged by Rex AND by her? Especially when Alan had a fairly raunchy sex scene with Jill that was going to be impossible to dumb down. Jesus!

She must have sensed my discomfort because she smiled and lowered her head slowly to her book. She didn't drop eye contact with me until the very last second, reading my fear like a well-thumbed novel. Now I was really nervous.

"Right," Rex said, his tone slightly less fervent and more direct. "Today will be the only day when you are allowed to fuck up. After today it will be considered a sackable offence. So we'll have a short break and then we'll begin our read-through. I'm expecting you to have a good grasp of how you will play the characters, how they will communicate with each other, and how they will exist in the world we are creating. Nothing can be faked, it has to be real, it has to be lived through, and it has to be felt. Anything less than that is a waste of my time. There will be no room for try-hards and pretenders. Remember that."

I understood that in allowing us to cock up, Rex was daring us to do it. I wasn't falling for that. I was still standing up, squirming as if I was desperate for the toilet.

"Of course," he continued, "some of us are used to this process and will therefore have all the tools in place. Others will have to work a little harder to convince us."

He was looking at me. No pressure or anything! That thought hung in the air while he eyeballed me carefully, then he jumped up.

"Half an hour," he said, and with that he was gone. The others started chatting among themselves, no one even attempted to look at or approach me. I feebly meandered over to a seat and pulled my copy of the play out of my bag. In a room that was full of people, I suddenly felt very alone. As I read, I could feel a pair of eyes on me. Everyone except me and Cecelia was chatting away. She was sitting watching me patiently, perfectly aware that I knew she was staring and unapologetic about it. After a few minutes she performed some kind of ballet manoeuvre to lift herself out of her seat and walk over to me in a swan-like manner, her feet just brushing the carpet as she moved. I was trembling. Having Rex breaking me down from the outside was enough, I hadn't bargained for a female version of him to be breaking me down from the inside. She stood over me, waiting for a response. Fuck this! I wasn't about to be intimidated by her, she didn't even know me. I had earned my place in this group and I wasn't going anywhere anytime soon. I looked up, my confidence beginning to wane under the weight of her nonchalant glare.

"Hi." I managed to choke out. "Hi, Cecelia. I guess we'll be working together a lot over the next few weeks."

She just kept on looking at me, her head twitching slightly from side to side like a goose that had found something in its path and was about to peck it into submission. A few painful moments passed.

"I just HOPE Rex knows what he's doing," she said, as her painted-on perfect eyebrows moved up her forehead.

"Sorry?"

"Casting you." There was no tremor in her voice; it was smooth as though she said this every day.

"I'm not sure what—"

"I have been given the part of Jill because I have aced every part I have ever been given and as you heard earlier, I have played some heroines that most two-a-penny actresses would give their shrivelled-up clits for."

The thought of it made me balk slightly. I didn't interrupt her; I had a feeling that it was more than my life was worth to do so.

"And the reason I have smashed the part every time is not just that I come straight from the Sydney Academy for the Dramatic Arts or that I am an incredibly versatile and accomplished theatrical actress or that I have been in the Australian Youth Theatre since I was PRACTICALLY a babe in arms. No, it is because my co-star has been as accomplished and as completely and utterly infallible as I am."

She stopped. It was like I was watching a monologue. She frowned and searched my eyes, looking for something, maybe she could see my soul twisting inside my body. She looked pained.

"You have no spark," she said, defeated. "You are too weak for this. You are an imposter and I shall deign to work with you until Rex sees sense and throws you out. Until then, I shall speak to you in character only."

I wanted to defend myself, I wanted to stand tall and tell her that I didn't care what she cocking thought and how dare she be so arrogant, insolent, cold-hearted and churlish. I wanted to rip those curls right off her stupid skull. But I didn't, I nodded and dropped my head.

"Good," she scoffed, "then we understand each other."

I nodded again; I had never felt so deflated. As she moved away, the door opened. Had it really been half an hour? No, but then Rex wasn't so kind as to stick to his word. The room quietened instantly. He swept in, fished around for a dog-eared packet of cigarettes that would be his movietime refreshment and lowered himself into his seat. I was beginning to think that this group was one thing and one thing only, bat-shit loopy. A flutter of pages followed and Rex opened his mouth to speak the immortal words:

"In black... AND!"

Well, it hadn't been a total disaster. It had started off pretty shambolic until the mood had been broken by the arrival of someone new. She bumbled into the room apologising, reminding Rex that she had had to go and sort out a headshot issue somewhere in East Dulwich; apparently, the first lot had come out smudged and Rex had made her go straight there and demand her money back. The girl was pretty and voluptuous, with long red hair and bright crimson lipstick. She had an ample bosom that she had managed to contain in a sexy, fitted, fifties-style dress with a cinch belt. When she spoke, her voice was high-pitched, almost as if she was ditsy, though I could tell instantly that she was anything but. She didn't seem fazed by Rex's dagger stare, and she certainly didn't notice the eyes of her female colleagues rolling as she pleaded her case.

"This was the only day I could do it, Rex." She was practically wagging a finger at him, which he seemed to enjoy.

"Oh, spare me the hackneyed gibberish, Sorcha. You've already disrupted an uninspiring and turgid read-through with your trite excuses. Now we're going to have to gear them all up to get them to rise to the dizzy heights of 'average' all over again." Rex was annoyed.

"Sorry," she squeaked as she sat down next to me.

We did start again, with no more chemistry than we had had before, and Rex managed to huff, puff and fidget more in that first thirty minutes than if he had had a bag of cockroaches poured into his Farah slacks.

"Hilary." He pointed an accusatory finger at the dumpy girl to my left, who I thought had read quite well. She looked slightly panicky. "I am asking for someone with an obsession, an unnatural obsession with religion. So much so that it is having a negative impact on the relationships she has with her family. What you are giving me is akin to someone who is LOOKING FORWARD TO BINGO."

She nodded and went back to the book to start again. It was as if she had had to respond to this kind of rebuttal a million times and simply went into default mode. When she read again, something had changed. There was more conviction to the words, more strength.

When my turn came, I felt as if my tongue was made of wood and my throat was made of sandpaper. The words were thin and dry. Rex let out so many exasperated sighs that I began to search in my bag for something, anything that would give me a bit more moisture. I couldn't go on with a mouth that was sponsored by Ronseal. After a frantic couple of minutes, with a wink Sorcha handed me a bottle, which I gratefully accepted. A few more scenes in and the insults were coming thick and fast.

"Brian, trying to direct you is like trying to piss in a cyclone."

"So THAT'S your insight is it, Lisle? Well, thank you very fucking much Bertolt fucking Brecht."

And poor old Hilary wasn't getting away with anything.

"If only you paid as much attention to the script as you pay to the menu at Burger King." Bit harsh.

"That delivery was about as balanced as an elephant on a jet ski."

325

"Oh, DO share that line with us again, Dame Judi, it was a real fucking blinder."

Although I was butchering my lines left, right and centre, I was getting more sighs than vicious words. I didn't know whether that was a good thing or a bad thing. It was like being directed by a helium balloon. And after a strained exchange between myself and Cecelia that was meant to be crackling with sexual tension but lacked so much chemistry that even Gary Glitter would have lost his hard-on, Rex was beginning to sound like a bouncy castle with a puncture that none of those still bouncing had even noticed.

I had a feeling that this was Rex at his most restrained. He must have smoked at least fifteen cigarettes; their butts were assembled in a mini-tower in the ashtray.

When the last line had been read, it was a few moments before he gave his summary.

"Well," he said to no one in particular, "that was about as atmospheric as a whitewashed wall. Same time tomorrow I guess for more purgatory." He forced the door open, walked through and then popped his head back around.

"Oh, and if any of you want to bring SOMETHING that comes CLOSE to decent acting, then be my cunting guest," and he was gone. Well I guess that solved the mystery of what the adjective from cunt was.

The group heaved a collective sigh of relief and we gradually filed out. Cecelia was first out, strutting across the room like a peacock. She didn't even bother to bid anyone farewell. Sorcha slunk up to me. Her smile sweetened the pill a bit.

"Hello there, are you new?"

"Yes, Simon." I had no energy. As it stood, I was embarrassed to even suggest that I was still in the room, never mind part of the group. It was like I had just started a new job after years of service in another position and I was supposed to give a shit about the photocopier and the filing systems in the same way as the others did.

"Look, as you can see it's a bit hard going in here. You've just got to keep fighting." You couldn't help but applaud her optimism. I felt like my world was ending.

"Thanks for that." It was all I could do to not erupt into hysterical sobbing all over her and ruin the shoulders of a perfectly good dress.

"It gets easier. I was a wreck when I first started. Then I stopped taking it all so seriously. I mean, for Christ's sake – we're not saving lives here." Very true.

I hadn't been shown kindness like this in about four hours and I lapped it up. I leant forward to whisper in her ear. "I know, it's just, no one seems to want me here."

"Oh, that's not true." It was the verbal equivalent of patting me on the head. "They're just frightened for their own safety. You got here on merit, which means more people will so they might get booted out. It's all mind games, let them get on with it." She removed a compact mirror from her bag and began powdering her nose.

"But," I whispered again, "Cecelia..."

As soon as the word fell out my mouth, she snapped the mirror shut and gave me a hard look.

"Well, Simon, you can always come to me if you want advice or a bit of support. I'll never turn anyone away, but if you start listening to the supercilious claptrap from the likes of THAT jumped-up little whore, then I'm afraid you're on your own." She dropped the mirror into her open bag, pulled the handles up over her shoulders, and then dragged me down the pub.

327

We thought it best to limit ourselves to two drinks, which we drank slowly. I was mainly trying to forget the turmoil of the last four hours and Sorcha was chatting animatedly about her last six months as part of the elite. Of course, they didn't refer to themselves as the elite, that was the name we mortals gave them. They just called themselves Rex's group. I had to stop myself from referring to them as the elite about three times. Sorcha had played Irina, the younger sister of the now infamous Masha, in *Three Sisters* and had had to endure acting alongside Cecelia for three whole months. She tried not to say too much, but she more or less suggested that Cecelia didn't get on with anyone, probably because she was so exhausted by having to hold up her enormous head for hours on end. I had seen Sorcha around before. She had said that she had watched me in *Hay Fever* and could understand why Rex wanted me. I liked her, she was very sweet and entirely genuine, or so it seemed. She apparently had Rex all sorted out, and once you managed to get yourself into that position you didn't really have much to fear.

"Rex instils fear in those who feel that this is the last chance saloon," she said, clutching her glass of rosé with both hands. "If there was an opportunity out there for more regular Joes to get into the more established schools, then he wouldn't have a leg to stand on and he knows it. The less people feared him, the less motivated he would be and the school would close. Its whole reputation is based on his tyranny."

I nodded, absorbing all the information I could. "So what's your advice for me?" I asked, desperate for a quick fix answer.

"Well," she said, draining the dregs of her wine, "first of all, read the play then read the play again and again... You get my drift? Then decide how you want to play the character and stick with it. Oh sure, Rex might not agree with your interpretation, but if you argue and stand your ground with a feasible defence, then you can prove him wrong. I mean, the guy loves to be right, but likes to be proved wrong even more. Except no one ever has the balls to do it. Come on, let's go."

As we walked out of the pub and I moved to go in the opposite direction, she grabbed my arm. "Oh, and don't even THINK about watching the film of *Equus*, it will ruin your style. If Rex gets a whiff of that, then he'll kick you out straight away, no question." She released her grip. "Now off you go. Get that play read and I'll see you tomorrow evening."

I smiled and thanked her before going on my way. I hadn't seen any of the others from my old classes tonight; they were in their own sessions. I looked at my phone, no one had texted. I suddenly felt incredibly isolated.

When I got home, I walked into the kitchen to find a note from the Gorgon upstairs: "Can we all chip in for water filter cartridges? Five pounds a month." I was happy to drink water out of the tap or drink my own urine if it meant not having to give her any more money.

I sighed and opened the fridge to make a sandwich. Freya was out so I watched *EastEnders* on my own, tutting to myself about the appalling acting. I thought of the crazy money these actors were making to just stand there and deliver lines while I was working my backside off to try and make all my scenes as real as they could be. Where was the justice?

It was still early so I figured I'd better start reading the play. I was so bored with it that I could barely bring myself to open the book. Perhaps if I attacked it with fresh energy, that might make it seem less of a challenge and more of an achievement. I spent two hours working on various speeches with different intonation and with various approaches. I was worried that each one was confusing the concept of the one before. Eventually, I collapsed into bed, happy with the work I had done and slightly looking forward to the hard day's work ahead.

2

I woke up in better spirits. It was a new day and I was ready to face it head-on. I ate a hearty breakfast, managing to surreptitiously avoid Flowers, who would always judge everything I put into my mouth against her own strict vegan values, from the porridge oats I devoured in the morning to the cocks I sucked at the weekend. Sorcha's inspiring words and fighting spirit saw me through a torturous bus journey where a filthy-looking rugrat, who was faceless behind a shroud of steamed-up PVC hanging over its buggy, screamed like it was being repeatedly thrown against a wall. I walked into the office on tippy-toes.

"Morning!" I sang at Sandra. Today's outfit needed only one adjective: citrus. I didn't know whether I was looking at my respected colleague or at the man from Del Monte's ex-wife. Orange top, lime-green stretch skinnies, and banana loafers. Alone, each piece might look acceptable. Together, they were retina-searing, death by neon.

"Oh, morning." There was a distinct note of disdain in her voice, like she was talking to somebody she barely knew.

"What's up?" I thought it was probably best to discuss the problem now and save ourselves a lot of dancing around the subject later.

"Nothing's wrong with me." Her tone suggested the exact opposite.

"I don't believe you." I remained on my feet, I wasn't about to buckle under the pressure and sit down.

"Well, okay, I'm not happy."

"Why, what's wrong? Is Leon's ailment flaring up again?"

"This has nothing to do with Leon." She spun round in her chair and her nails flashed in my direction, a cacophony of pink and orange.

"It's you."

"Oh?" I could feel myself going red but I tried to ignore it. If I had to get angry, then I didn't want any obstructions.

"You're like a different person, Simon. I don't recognise you at the moment. The last couple of days you've been absolutely vile. It's not like you."

"Okay." I took a moment to absorb this information. I didn't really want to answer her so I didn't, I just sat down and we both went back to our screens. After a few moments, I broke the silence.

"Are you talking about the fight with Clarissa, because she was asking for it," I said.

"It's not just that. You've been storming around, banging things down for days now. Poor old Pepe's been jumping around like he's been sitting on an electric fence. It's creating a horrible atmosphere."

I'd never heard her refer to him as "poor old Pepe" before. Usually, he was Pepe le Pew. How dare she start taking the moral high ground now just because I wasn't giving her any attention. I calmed myself, I didn't need this shit but I didn't want to fall out with Sandra – this was her place of work and to be fair to her, she never aimed to upset anybody. If anything, she spoke her mind and if people got in the way, then that was their problem. I was more likely to look for reasons to get mad at somebody.

"Okay," I sighed, "but no one appreciates the pressure I'm under at the moment."

"No, you're right," said Sandra, "but the one has nothing to do with the other. I know school is hard and the guy who runs it makes Hitler look like Mary Berry, but we're innocent here, we're not him. We're just getting on with our business." She was uneasy broaching this topic with me. I could tell that my behaviour was really affecting her. And I had to admit that we had become somewhat estranged over the last week.

At that precise moment, Clarissa flounced in. She looked like a mobile jumble sale with all the bags and the various trinkets that were dangling from every available patch of cheesecloth.

"Morning, SANDRA," she said, before wrinkling up her nose at me and plonking her posterior in her chair with such force that a cloud of dust erupted from the back of it. It was all I could do to not tell her to sod off and ruin this rather tender moment.

*

The altercation with Sandra stuck in my craw all day. I was annoyed with her for not taking my side and for not being a better friend. I knew that she was hard-nosed by reputation, but that didn't mean she couldn't thaw a little when she saw that her pal was struggling. Instead she chose to attack me. Besides, it was Clarissa who had started it. As a matter of principle, I wasn't going to apologise to her – she was no longer part of Eco Scene anyway. Apart from a couple of walls, she would practically be in another office and I wouldn't have to face her at all. Throughout the day, I could hear her breathing. I'm sure she always did this, but today it was like tinnitus in my ears and it was annoying the hell out of me. It was like someone squeezing an overstuffed Hoover bag. I put my headphones on but I found myself typing out the words Kylie Minogue rather than the invoice I was meant to be generating. Who was I kidding? I wasn't MEANT to do office work. Why was I lowering myself just to make a pittance to live on? Even prostitution seemed a better option at this point; at least you could lie down and have a fag after. And even though you might get taken roughly by fat old perverts once in a while, at least you wouldn't have to deal with your colleagues' shit-storms. Don't tell me that John Gielgud put himself through RADA by stuffing envelopes with invitations to a lecture on the use of pesticides in arable farming day after pigging day.

Craig drifted past for the third time that afternoon. If I didn't know better, I would have thought that he wanted me to notice him. God, how many other people could I piss off in this office? Cordelia, Craig, Sandra, Clarissa. Soon even the pot plants would be against me. Oh, bollocks to them all! I was part of a new world now, a world that was going to take me places and I wasn't about to hang around with any hangers-on. If I could afford to, I would get up and walk straight out, with my coat over my shoulder like a Melanie Griffith *Working Girl* kind of scene. But life isn't like a movie; not even going to drama school is like a movie, no matter how much they try and make it like one.

*

I bumped into Tim on the way back in from lunch.

"Hey," he said as he stopped me, "I saw you sitting on the fire escape earlier immersed in a book. Any good? Something I should be reading?"

There was a little bit of sauce on his lip from whatever he had been eating. I just wanted to lick it off and rip the faded t-shirt from his body.

"Just a play I've been cast in, I need to learn my lines." In truth, I had been saying them aloud to myself, but he was gracious enough not to humiliate me with that observation.

"Aha! Anything I might have heard of?" He sounded genuinely interested.

"Not unless you're into animal mutilation."

He frowned, pointing to the slogan on his t-shirt that read *Save the Tiger*.

"Didn't think so." I blushed. "Oh well, its only fiction."

"As long as no animals were harmed in the making of the thing," he joked.

"I can assure you of that. Lots of egos have been bruised but the animals escape unscathed." I was impressed by my joke. Normally, I just giggled and pirouetted on the ball of one foot like a bashful schoolgirl. He winked and we went our separate ways. If I could be any animal at this precise moment, then I would be a tiger in need of saving.

I arrived early at school. Sorcha was nowhere to be seen, which was a shame as I felt I had found a kindred spirit in her. As I was looking around the room hoping for some hidden cavern to open up in one of the four walls I had been staring at for the last ten minutes, there was a giant whack on my left shoulder.

"Alright, lad." It was Brian, with a thicker accent than I remembered.

"Oh hi, Brian," I said, rubbing my sore shoulder. This man had hands that were the size of mallets. "How are you?"

"I'm alright. Looking forward to tonight?"

"Is that a genuine question?"

He laughed; it was a belly laugh that seemed to rattle the window frames.

"Oh, you'll be fine, it takes a bit of getting used to but you'll get there."

"Then why does it always feel like somebody's died?"

"Because that's how you make it feel. You can't change Rex; you can only change your attitude towards him."

He shrugged and strode off in the direction of the coffee machine. It was good advice but I feared that it had come too late. I was afraid of this whole process, and once fear had set in at the tired old age of thirty-one, it was going to be an absolute shitter to get rid of it. I went out into the hall to find a bit of breathing space. I could hear various voices coming from the other rehearsal rooms. They would be getting ready for movement class by now. Camilla would be tapping that bloody cane on the floor and they would all be moving forward, the trained dancers gliding as if they were on casters and the larger, dumpier girls stomping forward with all the grace of a row of elephants with painted toes. It's not like I ever enjoyed movement classes, but I wished I could be in one now. It was strict but they were a laugh, stubbing your toe and trying not to scream or laugh. Flicking Vs behind Camilla's back and twanging someone's jockstrap every time she left the room. But where was that ever going to get me? Arsing around wasn't going to get me a stable career with a reliable source of generous income, was it? If I was going to go for it, REALLY go for it, then I was going to have to take acting seriously and not just dick about with it. This is what I had to do.

"Simon." I looked up. Lulu was standing in front of me. It was like I was looking at a different person. Her hair was piled on top of her head in a scarf and she wore a cool denim jacket over a red dress. Her face was beautifully made up, like a siren in an American movie. Though she looked the same, I saw her through different eyes, though it was me who had changed and was no longer recognisable according to Sandra.

"Lulu." I could hardly say the word, the guilt made it sound feeble and insincere.

"So when were you going to tell us?" Her whole stance was accusatory.

"I don't..." I didn't have the energy to argue with her. She was a force to be reckoned with, even when she was weak.

"Didn't you think we'd be happy for you? Didn't you think we would congratulate you? You made us feel like we're the worst friends in the world." She spoke slowly, they were words of pain. "You could have called us, texted, anything. We had no idea where you were, what was going on. This isn't you. You're acting like a different person."

I swallowed hard. "I-I didn't know what to say." I wanted to throw myself at her mercy. I felt completely pathetic. "I thought you might think that I'd sold out."

"How on earth would you know what we'd think? Do you think that we would be so heartless? We were proud of you, Simon. We were proud of you." She emphasised the words to give them more weight. I felt tears prick my eyes.

"I'm sorry." God, this school was so hard. You couldn't do anything without upsetting someone and them piling a few tons of guilt on your back.

I looked down.

"Simon." Was she calling me again? That wasn't Lulu's voice. I looked up just as Cecelia walked up to me and put her hand on my shoulder.

"Is this girl troubling you?" Was Cecelia for real?

"I'm sorry, but who the hell are you?" Lulu was riled. She started to puff herself up, which was never a good sign. Watching these two going at it would be like throwing two alley cats into a bag.

"I asked you a question, Simon." Cecelia wrapped her arm around my shoulder but it felt less comfortable than being encased in an iron lung.

"I'm talking to my friend," said Lulu. "This is a private conversation so I'd appreciate it if you fucked off!"

Cecelia spoke calmly while I just hung in her grip like a wilting wallflower. "Firstly, to answer your question, I am Cecelia Muntz. Secondly, I will not leave if I think that a member of my group is being berated by another student, particularly by one who is of neither the standard nor the breeding to even come close to one of us. We look out for our own and we are under immense pressure to perform to a certain level, which requires complete and utter self-quarantine. Therefore, I will not just fuck off. If you were any kind of friend to Simon, then you would piss off and let him get on with his important work, work that cannot be compromised by the incessant ramblings of some… fishwife."

Lulu was speechless; I had never seen that. I didn't agree with Cecelia's front but at least she had achieved the seemingly unachievable.

"Now if you will excuse US, WE have a play to rehearse. We are not just going to spend our evening practicing how to roll our Rs and playing Follow My Leader like a bunch of uncontrollable children. What a way to waste nine grand!"

And before I could say anything, Cecelia steered me back into the room, her vice-like grip fastened to my shoulder. Lulu just stood there with her mouth open as the door slammed shut.

When we were safely inside, Cecelia practically threw my body from her hands. She then rubbed them together as if trying to rid herself of some invisible film I had left on them.

"For God's sake," she spat at me, "I have enough drama to be getting on with without getting personally involved in your little scenarios. You are not making your life any easier by pulling stunts like that. You are meant to be setting an example to people like her not shacking up with them pretending you're the same. Well, for now at least. I am sure you will both be the same again very shortly when you are side by side in the dole queue." And off she went.

I looked back. Lulu's silhouette behind the frosted glass had vanished. It had been replaced with another; Rex's face was distorted through the glass, but his anger was still visible. Tonight was going to be tough.

Rex sat with his head in his hands for most of the first hour. It seemed he was attempting to try and ignore a disgusting hangover that just wouldn't go away. Poor Lisle had been up for the first half and even though his part had been a mere paragraph, Rex had not let him leave the stage until he approached somewhere near "living in the moment". Every word that came out of Lisle's mouth had elicited different responses with the same attitude: a huff here, a puff there, a fidget, a grunt. Rex even yelled "no" at one point, which frightened us half to death. After an hour that was so mortifying that I would rather have watched a public hanging just to cheer myself up, we were allowed a break. Lisle looked red, exhausted, defeated, but not hopeless. He went calmly to the toilets, wet his face and came back into the rehearsal space.

I had watched a couple of the girls smirking as they watched him turning on a spit. At one point, the girl I remembered as Kerry looked at me with an antagonistic expression. She had a pinched, almost evil face, with long bottle-blonde hair and eyelashes that were so mascaraed that they looked like she'd attached two toilet brushes to her face. How someone could be so insensitive, so inhuman to one of their own, just astounded me. But I didn't retaliate; I just glanced back down at my open script.

After barely enough time to have a few nervous sips from a cup of coffee, Rex strode into the room. He appeared to have a different energy. Maybe he'd snorted a line of coke and was now ready to give me a bit of praise. I doubted it.

"Simon, you are up." He threw his hand in my direction and waggled his wrist like he was shooing an apprehensive sheepdog around some pretty stubborn ewes. I got up and shuffled over to my place, book clasped in hand. Brian was already there.

"You will start upstage left, come out of that door and make your way over to Dysart. Dysart will continue to speak but you will NOT look at him because, obviously, this is a flashback scene." It was all pure instruction but I was so wracked with nerves that I wasn't following a single word he said. I had a million questions about this blocking but I couldn't think of one to ask. I made my way over to where Rex had gesticulated.

"Got that?" I nodded. "In black... AND!"

Lisle said his line. There was silence. It took a second before I realised that this was my cue.

"Sorry Rex, I–"

"No kidding. Start again, please. In black... AND!"

Lisle said his line again. I tried to visualise, push past the nerves and look through Alan's eyes, the eyes that I had been looking through for the last few days. I walked on. Well, that's to say, I took two steps.

"Stop!" Rex was looking at me like I was the village idiot walking onto his land naked from the waist down.

"And what was that?" He was looking directly at me, as were the others. I could feel myself flushing, the old familiar lump rose in my throat and my eyes instantly watered. "I asked you to make your way over to Dysart. Did I not say that in English?"

It was a question that didn't require an answer.

"WHAT?!?!" he shouted. "Are you going to answer me or not?"

I nodded, I felt like I was an orphan being reprimanded by a Nazi.

"Oh, okay. I'll just wait until my notes sink into your thick skull, shall I?" Sarcasm dripped from every word. I instantly got tunnel vision.

Though the room was ostensibly small, the space between me and Rex opened up like a long, grim corridor, one that was paved with failure. This was horrible. Any pleasant feeling I had about this man, any exchange of words, any stupid hope I had that Rex could possess any kind of empathy or sympathy was gone. At home I had mused that he may just be a pussycat and that I would learn how to play to his better side and somehow make him respect and like me. How foolish I was. There was no such side to him. The man was deranged.

"Are you ready to try again or will you keep the company waiting for another ten minutes?" His face bore an expression of pure loathing. I just wanted to run.

"I'm ready," I said and walked over to my place, determined not to be beaten down and to stand defiant, as Lisle had so honourably done for the last hour or so.

"Right, in black... AND!"

With those three words I closed my eyes and imagined, tried to imagine, but Simon was shaking so much that Alan was not coming through at all. I took the few awkward steps.

"No," he said, getting up out of his seat, "that was exactly the same." He didn't seem to be enjoying this, he was actually angry. My walking was riling him and I didn't know what to do about it. This whole process required more strength than I could give.

"You are so full of tension that you are practically rigid." He paced the small circle immediately in front of his chair. "No one in the audience is going to want to watch a fucking tin man stroll around the stage. They will come here to watch Alan, NOT you with a rod up your arse pissing about in the middle of my play!"

I stood there watching him; I literally didn't know how to retaliate. I just had to take it, try again and live in some vain hope that it would be better the next time. "Can I try again?" I asked, like the words escaped me before I had the chance to think about it.

"What's the fucking point?" he asked, as if I'd committed the worst sin in the world. People around me began to look away. Even the hardest of hearts felt sorry for me now... apart from Cecelia's swinging brick, no doubt.

"I'm just nervous," I said, hoping that honesty would be the best policy.

"Well, that's no fucking secret, is it?" He turned to the company. A few scoffs were audible but I didn't dare look at who it might have been in case I turned into a pillar of salt.

"But why aren't you using your nervous energy to channel into the character? I'd happily watch a nervous Alan, but instead I've got some stupid quivering retard ruining my production." His eyes seared into me.

This was worse than any humiliation I had ever endured, even worse than when my sister walked in on me wanking in front of an old episode of *The Bill*. The saggy-titted old policeman was half-naked and I was about twelve and discovering my sexuality for the first time. That had nothing on this.

"Can I just try?" I gulped. I'd taken a grand total of four steps; God knows what it would be like when I opened my mouth.

"Well, let me see." He paced again. He stopped in front of a stool, thought for a moment and then picked it up with his right hand. "Try again, and if it's satisfactory, then you'll know because I won't throw this stool at you. How about that?" He raised it in triumph over his shoulder, eyebrows raised, face calm. This guy really was a whole barrel of nasty.

I nodded and resumed my place. I closed my eyes once more and breathed in and out, tried to see, tried to think and believe.

"In black... AND!"

Something was pushing to come through but I didn't know what, something different. Shit, I'd have had Stalin if he'd wanted to give it a go. I

341

took a step forward, then another step. I was so off-balance that I nearly fell over, but I opened my eyes just quickly enough to dodge the metal stool that flew towards me with an almighty crash. I looked at Rex, whose face remained calm.

"Fuck you!" he said, and promptly left the room.

Sorcha put her arm around me in the break-out space. Rex had simply refused to direct me anymore, suggesting that I get out of his cunting sight before he does something he regrets.

"Don't get despondent," she said, pulling me closer into her heaving bosom. "He's like this with everyone when they first start. It's like he's disappointed that he has to put in any work himself."

"But it's so silly," I snivelled, unable to really cry, just look bright red and be consumed with feelings of inadequacy. "I mean, I couldn't even get the first few steps right."

"Oh, that's rubbish, you were nervous that's all. Once you've gone the first round with him it gets easier, you just need to get used to his tirade of abuse."

"But I don't want to have to get used to it, I don't want to be spoken to like that, it's totally unnecessary."

"Sorry, hon, that's his method and you have to accept it." Her comfort was sympathetic but her tone wasn't. "If you can't, then it's best if you just go. It's not worth putting yourself through it unless you are really serious about it."

"I don't want to go. I just want to go back to how it was, dicking around in class, having a laugh, being with my old friends. Dealing with Rex in minimal doses, that's all I want." I was moaning now. I was going through the stages of denial incredibly quickly.

"Sorry, Simon, that's no longer an option. You've reached the Faustus point, sold your soul. It's either forward or nothing. And you have to act fast because Rex won't wait around for you to buck your ideas up. The play itself is in two and a half weeks, you think he's got time to spare? He's probably already signing up your replacement. You have to toughen up and it has to be now." She moved away. "And as for your friends, they won't understand your plight. It's probably best to forget them for now. I had to leave so many behind when Rex offered me this opportunity. They got so jealous, tried to make me feel bad about moving forward, and I didn't have the wherewithal to put up with their bitterness. It was tough but I feel better for it."

I wondered whether that was what Lulu had been trying to do to me earlier. These mind games were driving me mad.

"What about the people in the group?"

"The boys are nice, Patrick, Lisle and Brian, Philippe's a bit of a bitch. Kerry can be a bit hard-nosed but she's harmless really, Isabella's a bit of a dumb slut and Sharron is quite a pointless entity. Hilary is a case; poor girl struggles to keep up with the others but she's perfect for the older matriarchal roles that often come up. You know my feelings on Cecelia, a horrible, vicious cowbag. I keep my friends and my study separate now, it's easier. I'm glad you're here though." She smiled and I immediately wanted her to adopt me I was so in need of a bit of support.

"I'm glad I found you too. I'm sure I'll be fine." I had a mini-rush of elation that spurred me on to think positively for a split-second.

"You will. Come back tomorrow, and if it goes the same, then see what he says, but don't you dare come in with no fight. You can't let him get the opportunity to make you feel like shite twice in as many days."

We walked out together and she patted me lightly on the head.

"Now go get 'em tiger!" she laughed and off she went. My thoughts immediately went back to Tim's t-shirt.

As I walked, I turned my phone on, feeling a touch better. There was a text from Beez:

Here, queer and loving it dear! Weather is sublime, surf school is total dive. Don't think he wants me to teach after all, we have to build the fucking thing first. Now THAT I can do! Will call soon. Big love. Xx

I had to laugh. There was Beez grabbing life by the horns, doing something he wanted to do no matter how risky, expensive or crazy. I wished I was like that. Instead I was the first to put obstacles in my way and make excuses for reasons to play safe. I needed to break out of this mould and go for it; stop hiding in the shadows, stand up on that stage and do myself proud.

*

The next night I triumphantly got to the second line before Rex stopped me.

"Er, Simon, kudos on making it into the centre of the fucking stage. How about we have some worthwhile acting now?" His tone was less abrasive.

"Don't take it personally, don't take it personally, don't take it personally" was my new mantra for the evening.

"In black... AND!"

I went to open my mouth to speak, but to avoid making a complete twat of myself, I stopped.

"Sorry, Rex," I said, dropping my book to my side, "I don't know what I'm supposed to be doing."

Surprisingly, he didn't glare at me like I'd committed a cardinal sin, he looked rather taken aback. "Well, anyone watching will have guessed that by now, won't they?" He directed it towards me rather than the company. I chanced it and stole a look at them. Kerry was sneering, while Philippe was leaning forward, transfixed by my actions.

"No, what I mean is that I've been trying so many ways that I'm unsure of how you want me to play it. I feel I'm getting a bit frazzled by the lines." I'd heard the buzzword "frazzled" being tossed around hither and thither. I thought I might impress him by using it in a sentence of my own.

"Well," he said, more relaxed than I had expected, "it takes balls to ADMIT that you're fucking useless, so I'll give you that one. If you'd bothered to do any research, then you would see that Alan IS confused, he IS frazzled, he IS exactly what you fucking are. But since you are more interested in playing the part as Simon, a dull twat trying to unsuccessfully suppress his mania, it's making for incredibly frustrating and banal viewing. In other words, YOU are not allowing yourself to be ALAN. YOU are portraying a shit version of how you think ALAN should be. Consequently, you are neither, just blah and completely unwatchable. Let yourself go!" He stopped.

My God, had I just asked for advice? Had he just answered me? There were a few more expletives than I would ordinarily care for but at least we had got close to having a successful exchange between actor and director.

"I tell you what, let's give you a little tea break to let that information sink in. I know how your type like to be mothered before you can get anywhere. We'll reconvene in ten minutes, when I'll be expecting a minute step in a better direction. Okay?" His words were acid, but he swept out of the room with a tiny grin on his face, his sandals squeaking down the hall as the door slamming echoed behind him.

I cast another glance towards the back of the room. Cecelia was looking at me like she might be able to kill me with her retinas alone. Sorcha, sitting behind her, smiled.

For the next ten minutes I stood on my own to collect my thoughts so that I could go back in and do a steady job. I started to think about my own situation; I was tired, emotionally blasted, weak and troubled. Rather than heighten these emotions, I thought it best to just play them as they were within me, raw and muted.

Rex still stopped me, made me do things again, but I tried to zone out his threats and tune more into the pain and the struggle. The whole thing took another two hours, by which time I was beginning to see the light but using so much emotional energy that I was totally worn out.

"Well, you're a step away from trite," he said at the end of the session, "but at least you've experienced something real. I'm not impressed but I'm not disgusted by your performance. I'm expecting more, much more, which I am now in doubt that you are able to give."

It was something I could use, a sort of backhanded compliment. He strode out of the room.

While I was collecting my bag, I felt someone behind me. I turned and stared Kerry straight in the eye; she was flagged by her two blonde sidekicks, who looked like gargoyles on either side of an ugly steeple.

"Hi, Simon," she said, her voice slicing its way towards my ears. She kept pursing her lips and tossing her head like she was in too much discomfort to speak to me at all.

"Hi... Kerry." I looked across at the other two. Isabella's generous breasts were spilling out of a low-cut top, and the other one, Sharron, was so skinny that it looked like breasts had been the last thing on God's mind when he created her body. A brain was also conspicuous by its absence.

"Yeah, look, I wanted to say that I know you're being given a tough time and I think you should just get on with it."

I didn't know where this conversation was going. As openers went it was fairly lousy. I kind of suspected that now I was beginning to make progress, this vile little climber was after a piece of the action. "Look, Kerry, I don't need another lecture. I've had quite enough for two days, thank you."

"I'm not having a go. I just think you might benefit from having a helping hand. I know it's not easy to be put on the spot in such a pressured situation."

"I'm sorry, why do you care? You've done nothing but look at me like I'm a skid mark in your boyfriend's pants for the best part of three days." I was not in the mood for any more shit, least of all from this one and her two idiot stooges.

Kerry smirked. "I do care! I might be a little standoffish at first, but that's only because you have to be in a place like this. Show any kind of mercy and no one takes you seriously."

I applauded her for owning up to that; maybe she was harmless after all. "Okay, well you could have cooled it a little; it hasn't exactly been easy for me either."

"Well, I'm extending an olive branch now. Aren't we, girls?" The other two nodded their heads. It was like watching some low-rent *Thunderbirds* episode.

"Okay, well thanks."

"Look, I thought I'd give you a heads up. I can see you're looking a bit tired and I think the whole thing might be getting to you a bit, so to get yourself up to speed, I'd recommend these." She presented me with a cylindrical tube. The label read: "High Wire – Caffeine Supplement".

"Sorry, what is this?" I was confused as I studied the tube for a moment.

"They're pep pills, a slight pick-me-up. I'm guessing you're not sleeping too well, spending endless nights poring over the script."

"Well, yes and no." I didn't really know how to take it all.

"These will just give you a boost. Take one before rehearsals and you'll perk right up. Rex's insults just drift over your head. Honestly, they're amazing." The other two nodded in unison again.

"Why are you giving me these?"

"Someone gave them to me when I first started and they made my life so much easier. In consequence, the rest of the company felt at ease too."

I took a moment to think about what she was saying. Being continually berated by Rex had given me a certain fight, a surge of confidence that I had not possessed before.

"So let me get this straight," I said. "You want me to drug myself up so that you get a chance to get on the stage quicker? You're unbelievable."

She sighed. "Fine. If that's what you think, then I'm not gonna argue with you. Do it your own way, let's see how that works."

"I will. If I'm going to smash it, then I want to do it because of my talent, not because of mind-bending narcotics. Where's the skill in that?"

"Like I said," she leant closer, "do it your way, see if I care."

Her minions looked me up and down like I was the biggest fool to ever walk the earth, and then the three of them spun round and sashayed off. The sodding cheek of it! She wasn't harmless at all, she was dangerous! I shoved the pills in my pocket; I would throw them in the bin on the way home. I had better not leave them around the house; Flowers was bad enough without added caffeine. I had caught her dusting an aloe vera plant before now, heaven knows what might happen under the influence of High

348

Wire. I blew Sorcha a kiss before I left, and she mimed grabbing it and throwing it at the back of Cecelia's head from behind her.

I smiled and looked at my phone. There was still no word from Lulu; I had texted her on my way home last night apologising for yesterday's drama. She was choosing not to answer me. Maybe she was jealous; maybe she was trying to make me suffer. Maybe I should call her or Sophie, Ricky or Liana. I felt like I hadn't made contact with that world in years, not just days. I suddenly thought better of it, remembering Sorcha's words. Perhaps it was better to forget that they ever existed.

I spent virtually the whole night reading the play; the words were barely going in. I was so used to the page layouts now that it was like watching an old movie like *Dirty Dancing*; you know it frame by frame so the plot loses all meaning. Not that it's got much plot!

I had hardly seen Freya this week; she must think I'm such a terrible friend. Normally, we would sit and watch at least one *Great British Bake Off* episode together but this week, nada. I thought about her when I was watching a profiterole tower being assembled without anyone there to discuss it with. Before I knew it, it was three am and I was no nearer to sleep. I had to be up in four hours, it didn't bear thinking about. I ploughed on regardless.

One, maybe two hours' sleep meant that I was almost asleep at my desk. It was only when Pepe asked me to do something that I realised I was actually nodding off and a translucent stream of drool was running down my arm.

"Wha—?" I asked in a slumber-induced haze.

"Could you sort out the subscription spreadsheet if you please?" he whinged. Surely "if you please" was a catchphrase from a hideous sitcom based on ethnic stereotypes. People didn't really say it, did they? I did as he asked by making up a few numbers and throwing them onto an Excel template. This wasn't like me. Normally, just because I didn't care it didn't mean that I wasn't diligent.

I noticed that Sandra and Clarissa had started to bond over the photocopier. I could hear their guffawing from all the way over here. I didn't feel angry or annoyed; I felt upset and left out. Despite all my moaning I did appreciate Clarissa, and I had now driven a wedge between us for no real reason. But I couldn't back down because backing down would mean that I lost the fight, and if I lost the fight here, then I would lose the fight with Rex. I wanted to go up to them and say something witty as I would have done in the past; teased Sandra about her crazy dancing or told Clarissa about some dreadful play that I had seen with midgets in it or something. But my world had changed, I had changed and I couldn't go back. As Sorcha had said, it was forward or nothing. So I grabbed my bag and lowered my head as I walked past them to the exit.

Here I was, back in the space, exposed for Rex to pick at. Kerry had nodded to me as I walked in. She and the rest of Team Vacuous were unsure of how to play it with me now that I had tangled with them. I would have to watch my step with Kerry; she was clearly willing to do whatever it took to get on top. She would probably even consider getting on top of Rex.

"Well," Rex exclaimed when he saw me, "you look like shit."

Never mind the Old School, I'd have settled for the charm school at this point.

"I've been up learning lines," I mumbled.

"No one's asking you to sacrifice your sleep, Simon. If you're doing that, then you're never going to get this acting lark up to any standard. You'll never be able to keep your bastard eyes open."

What did he want from me? I couldn't work it out.

"Nevertheless, in black... AND!"

I didn't get far.

"Back in Dullard Town, are we then? Are we going to make any sense of the part or are we all just standing here wasting our fucking time? And again."

It was no better.

"You know the thing I hate most about you?" he said, after a few moments of painful contemplation. "It's that you're a pretender. You don't even try to go to the places that one should try reaching. You're just a run-of-the-mill, common or garden pretender. And I don't have the space for pretenders in my school."

He started to walk out. Surely this was going to be my last chance and I couldn't let him win.

"What am I meant to do?" I called out after him. He stopped at the door, his face contorted with rage.

"Do you want me to GET UP THERE AND DO IT FOR YOU?" he roared. "Okay."

He strode over in a whirl of madness and sweat. He snatched the book from my hand so fast that I nearly lost two fingers in the process.

"This is how you're doing it." He began to read in a high voice, mincing around the stage and flapping his arms like a crazy pigeon. It was mortifying and totally inaccurate. "Could you watch that SHIT for an hour?" He threw the book at me. It hit my chest and fell to the floor.

Again he made for the door.

"How do I make it better?" I asked.

"Well, let's try ACTING for a start, shall we?" he said, and waited for an answer. When no answer came, he continued. "Because quite honestly I think you should fuck off elsewhere if you need to go back to basics. I'm certainly not a kindergarten teacher."

He left the room. All eyes were on me. I was exhausted from it all; I thought that this was probably the end of the road and the thought hit me so fast that I ran from the stage and into the toilets. I threw myself into a cubicle and sank to my knees. The crying was silent, a flood of tears came out in short, intense bursts. When I saw that there was no toilet paper, I fumbled in my pocket for a hanky. I pulled out something else, the pep pills that Kerry had given me. I'd not yet thrown them away. Wiping my eyes with the back of my hand, I stood up.

"To hell with it!" I thought and pulled the top off the bottle, shaking two small, brown, circular tablets that looked like little sheep pellets into my hand. Before I could stop myself, I threw them back and stumbled over to the sink to drink some water from my cupped hands. I looked at myself in the mirror. As I saw my eyes, red, puffy and swollen, and the tracks of my tears running down my pale face, I saw a different man staring back at me, one who was almost broken. But I wasn't broken yet. I was still breathing, I was still standing. Hell, I was even crying. "So you will not break me Rex," I said aloud. "This, my friend, is the last time you'll see me cry. I'll see you die before you see me cry again. This is on, the game is on." I got closer to the mirror and took a long hard look at myself. After a few moments, I walked out of the bathroom with my head held high and a stream of toilet paper stuck to my shoe.

3

A ripple of gossip was making its way around the room. Would I last? Would I crumble and beg for mercy? How would I ever make my way back from the hell of my own making? Rex had not come back into the room last night and I had been forced to listen to the half-baked advice from my peers:

"You'll never survive if you give in so easily."

"You need to block out the insults, breathe, start again."

"Go and see him, defend your honour."

"Forget that Rex is there, he's forcing you to ignore his presence."

There were so many handy hints and tips that I felt utterly weighed down by it all. With that and the added pressure of having to do a good job, I believed that I was metamorphosing into some subhuman species, functioning only on nervous energy, guilt and misery. I had swallowed another two tablets on the bus home and they had started to kick in around eleven pm, when I got a sudden explosion of vitality and had a strong desire to do something creative. I spent all night rehearsing my lines in various ways, crawling along the floor, acting the fool, in floods of make-believe tears. If Freya had been up, then she would have probably thought I was having a nervous breakdown. I automatically felt better about being more prepared but I'd had absolutely no sleep. It didn't seem to matter. I was sprightly, focused. I didn't care that my body and mind had had no time to rest and recuperate, so I continued and wouldn't stop until I dropped.

I decided to take on a massive mailmerge at work: writing to all of our members and asking them to update their details so that I could amend the database. Sandra nearly fell off her chair. She could tell that ordinarily I didn't give a flying crap about the database, but it would give her something to muse on with Clarissa. Now that we were drifting apart, I needed

SOMETHING to keep myself occupied. I even gave Cordelia the letter to proofread. She was so taken aback that I swear she had to look up "proofread" in the dictionary just to make sure I wasn't having her on. When she handed it back, I was already sticking down envelopes.

Pepe smiled up at Cordelia with a sickening smile as if he had whipped me into shape, not over-the-counter zing pills. At lunchtime my teeth began to chatter so I threw another tablet down my neck. What the hell! It was only caffeine and caffeine isn't dangerous. I'm sure I'd read about people drinking cup after cup of coffee before now, this couldn't be that different.

When the day was over, I practically skipped to school and up the steps. I had learnt not to look at the people out front from my old life who were watching me. If I made direct eye contact, then they had the power to disembowel me with their hard, judgemental stares.

And here I was, standing in the elite's rehearsal space, being judged once again. It seemed there was nowhere to run from the big monster of scrutiny. My turmoil seemed to amuse Cecelia. She took great comfort in knowing that I was all twisted up inside, a twist that was emphasised because of the amount of caffeine coursing through my veins. Surely it was enough to send a hippo into a disco fit. I had visions of just going and slapping Cecelia, channelling all the energy I had, all the torment and rage, and planting the biggest handprint straight across that smug face of hers. A smack that was so hard that she'd have to spit a few teeth out in the process. Then I'd grab that stupid hair of hers and smash her face repeatedly into the nearest available wall. And the worst thing, I'd feel absolutely no remorse. Kerry sauntered past. I could smell her cheap perfume a mile off.

"God, Simon, I recommended that you took one or two pills, not the whole bottle. You look like crap." She was right but I wasn't about to have that. The pills wouldn't allow me to feel fear.

"So what's your fucking excuse?" was my impeccably timed response. She scoffed and walked away. As she did, the door opened. Rex's aura came in first. It was one of regal defiance; he was going to be firm in the face of adversity, the adversity being my crap acting. He strode in, rolling the ever-present cigarette between his forefinger and thumb. I could see from here that his fingers were beginning to turn yellow. My God! How much did you have to smoke before it started colouring your skin? He looked calm; I thought maybe I was off the hook. How naïve!

"Sit down, company." We all did as we were told. I was starting to have funny little hallucinations from all the caffeine. The pattern on the disgusting carpet looked as though it was moving in straight trenches up and under Rex's feet.

"I chose this play," he began, looking purposefully up into the air, "because of its depth. This is not a common or garden retelling of a banal foray into the world of mental health. Neither does it serve as an agitprop for some kind of political viewpoint on behalf of the writer. It is neither psychobabble intended to shock or encourage controversy nor a piece that is played purely for entertainment with its nudity and brutalism. I chose it because it is a play that needs to be uncomfortable, that needs to twist and turn in the actions of the actors and the audience. It is a play that sits unnaturally within the cerebral imagery that one might encounter within their lifetime. It is not merely a bitter pill that someone swallows and is then passed through the course of their system only to be expelled after a good meal and a good night's sleep."

As he went on, I began to drift in and out of consciousness. His figure blurred then sharpened as the crazy shapes continued to move beneath him.

"This piece is a tragedy, but not like you might hear a child's scream in the night. It is seeing your loved one hanging inside an open closet, seeing your family pet drowned in a swimming pool, watching the love of your life fucking another person and looking at them with the same passion that they once used to look at you, being told your baby hasn't survived, cutting the name of the bullies who taunt you into aggressive marks across your skin."

I swallowed hard. I hadn't considered this kind of weight. Through my high haze I knew instantly that I had taken the wrong path. From day one I had taken the wrong path, and my current state was just about the worst place I could be at this very moment. Rex stopped and looked at the floor, letting those hard-hitting words sink into every one of us. He then turned his head towards me. His look was one of total abhorrence.

"And you have the barefaced nerve to show up today," he said, looking me straight in the eye.

I burst through the door, wrestling the pills out of my bag and throwing them in the nearest bin. That had been intense but not hopeless. Rex had thrown down the gauntlet and it was up to me to pick it up and run with it. Clearly this was a different league altogether and I had to work even harder to survive. It was not enough to simply walk into the room with the lines down, having stupidly practised the part in myriad pointless ways that made no sense whatsoever in the grand creative process. I had to live this not clown it like I had so many times before. This was a real and dangerous process, anything less would simply not be tolerated. I hadn't argued the toss with Rex. I had merely pushed past him and left the room, which was a big risk to take. He might already be recasting me as I walked out but that wasn't my issue. All the time I thought I had been fighting, I hadn't been fighting at all. I had been merely playing. Fighting came with taking risks, jumping without a parachute into the abyss, not knowing whether you'd even come up for air. If this was going to happen, then it was no good going home and reading and reading until my eyes and my head were sore. I was going to have to do something far more earth-shattering, I was going to have to live like Alan, breathe like Alan, become Alan, the petrified little boy who is so confused and plagued by religious and sexual dark images that he feels compelled to pick up a sharp object and drive it into the eyeballs of his favourite animals to hear them scream out in tumultuous agony. Then and only then would Alan's torment be appeased and his spirit laid to rest. This was heavy shit, the kind that would never be resolved though pep pills, late nights and endless study. This was down to life experience.

I pulled out my phone and started dialling. It went to answerphone.

"Hi, Ricky, how are you? Look, I know you're in class and I'm so sorry that I've been out of the loop. It's been a bit of a struggle trying to juggle everything and I just want you to know that it was never personal. I just didn't know what to do. Erm, I'm wondering whether you can get your hands on any coke, mate? I'll pay. I just fancy a few lines."

I knew that Ricky would never turn down the offer of having a night out on the grams. Even if he wanted to, the temptation wouldn't let him.

"I'm going to go to Davy's now. Give me a call and meet me in there after school if you can, mate. We'll make a night of it."

I hung up. I didn't know whether I was doing the right thing. All I knew was that I had to get into an unrecognisable state to really give this part gravitas. I couldn't go into that room tomorrow like a frightened little lamb. If necessary, I would try every single thing out there to get me suitably fired up for an uneven and unpredictable performance. For one second I realised the opportunity I had been given, and in total secret I thanked the cunt that had

357

given it to me.

I was just downing my third vodka when the door opened and a gust of March wind blew out the candle on my table. I had spent the remaining time between leaving school and sitting here taking a walk down a distressing memory lane. I knew who the best person to think of was: the witch, aka my ex-stepmother Faye. Although it had been fourteen years since I had last seen that woman's face, the mere thought of it would make my hands involuntarily clench into bloodless fists and my teeth begin to bare all on their own. I remembered her pinched nose, her dry hair, her terrible dress sense, and her acrid breath from the multiple bridge work that she had had done as a teenager. The way she used to rub her hands in glee as my sister Martha and I cowered at her mercy, the way she circled us as a bloodthirsty vulture might circle two vulnerable and frightened deer. The way she used to pile on the guilt after we had asked whether we could spend more time with our mother:

"You must really HATE your father to act in such a way."

"Your father and I have decided that you are the most conceited, spoilt little children that were ever given the opportunity to walk the earth. You will sit at my table, but you will not dare to eat my food until you have apologised for being so rude to me in my own house."

It wasn't her house, it had been my father's, but as children we had never known the ins and outs of their financial situation. In years to come we were to realise that that money-grabbing, horrendous streak of muck had clung onto our father like a limpet, fleecing him of every bit of money he had and purging every emotion he had ever felt and any bond he had ever had with his children. How could someone have acted in such a way towards two defenceless kids? But then, one can be dangerously contorted with jealousy, and Faye was so jealous of our mother that she could barely see straight to tie the laces on those hideous dance shoes that she always insisted on wearing. She could see our mother in us, in our faces and mannerisms, and she thought that by getting to us, she was getting to our mother. Dad had not known which path to take, dominated as he was by such an evil force. She was like the hard-nosed schoolmistress in a Dickensian novel, punishing the children unfairly with any weapon she could lay her hard hands on. All I remembered of Dad was that he had looked tired, emotionally drained and weak. He had dangled on her puppet strings for so long that he looked as though he had fought enough between his heart and his conscience to break a little of his spirit.

Once when I was eleven and off to a party, Faye grabbed me and started telling me about where she would be when I got back. She talked a lot with her hands and, to better understand, I watched her many gesticulations. Out of nowhere she went to slap me hard around the face.

"Don't you EVER make fun of me when I am talking to you," she spat, her eyes wild, bloodshot and watering. The woman was so full of hate and rage that she was practically in tears. I went red and fought back the tears but I was used to it, this kind of situation happened often. I used to hear her talking on the phone, telling people that when we came to live at their house, we could barely use a knife and fork and we didn't know how to brush our teeth or wash properly. It was all rubbish of course but it made her look better, like our saviour. She was so full of shit that I swear she'd even convinced herself that these lies were true. Little did she know that I would regularly sneak into her wardrobe while they were both at work, pick my nose, and wipe it down the insides of her dresses. It helped a little knowing that while she was berating me in front of my father, she was oblivious to the fact that she was covered in my snot.

Once she even found a story that I had written, one that documented my life with all the names and places changed. She read it out at a family dinner, much to my horror, parading around the table and shrieking the worst bits in a mocking tone that sent shivers down my spine. She then threw the script at me and promptly ignored me for the next three days, only to then act as if nothing had happened. Sometimes I wished she had hit me. At least with physical pain, it is temporary. Once you feel the sting of a punch or a slap, you know what you are dealing with and it is easier to manage. Words are harder to gauge; you don't know how deep the conviction is behind them, how dark a person's motives are, what they really think of you and what they might do next. Living with her was like sleeping with a ticking time-bomb under your pillow, never knowing when it was going to explode or whether you would survive the fallout.

In the end I left, ran away to my mother's. It was so easy; I couldn't understand why I had never done it before. I had waited in the hope that it would get better, believing that she would see the good in me and that all those years of abuse and neglect were just because she loved me and wanted me to be the best that I could be. But her treatment never changed. One day I just decided to leave. I had started college and the school bullies that had tormented me all through my teens had disappeared. People were no longer seeing me for what I was but for who I could be. I was no longer the filthy poof, the queer who had no personality, who was just wrong and rotten to the core, a belief that Faye seemed to support. They started to see me as Simon, a person who felt, lived, breathed, saw beauty, loved and created. I got stronger and decided that if I was going to rid myself of people who were unwilling to give me a chance, then I would have to get rid of their master. I packed a bag to stay at Mum's and never went back home. I didn't know I was going to do it, I just did it. I didn't know that the final goodbye I said to her was to be the last so there was no weight behind it; it was just an ordinary goodbye. Perhaps it was better that way. I often fantasised about saying goodbye and pushing her down the stairs, listening to her neck break against the final step and merely walking over her limp, lifeless body to get to the door, or taking a baseball bat to the kitchen and aiming a swift blow at her smug, ugly face. But maybe I did it the best way possible. In time, Dad told me that he was glad I had done it and that I had been brave to withstand it for so long. All I could do was nod. If I had learnt to be brave from anyone, then it certainly wasn't from him.

I very rarely went back to these memories; they just used to anger me so much. They were full of questions and very few acceptable answers. I felt that moving on from this difficult time was a much better option, but then I think that it has coloured my relationships and affected my confidence because I never, ever felt good enough. Perhaps this is why I couldn't ever let something in and the emotion out in acting classes. It seemed that I was so hell-bent on protecting myself that I had constructed an inner guard that was solid and unmovable. As I sat here, getting more and more inebriated, I began to see a dark shroud envelop me. I believed that this was where I was meant to be going in order to reach out to Alan a little more.

Ricky came over to the table.

"Wotcha!"

"Hi, Ricky, you got my message, excellent. You want a drink?" This wasn't the time to be maudlin, I needed to convince Mr Hellman that we should go on the bender to end all benders.

"Yeah, I'll have a drink. Want a line?"

It was music to my ears. As he chuckled and I made my way to the bar, I was partially satisfied. This little experiment had better work. If I could convince Rex that he had been absolutely correct in choosing me to play Alan, then I might prove my worth not only to him, but also to the bitter memories of my stepmother. I was going to do this by going to an unrecognisable place, a place where fear, torment and anguish reigned supreme, the deep, dark recesses of the human spirit. I was going to attempt to go to the place that most human beings spend their whole lives trying to avoid. I was heading for rock bottom.

Luckily, Ricky had been easy to convince. We started off with a few lines in Davy's. The barmaid had eyed us suspiciously as we took turns to nip to the bathroom, but Ricky turned on his million-dollar smile and she beamed back as all the ladies did when they succumbed to the old boy's charms. Seeing as Ricky had kindly supplied the drugs, I paid for the drinks. I was perennially careful with money but I thought it would do me good to not count every last penny tonight. If I was going to step out of my comfort zone, then I would have to go at it hammer and tongs, do without all the creature comforts that I held so dear.

"So how did you get yourself into this pickle then, mate?" Ricky asked. The coke was making us feel very uninhibited. Suddenly, any ill feeling or self-consciousness between us was gone.

"Mate, I didn't know what to pissing do! Rex had me over a barrel. I couldn't just carry on as normal. I had to get on with it and I'm afraid it meant upsetting a few people. It was never personal."

"How is it, you know, on the other side?" He winced as he downed a hefty slug of bottled lager.

"I can't explain it, buddy, I really can't. It's like nothing you've ever experienced, abuse on another level. You know what that bastard is like." I hesitated a moment before asking, "I expect everyone hates me, do they?"

"They'll get over it. Jealousy is a lonely emotion."

It was at that moment that I realised how much I really did love Ricky. Not in a sexual way but in a real brotherly, no shit, supportive kind of way. Of all the people you could meet in such a fickle place as drama school, I had someone here who just allowed me to be me. And though we seemed poles apart, we had a similar vision. We were both trying to make sense of our crazy selves. I had a sudden urge to kiss him.

"You know, Ricky, you really are bloody fantastic."

"Simey boy, if I liked pricks up my arse, then you'd be the first one I'd ask."

I didn't have the heart to tell him that if we ever did end up in bed together, it would probably be the other way around.

Ricky managed to get us into some seedy club in Soho. The kind of club that was so exclusive that it was just a door on a street. He seemed to know the bouncers, who nodded us in and gave Ricky some kind of secret handshake. I wondered whether it was some kind of Masonic gesture but I kept quiet.

Inside was pure debauchery. The walls practically dripped lust and sweat brought on by the copious amounts of drug use. Wide-eyed, slack-jawed women were draped over beefy black guys who were decorated in gold jewellery. Unsteady stick-thin, fake-breasted waifs swayed uneasily to the thumping French house music. Ricky saw someone he knew so we made our way over and positioned ourselves in his group of friends. These people were chewing their lips and talking in riddles the whole time. I sat next to a girl who said that she worked for the AA breakdown service. She was so off her tree that at various points in the conversation she put me on hold and asked me to give her my registration details.

I was loving it, not worrying about money or the world outside, being a part of this pure, unadulterated hedonism that lived in the moment. Ricky managed to score some more drugs so we spent the whole time riding a sea of euphoria. I'd had no sleep and was happily running on empty.

When we left at five am, my head felt like a big vibrating ball. The bin men and road-sweepers looked at me with big glacial eyes, unfazed by the bedraggled night cat that walked towards them with a vacant look on its face. The natural light burned my retinas; it looked superimposed, as though someone had painted the sky. It was only when I reached the bus stop that I realised Ricky was not with me. I thought I had had a full conversation with him while we had been walking, but obviously not. When I got home, Flowers was on her way out. She did little to disguise her horrified look as I staggered to the front door and launched myself through it. She wasn't my bloody mother so she could piss right off. I would have said as much but I didn't want to argue with her at the moment. I was still a bit loved up.

I splashed a little water on my face and wrestled myself into a change of clothes, careful not to look in the mirror and face my reflection. As I threw my jeans onto the bed, a small wrap of white powder fell out. It was wrapped in cling film. I couldn't remember where it had come from. I picked it up and examined it. Oh well, if I was going to do it wrong, I should do it right. I racked up a line and snorted it through an old flyer that I had fashioned into a straw. It wasn't coke, it was far too aggressive. I stumbled to the toilet and retched into the bowl. My head spun in all directions, a searing pain shot through my temples. I slumped at the end of my bed and massaged the sides of my head. I don't know how, but while I waited for the agony to subside, the words from the play began to spill out of my mouth. I knew they were in the right order but I didn't know what they meant. I kept saying them as I got to my feet, grabbed my bag and made for the door, ricocheting off the walls as I did so. The pain started to dull and as it did, the nasty, bitter powder slipped down the back of my throat, making me gag a few times. With the pulsing throb almost gone from my temples, I felt a rush of something else, something new. It was making me bleary-eyed and my limbs flaccid.

I wobbled out of the front door; the sunlight was like razorblades to my eyeballs. My brain sloshed around like a spongy ball inside my skull. I kept repeating Alan's words and I would do so until they sounded like my own. People were looking at me but such was London that they were not really moved. They'd seen it all before. I sat down at the bus stop and watched the traffic going by as if it was some kind of film. The most depressing thing was that even though I felt as though I was brain-dead, I knew exactly how I was going to get to work.

The words on the screen merged into one. I could barely focus, and when Pepe shuffled into the office at ten, I kept my head down so that he wouldn't see that my eyes were the size of dinner plates. I must have looked like something off *Dr Who*. I still didn't have the nerve to look at my reflection. I remembered seeing my friend's face the first night that I ever tried Ecstasy. It was the late nineties and we were in a terrible student dive in my home town. My friend Harvey was totally out of it and was staring at me, wide-eyed and loose-jawed. I was a little out of it myself but not enough to not notice how much his face had changed. It was frightening and intriguing all at the same time. We all sat there looking like it, spitting out random words, our eyeballs rolling and teeth gnashing like a bunch of cartoon wolves. We once invited a girl who was totally anti-drugs back to the flat. In secret, we were all popping pills in the bathroom. Hours later she ran screaming from the place after describing us coming towards her like a pack of zombies, chatting away about nothing and reaching out to hug her with a million arms.

I was worried that I might feel like that poor girl if I caught sight of my reflection this morning. Horror of horrors: Pepe didn't just go to his desk; he began to shuffle over to my desk.

"Er... Seemon." I hated the way he said my name. If I thought about it too much, then I'd lay into him and probably be fired on the spot. "I need that report for the memberships, the one that you does every year. I need it last week."

I vaguely recalled doing something last year, some kind of round-up of all the membership sales for the last fiscal year. Sandra and I had completed the report together, but it seemed that she had conveniently forgotten to badger me about it, probably because she now didn't care whether I got in the shit or possibly because she didn't want to spend another second in my company. Either way, it made me feel down. I was careful not to look up at Pepe. If I did, then it would be like that moment in the vampire movie when a friend sees the undead for the first time, a trickle of blood running from its mouth. Not that I was a vampire, and not that Pepe was any kind of a friend.

"Sandra is happy to go through it with you this afternoon. We really need it done."

He was speaking for her now, was he? I wanted to reply with some kind of clever quip, but all I could manage was, "Fine".

I kept my eyes fixed on Pepe's shoes. He was hesitating as if he wanted to broach a topic with me but didn't have the nerve. He was probably intending to tell me that I looked like shit or wanting to check that I hadn't died because I hadn't moved all morning. Maybe he had the same thoughts about my possibly being a vampire because he didn't bother in the end. He just shuffled back to his desk. For once in all the time I had been there, I actually considered reaching out to him, telling him I was losing control. I don't know why, I just felt vulnerable now I was taking risks for the sake of my art. In that split second I longed to return to the normal world. I somehow felt that it was a little too late. Whatever chemical I had consumed was now wearing off and I needed someone to tell me that I would be okay. If only Pepe could promise me that he would keep me safe until this sorry business was over. But then London isn't like that. When you're off the rails, people don't sympathise. There would be a queue of people outside who weren't off the rails and they could jump into your shoes as quickly as you leapt out of them.

I still had the wrap in my pocket. If I could just nip to the loo and dab a bit on my gums as a little pick-me-up, then I would be a bit more sorted, I might even be able to sustain a lucid front throughout my meeting with Sandra. I waited until the coast was clear before casually strolling out through the door and into the toilets on the floor below. As the door opened, I nearly crashed into the person on the other side. It was Craig. I had forgotten that he even existed. I committed the cardinal error and looked up. He went to ignore me but he took a second look and his face went from a look of disgust to one of horror. I couldn't ignore it, but I didn't have time for this bullshit.

"Yes?" I barked.

"Nothing." His tone was equally dismissive.

"Good." I pushed past him to the toilet cubicle.

"Simon!" he called. I turned and looked at him. He'd seen my face now, there was no point trying to disguise it.

"Yes?"

"You look... terrible."

I didn't know whether this was concern or whether he was just stating a fact. I went for the latter.

"Why thank you, how charming!"

"Okay, I was just saying." His attitude was so immature. He bored me. I just wanted to get into my little den of iniquity and get back on the road to escapism.

"Well, don't just say. I'm not interested in anything you have to just say."

He shrugged and shook his head. "Okay. Well, I thought I might just say that you look like a pile of shit today but, hey, it's obviously a look you're going for." He went to leave.

I couldn't stop myself, before I knew what was happening the words had escaped my lips. "And I must say that you're the crappest shag I have ever had and you should keep your opinions to yourself. Now piss off!"

He didn't expect that; it threw him totally off guard and he looked close to tears. I didn't wait for a response; I just wrenched open the cubicle door and pushed my way in. I heard the door slam outside; I was surprised that it didn't come off its hinges. I was sad that I had hurt him but I couldn't allow myself to feel remorse now. If one regret came into my head, then I'd regret it all. Alan didn't regret anything; he just acted on pure impulse. And with that in mind I racked up two lines of the vile white powder, one for Pepe and one for Craig.

The meeting with Sandra was hell itself. My head began throbbing halfway through and none of the numbers made sense. I would have struggled to remember one to ten, never mind the complex figures of all the varying membership fees that Eco Scene had managed to dream up seemingly at random that stretched out before me. Sandra was tight-lipped and impassive. I could feel our relationship shrivelling up in front of our very eyes like an overcooked onion.

"November, eight pounds, Mrs Stallett," she said; the words were dry and bereft of feeling.

I looked down at the spreadsheet. I had created the damn thing but I could have written it in Arabic for all the sense it made to me now.

"Erm... I'm not sure."

She drummed her nails on the desk, which was not only rude, but with my headache in full swing, each nail sounded like a donkey being thrown at a double-glazed window. After a minute I wasn't getting any closer and I needed someone to blame. I took my head out of my hands and nodded towards her fingers.

"I'm sorry, can you stop that, it's really annoying." She huffed and folded her arms. She was clearly another one who acted like a two-year-old when faced with confrontation. "Look, I can't see the – oh, here it is! Did you say Mrs Taylor?"

"S-T-A-L-L-E-T-T." She spelled it out like she was talking to an imbecile. Oh God, this was awful!

"Look, why don't I just complete this bloody thing on my own, you're obviously not with us today."

I looked up a little too quickly and all the colours from her chequered shirt blended together for an instant.

"What's that supposed to mean?" Even though I felt like hell, I was not willing to back down from this fight.

"Well, you're fannying about with those papers and we're not getting anywhere so it might just be easier if I do it myself."

"What's with the attitude? I'm trying my best." I suddenly had the urge to throw up.

"Don't you DARE talk to me like that, who do you think you are?" Her look was intense and full of rage. She began to bare her nails like a puma ready to pounce.

"Well, I'll tell you who I'm NOT; I'm not one of your kids so you don't have to talk to me like I am one."

"Don't bring my kids into this. How dare you bring—"

"Oh whatever, Sandra." I pushed the papers over to her side of the desk. "Do the thing yourself then if you want to. In fact, enjoy it. I've got other work to do." I got up to leave.

"I doubt you'll manage to do much other work in the state you're in." She had waited this long to really stick the knife in and she was savouring every word.

I stopped, seemingly to process this information. In reality, I was letting a wave of nausea pass. How had we got to this stage? Weren't we friends at one point? How could she treat me like one of the others in this place who we used to collectively tut and roll our eyes at?

"What are you insinuating?" I challenged her, leaning forward. I fought hard to focus on her. It was a miracle that I could focus on anything at all.

"You look like you've been hitting the pipe." It was her turn to lean forward. Had we had them, our horns would have been locked.

"Is that the voice of experience?"

I was giving as good as I got. It was about time someone stood up to this woman. She was all mouth and no trousers. Her nostrils started to flare as she went to stand up.

"You little—"

"I tell you what. I've got a better idea, how about you mind your own damn business and keep your nose, your stupid hair and your fake talons OUT

OF MINE!"

The voice belonged to me but it sounded like a thing possessed. It was loud, cracked and enraged. Even Sandra looked a bit scared. She'd never dealt with anyone on the edge of insanity before and for once she felt out of her depth. I whisked round and stormed out of the room. I didn't even stop off at my desk; I went straight to the toilets.

"Selfish bitch," I muttered under my breath. I don't know whether I was referring to Sandra or myself.

I sat with my pounding head in my hands for the majority of the day. I hadn't eaten, I hadn't slept. I had had two fairly intense arguments with people that I used to trust and I was totally spinning out. Deep down, however, I could feel it was working. Alan's lines kept resonating in my head, like something was being born within me that I was nurturing.

I was uber-careful to look normal in front of Pepe. Cordelia came to see me at some point about the report. They had obviously caught wind of the fact that I was looking off-colour and behaving erratically and were monitoring me closely. I was certain that it wouldn't be long before I was given my marching orders, but I braved the paranoia until five when I somehow managed to drag myself to school. Doing my usual bull-like stride, casting off looks as I sauntered into the building, I barged my way into the rehearsal room. People looked shocked to see me there, Cecelia in particular. She was probably hoping I'd done the right thing and topped myself.

"God," she scoffed as she passed me on the way out of the door to her locker, "you look like hell. Did somebody die?"

I grabbed her arm, my grip was tight but I didn't care. I pulled her back with such force that even she couldn't help but look surprised.

"Not yet," I snarled at her through gritted teeth, "but if you don't get off my back pretty fucking soon, then you'll be the first on the slab."

She tried to wrench herself free but it only made my hold tighter. "Is that a threat?" she spat, trying to sound calm. She had the grace and elegance of a swan but I could tell that underneath she was paddling frantically in the water.

"You bet!" I said, and threw her arm back at her. She had more sense than to argue with me. It was the first time I had grabbed back my power and I loved it.

When Rex entered the room, he took one look and understood the situation immediately. He didn't question my appearance; he didn't mention my presence.

"Company, we will be going from the top of Alan's scene," he said. "Simon, Lisle, please take your places."

I moved towards the back of the room and stood on the spot. I didn't look at Rex or the others. I didn't even look at Lisle, who was sharing my scene. I waited for Rex's introduction. As if I was hypnotised, I told myself that when the words came, I could let it all go: the altercation with Sandra, the pain on Craig's face, the fact that I was going to lose my job, that I was probably addicted to a white powder that I suspected was probably not what I thought it was, the look of anger and disappointment in my stepmother's eyes all those years ago, full of resentment at the fact that I had been born, the fact that I was violent, aggressive, unhinged, and dangerous to those that stood in my way, and more importantly, that Rex had won the fight.

The words came and I twisted, writhed. I saw little through the dark fog of desperation, my head awash with torture, remorse and anguish. The Alan inside me was like a frightened child searching for a way out of my demon skin. He contorted and screamed in agony. The words belonged to Alan, but they were the voice of the demon, the demon that plagued us both.

Lisle's cool, soothing words seemed to quench the panic just for a second but there was no stopping, there was no end. But then Lisle's and Alan's words stopped and I felt the demon shrink. He backed away, his teeth locked in a crooked smile with sharp teeth, his eyes vacant, his pose rigid. I looked down and realised that I had fallen to the floor. My palms were sore and saliva had dribbled out of my mouth like a leak from an unscrewed bottle top. I could see the company of disbelievers sitting before me with their mouths open. Rex was on his feet, standing over me. I looked up at him with streaming eyes. For a split-second, there was a slight change in his expression before he wiped it off and went back to default. I looked at the clock. The scene had taken minutes but it had felt like hours. There was an eerie silence and all eyes were on me. The shroud of mystery enveloped me like a cloak and I instantly felt cold and vulnerable. What I wouldn't have given for a blanket of some description!

Rex was the first to speak. "Tomorrow we continue," he said, his face unreadable. With that, I watched him promptly leave the room. I didn't want to stay around and face the crowd, I craved solitude and warmth. I wanted to crawl back into the dark hole and wait until tomorrow. If I lost Alan's soul inside me, then it would die and I would never be able to go to this place again. I would lose this moment forever. I grabbed my bag and dashed to the door, hearing Sorcha's voice behind me.

"Simon, WAIT!"

But I didn't. I raced out. Suddenly, I felt like a vampire, fleeing civilisation for the comforting desolation of the dark, cold night. I found myself crouching on the ground in the doorway of a derelict building off Kings Cross, dabbing frantically at the last remnants of the powder and rubbing it into my gums. I had no idea where to go from here. I couldn't mix with the normal and I couldn't go back to the life I had before. I had to get hold of Ricky and get some more of whatever this was. I called him.

"Mate, it was a new one. I don't even know its name but it's cool."

I'd heard the word before but I was pretty sure that it was a new drug to me.

He went on. "Yeah, I can get you some but I'll have to see my man. Are you sure you want more, it's pretty heavy stuff?"

"Ricky, please don't question me. Do you think you can get some tonight?"

"I'll have a go but—"

"Good, I'll meet you after school, yeah, and come with you. I don't care where it is or how long it takes."

He sounded apprehensive, like even he thought this was all a bit hardcore.

"Please!"

He could hear the desperation in my voice.

"Yeah... alright, mate. Give me an hour."

4

A good night's sleep seemed like the furthest thing from me at present. The last two rehearsals had not been perfect but a damn sight better than anything I'd produced before. I had practically given Ricky power of attorney by handing over my debit card and making several withdrawals from the Bank of Trollied.

The paranoid guy who used to check his bank account every three or four minutes was dead; I was his new *don't give a toss* alter ego. I had ignored so many texts from people I hadn't spoken to in ages. I'm surprised that a poster with my face on wasn't posted up around the place. My dad, my mum, my sister, even Beez had texted me a couple of times. It hurt me not to respond to B**eez**, but it would all be to the good in the end.

My days were taken up with trying to act normal at work in between popping to the toilets to shove a bit more horse tranquilliser up my nose, a nose that was so numb with narcotics that it could have dropped off and I wouldn't have felt its absence. Me and my schnoz had become distant companions. Ricky didn't argue with me even though I was beginning to look bedraggled, grey and desperate. He had a moral dilemma on his hands: whether to save his friend or keep on earning enough commission to keep him trussed up in All Saints' tight-fitting gear for yet another season. All I asked for was his trust; it was a win-win situation. I absolved him of all moral responsibility and I got what I wanted. I didn't really know where I was going to go from here. How would this all end? Was I killing myself just to play a part? What would happen when it was all over? Would I just come off the drugs and booze and go back to playing the wholesome parts that I was accustomed to? Didn't Renee Zellweger put on shitloads of weight to play Bridget Jones and then lose it all when filming stopped? This was the same;

after all, she was dicing with her cholesterol and no one around her gave a damn as long as she was true to the book and spoke with a convincing accent. I never saw Freya. I would shrink into my room like I was lurking in the shadows, frightened of the light, condemned to the dark. The plan seemed to be working. It wasn't much fun but I was getting somewhere with Rex. He was becoming more and more excited by the performance I was giving. Yesterday I had had to block the scene where Alan eats with his parents. Brian and Hilary had been like puppets, just as they were supposed to be. I had imagined them as people in my life, Cordelia and Pepe, forcing me into a mundane charade of pseudo-smiling and small talk when mostly I just wanted to smash their skulls against the nearest brick wall.

Rex's direction had been minimal. He hadn't said much except for asking me to rein it in at times when the piece had been a little too self-pitying rather than confused, too knowing rather than oblivious. After each session, he had left the room and I had followed soon after, never allowing those around me to penetrate my concentration. I was a lone ranger in this mission and it seemed to be effective; I couldn't allow anyone to scupper this method.

Clarissa and Sandra now barely registered me. Sometimes I could feel their judgement as I passed them in the corridors but there was nothing they could do. There was no real work on so I wasn't exactly doing anything wrong. A couple of times I nearly bumped into Tim but I had purposefully walked in the other direction to avoid eye contact. In team meetings, I kept my head firmly in my notebook and scribbled Alan's words instead of writing minutes.

My time in the office was limited and I knew that, but then hadn't it always been? Now at least if Cordelia read the riot act, then it would be justified. The same walk up the steps of the school was now a straight road into the pit of Alan's demon and I already felt as though I had crossed my arms across my chest and spiralled into the gaping chasm.

Cecelia was avoiding me at every turn; she knew I was metamorphosing and that my resolve was strengthening. I was beginning to snarl back at her, nip at her heels and let her know that two people could sell their souls for success in this company. She was no longer the only one and she didn't hate me any less for it. I knew, however, that coming up soon would be the scene where Alan was to have sex with Jill, and I would have to work hard to take Cecelia in my arms and kiss her. The kiss in *Hay Fever* with Maeve had been nothing compared with this. This would have to be a different level altogether, the lust furious, wild and climactic.

Today, however, my energy began to wane, something in me began to break and I found the words failing me with each sentence. I knew them but I had reached a peak, a point from which I could now only see the spiral down and not the climb up. This experiment that had been so effective up to now was beginning to take its toll and I was feeling the effects, my throat was dry, my eyes were sore and tired. I felt sick and weak and could barely pull myself up off the seat to drag my feet into position. Rex allowed me to fail twice before he asked the company to leave. Sorcha looked at me. She was concerned but I didn't return her gaze. Even Philippe, who had seemed so cold to me before, now came to ask me if I was okay. I held up my hand to signify that I didn't want to chat even if it was just to check on my well-being. The world around me just seemed to melt. There was only one answer. I waited for the room to be vacated before I frantically tore around in my bag to find my stash, fumbling desperately in every corner until the small white pouch was located. I carefully opened it and hungrily ladled the powder onto my gums. It was so haphazard that flakes cascaded onto the mucky floor, leaving little white deposits. As I scooped it up, the door began to open. I scrunched the wrap into the ball of my hand and wiped my mouth, removing any traces of dust from my lips.

Rex's cigarette entered the room first. The clinical glow of the yellow walls coupled with the brown, scratchy carpet and the smoke created a sort of lomo effect as the drugs began to kick in.

"My office," were the only two words he spoke as he disappeared.

Did I imagine that he had been there? How did he know that I was still there? Straightening my jaw and checking for any trace of white trails on my person, I stood for a moment or two with my head back and my mouth open, letting the soothing wave of the euphoric drug-addled sensation flow through my blood to the tips of my fingers and toes. I had consumed more than I thought and I wasn't sure that I was even going to make it to Rex's office, let alone inch myself into a chair and sit facing him for the next ten minutes. I concentrated on my breathing, in and out. My eyes were heavy and sticky but I forced them open and gradually concentrated on putting one foot in front of the other, even though I must have looked like a giant marshmallow in a Superdry coat. The more I walked the easier it got, until I found myself approaching the correct door. It was open, and the obligatory plume of smoke was making its way into the hall.

I fought to gain composure and entered. He sat, the angles of his face illuminated by a small table lamp placed in such a way that made his shadow take up the whole room. As he turned, I'm sure I saw his shadow stay put, cackling behind him like a silent maniac. His glasses were perched at the end of his nose as he leant forward to examine his computer screen. I was glad of the minimal light; hopefully, he wouldn't notice that all the parts of my face had made a collective decision to swap places. I sat down, coming closer to him, his aura surrounding him like a thick, dense bubble. I looked at the walls, trying to steady my focus. The large *Three Sisters* poster that hung to my right seemed more three-dimensional than usual. Each of the stencilled women seemed to be jutting out, mocking me with their pencilled frowns.

He took a few seconds to speak. "You're going too far," he said. He didn't elaborate; he was clearly waiting for me to defend myself. I wasn't sure that I could. I felt the ambience of the cramped room, the shadows and the smoke. I was tripping out in ways that Jack the Ripper's victims might have. I just sat and watched him for a moment. Suddenly, as if an egg had broken inside me, I felt a sense of clarity as if all his words, all the insults he had ever said, everything I had ever felt, every dark crevice of fear that I had crawled into when I thought of Rex Bamber had opened up into a wide, lighted cavern. I wasn't going to play this game anymore. I had given up my relationships, my work, my money, my health, and now he was saying that I was going TOO far? He wanted me to pull back? NOW he wanted me to pull back?

I folded my arms, which he saw in the flicker of his eye but he still didn't tear his gaze away from the computer. He picked up the cigarette and took a long, calm drag before opening his mouth and letting the white strings escape and climb upwards in a swirly ascent.

He broke the silence. "You know you're going too far." He stubbed out the cigarette.

"I'm trying to see inside the character." The sound I made was raspy and my breathing irregular, after every word there was a heavy pant.

"Yet you are losing the plot. I didn't ask you to sabotage yourself." His tone remained muted; his gaze remained fixed away from me.

"Then what did you ask?" I found my voice from somewhere, maybe it was from within the small white baggie that was still in my fist. I went on. "What did you expect me to do, Rex? Just waltz back in here and perform this intricately woven part without ANY kind of help?"

He sneered. I'd just about had enough of his sneers. The chemical that was coursing through my veins was giving me drive, a motivation to claw back all the confidence that had been sucked from me ever since I had first walked through the school doors. I couldn't back down from this one. If I did, then all my losses would have been in vain and I couldn't let that happen again.

"Don't you laugh at me," I whispered, looking him straight in the eye. His pupils seemed to dilate slightly before returning to normal. In that split second, I saw my stepmother's glare, her vitriolic expression full of anger and hatred.

"I beg your pardon?" His speech was slow and contained.

"I said, don't laugh at me." I was fighting Rex and I had the little boy fighting against his stepmother at my side, giving me the power to continue. "I have been doing the only thing I knew how to do. You haven't taught me ANYTHING! I am just using what I have at my disposal to create the results that YOU wanted and now you're saying I'm going too far? Fuck you!"

I could feel my heart thundering in my ears, the sound was deafening. I stood up. "Fuck you, Rex!" I spat the words out as if I was trying to shake my tongue from its root.

Rex's expression was one of shock and delight. He had loved setting up this drama and I had just walked into it with my eyes shut and my arms wide open. My instincts told me to leave it there. And so I did. Picking up my bag and pushing the chair aside, I spun round and marched out of his office into the corridor. Even though the drugs were meant to disable my sense of reality, I had managed to fight my corner. I was proud but I felt totally wiped out. Looking down at my hands, I noticed that the white ball of bagged powder had reduced in size since I had been squeezing it so tightly in anger. I rushed to the toilets to try and salvage what I could. I had sobered up somewhat and I needed the last few bits to get me home or I'd surely pass out on the bus floor. As I went to open the door of the toilets, something made me stop still. Though the rest of the school was quiet, a muffled sound seemed to be coming from somewhere. It was like the sound of scraping and knocking coupled with a short, sharp high-pitched cry. It was almost rhythmic, as if someone was trapped somewhere and had been trying to get attention for so long that the only way out was to tap out a beat in the hope that someone would notice.

I looked around. There was no place small enough in the direct vicinity for someone to get trapped. Perhaps they were trapped in the toilet cubicle; it had happened before. I went to barge through but the sound changed; it was no longer one of anguish or pain, but suddenly one of pleasure, of ecstasy, of submission. I opened the toilet door slightly and the sound intensified. It was a woman's voice, together with a knocking sound and deep moaning. It was suddenly all too clear what the noise was. I began to feel aroused. I had never caught anyone having sex before, least of all in a public place. I had to see who it was, who had the brass balls to copulate in the toilets of the school when Rex was but a heartbeat away. I opened the door ever-so slightly so that a crack of light shot across my face and brought my eye close to the exposed scene. I saw a beautifully tight hairless bottom moving ripple-like as it ground forward. A white hand with perfectly polished nails gripped the left cheek tightly.

"Oh Jesus!" Another ecstatic female gasp made me look up. I saw the perpetrator's cherry red lips and alabaster skin and her copper hair in disarray on her face. The huge, dark sweeping eyelashes were shut as she bit into one of her lips and jerked her head backwards against the hardboard wall. The other hand gripped onto the t-shirt of the pert-bottomed assailant, who moaned and thrust further into her.

"Fuck, yeah baby, fuck, yeah."

My cock instantly stiffened in my trousers as I watched my friend Ricky knobbing the life out of my movement teacher Camilla, working her with a controlled, intense manoeuvre. I let the door close and the image sink in for a second. The experience had made me horny and I was surprised that I was able to sustain such a feeling when I was so out of my mind on special K. Was what I had just seen ACTUALLY real? Was my friend Ricky ACTUALLY having an affair with Rex's wife? I moved away from the door and, as I did so, my sexual arousal slowly turned into savage revenge. If I was savvy, this little scenario could work in my favour. How wonderful to be privy to information that brought Mr Smug down a peg or two. I pulled my bag further up my shoulder and turned, striding purposefully back up the corridor, making my way to the now shut office door. I pushed it hard and walked in, taking Rex completely by surprise by slamming my fist down on his desk. He jumped a little but kept his composure. The light flickered as he tried to retain his equanimity.

"I think," I began, "that before you tell me how far I am going, you might want to see how far your wife is going right now in the toilets. Have a good evening!"

And with that I left the building. I didn't stop, I just marched straight through and out, opening the small white packet and letting the wind take the powder with it. I made the decision right there and then to have a good night's sleep tonight, to try again tomorrow.

I had felt the necessary emotions, I had been to hell. I had probably screwed myself over a million times in a short period of time and I couldn't do it any longer. I would sleep on it and see where I was tomorrow morning. I would try and make amends with those I had wronged, try and make peace with myself. This whole situation was a joke. I was a nice, funny, charming guy and yet I was allowing myself to travel to a darker, more hideous side to gain the respect of someone I hated, someone who was being shat on by his own spouse, who was screwing the guy who was giving me the tools to screw myself. This world was just not my world and I had to accept that. Tomorrow I would attempt to go back, back to safe, secure and steady. No more hiding in the shadows waiting for my demons to come knocking; this was drama not real life. I had had enough. I got on the bus and immediately texted Beez. I missed him, for once in this string of miserable consequences, I really missed him. I didn't really know what to say. *I miss you x* did the trick perfectly.

*

Of course, I didn't get a good night's sleep. Aside from the tossing, every time I turned it was like a bag of nails was being emptied inside my head. I pined for one more line of powder just to see me through the night, but then I remembered that horrific scene in *Trainspotting* where the baby crawled along the ceiling and I squeezed my eyes shut and tried to block those feelings out. When I eventually woke with a start, drenched in sweat, my tongue crying out for moisture, it was light. I sat staring up at the tops of the walls, but they didn't match. The after- effects of copious amounts of opiates and the lack of sleep had robbed me of the ability to generate simple forms in my brain. I drifted between panic and calm. I was jittery and cold. The only answer was to shower. The water felt like insects crawling over my body and I scratched and scratched to try and feel the soothing flush of its powers again, but my skin was used to something else. I dried myself and pulled on some clean clothes.

This time I forced myself to look in the mirror to see what Rex had done to me, what I had allowed him to do to me, and what I had done to myself. I was grey, like an old white sock that had got caught in a coloured wash one too many times. My eyes were red, like freakish Halloween gobstoppers. My pupils were huge and unnatural. My skin was beginning to break out in spots, primarily around my mouth, which glowed a sharp pink. My lips were cracked and my hair was heavy around my head. I wouldn't have looked out of place in the Gorillaz. Blindly, I scrambled around in my cosmetic bag for concealer. Would it work? Or would I look like a half-painted, exposed plaster wall? I used it sparingly. Perhaps if I was looking for sympathy and forgiveness today, it might support my case to look utterly bedraggled. There was such a fug in my brain that it was hard to believe that my brain was in there at all. It had temporarily moved out and was quite happily resting in its new home at the pit of my arse. Running a brush through my hair and pulling my hoodie up over my head, I set out into the day. I was hours early but I might just try and eat something or at least let my eyes adjust to the light, take in beauty again, breathe.

*

When I got into the office, it looked different, like returning to your home after the burglars had defiled it. My desk was no longer a little sanctuary, a home of idle gossip and playful taunting. It was the place where dark deeds had taken place and horrid thoughts had manifested themselves and the place where I had fallen. Sandra was in, I recognised the denim jacket that was two sizes too small and adorned with original 1970s badges that had been thrown in the wash with it and left perfect rust-coloured circles all around the lapel. At least if she ever took them off, she would have a perfect guide as to where to pin them back on. The jacket was slung over the back of the chair but she didn't turn round. The tap, tap of the keyboard seemed to signify that she was actually working rather than writing more articles for her precious *Coffee Break* magazine. Maybe she was just tapping away for my benefit. She could have started adopting the tactics that we had used when Pepe walked into the room; ergo she was pretending to work so she didn't have to say anything to me. I dropped my bag in its usual home and stepped forward towards her desk. She had stopped typing and was examining the screen.

"Er, Sand?" I spoke but my throat felt like it was made of sandpaper and the words got choked. I tried again, she didn't respond. Maybe she was ignoring me to humiliate me. Couldn't she see I was offering her a big sodding olive branch here? How could she be so heartless?

"Okay," I sounded more crestfallen than I had wanted to, "I understand you don't want to talk to me. I totally get it. The way I've acted has been... unforgivable."

There was no movement; her head remained fixed in front of the screen. I suddenly found my neck incredibly itchy and scratched it just for something to do with my hands. I was red, thankfully any other colour than grey, and my eyes were watering. I hated confrontation but I hated apologies even more – they always showed my true weakness.

"But if you would just–"

"That school of yours," Sandra said, her tone direct but warm, "it's on the news."

"What?" I forgot my discomfort and leaned in to get a better look over her shoulder. The headline of the *Haringey Gazette* website spoke for itself:

WOMAN FOUND HANGING IN NORTH LONDON DRAMA SCHOOL

Sandra turned to look at me; there was a smidgeon of sympathy when she saw my state but I was too enveloped in the words I had just seen.

What the hell was going on? We exchanged confused glances.

"You'd better get down there," was all she said.

The building was cordoned off with police tape, yellow and black diagonal stripes blowing in the chilling wind. A single police car was outside; it looked like they were not letting anyone in or out. The bullish policewoman wouldn't give anything away.

"You don't understand. I'm a student at this school. I need to get in. I need... to get to a class."

"I've heard it all before, mate." She chewed her gum defiantly. "No one's going in; it's a crime scene until stated otherwise. Loads of your little friends have tried to get a butcher's at what's going on inside but they can't. It's for us to decide when people are allowed access. If I were you, I'd go home and wait for them to call you. Now, please, let me carry on and do my job."

Her "job" appeared to be standing there looking like a Staffordshire Bull Terrier with sore testicles, but I didn't argue.

"Can you just tell me what's happened?"

"All I can tell you is that a female was found in a critical condition. She was taken to hospital and we're examining evidence. Nothing's clear yet. It happened in the early hours of this morning. We probably won't be finished here for another twenty-four hours. Before that I doubt that acting like a tree will be very high on the owner's agenda."

She seemed happy with her little joke. I wanted to say something like asking whether my taxes paid for all her Bernard Manning DVDs but I kept my mouth shut. I just nodded and walked away. The school had never looked so desolate; not only the place of broken dreams, but now the home of broken lives.

I shuddered, wondering who it could have been or what could have happened. I had a good idea but I didn't want to think about it. What had I done? Had my actions put this near-fatal wheel of events into motion? I had to find out. There was only one person who could tell me, but could I bear to make the call? I had to. I just had to or else the guilt on top of everything else would have eaten me up. I fished in my bag for my phone and took it out. I dialled the number.

"Hi, Ricky."

There was sniffing down the phone. The voice that answered was weak and defeated. "Mate, it's bad," he said in barely a whisper, "it's really fucking bad."

*

I took a train all the way out to Reading; my nerves were totally shot to shit. What could I say to him? The last time I had seen him, he was bare-arsed and shagging a tutor on the sink of those filthy toilets, his bottom bobbing up and down between the handwash and the cold tap. I had called work and said that the police had wanted to take statements from those on the scene; I would make up the hours some other time. Thankfully, Sandra had taken the call and had at least feigned concern in lieu of the real thing. In truth, I think she had appreciated my half-apology. Presumably, it was a baby step towards some kind of reconciliation. At least, that's what I had hoped.

I'd never been to Reading before, it was bleak and slow. I wasn't familiar with the area so I just got a cab to the front door. The cab driver attempted to make conversation, which I wasn't used to after years of silence from the London cabbies.

"What brings you here then? You local?" he asked through the postage stamp-sized gap in the bulletproof glass.

"No, I've come from London. You see, I caught my friend shagging Beelzebub's wife in a public convenience so I spilled the beans. She tried to top herself last night and now I'm here for some kind of redemption. Keep the change."

Of course, I didn't really say that.

"I'm here to see a mate. Three fifty was it?"

Ricky's mum answered the door, an attractive lady with blonde curls and a wrinkle-free face. She wore a glamorous sparkly top even though she was clearly just hanging around the house, and her wrists were adorned with silver. She looked as though she should be walking down a red carpet rather than running the Dyson over her own.

"Hi there, Simon is it? I'll just call our Ricky. Can I get you a tea?"

I felt like asking for a brandy, but I expected that eleven am was still too early for spirits, even in the Hellman household. She shouted up the stairs as I looked around the kitchen. It was brand new with black marble worktops and terracotta tiles. What my mother would have called "garish" and "new money".

She bustled back into the kitchen. "He's been up there all morning, won't let me in. He's even made me call in sick to work and his dad won't be happy. He's already a bod down and they're supposed to be laying a big black one today in Basildon."

I looked at her blankly.

"Carpet, dear, he's a carpet fitter. Well, Ricky is. His dad owns the business but he'll have to get stuck in today. He can't afford to lose the job and what with the economy..."

Nice as she was, I wasn't here for a political debate, particularly about the fiscal downturn of the home furnishings industry.

"Mrs Hellman."

"Lynne."

"Sorry, Lynne. Do you mind if I just go up? He is expecting me."

"Oh yes, dear, of course. I'll just get on with me dusting. Now where did I put me cloth?"

I could see that it was sticking out of the pocket of her tabard but I left her chasing her tail for a few minutes while I made my way up the stairs. I glanced in a few empty rooms before tapping on the closed door.

"It's me, Ricky, Simon. Can I come in?"

"Yes, mate." He sounded a bit more chipper.

I pushed the door and went in. The bedroom was stuffy. A big wardrobe stood in the corner, spilling fashionable garments out everywhere, a poster of a lesbian kiss, and black sheets no doubt spotted with tell-tale marks. It was just how I expected. Ricky was sitting hunched on the end of the bed with his back to me.

"Hi," I said, inching my way in and sliding onto the bed next to the pillow. He turned to face me; he looked worse than I imagined. Puffy, swollen eyes and dried tear tracks down his face. I let out a deep, sympathetic sigh.

"Mate, you look worse than me." He managed a laugh, which was something. "I don't know what to do, buddy." He looked as if he was about to start crying again.

"Do you want to talk about it?" I shrugged, not really knowing how to broach it without asking him straight out whether he had seen the action unfold with his very eyes.

"I'd rather have a line," he said. His expression suggested that he was asking me to join him. I'd lasted nearly twelve hours and I was doing relatively well, did I want to ruin all that now?

389

"RICKY," a voice came hurtling up the stairs, "I'M OFF OUT WITH AUNTIE MARGOT. THERE'S A PIZZA IN THE FREEZER. DON'T YOU GO LETTING SIMON GO HUNGRY NOW."

"Okay, Mum."

"SEE YOU LATER." There was a shuffle and the door slammed.

He looked at me and shrugged. "Well?"

An hour later I was well on the way to being totally incapable of holding my shit together. We had tooted two lines each and I had fallen back into the old habit like a tramp on a sandwich. Granted it had only been half a day, but if I was going to be able to cope with this nightmare, then I was going to need a little pick-me-up. Unfortunately, "little" didn't come into Ricky's vocabulary where white powder was concerned. The lines looked so big you could have double-parked on them. Ricky had produced a box, a charming wooden shoe box with a sliding lid. Once the lid was opened, the party had begun. Various bags of suspicious granulated chemicals were in it, together with a small bong and a long, thin tube of glass, which Ricky had pulled out and examined with care as if he was a museum curator exhibiting a rare historical artefact.

"This is the Soul Pipe," he said, his speech beginning to slur. "Only my friend Badrock gets to sit on this baby."

It sounded salacious, filthy. I wondered who Badrock was. I didn't have to use my imagination too much.

After a bit of giggling and general schoolboy behaviour, we settled back with a large spliff and Ricky began to get reflective. It was the first time we had mentioned what had happened since I arrived. I was glad I was so out of it that I could disassociate myself from the whole thing. We sat in silence for a bit before he spoke.

"It was horrible, mate, just horrible."

"What was?" I had a feeling that I was going to have to fake surprise and was careful not to overdo it.

"Well, you said you saw the local news, right?"

"I saw it online, the article was vague. I couldn't really tell…"

"Mate, if I tell you something, you've got to swear you ain't gonna tell no one." His eyes were wide and pleading.

"Ricky, who am I going to tell? My old friends don't speak to me and my new friends treat me with similar contempt. Other than you, there IS no one else."

"Okay." He looked around as if the walls were about to lean in for a good old listen. "I've been banging someone at school, someone… important."

"Okay." I thought the best way to play this was nonchalantly. That way, I looked cool and no theatrics would be necessary.

"It's um…"

"Oh God, Ricky, spit it out."

"It's Camilla."

He waited for the gasp, but there wasn't one.

"Okay."

"You're not shocked?"

"Not really, Ricky. I work in close proximity to Rex, nothing shocks me anymore. I've heard tales that would turn your hair white." Ace, Simon, ace. I felt bad lying to Ricky, he was a good friend and I had deceived him. Now he wanted my help and all I could concentrate on was to how to cover up more of my deception.

"Well, last night he found out."

"Oh shit!"

"Yep. I went to the pub after class, and if I'm on my way to Archway station and need the loo, I pop in and use the school's. It's such a long train journey back here and I don't wanna get caught short, you know? Anyway, last night she followed me into the cubicle. I didn't even know she was there. She came in behind me and just shoved her hand down my trousers and started playing with my cock."

I licked my lips; I could feel myself getting aroused all over again, imagining Ricky stumbling around pissed and horny, unable to stop her sexual advances. She whispers in his ear that she's wet as she pulls her skirt up. Her pussy is totally bald like an eighteen-year-old's. She says something suggestive to lure him in, tell him she wants him to play with her. She grabs his hand and puts it on her, inside her. They know they might get caught but it just adds to the thrill. She tells him that Rex never comes out of his office, says that he sometimes sleeps in there, that he stays up all night playing online poker and drinking whisky. She speaks while vigorously jerking him off inside his clothes. He can't help himself. He drops his trousers and puts it in her. The drugs made me fantasise. I watched the scene play out in my head as Ricky's lips moved and I nodded in all the right places. But then Ricky's speech took a different turn, as though he was no longer speaking to me but letting himself think aloud. He was looking off into the distance; his eyes glazed over.

"And just as I'm about to climax, the door opens and he's standing there like a ghost. And I'm coming, it's spilling out of her and she's trying to adjust herself but she can't, I'm still in her. My dick slips out and squirts a jet of come over the floor. He stands looking at us, looking at my dick as I'm trying to push it back into my flies, and she's horrified. She starts apologising, apologising like he's about to kill her or something. Saying she didn't mean it, it meant nothing. He just stands there watching us dance around eachother. She jumps off the sink and slips a bit on my cum, steadying herself with the sink. And I'm squirming, not knowing what to do with myself. And all the while he's staring at us like a man possessed, like there's some kind of devil in his eyes. After a moment, he just reaches forward and grabs her by the hair. She lets out an almighty scream and he's pulling her to him and out of the door. She's twisting and turning, begging him to stop, and he just forces her down the corridor. I run after her, trying to stop him, pulling his arms, but he's too quick and I'm still in shock. And I'm shouting and she's screaming blue murder, begging him to stop."

My eyes widened at the true horror of what I was being told.

"He pushes her into the office door and lunges at me with one hand to get me out, and the door slams. And I'm banging on it, telling him to stop or I'll rip the thing off its hinges. And after a while the screaming stops and I'm out of breath and panting. I try to listen but there's no sound. It's deathly quiet. I call his name but there's no answer. I wait a second and the door opens slightly. It's her. Her hair is a fucking mess and her lipstick is across her face. Her face is streaked with mascara and tears. And she tells me to go, tells me it was a mistake and she was sorry that I got caught up in all of it, tells me that her and Rex need to talk and that I should just go. I can't see into the room, but she looks terrified and I make her promise me that she'll be okay. There's nothing else I can do." His face began to crease again. "So I just fucking left man, I just fucking left. I couldn't do anything else, I couldn't, I just couldn't." He began to sob, big loud cries of pain. I moved up to him and put my arms around him, pulling him into an embrace. He wept into my shoulder. "There was nothing I could do, nothing." He kept repeating these words until they began to be mere sounds. And all I could think of was how I had caused this and wonder what the hell I was going to do to get out of it.

He'd cried for a good ten minutes before I laid his spent frame down on the bed. He was so tired I think he'd managed to sob all the drugs out of his system. Two patches of wet seeped into my top.

This was truly horrendous. No one knew that it was me who had given the game away to Rex, there had been no other third party involved and, as far as I knew, nobody had been around in the school when I had made my little discovery. Now Camilla's life had been ruined and Ricky's came a pretty close second. I didn't even consider my life. I'd jumped back on the wagon without even bothering to think about using my willpower. I was back to square one, dazed and confused and feeling utterly helpless. Maybe no one else knew that it was me, but I knew. I knew that I was leaving a trail of destruction on my way to the top. I was throwing bodies to Rex, including my own, and he was using them as puppets to act in his own little theatre of the macabre. I watched Ricky's chest move up and down as he drifted into sleep. I ruffled his hair, my little Ricky. A child trapped in a man's body, still hoping to play the field with anyone who comes along, not caring about what the husband might do if he caught her with his wife. Or what she might do to herself. Oh God! My nerves intensified. I would have to see Rex. I had to know what the consequences of my actions really had been. Did he blame me? Was he going to make me suffer even more than I had suffered already? Or did he respect me for telling him the truth? Had I thrown my friend into the fire to spare my own fate? This was too much.

Desperately, I scrambled through the open box, picking out the half-bag of white dust that we had been snorting. I pulled it open and dipped my finger in. It came out with a coating of crystals glistening on it, like dipping a biscuit in chocolate. It looked too beautiful to be so harmful, but then most things that kill you possess dangerous beauty: vanity, love, desire, the three things that had prompted me to take my integrity in both hands and cock it all up, all for the sake of looking good to Rex and his company. I should have declined his offer, gone back to my normal little life, climbed up the admin ladder to now be sitting at the top of the organisational tree, frowning on people like me not celebrating them. I put my finger to my nose and sniffed. The crystals were so fine that they rose up my nasal passage and straight to my brain. This was a new type of euphoria, it was enlightening and empowering and it made me feel amazing; truly great cocaine.

While Ricky slept, I poured a healthy ration into a separate bag and stuffed it into my pocket. That should keep me going for a bit. I left him sleeping on the bed while I made my way downstairs and into the kitchen.

Where do people normally keep the brandy? These people were likely to have a cocktail bar in the front room, I thought, so in I went. Sure enough, it wasn't a bar but more of a cabinet. I swung open the door and picked up the first bottle of brown liquid I could find. I shut the door and wiped the handle with my sleeve. I'd seen them do it in movies so I repeated the action, more for effect than anything else. Then I made my way to the door. I didn't know quite what I was going to do. I just knew that I had to be off my head while I was doing it.

I walked to the station in driving rain. By the time I got there, I was drenched and a little sozzled, having had a good few slugs of the dark rum I had pilfered in place of brandy. I put my return ticket through and boarded the train.

Getting back into Paddington at four pm, I thought it was probably best to go straight to school. If I had to hang around for much longer, then I would be sure to fall foul of my own curiosity and begin the slow descent into a pit of paranoia. I wasn't even sure whether the school would be open, whether classes would be on. We were always told that unless the Four Horsemen of the Apocalypse were making their way up the stone steps, we must always assume that classes would be on. I wondered whether at least one of them would be waiting for me outside, smiling at me from his steed of death.

When I got to school, the half-drunk bottle of stolen booze and untouched bag of smack burning a hole in my bag, a crowd had gathered. It was only five pm but obviously other people had used my excuses and used the situation to bunk off work early. The striped tape and the cop with the attitude had gone, and everything looked as though it might be back to normal, whatever normal was. A few people from my old life were scattered about chatting, not really knowing where to go. I went to push open the door when I felt a sharp tap on my shoulder. I turned round, hoping it might be someone from the elite group ready to give me the lowdown I so desperately craved. It wasn't.

Lulu stood there, hands on hips, looking as unimpressed with me as she had been a few nights ago. It was odd but she was like a total stranger to me now; she was cold and unfeeling and therefore I had removed her from my mind.

"I want a word, Simon," she said, as if she was summoning me to her office. I shrugged and followed her to a quieter area of the street. She led the way and I skulked behind her. I was ready for an onslaught, there was no way I could avoid it now that Lulu had decided that she wanted to give me a dressing down. Compared to one of Rex's tirades, a ticking off from her would be like getting a knighthood from the Queen.

She stopped and turned round. She didn't look angry; she looked as though she was at a loss.

"Simon, forget the other night. I didn't mean to get angry at you."

This was a revelation, she never apologised for her actions. If she was wrong, she might make it up to you by doing something nice, but she would never admit it. God forbid. It was more uncomfortable for her to be nice.

"Okay." I didn't really know what to say.

"I just… well, I want you to know that I am worried about you." She dropped her hands to her sides. "I mean, look at you. You're pale, you're spun out. You don't even appear to be on this planet."

"Oh, thanks very much."

"I'm serious. I'm concerned that this part is consuming you, threatening you. It's killing you, Simon. You're not even a shadow of who you once were. You're a shadow of that shadow."

I could feel the anger bubbling up inside me.

"And what do you want me to do then, Lulu?" I was straight on the defensive. "I mean, what would YOU do in my position? You got a few lines wrong in a show last term and you practically imploded! I am trying to get some kind of insight into how an extreme character should be played. Okay? I mean, I'm taking risks and applying methods that may seem a little unorthodox to you but at least I am trying. I have been given a golden opportunity to do something different, something that could change my life forever and you are saying that it's killing me?"

I stopped to look at her. She was taken aback, slightly put out that someone had dared to fight her concern with a valid point.

"Lulu, it's SAVING me, saving my career, my dream, my aspirations and my ambitions. Half of this school will be down the job centre when the year is out but I have been given the chance to reach for a higher goal. So thank you very much for your concern but I do not need it. I am doing fine by myself and if you can't accept that, then maybe I don't need and never have needed you."

The speech was my best performance ever. I think I had even left Lulu temporarily gobsmacked. I wasn't finished.

"If YOU stopped throwing paint all over your face, hiding behind your laugh, your threads and your ARROGANCE, then maybe you might open yourself up to a new experience. You might let something in that wasn't already there, feed a bit of potential with the correct nutrients to make it FANTASTIC, but you don't."

I gesticulated towards her headscarf tied in a perfect bow at the front of her locks. "All this, it's keeping you in. Nothing is getting out. Being an actor is like being a vessel, full of experience, knowledge and power of the human spirit and condition. Your mind and body become conductors of thoughts and manners based on REAL FEELINGS, not just superimposed shit that you've picked up from some Channel Four reality show. And I don't need a lesson in how to do that from YOU, Lulu. You should be learning from me."

I was done and I pulled my bag close to me to make my way into the school. Her hand shot out and gripped my arm, her teeth were bared and a snarl burned across her lips.

"I know it was you," she whispered. "I was rehearsing late and I saw you watching from outside the toilets. I saw you going into Rex's office. You can't hide from this one, actor boy. You killed Camilla and you ratted on your friend. How can you live with what you've done?"

I was shell-shocked. Her hand maintained a tight seal around my forearm.

I scrambled around for the right words. "I don't know what you're talking about."

"Like fuck you don't. I was in the ladies toilets when I saw you. I followed you to the office and hid when you left. You're the selfish cunt who stepped over others to save your own skin. I don't know what game you and Rex are playing, but I'll get to the bottom of it and expose you both." There was pure rage in her eyes.

I shook my arm free but her hand remained in the air like a threatening claw.

"You don't know what you're talking about," I said, regaining a little composure. "No one is going to believe the ramblings of some deranged, jealous actress with a vendetta."

"We'll see," she said, but I laughed at her.

"No proof and now no argument. Oh dear, Lulu, your motivation in this is as ill-conceived as it is on stage."

And with that I turned and walked away, the nerves building up in me like red-hot lava, threatening to spill out of my mouth and trickle down my chin. The game was up. I had to ask, no, plead with Rex to help me out. Okay, I didn't wrap that noose around Camilla's neck but I very well might have kicked the chair away. Lulu didn't follow me, thank God. I picked through the throng and pushed in through the door, not stopping until I had passed the scene of the hideous crime and barged into Rex's office, the door slamming shut behind me.

He was sitting in his usual place, but this time the computer was not on. Instead he cradled a glass of red wine and sat looking into nothing. The bottles littering the desk made me think that he had probably spent the majority of the night in here, not playing online poker I might add. He already had a five o'clock shadow and his pallor was yellow. There was a tell-tale dribble mark of wine down the front of his linen shirt that looked deceptively like blood. I stood there like a lemon for a good few seconds. I was tired of these pregnant pauses; it was as if we were constantly in a big yawn inducing Pinter drama all the time.

"Well?" I thought since I had barged in, it was only polite to begin the conversation. He didn't flinch. As if on a thirty-second delay, he jerked his head upwards.

"Well what?" His tone was caustic, as if I'd said the most stupid thing in the world. I didn't want to have to ask him outright, knowing the answer and the part I had played in it.

"What happened?" I asked. I felt as though we were in some kind of murderous tag team and I didn't like it. Being associated at all with this man and his erratic and shameless behaviour was almost too much to bear.

"What business is it of yours?" he asked, calmly fishing around in his Golden Virginia packet and pulling out strands of tobacco that looked like pubic hairs. "Do you think that we have entered some kind of tryst? Get a hold of yourself."

I wasn't going to get anywhere and he was right, I hadn't been there. I was the coward that had fled the scene so it really was none of my business.

"After a shambolic performance yesterday, you drop a bombshell and then come back looking like the wreck of the Hesperus to pick at the bones of the mess you've made. Your gall knows no bounds, does it?" This was delivered in a serene manner, which was much worse than if he had shouted at me.

A few moments passed as he licked the paper and rolled the cigarette into a perfect cylinder.

"So you'll get no ammunition from me to feed your salacious little gossip-peddlers outside if that's what you're after."

"I'm not."

"Then why are you here?" He breathed in and raised his eyebrows. "Go on, tell me."

"I... was wondering... about rehearsals. Are they on tonight?" He'd never fall for that one. I was pulling it out of my arse so fast that half of my internal organs were about to come with it.

"Not for you. You have no place under the roof of my school." He inhaled deeply and let the smoke just drift out of his open mouth. He couldn't bear to look at me.

I didn't move in the vain hope he might change his mind. But why did I want him to? Perhaps for verification that my disloyalty had been my only mistake, that I had done everything else right. I didn't want to leave the building forever without hearing that my time hadn't been wasted. It didn't come. This was it, it was over. I had come, been ruined, and now I was about to leave. How could someone who just faded into the background now be responsible for bringing the whole place to its knees? I turned and reached for the door handle.

"I know what you're thinking," he said, looking up to the ceiling as though he was addressing a room full of people. He had a smile on his face that was so patronising you couldn't help but want to wipe it off with a left hook.

"You're thinking that for the number of sacrifices you've made this hasn't been worth it, that you don't deserve this punishment. You think that the sacrifices you've made have earned you the part of Alan, but you're wrong."

I shook my head, involuntarily agreeing with him, hypnotised by the stream of smoke escaping from his lips.

"But there are sacrifices and there are sacrifices. You've made one vital error in your quote-unquote wisdom."

I was confused.

"Alan makes the ultimate sacrifice. He stabs the horses through the eyeballs to give them salvation. He offers up his favourite animals to save himself. Yet he doesn't harm himself, he doesn't flagellate himself as you do. He's not a coward, a miserable, snivelling coward who thinks that self-abuse

401

and telling tales on others for redemption is the key. He's realistic. He proffers something far greater." Rex rolled the cigarette between his finger and thumb.

"What are you saying, Rex?" I had no idea what he was suggesting but I began to be aroused by the temptation.

"What lengths would you go to in order to protect yourself in this performance, to seal your career, to carve your name in the industry?" He looked down at his fingers as they worked the tip of the cigarette into a tight hoop.

"What or WHO would you sacrifice?" He waited for my answer.

"Are you saying that you want me to sacrifice someone to save myself? Didn't I do that last night?"

"Unwittingly," he said. "You weren't to know that that crazy bitch would pull a stunt like that. In order to truly play the game, you must already know the consequences. You must know that the person you banish will never be allowed back into the fold, publicly humiliated, and blacklisted from the profession. Are you willing to make that choice for the sake of your own development? Because if not, then you're not willing to let Alan's tortured soul in. It's all about feeling real emotions here, Simon, not petty drug-taking or tittle-tattling. This is about your direction and control."

"What are you saying here?"

"I'm saying that if you're willing to take the necessary risk, then I am willing to offer you a golden ticket to stay in Alan's shoes."

"You mean some sort of pact? You're bribing me?"

"If that's the kind of language you speak in..." He shrugged.

I thought about it and it made sense, but the thought made me sick. How could I do even more damage? Just how many people would I tread on to get further up the ladder to Rex's position on high? But then I was guaranteed entry into my dream career, the champagne lifestyle of easy money and the opportunity to mix with like-minded, talented and creative individuals. And playing Alan was just the beginning, a path towards being the name that people remembered, the name written in lights above the door and across the posters. And the opportunity to finally show the horrible woman from my past that she might have won a battle but it was I who had won the war.

"I see your potential but I don't see your balls," Rex said, enjoying every second of this.

I couldn't stand the pressure. Who would feel it most? Whose life would I potentially annihilate? Who would never forgive me for what I had done? Who did Rex expect me to choose?

"Oh well, it seems that you don't—"

"Lulu Harries," I said. "Get rid of Lulu."

5

Had I hammered the final nail into my coffin? Somehow there was so much guilt involved in my current situation that I had become immune to it. I was numbed by it and there was no other explanation. Why couldn't there be some kind of respite in this cavalcade of misery? This was supposed to be an empowering, enlightening experience, but so far I had felt nothing but turmoil, torture and pain. So had Camilla, so had Ricky, to an extent so had Rex, and now so had Lulu. I imagined her face as she was escorted off the premises, violent thrashing about and blood-red lipstick. She would have known that it was me. She was probably sticking pins into my voodoo doll as I sat here, drinking the dregs from the bottle of rum and studying the pages of the play. I was beginning to feel acceptance of my sealed fate and of my certain future. Yes, I had had to make sacrifices but I had been saved. If I hadn't, then Lulu would almost certainly have spread vile words about me. Now she was blacklisted and I had power over her. Camilla and Ricky had had to be sacrificed to get me closer to Rex, to form a bond that would now be unbroken. He trusted my mettle, my ruthlessness, and my commitment to the cause. I had passed every test and though I didn't feel good about it, I felt as though I had done something productive. I had made an investment in my professional development. The fact that some people had had to suffer was not my problem; they should not have got in the way. A few weeks ago, I would have quivered at this thought, banished it from my brain. But this experience had made me realise that life is not about pandering to the needs of others, it is about doing what is necessary to better yourself. When the ship is sinking and the lifeboats are out, you must jump in yourself and start rowing. When life is so hard to navigate through, why die to let someone else live? It was a childish and frankly pathetic notion to think that someone wouldn't climb on your back to get away from the water and make you sink.

Rex had shown me that the power of people's success lies in the risks they are willing to take. I had made a few and gained the ultimate prize: I would play the part and play it well. After that I would continue, taking the next set of risks to receive higher and higher accolades. I was beginning to understand the pattern of becoming a successful actor. Cecelia was doing it and she was an utter bitch. Yet she didn't care. Look after number one and eliminate the competition. I had to be careful, however, that I didn't destroy myself in the process.

The office was quiet. I had permanently silenced my phone; I didn't want to be contactable by anyone. The phone was for my convenience not for the convenience for others. If I want to be traceable, I'll shove an aerial up my arse, thank you very much.

My words to Sandra were civil but cold.

"How was it?"

"Oh, it was nothing in the end, some girl causing some drama. She didn't even go through with it. Bloody actresses!"

This blatant lack of compassion was so far removed from the Simon she knew it frightened her and she went back to her work; no further conversation was exchanged between us. The day wore on and I secretly read my play under the desk, wondering whether to sneak off and have a secret toot to make the hours go more quickly. I thought about it twice and decided that it probably wasn't the best idea. I was running on completely raw emotion at the moment and I wouldn't want to tip the balance in case it didn't work. At ten am, I felt a cold presence over my shoulder. It couldn't have been Clarissa as there was no stench of sandalwood, plus I hadn't spoken to her in weeks so there would be no reason for her to tower over me. Whoever it was, I had been busted reading, but I was past caring.

Taking me totally by surprise, I was faced with Cordelia. But it didn't really look like Cordelia; it was more like a bedraggled mess. Her hair was not the usual tightly-wound knot on top of her head; it was half cascading down her shoulders. It was as if a tiny bomb had exploded within and sent all those locks that weren't stuck in place into disarray. Her cheesecloth blazer looked like it had been pulled on by blind dwarves and her pearl necklace was on back to front, the clasp making a far more attractive centrepiece than some of her hideous neckwear. She was out of breath, not with exhaustion it seemed but with anger.

"Simon." Her voice was off-kilter too, as if she would start screeching if given free rein.

"Morning," I said, irritatingly cheerfully. I had no idea why she was in such a state but it was highly amusing. I had to stop myself laughing in her face.

"Can I see you in my office for a moment?" That was a joke; her office was not an office at all, she had a bit of floor space in OUR office!

"Sure." I wasn't apologetic in putting my book back in my bag. I threw it in and followed her through. What she meant was the meeting room. It was the scene of many a painful team meeting and, of course, my infamous altercation with Sandra. I knew this was bad. I had seen a couple of people enter that room with her and then fly straight out through the front door, never to darken our door again. To quote Martine McCutcheon, this was my moment. She led the way and I closed the door behind me.

"Sit down," she said, trying to sound composed but, in fact, sounding a little more like Bobcat Goldthwaite.

I did as instructed while she fished around in her organic satchel. Rummaging around with an enraged expression on her face, she spoke as she fought a losing battle with the bag in question.

"It is no secret to you, me or indeed the rest of the organisation that your standards have been slipping a little of late."

"Is it not?" I was going to play this game for as long as I could. There was no need for politeness, I was fucked.

"Well, perhaps it is a surprise to you but I have been inundated with complaints about you from other team members, complaints about your poor appearance, rudeness, apparent bewilderment, antagonistic behaviour and, more importantly, complete and utter lack of interest in the work that you are contractually obliged to do."

"Well, that's not news," I shrugged.

"Since we at Eco Scene regard the latter as the minimum requirement of all our employees, I have no alternative but to let you go."

I waited a second.

"That's it?"

"That's it." She was defiant. She had stopped scratting around now and was looking at me with a face that expressed defeat as much as anything else.

"Well, I don't think you can do that, Cordelia," I said. "I know my rights and I do believe that you have to issue me with a written warning before you just blurt out my dismissal on the spot like that. If you have no paper evidence that I have done anything wrong, then I'll go straight to the Board of Directors and plead my case."

She was bubbling up. I was just getting started and I was enjoying watching her squirm for once. Unfortunately, employment policy had her by the balls, the balls that should have been dangling from her stupid head.

"Paper evidence?" Her voice started to increase in register as she went for one last fumble in her bag. "I'll give you PAPER EVIDENCE."

With that, she brought her hand out of the bag and threw a small sheet of paper at me. It slid across the table and landed in front of me. I looked down. On it were my eyes, my nipples and my arms. It was my penis, but her bedsheets. It was the photograph lifted from the other night's frisson with her nephew that I had forgotten all about. At least the developers in Boots had had the good sense to stick a "quality control" sticker over the offending gloop dripping from my fingers into my mouth. Oh my good God! Even with my new devil-may-care attitude I was shocked and embarrassed. Cordelia swept a hair back from her big red face. She was shaking, like she was about to erupt. I looked up at her open-mouthed.

"Now do me a favour and get the FUCK out of this office!" she shrieked.

I just left, taking a few of my photographs off the board in front of my desk, photos of happier times. Well, they looked happy but I don't know whether I really was. The last shred of my old life was gone now. My job, though by no means important to me, was at least money in my pocket and that's why I had held on for so long. The fact that they had let me continue was something else entirely. I hadn't said goodbye to Sandra, I doubted she would miss me, and no one else had been in, not even Pepe. I expect Craig had been sent back on the next train to wherever he came from. Good riddance! Little shit wasn't worth keeping.

It would probably take Cordelia a while to get over this. She would have to train somebody in my place, discovering all the horrid emails I had written to Sandra slagging her and Pepe off to the hilt. Sandra might even get into trouble.

Oh well, it wasn't my problem now. I had brought the white baggie with me today; I had a strong urge to celebrate my new-found independence with a large toot up each nostril. I had all day to play. Maybe I could camp out in a park somewhere, read the play, and chug on a bottle of spirits and a few lines of mystery dust.

What a life I could lead without full-time shitty employment hanging over me like a black cloud, sucking out my energy and creativity! Perhaps now I would have more time to concentrate on other activities like painting, drawing or writing. Get my old job back at the Boadicea and doss around like Beez did. Not answering to any man, no longer feeling the capitalist pull into habit and disintegration.

My confidence wasn't up for long. After a few hours, the reality began to creep in and I realised the position I was in. I was ruined and I had ruined. Poor Lulu, she would have been crushed – I would have crushed her with my actions. Ricky would be devastated, gutted, and left out to dry. Then at his lowest ebb, he would realise that his friend had stolen gear from him as well as booze from his parents. Camilla was probably in some hospital somewhere, an angry purple mark around her neck, her signature make-up absent, her eyes hollow and her face gaunt. Craig was being shunted off back home, mortified by his actions and disowned by his family. I even felt sorry for Pepe, who would now be frantically calling temp agencies to find a temporary Senior Administrator. I piled on the guilt layer after layer until I started crying. And when I did, the words that came out of my mouth in dramatic bursts were Alan's words. I was suddenly beginning to feel that this sense of desperation, guilt, fear and torment was no longer mine; it was the alter ego of a boy undone, plagued by destructive thoughts and banished to the dark recesses of his poisoned mind.

I went into the grubbiest of public toilets off a Camden park. There was shit up the walls and the tiles were filthy. It reminded me of CXR. And that made me think of Beez. Oh, what I wouldn't give for a night out with my friend now, to go and laugh at the tragedies in that darkened room and dance to Rihanna with the sweaty minotaurs on the sticky dancefloor. What had happened to those days? How did I end up like this, undone, manic, frightened and alone?

I snorted two fat lines and sat on the toilet seat. All along the walls were scribbled the names of various boys and what they were into with phone numbers and crude drawings of ejaculating penises; the seedier side of gay life. Suddenly, it seemed fitting that I was in a filthy toilet shoving filthy chemicals up my nose. It wouldn't have seemed right anywhere else. We come here to expel shit out of our bodies and to pump more shit into them. We expect and demand privacy to do both. Oh, the glamour of drugs!

It was a few more hours before I arrived at school. My eyes were like pinholes and I was sweaty and on edge. Wired and confident, I strolled around. The drugs were giving me false confidence so I grasped the opportunity and laughed at Cecelia, who tried to regard me with contempt. I threw my arms around Philippe, who looked as though some vile dog was attempting to jump up at him.

"You are sooooo fit," I croaked into his ear. I was showing off, surely making more enemies, but I had had Rex's word now so it didn't matter that I was making an utter fool of myself. I was untouchable.

I gave myself a few moments to get with it, to channel a bit more into the things I had lost, the lives I had wrecked, the position I was in. Rex had seemed unmoved when he saw me, half there but firm, standing tall and shivering slightly with nausea. We were going from the top of the play. I knew it well. I strode to my place. He sat, hands clasped between his knees, leaning forward. He was expecting perfection tonight, expecting a solid, definitive performance from me. The others might as well have not even been in the room. I stared at the floor as my breath pumped in and streamed out. The floor began to swim, and as it did, the face of Camilla appeared. Not as I remembered her, but almost as a ghost. A tear fell from her face as the rope around her neck broke and she fell, rasping, coughing, broken to the floor, begging for mercy, for her life to be over, for something or someone to help her, for the nightmare to end.

"In black... AND!"

I opened my mouth to speak.

Camilla had followed me around that room, through every inch of space that Alan covered, every word he spoke and every person he spoke to. She danced through his psyche like a trickle of oil through water, her neck severed and her limbs disjointed. At one point, she was so broken that she crawled with him and lay with her throat bared, pleading with him to finish the job and end the suffering. Alan whispered, "I can't". She had lain on the hard floor, barely alive but certainly not dead, every rise of her chest agony, her hair unravelled and like a pool of blood beneath her head. Alan retreated into the shadows, unable to help, enraged at her and frustrated that she had governed his thoughts even when he had tried to make sense of the world around him. She promised that she would be back tomorrow.

When I had opened my eyes, Rex's were glassy. He had not moved. The floor around him was littered with cigarette ends, and those around me were standing like marionettes in some puppet show.

"That," Rex addressed us all, "was exceptional."

I hadn't seen any of the other actors but I had known who they were. I had known that each and every one was there to hurt Alan, and no matter how much they had wanted to help him and save him, in reality they were ready to hurt him, to savage him with their words.

"Tomorrow," Rex said, "we shall tackle the scene where Alan's demise comes to its harrowing climax. Please be prepared for a very intense and dramatic rehearsal. Many thanks." Then he left the room.

Brian was the first to speak.

"Many thanks." He turned to his peers. "That's a glittering surprise; we've never had one of those!"

While I was gathering my things, Cecelia made her way over to me. Instead of looking stern she was calm, almost pretty.

"Simon," she said. I could tell she was attempting to sound sincere. It was patchy but I gave her credit all the same. I tilted my head towards her. She stopped as if she was going to say something but thought better of it. She simply said, "Good job" and left the room. I appreciated the sentiment even though it was forced.

The next to pass on praise was Brian, who patted me on the back so hard with his gargantuan hands that it brought on a mild coughing fit.

"You've got to come out for a drink with us, come on, lad," he chirruped.

"No, I don't think—"

"Look, I insist. We've nearly finished rehearsals. Tomorrow's the last day before the dress."

He was right but I didn't know if I was quite up for celebrating. The last few hours, days, weeks even had been so emotional that I thought that having to spend another minute in anyone's company, even my own, would be enough to send me into a blind panic. Brian clearly wasn't taking no for an answer and I narrowly escaped him grabbing me in a headlock and dragging me to the pub regardless. I begrudgingly agreed and followed the throng up the road to the pub, praying that I wouldn't bump into anyone from my old life skulking around outside. Lulu's sudden departure was sure to have hit the newsstand, so to speak, and I wasn't yet prepared for the onslaught. She was bound to have gone viral with the news and I wasn't sure how I was going to handle the pressure. Luckily, my stolen stash from the previous day would put paid to any jitters on that score.

The table in the pub would have been more or less silent if it weren't for Brian's incessant booming.

"I couldn't believe it," he said. "When you were rolling around on the floor in scene two, it was like you were speaking to another force."

412

I was gulping down pints like Prohibition was coming in tomorrow. Nothing is more uncomfortable for me than having to take a barrage of compliments. The three waif-like blondes supped their shorts and smiled in all the right places. Though it seemed to pain them immensely, they were forcing themselves to agree.

"I mean, your performance made me want to do a better job," he went on. "You were dragging me into the drama. Just incredible!"

A few nods rippled around the group. Cecelia had not deigned to join us, she was probably fiercely preparing to try and outshine me in tomorrow's rehearsal.

"What's your secret?" Brian asked. At which point, many people leaned forward. I found it hard to believe that anyone was really that interested. They had all seemed to resent me from the get-go and now they were eager to hear about my motivation. It was all a bit bizarre. I took a massive gulp before I answered.

"I don't really know. I've had to go to a lot of dark places emotionally. It hasn't been easy." It was the truth.

"Well, it's no secret that your... demeanour has altered considerably." That was very diplomatic of Brian.

"Uh, yeah. In order to really get under Alan's skin, I had to put myself in a lot of risky positions. You make a lifestyle choice. You either try to play the part as best you can with little experience or you gain some experience to help you play the part."

Lisle put down his glass of wine.

"It's a credit to you, Simon, it really is. I mean, some days you've come in looking like hell, I can't lie. But then you've just knocked it out of the park. It's a real testament to the pros of method acting. Your performances have really been jaw-dropping."

I literally couldn't take this in. All this time I was singling people out, thinking I was being ridiculed and mocked and in truth I was admired? Surely not.

As the beer flowed, the talk flowed too. I was drinking twice as much as everyone else but I was enjoying basking in my glory, so much so that I was doling out praise myself:

"Oh, Hilary, I simply couldn't have done that scene without your input."

"Lisle, your portrayal of Dysart made my character feel safe, and in turn I felt safe."

It was all becoming so easy. I was beginning to act and sound like a pro. I was fast becoming elite.

*

As I walked towards the toilets, I felt the full effect of the last few hours' drinking. I must have had six pints on an entirely empty stomach, and now I was swaying slightly from side to side. I felt like a hero, unbreakable. I had won the respect of Rex, I had won the praise of my peers, and I had just given a career-defining performance. There truly was no stopping me now. I glanced in the mirror in the gents and smiled back at the virtually unrecognisable fiend staring back at me. Fuck them all, fuck Cordelia, fuck Craig, fuck Sandra, Lulu and Camilla! I just didn't need them now. I was what I'd wanted to be from the very beginning, a star. And if drink and drugs had got me there, then so be it, they would be included in the cautionary tales in the autobiography that I was sure to have commissioned after my long and successful career as a West End stalwart. I had achieved the seemingly unachievable.

As I left the toilets and went to join the others, I grinned to myself. This was just the beginning of something massive, and all the little things that had happened, the attempted suicides, the sacrifices, had all been necessary footholds for me to climb up. Without looking where I was going, I bumped into someone.

"Sorry," I mumbled, looking up. I stared straight into the large, glassy eyes of someone I hadn't seen for a long time. Sophie stared back at me but she didn't speak. I stopped in my tracks, not really knowing what to say. The glow from the open fire roaring to our left illuminated her dark eyes. Her expression was one of utter disappointment, as if I had just kicked her guide dog.

After a second or two of uncomfortable silence, she spoke. "Did you do it?" Her voice was not the usual weak, thin voice of old but bold, accusatory, shaking with emotion.

I babbled some kind of feigned ignorance.

"Don't you lie to me, did you do it? Did you do that to Lulu?" Her face was twisted with rage. It was a Sophie I had never come into contact with before; she appeared to have acquired some bite.

"Do what to Lulu?" I was going to fight back. The beer had got me all worked up and if I was going to take Lulu, Camilla and Ricky down, then I'd wipe the floor with Sophie as well.

"You know what," she said. "You got her thrown out of the school. She saw what you did and you got her cut. She is a total and utter mess. She has had to move back home because she's so upset, she told me she wanted to kill herself."

Oh, what is it with bloody suicide? I mean, can no one handle their own life anymore?

"I don't have to listen to this," I said, trying to push past, but Sophie grabbed my shoulder. Her touch was light, her face softened, her eyes teary and her voice dry.

"Please, Simon, just tell me you didn't do it. I need to know that you didn't do that to our friend. That you didn't make a pact with Rex to have her ejected."

This metamorphosis back into doormat Sophie irked me. Why couldn't she just accept that that had been the game all along? Never mind this who's next to leave, what can we do to save our place at the school, this isn't fair, boo hoo hoo. Sophie had to get it through her thick skull that in this world it was shit or be shat on.

I leaned in closer, so close that my words were accompanied by big globules of saliva.

"Yes, I did it," I spat. "She had it coming to her so I did it and I don't for one minute regret it either."

She looked as if she was about to cry, as though all the suspicions that she didn't want confirmed were being laid out for the world to see.

"And if you know what is good for you," I went on, "you'll drop the little girl lost attitude and start making some changes of your own, because if you want to survive on this course and in the real fucking world, then you're going to have to break a few hearts."

She took her hand off my shoulder and put it on her chest.

"Never!" she said defiantly. "I could never do that to someone. I could never become what you have become. This isn't for me at all. You're not the same person. You're... twisted!"

The fire died in her eyes as she moved away, and as she did so I realised that I was losing her. She was going to where all the others were, somewhere that didn't include me anymore.

I was twisted. How expertly put. The only other person to ever call me that had been my stepmother. Perhaps she had been right all along.

6

That revelation had been the most shocking. Twisted: is that what I had become? Is that what I had always been? The very sound of the word was offensive to me. To see Sophie, a dear friend, so appalled by my behaviour that she had decided to brand me with the same moniker that had been thrown at me twenty or so years earlier by someone I was meant to place the ultimate trust in. Surely that had sealed my fate. It ran around in my head like a freight train.

When the alarm clock went off, I almost sleepwalked into the shower to get ready for work before coming to the sudden realisation that I was no longer welcome there, so I went back to staring up at the ceiling.

Tonight was the final dress rehearsal where we would tackle the denouement at full pelt. The chorus had begun blocking the majority of it in the sessions before I had been needed; they merely had to slot me in somewhere. The final scene where Alan sees Jill as a sexual being and becomes so consumed with guilt and emotion that he takes something sharp to the eyes of his equestrian saviours had to be so raw that Rex was hell-bent on keeping the rehearsal of it to a bare minimum. As long as we knew where we were standing, the rest had to be purely organic. The improvised passion of the scene would add to the sincerity of the piece. Cecelia would be sure to flounce around the stage with all the necessary theatrics. The fact that we had barely played a scene together yet weighed heavily on my mind. What if we danced awkwardly around each other and undid all of my previous good work? Rex was directing on a knife-edge. Surely if it was shit tonight, then we had very little time to put everything right before the first show. It was an interesting method but, since he trusted it, who was I to argue?

I couldn't shake last night from my conscience. Every time I breathed in, it was like a new ache in my breast. After Sophie had left, I had run back to the table and grunted my goodbyes before escaping into the night. Even though I didn't want to admit it, it hurt me that I had hurt Sophie. She hadn't done anything wrong, she was just concerned for her friend and, if I was honest, I was concerned for Lulu too. I hoped that she would somehow see a light at the end of the tunnel. Who was I kidding? Who on earth could justify my behaviour and even consider my absolution? I was twisted, a bad boy, and the evidence of that fact was mounting up. I might as well accept it.

*

When I got to the rehearsal, Cecelia approached me.

"You know that friend of yours quit the school," she said, as if it was the most natural thing in the world. "Please don't fuck this up for me today."

I don't know why I had expected an extension of the kindness to have spilled over from yesterday. The girl was a ruthless caniving bitch, and it takes one to spot one.

So Sophie had left. I wasn't sad, I wasn't happy. Somehow I had forgotten to feel anything for anyone anymore. Inside I was numb. I fumbled around in my bag for my script and stumbled upon my little white stash. I was carrying it around now like a wallet just in case I ever needed it. In order not to cock up this scene, I was going to need to be wired, so wired that the fury in Alan's actions would be unbridled, irrational, ugly. I made a long trip to the toilets; it was like retuning to the scene of the crime. I found myself imagining pushing Camilla's limp, hanging body out of the way just to get in. I think I overdid it, if you can call a third of a bag overdoing it. When I came out, my senses were swimming.

419

Rex paraded up and down the room.

"So far I am pleased with this production, very pleased. It is truly worthy of showing the public." His hands were laced together and he took slow, confident strides. He was zooming in and out of focus but I was trying to avoid his gaze, saving my mania for the upcoming scene.

"Tonight we shall be tackling the final scene when Alan sees Jill as he has never seen her before. Energy must be at optimum level as we must be living this fear, this torment. I am expecting to be gripped, scared, hypnotised. This level of drama is exceedingly difficult to achieve and I am EXHILARATED by the prospect of witnessing something raw and real, passionate and haunting tonight."

The company collectively shifted in their seats. No doubt the pressure was on me to nail this. The tension in the air was palpable but I was actually slipping out of reality. Drugs had never made me feel this way before. I had surely consumed more than I had intended. Drool was starting to escape from my mouth.

Rex sat down in his usual place; he glanced at me and looked visibly shocked by the mess I was in. For a split-second he seemed to toy with whether to go ahead with this. It could be potentially disastrous putting someone so manic into such a powerful position. I could, however, see that he was willing to take one last risk. Rather than stop the play and save himself and myself from making a grave mistake, his curiosity got the better of him. I was twitching and starting to convulse slightly. The words were bubbling up on my lips before I heard him speak.

Cecelia began circling me like a wolf might circle its prey. Her words were inhuman, like knives being sharpened and bared ready to scythe at my skin, her eyes wild like fire. Her breasts thrust in my direction and her face contorted into a still mask midway between rage and lust. The Alan inside began to stir. He awkwardly got to his feet and surveyed her for a moment. Was she mocking him? He stood watching her. There was something pulling at Alan, a force stronger than the demon, taking him away from himself and into a realm of fantasy, one where Jill was stripped bare, enticing and arousing, her breasts exposed and her skin hot and silky. She ran her hands up and down her body, over her breasts, between her legs. His fingers longed to touch her but he did not know how. He didn't know whether to kiss her or rip into her, tear away the parts of her that beckoned him in, rip her to pieces so that she could no longer tempt him to a point of no return. As she came closer, he could feel her breath on him, her hair slightly brushing his hand. What was between her legs? Could he discover it? Would it bring him pleasure or pain? Could he withstand the pressure of satisfying her or would she laugh at him, mock him, and then leave him naked and alone?

Alan's focus on her blurred as he traced her with his eyes, the lines and contours of her body dispersing and re-joining, her long, slender waist, the curve of her breasts, the tender throat and tight neck, the chin and soft lips. Suddenly, like a jolt of electricity, I began to feel something different. A hallucinogenic pull that dragged me into a fit of shock and disbelief; Jill's face was not Cecelia's anymore. Though it was her neck, the face had twisted and turned into something else. A vile monster stared back at me. The eyes were Sophie's, the huge glassy domes that bore disappointment and remorse; the lips were Lulu's, tight, unforgiving with teeth bared and an accusatory snarl on them; the skin was Camilla's, white with dried blood seeping from the nose and throat. It was a hideous beast, an abhorrent amalgamation of all those I had denounced, judging me, attacking me. I lashed out with one swipe, knocking it to the floor, and while it was down and writhing I crawled on top, pushing it down, restraining its limbs as it flailed in protest.

With another chemical rush, Alan placed his hands on Jill's body, gently caressing her as she started to ease into him. She softened, her eyes closed and her lips parted. Her hair fell to the floor and she put her hand on his arm to steady him. But then I was battling with the beast again, it started to jolt as I brought my hand to its waist, gripping it tight so it couldn't wriggle free, and as it cried out in pain, I brought my hand up and over its head.

"IF YOU DO NOT LEAVE ME," I screamed, threatening it with my clenched fist as it cowered and yelped in pain, "I WILL KILL YOU!"

"STOP!" The voice rang outside my head and snapped me back into the room. I was lying on top of Cecelia; she was shielding her face and shuddering. My fist remained in the air over her; a few strands of her hair danced between my fingers. She sensed the tension go out of my body and frantically crawled backwards away from me, holding her cheek and wrapping her torn shirt more tightly around herself. She began to sob, real cries of terror and shock, sharp and intense screeches amid little pants of breath. I turned my head towards Rex.

He was in shock too; the whites of his eyes were illuminated in the light above him.

"I mean… What is… are…" He couldn't find the right words. He just stood there taking it all in.

I had no idea what had happened. I let my hand drop to my side and, as it did, the blonde hairs drifted to the floor. I swallowed hard and fell to my knees. My breathing was fast and laboured.

"You have… You just…" He didn't finish the sentence. I sensed something shift in the way he was addressing me. It was an emotion I had not detected in him before. It was fear.

We sat looking at each other for a few seconds before he turned and strode out of the room, slamming the door behind him. Cecelia was being comforted by Hilary who had rushed to her aid. Her hair was bedraggled and she attempted to straighten it with her fingers as she scrambled to her feet.

"You're an animal!" she screamed, wanting to come nearer but fearing the consequences, "An ANIMAL!" And with that she ran to the door, wrenched it open, and ran into the corridor.

I just sat; slack-jawed disbelief was etched across the faces of the rest of the company staring back at me.

"What?" I asked them belligerently.

"Oh, Simon," said Brian finally, looking at me as if I had just committed a cardinal sin and I was to be burned at the stake.

"Oh, shut the hell up!" I spat, not knowing whether I was being defensive for protection or for mercy. "If you put HALF of what I put into this play—"

Brian didn't wait for me to finish, he just hung his head and made for the door. I watched while others followed suit and soon I was the only one left. The dim buzz of the yellow light above my head cut through me like a knife through butter. I had gone as far as I could go and now I really was alone. I had hit the bottom. And once you hit the bottom, you have no choice but to stay there awhile.

*

After I had drunk about half a bottle of whisky, I went home. When I got in, I crashed around in the kitchen looking for a glass. I didn't know whether I had woken Flowers, she could rot in hell for all I cared. I'd probably meet her down there. Knowing my sodding luck I'd still be renting a room off her.

I got to my bedroom somehow and poured myself a good half pint of the stuff. Then pulling my magic bag out of my pocket, I did a little assessment. What if I poured the rest of this bag of disco crystals into my whisky and downed the lot? The assessment didn't take long and the experiment took even less time. Before I knew it, I was wiping the foul-tasting liquid from my mouth before retching and swallowing, retching and swallowing. I wasn't perturbed. I continued this process until the whole lot had gone. Then I remember laughing, laughing for no apparent reason. If you didn't laugh at these things, you'd just cry. Tonight I might just die.

7

The morning seeped into my consciousness like a dark snake, slithering into my head with a searing pain, in through my closed eyelids, up my nose and through my veins. As soon as my brain registered that I was in fact alive, I began to convulse on the bed. My skin was drenched and so was the sheet underneath me. After dry heaving and eventually expelling foul-tasting bile onto the floor at the side of the bed, I dared to open my eyes. Instantly, I felt fear, a fear of not knowing what would be waiting for me when I opened my eyes, what had happened, where I was. All I knew was that I was breathing and I was feeling intense pain from both my head and the inside of my arm, not to mention my eyes themselves, which felt as if they had been gouged out, rolled around a bit, and then returned to their sockets. I couldn't deny that there was some kind of bright light behind them – I could very well be dead. But surely after what I had done, I would have been lucky to have escaped ending up in hell. I opened one eye and looked around. I saw curtains, torn and hanging limp from the windows. A burst of red smears adorned the opposite wall. It wasn't paint, I knew that much. Books had been ripped from the bookshelf. The sheet beneath me was grey and red, dull, uninviting colours. I shut my eye again. God, the pain! I felt like my soul was on loan and the cords attached to it had been severed and left to bleed.

What had happened last night? The last thing I remembered was ricocheting off the walls down to my bedroom. Everything else was a blur. Oh no, here came the vomit again. Another bucketload of venom spilled from my gut through my open mouth and onto the floor. I purposefully swung my head to the other side at the expense of a lot more physical discomfort. This time I opened the other eye. It appeared that I had been quite liberal with the red smears – they were dribbling down the walls. And on my door, my heavy, wooden door there appeared to be... scratch marks, as if a giant cat had been swung around my room one too many times and was trying to claw its way out. I shut the other eye and internalised my feelings, wanting to steady myself in the effort to move. As well as the extreme throbbing of my head, the unspeakable sting from my right arm was truly indescribable. The rest of my limbs cried out in protest as if they needed moisture and warmth to function and I was starving them of both. I was fully clothed; I could tell this because my clothes were so wet and heavy that they had practically pinned me to the bed.

It was no use, I was going to have to move and it had to be now. I kept my eyes shut and made the first attempt to put my arms out to lever myself up. I cried out as I pulled myself up into a slumped sitting position. I felt like my backbone had broken and I was just a collection of cracked bones held together by wet, cold skin. My hair was stuck to my head, a head which thumped like there was a party going on and I was the only one NOT invited. I felt like hell, hell's mother, hell's rapist grandfather. Whatever I felt it was inhuman and brutal in its ubiquity. My body swayed on its own, ready to slump back down at any second, so I decided to fight it and open my eyes. The light hit me first and I retched yet again. This time careful swallowing curbed the onslaught of the bile. The full force of what awaited me came into focus: pure destruction. Torn paper was strewn around the floor, striped red and jutting out like teeth waiting to incise my feet. The walls were streaked with the same angry vermilion, like the daubs that decorated some serial killer's bedroom. I was lying on a patch of red, murky green and translucent circles of stain, the secretions of torment from a body attempting to exorcise its demons. The set of *The Exorcist* surely had nothing on this.

I had to keep going. If I was going to live today, I was going to need to persevere with my movements, no matter how bad the pain. No matter how hysterical the desire to lie down and shut out the world was, I was not going to succumb. As I went to put one foot down, I noticed it, the jagged shard of glass from the broken bottle of whisky discarded on the floor like a broken bone, threatening, snarling, an all-too-real reminder of my implosion. It was streaked with the same red as the walls. I reached down and picked it up. Holding it up like a zombie with my eyes half open and my mouth hanging like it was unhinged and left to dangle, I examined it. It was a thing of beauty, its crystal grandeur glinting in the light, a small weapon, a tiny sword. It slipped from my fingers and dropped to the floor. I had reached the final step. I had inflicted pain on others, many others, but now I had inflicted it on myself. The drugs were gone; the glass was just a piece of glass. I had made the ultimate sacrifice by offering my blood, my sanity, my integrity. And I had lived, I was breathing and I was alive. Even through the fug of last night's cocktail of violence and abuse, I saw a way out. Today, I was going to try and put something right.

*

Though my two flatmates were out, I was sure that they must have heard last night's dramas and that I wouldn't have a home to go to by the end of the day. If by any chance they had been out all night, then I might just be spared. If it had been that bad, would they not have called the police, a doctor, anyone? Maybe my luck was temporarily in. I had scraped up the paper and removed the disgusting sheets from the bed. The stains had seeped into the mattress. It would have to be replaced. There was no way someone else would be able to stomach the remnants of horror that streaked that sorry furniture. When I got some strength back later, I would turn it over.

No doubt the stains would beckon me from the other side while I slept with one eye open. I decided not to try and remove the red from the walls. It was not my priority today, today I had to do something else; I didn't know what it should be but I did know that once it was done I would feel something within me change. I dumped the sheets in the large bins out the front. I had tried to shower but, hot or cold, the water had burned my skin like a thousand flames. I didn't look at my body as it begged for mercy. I didn't want to see where my blood had actually come from. I kept my eyes in front all the while. Even as I wrestled my saturated clothing from my body, I kept looking forward through half-dead eyes. The clothes went in the bins too. I never wanted to see them again. Fresh clothes were put on. I scrubbed my carpet as best I could. Luckily, the colour of the carpet was darker than the bile, but when I had finished, the water told a different story. Two angry dark patches glared up at me. I opened the window to let the vomit smell out and fresh air in. At first it made me cough, wheeze and double over, but soon it replaced the fog in my lungs with something new, something soothing and reassuring.

I picked up my bag and escaped from the house. There had been no sign of life there, so I think I had got away with it for now. It had been a struggle putting one foot in front of the other. My head felt as though it wanted to make contact with the ground more than my feet did. I wobbled from side to side. Some kind of sludge overtook the space where my brain was, and as the tide went in and out, my motor system went with it. I was like a rag doll. People would surely be staring at me but I didn't care. All I cared about was getting out, finding the source of what had allowed me to live, finding the purpose that had kept me alive, and honouring it. It could have been a number of things. I made it to the bus stop and heaved myself down. Taking a moment to breathe, a flashback entered my mind, restraining a beast, a beast that had different bits borrowed from other people's faces. Whose faces? The eyes, those piercing, crystal eyes.

I pulled my phone out of my bag. My battery was nearly dead but I had to do this. Frantically, I scrolled through the list of names until I reached Sophie's. I pressed and held the phone to my ear, my hand struggling to hold it in place. Each ring was like a hammer to my skull. It rang and rang and eventually went to answerphone. Hearing her sweet voice on the message brought tears to my eyes. By the time the beep sounded I was weeping.

"Sophie, Sophie, it's me," I began. I didn't know what to say. At least, what to say normally, the words spilled out of my mouth like on overfilled pint glass. "I can't explain, and you probably wouldn't want to hear it if I could, I just can't say this enough but... I'm sorry. For all of it, what I did to Lulu, how I behaved in the pub the other night, rejecting you, humiliating you, I just—"

The beeps ran out. I had tried to make amends for every sorry act in the space of a few seconds. The tears were running down my face and snot was cascading from my nose. The only thing now was to leave a similar message on Lulu's phone. And when I did, I was a broken man, a broken man with an aching head and a sting in the heart. No words could put it right, but maybe the wheels of forgiveness would begin to turn.

*

I found myself outside the Eco Scene office, watching as the sliding doors swung back and forth letting people into the foyer of the shared building. It was late morning so everyone must be in the office – I didn't see anyone I knew. Why was I here? Was I really going to try and put some kind of apology together for Cordelia? Would appeasing her settle the score with the underlying guilt and discord that I felt? Or was it Sandra that needed the apology? Or Clarissa? I just didn't know any more. All I knew was that I didn't have the nerve or the energy to go in just yet. I guessed I would have to hang around until I did. I really wanted a cigarette – I felt like that was the only thing that would curb the jitters and give me something to focus on while I built up my resolve to enter the building. Of course I didn't have any; I barely had the money to pay for a box of matches. Perhaps if I hung around the smokers' corner looking forlorn for long enough, someone might give me one. Hell, if I dropped to the floor, I might just pass off as a tramp and be given one as a kindly offering from some charitable well-wisher. It would be good practice for when I had to do it for real. Having no home or job was sure to force me onto the streets sooner or later. I shuffled around the side of the building to the banished area. There was no one in sight. Old Street was like a ghost town this morning. Fuck! Just as I was about to cave in and climb the stairs to the sliding doors of fate, a figure stood in my way.

"Simon?" I recognised the voice. It was the voice of reason that I'd heard so many times over the partition in the office and the one that often snaked its way into my fantasies. Tim stood in front of me, devastating in loose jeans and an Amnesty t-shirt. I felt like I hadn't seen him for an age. Even though I was virtually at death's door, I'd still felt a compulsion to scrape my hair back and pop a bit of lipgloss on.

"Oh, hi Tim." My words were weak and pathetic.

"Buddy, what's up? I heard you were... well, you'd left." He walked over to me and went to put an arm around my shoulder. I felt like any physical contact would burn an everlasting mark on my skin so I shrank away.

"Yeah, shit happened... I... I don't know." I didn't know what to say. There was no nice way of saying that I turned into a massive bastard overnight and I regretted every moment of it.

Tim didn't look at me with a patronising glare; he didn't tilt his head to one side and sigh like he'd lost all faith in me. He just nodded. His understanding was more than I could bear and the tears came once again. I couldn't stop them and before I knew it I was crying into his leather jacket. It smelt of fags, must and the varying odours of his skin from the last six or so years. Only when I stopped for breath did I notice that I was holding him with both hands, my fingers digging into him. And he, well, he was holding me too.

"Look," he said, "whatever has happened you know it's never too late to make amends, never too far gone to claw it back, and people will understand that. Sometimes you have to go through pain to get to pleasure and, if you're a good person, pleasure will come to you. You just have to want to get it."

I lifted my head from his jacket and sank back into myself.

"We've all had the option to balls things up for people, but it's only the real bastards who never realise it."

I nodded. All I had needed was for someone, anyone, to give me some real, unadulterated, sincere affection. I had always thought that my success would bring it to me, that I would never have to earn it. In truth, I had had it all along. I didn't need Rex's approval, I didn't need the praise from Brian, Cecelia, anyone; all I had ever needed was my own.

"You're a top man, Simon," Tim said, his clear blue eyes sparkling in the crisp daylight. "Whatever it was that made you lose sight of that, make sure they know that you knew it all along."

And it was with those words that I left Tim with a somewhat strained but genuine smile.

I had to perform tonight, not with the aid of narcotics and nerves but because I could perform. I had been good all along. Rex's method of instilling fear and pain was just a smokescreen, it didn't work. It only worked to break the spirit and the mind. I was not going to jump from one stimulant to the next just to get a character right. I was going to face the fear, face him, tell him to teach me and not to be so goddamn lazy as to expect me to find it out for myself. He was a teacher not a barbarian, and I was going to make sure that I learnt something from him in this experience.

As I walked down the road with a slight confidence boost, my nearly dead phone vibrated in my pocket. I stopped and fished it out, pressing it to my ear, hoping it was one of the girls granting my redemption. The voice was male.

"Simon?"

"Yes, who is this?"

"It's Philippe."

That was a shock. I'd not really heard his voice properly for a long time. He had always been the beautiful but silent boy in the corner of the room.

"Oh, hi Philippe, what's up?" I was intrigued.

"Erm, I don't know how to say this..."

"Say what? Come on, my phone's about to die."

There was a long pause.

"Rex has fired you from the play," he said. The world around me seemed to spin.

"You what?" I couldn't quite believe it. Hadn't Rex promised me that I would play Alan no matter what? I was sure there was some mistake.

"Yeah, I'm sorry, but I've been rehearsing your part for ages. He asked me this morning to step in."

I had to steady myself against the wall.

"What do you MEAN I'm fired?"

"He asked me to call you and tell you. I'm sorry you had to hear like this."

"No, no, this can't be happening. I've put everything into this part."

"That's Rex, I'm afraid. He's a bastard. Look—"

And my phone died. Shit, shit, shit! I tried to turn it on and off again but it wasn't happening. How could this be? Had everything I'd done, all the sacrifices I'd made, the people I'd hurt, betrayed and disowned, had all that been for nothing? Fuck that! No way!

I began to run. I ran to the bus stop and boarded the bus that would take me straight to the school. Suddenly, my illness didn't matter anymore. I had to hear it from Rex. Thoughts kept flashing through my head. How could he do it? Why would he make me go through such hell just to drop me anyway? What kind of sick, fucked-up, nasty game was he playing?

The bus journey was like a never-ending rollercoaster ride to eternal damnation. The fire and rage built up inside me and threatened to spill over with a tirade of screams, angry words, and clawed swipes at the chest of the next person who got in my way.

As the bus stopped for the millionth time to let another group of people on, I threw myself through the doors and ran. I ran like I had never run before. I passed elderly women on frames who yelled at me to slow down. I ran into the path of a group of schoolchildren, sending their boxes of chips flying.

Finally, I reached the steps of the school. I tore up them like a thing possessed, flung open the heavy door, and hurtled down the corridor. The infamous office door was shut. I had a feeling that this was the last time I would stand in front of it like this. If I didn't leave this building as a criminal, then I wouldn't leave at all. It would be a question of who put up the best fight. That bastard had broken my nerve, I was now reckless, ruthless, and armed for battle, and if Rex was similarly armed, then so help me I would fight him to the death. If I had to drag his limp body out of this building with my own two hands, then I would. I pushed open the door and walked in. I had nothing left to lose tonight, except possibly my freedom.

8

I stood on the other side of the table. I could feel my heart beating through my chest, ready to permeate the thick cotton of my vest and squirt blood all over the floor. My pulse beat a dramatic thud in my ear and my face burned puce. Rex had been standing when I arrived, almost as if he had been waiting for me to show up. He didn't look surprised as I burst into his office. He just stood, musing, as though he had been watching the door for some time. Now, however, as we stood on opposite sides of the desk, I couldn't help noticing that he seemed slightly unnerved. It was the only time I had ever seen him lack a certain fixed control. He was breathing hard too, his peaked nostrils flaring. I half-expected jets of steam to shoot from them like the exhaust pipe of some fancy sports car. A curl had escaped from his usually perfectly coiffed hair and it dangled threateningly from his forehead. It seemed to invite me forward to put it back into place, coaxing me to step over the boundary and initiate the first attack.

I could taste blood somewhere in my mouth but I didn't know where from. Maybe I was biting too hard on my tongue, my stare fixed on Rex. We were both poised; one of us was going to make the first move, but to where?

He was the first to speak. "What are you doing here? You are no longer welcome in this building." He was trying to be calm but I could detect a squeak of agitation.

"What the hell are you talking about?" I didn't need to fear this guy anymore; I'd experienced so much fear in the last few days that the well was dry. I was pumped up and ready to beat him to death if I had to. Once you get to that point the only thing to fear is your own insanity.

"We made a pact," I continued.

Rex threw back his head and laughed. It was piercing, utterly manic, and seemed to last an eternity. His head flew forward as he took in air before laughing again. His whole face twisted into a sickening mask of mirth. If I ever needed evidence that behind the method there was utter madness, then here was exhibit A. And I'd had enough of a crash course in madness throughout this process to spot it a mile off.

His hand reached up and folded the curl back into place, but the beads of sweat on his forehead were the major giveaway that his crown had slipped. This was Rex as his psychotic self, warts and all. Gone was his composure, his pensive looks and guarded sneers. Instead I saw a crazy, possessed man in front of me, cackling like a pantomime villain and slowly coming apart at the seams. His demeanour was of a man on the edge, someone who would jump if they weren't pushed. I knew that while I had him in this state, without the airs and graces that he portrayed so well on a day-to-day basis, I could strike and scar him easily.

Being in this position was thrilling. I felt I could say or do anything, throw the furniture, smash the place up, whip my cock out and piss in his face. I felt invincible. The adrenaline was addictive. He stopped laughing and turned to me again. His face was red and his eyes were bloodshot. It suddenly dawned on me that this was all far too theatrical to ever be truly frightening. In the cold light of day, Rex was just an actor too, a plain old, run-of-the-mill, hammy, two-bit actor in a badly cast farce. But I wasn't about to be his cohort.

"Pact? Is that what you think? That our little PACT absolves me of my professional responsibility? I can do what I damned well like," his words were like razors, slicing through the air with a hefty spray of saliva, "for the good of the school."

This is where I lost it.

"WHAT SCHOOL?" My voice was loud and clownish, almost as if something else was crawling around inside me, shouting up from the pit of my belly. Now I was hooting like a crazy person. But it was only a decoy so I could search around, frantically scanning the office for something to rip, throw, or dismember before his very eyes. I picked some random book from the shelf and began to shred the paper between my fingers. It was so old it practically disintegrated in my hands.

"What, this? This shit? Is this what makes up your school?"

The book was not enough, there was no impact here. Rex didn't even look at my hands; he was watching my face all the while. I needed something else to destroy but I didn't have much time. Suddenly, I realised that the poster his precious high-flying artist daughter had drawn was hanging next to me, laughing at me with its precociousness. That bastard etching that had always towered over me like a guard dog whenever I was shrinking into his office chair. Perfect. I took it with both hands and wrestled it from the wall.

"This?" I teased him.

He knew what I was about to do and although he wanted to plead with me to stop, his pride wouldn't allow him to back down. His arrogance was very much still present even though he seemed to have lost a grip on all of his other characteristics. He would just have to let the poster go.

"This makes up your school, does it?" I asked, not expecting an answer.

It tore easily enough; once I started to rip I couldn't stop. And he didn't try and stop me, to ask for mercy. If anything, he began to look scared. Pieces of paper fluttered to my feet like the last dying embers of a devastating fire.

"This pile of dusty bricks, these rat-infested walls and filthy, shit-covered windows are what you hold so fucking dear, are they? They are your school?"

"I am not going to try reasoning with you, Simon. I don't reason with those who are unstable."

I smiled at the irony. Here was a man who took almighty glee in destroying the hopes and dreams of others telling ME I needed help.

"Or is your school made up of the people within it? Are we not the heart of the school? The ones who determine its success? The ones you crush? The ones you discard? The ones you barely give a chance to succeed? Are they not your school?"

The silence was long and in that time I concentrated on my breathing. It was deep and pregnant. I could tell that he knew exactly what to say next. He looked at me with a dipped head and direct, flaming eyes. Something inside me made me want to pounce and tear at them with my two hands.

"You didn't seem to care about those people when you stepped on them as you started to rise up though, did you?"

It was the perfect white-hot knife to stick into my soul because the bastard was right. The Lulus, the Sophies, the Rickys; all the memories suddenly came back to taunt me. How I wished any of the people I'd screwed over could be here now.

"They all got thrown to the side once you tasted a bit of glory, didn't they, Simon? What are they doing now, hey? Blacklisted? Heartbroken? Dead? Do you even know? You sold your soul the moment you picked up that script and slipped into Alan's shoes with the big boys, so don't give me the sanctimonious shit that you ACTUALLY care. What a patronising little weasel you are!"

I swallowed hard.

"I did care." I wanted the words to sound sincere but they were choked and feeble. "I had a few problems."

"Yes, you did, and you got rid of those problems, didn't you, by picking them off one by one?" He went to come around the table and half-expected me to move in the opposite direction. It was as though he was trying to turn this tragedy into a melodrama, acting it out like there were cameras on us filming our every move. Maybe there were.

I remained rooted to the spot. I couldn't play his little games anymore. I was worn out, exhausted from stretching too far, from being frightened, angry, intoxicated and weary. His last point had stolen my breath and I felt as though I no longer had enough strength to continue this battle, the battle against him, the battle against myself. This would have to be the last fight, but I had no idea who would win.

"What are you doing to me?" I was starting to break but I didn't care. Sophie had broken and I had practically laughed in her face. It was my turn.

"All I ever wanted to do was please you. That's all any of us wanted, to please YOU. And you beat me down, crushed me like an insect, simply because you could."

"I didn't crush you, any of you." His voice began to rise but there was no compassion or warmth. "So many of you are deluded. If you were weak, then you crushed yourselves. I only care about the school, the school and its success."

"There will be no success; no one wants to be associated with you. We all hate you. Everyone hates you."

"No, they don't. When they look back at their achievements, they will be thanking me. Those who I discarded should be kissing my feet. I am the only one who will tell them that they are wasting their time and money in a pointless endeavour. Any other so-called industry expert who says otherwise is lying."

"Well," I paused, "what about me?"

I didn't want to sound as though I cared but I did and I had to know.

He paused too, leaning on the desk to steady himself. He seemed to stop and think. Perhaps I was cracking something in the monster's skull, something that was going to force him into admitting something that he shouldn't.

"You," he said, "were an exception."

"I don't know what that means."

"I am not massaging your ego, Simon. I am not going to say what you want me to say. Casting you as Alan spoke for itself. Whatever you want to read into that is up to you. You took on the challenge. You seemed to be trying hard. You were beginning to reach levels that I have NOT SEEN BEFORE."

"Then why cut me from the play? Why undermine my work, my integrity? Why break me on the first night of the rest of my life? I have been through hell and high water to breathe reality into this fucking part. What more could I do? What IS IT that you are you trying to teach me?"

He looked pensive for a moment. I almost sensed an element of loss in his eyes, as though perhaps he felt pity but didn't want to say. I didn't need his pity; it only reignited the fire inside me.

"Last night's performance did not reflect your best work. It was outlandish, dangerous. You are a liability and I cannot be blamed for that."

This was where he was most comfortable, giving titbits of ambiguous critique in a cold and callous way, begging you to argue with him just so he could twist the knife a little deeper, twisting you up until you were practically on the floor, pleading for him to vomit into a bowl just so you could have something to curb your crippling hunger. What a bastard he was!

"That is motherfucking horseshit!" was the best I could come back with. "You promised that with the sacrifices I made I would be guaranteed to play the part of Alan. I kept my part of the bargain. And yes, my performance may have been a little misguided but I could have reined it in. I could have tried again. I know the balance now; I understand what I have to do."

"There isn't time for that."

"BULLSHIT! I'm a competent actor. I reached the point of acting close to reality by finding the truth in the madness. You know I did. I saw it in your face. I have it now; I know how to get back there. Let me prove that to you."

"You are not as competent as you think. You are not strong enough to play the part."

"So you cast Philippe, the most delicate fairy of them all? You are SUCH a liar, Rex. You go back on your word continuously. You cannot get away with this."

"Sorry, who do you think you are talking to? I can do what I like."

I stopped and looked at him for a minute. The figure before me was stripped of his armour and coming apart from all angles. I was beginning to think that Rex was not Rex at all but a devil in wolf's clothing.

"I don't know what I am talking to. Whatever it is isn't human, doesn't have a beating heart or warm blood trickling through its veins, just a dusty wheeze through the dry arteries, dark tunnels that stretch from the black hole where something that used to beat has crusted over through years of neglect. You are not even worthy of the word animal."

"Oh, shut the fuck up, Simon, you're embarrassing yourself! I am not continuing this charade. You are no longer required here. That is my decision and my decision is final. Now leave and shut the damn door on your way out of this school."

I remained still. If he wanted me out, then he was going to have to remove me.

"All I wanted was to gain your approval!" I started to scream at him. He was taken aback but not surprised. "I did everything, I fucked over my friends, I believed your words, your criticism, I even inflicted pain on my own body to try and DRAG the emotion out of me, only to make you satisfied that I could play this part. I couldn't have done any more." My voice was hoarse; the visions of all these moments came flooding back. Sophie's crestfallen face in the pub against the roar of the open fire, the red stains on the bedroom walls, the taste of the bile in my mouth, Camilla's ghost that had danced through the scenes with me, the monster that I had struggled with at length before I realised what I was capable of. It was like the flashbacks from a grizzly movie about a series of cold-blooded murders.

"It was all for nothing?" I was crying now, hot tears of regret and desperation. They burned as they ran rapidly from my eyes to my chin. I crumpled into a chair like a paper cup. "All for fucking nothing?"

I looked up at him. I wasn't expecting appeasement. I don't know what I was expecting.

He lifted his head slightly, peering at me as he had so many times before through those glasses perched so far down his nose. His eyes were black and his arms were raised. I couldn't help thinking that what I was looking at was nothing more than a demon.

"If NOTHING means stepping closer to the light, then yes," he hissed, contorting with each word he spoke. "If nothing means allowing yourself to be taken over by a force beyond your control, then yes. If nothing means changing your life from the mundane, the mediocre, the moribund into continuous flashes of crazy, fantastical, sadistic, euphoric, painful beauty, then yes; you felt nothing."

He was sweating profusely. The spit flew out of his mouth like hot lava erupting from a volcano, while his body convulsed and his face grew a sickening shade of purple. He appeared to be shapeshifting into something totally sinister. I was sitting opposite an utterly disturbed and unhinged psychopath.

"THIS is your final test. You will not be acting here tonight. If you survive this, then you will be another step closer."

I was overwhelmed by his metamorphosis into some kind of dark angel. I struggled to take in what I was witnessing. He towered over me, almost levitating.

"Closer to what?" I whispered, not really wanting to anger him further. I had no idea what might happen if I did.

He inhaled so violently that I half-expected the room to disappear into some sort of vortex. His whole body shook as he opened his mouth. His teeth were like little pincers in a cave of crimson.

"To me." It was an inhuman growl rather than a sentence, one of utter insanity. "You are nearly me."

This was it. This was the moment he'd been waiting for. It seemed as if some sort of evil being had been hard at work trying to prevent him from making this confession, but now it had escaped, it was clear that I knew too much.

"Rex?"

I was scared. He was visibly quivering as if powered by some other energy, one that was not recognised anywhere in this world. I had no idea where he would go next. Was he actually suggesting that I was as good as him? Having to admit that someone may be his equal was poisoning him?

"I have lived through the rejection, harboured the pain. I have been beaten as a child by the hand that fed me, been thrown to the wolves by the industry. I have been chewed up, spat out, defiled and left for dead. I have been dragged across the coals, told I was nothing. It was only when I began to break myself that I climbed back up. Since I first saw you I have been working hard on grooming you, training you, moulding you into the perfect specimen."

I suddenly felt a cold shiver shoot down my spine. Grooming me? Moulding me? What was this maniac talking about? Had he finally jumped into the abyss of lunacy?

"What do you mean?"

"Oh, come on. Do you think that they haven't been working for me?" he spat.

"Who? What? What are you talking about? You're deranged!"

"Do you think that Kerry just gave you those pills because she wanted to? Do you think that darling Ricky Hellman just happened to supply you with white powder out of the goodness of his heart?"

I stopped and stared as my life flashed before my eyes, the randomness of the events that had led up to this point, the hallucinations, the anger, the endless torment. Was it no coincidence that I had fallen so far so fast? Had Rex been secretly employing people to drug me all this time? I searched my brain for fragments of clues to piece this puzzle together, but I couldn't. Everything had been so readily available, and what was worse, I had taken it like a baby takes a rattle.

"You mean, my God, what have I been putting into my system?" I wanted to be sick, to expel all the poison from my stomach, from my skin. But it was far too late, the damage had already been done.

Rex's face came closer.

"What does it matter? It brought you here." His breath was like fire on my cheek. "You have totally submitted yourself to the art. You have done what was needed. And like Faustus before you, you will pay the ultimate price."

He started to reach into his pocket and I flinched, expecting it to be something sharp and threatening. But it wasn't. What he produced was small and brown. It had two arms and two legs and a bulbous head made out of hessian with a tuft of hair sticking out of its crown. The hair was black. The hair was mine. The face had two buttons tacked onto it for eyes and a ripped smile like an open chasm. The hideous doll smiled up at me from Rex's red, open palms.

"I knew from the moment you walked in that you were the next in line, the next for the empire, the next to sit in my seat, that it wasn't going to be easy convincing you. I would have to seek alternative methods. And now you really do belong to me." He was rasping. I could feel his hot saliva searing my skin.

The doll remained still, continuing to beam in my direction like a ghostly face in a cracked window. It was then that I noticed something red on its forearm, lettering, a word etched in crimson cotton. My heart leapt into my throat. It couldn't be!

I grabbed at my shirt and tore it open as I hoisted it violently up over my shoulder. I looked at the soft, white flesh underneath. I had scratched the word so perfectly but the wound had started to reopen and fresh blood trickled from the dark red letters etched across my skin.

I had written one word. The word that the doll proudly wore: Rex.

I balked at the sight and doubled over onto the desk. What could I do? What would he do? Now that he had confessed all to me before the final test I wasn't so sure that I would walk out of here alive. I had to remain calm.

This was not over. I would not follow this psychotic into his cult. He would have to kill me first and I'm almost sure that he would. At the very least harm me. But how could he harm me more than I had harmed myself? He may have pulled the strings, but I had held the glass. I had carved his name and I had smeared the blood, but I had survived and my thoughts were still my own. I had come out the other side and I still belonged to myself. I suddenly realised that I was his equal but not his property. We were neck and neck and there was everything to play for. I looked up and met his gaze.

"You evil, vile and sadistic torturer," I said in a calm voice. "I do not belong to you and I will do whatever it takes to NEVER EVER be like you."

Rex's head jerked back and he started to laugh again, this time the shriek was more horrific, more haunting, more terrifying. It was the laughter of Satan himself. It pierced through the walls and out into the street, through my ears and into my brain. It rattled the windows and shook the walls.

His throat appeared in front of me as his Adam's apple jerked up and down violently. There was only one way to stop this charade and it had to be now. With the stealth of a panther I dived for an empty wine bottle that rolled slowly on the desk to my left. With a swift flick of the wrist I smashed it against the wall until the glass splintered. A jagged, cylindrical, razor-sharp instrument was left in its wake. Like a medieval torturer I wielded my weapon above my head while Rex gasped for breath; his eyes were practically hanging from their sockets and darting from one side of the room to the other. He choked oxygen in and momentarily glanced at me while I stood over him, my weapon bared and ready to be used.

"I will never be you," I repeated calmly as I kicked the doll from his taloned clutch. He tried to grab it but I got to him first.

"In black," I whispered, "AND!" I raised the bottle high. And then I started stabbing.

I dabbed the sponge on my face. I looked perfect. My face was white, my lips were pink, and my hair was perfectly gelled into a centre parting. Alan stared back at me, handsome, erect and proud. I looked down at my costume; the cotton shirt was soft to the touch. I pulled it up to my face to feel it against my skin. It was cold. I caught sight of my hand. The blood had been quite easy to rinse off in the end. The movies would have you believe that it's quite thick and leaves terrible stains on your skin, but if you get it at just the right time, it rinses off with warm water no matter how much of it there is.

They would find him eventually. I was not a killer. I couldn't plan where to bury someone or burn the remains of a corpse or break their teeth and cut off their fingers so that they couldn't be identified from their fingerprints or their dental records. I'd read books on the subject but I didn't have the strength to do it. I'd been far too tired once the anger had subsided.

Before I'd realised what I was doing, I'd cut off two of his fingers and was sitting happily rolling them to and fro on the floor like cold sausages. They didn't look like fingers anymore, more like nails hanging onto skin. They were actually quite gross.

I don't think anyone will open that door for a couple of days, maybe he will have rotted away by then or maybe he'll be as I left him, naked from the waist up, skin punctured like a discarded Li-Lo on a rubbish dump, glasses broken and hanging from his nose, and stumps where two of his fingers should have been, amateurishly hacked off with a shard of broken glass.

I hadn't vomited, I hadn't even cried. How can you be remorseful over something you've dreamed about for months? I can't remember whether he screamed, no sound resonated in my head. I'm sure his screams would have haunted me had I heard them. I can't imagine him screaming anyway. Right to the last he'd be a proud motherfucker.

However, one thing you never read about in horror books is the smell. Maybe it's just bad blood that smells but I distinctly remember a nasty odour, the kind that hits you when you stick your head in an unclean fridge, the stench of something that is not quite right. Maybe the smell would lead them to him and then to me. I didn't try to remove my fingerprints from the office or hide the bottle under mountains of junk, I was far too tired. I just stole the key, locked the door from the outside and calmly went to get dressed. Phillipe had been inquisitive, I just told him that I had made Rex change his mind. Clever boy had the good sense not to argue.

I dabbed my face once more before the door swung open. My skin was ice-cold.

"Five-minute call," said Aaron, the student who had first presented me with the exuberating good news that had led me to into this lion's den only a few weeks ago. We didn't share glances of recognition; he didn't even look at me. The rest of the company were scattered around but they didn't want anything to do with me either. They were loyal to Phillipe, even to Cecelia who was keeping her distance. Measuring me now with fear in place of contempt – another thing I had risen to extremes just to earn. Maybe it's one of those things, you either try harder to claw back peoples affections after you tear them to shreds or you just move on from each cast and forget you ever met them. We would have to see how it panned out once Rex was found. I wonder whether they'd thank me or not.

Maybe my fate was sealed and I wouldn't need to know them again. My worth would be defined by the amount of head I would be forced to give in prison, my cute little ass being pummelled on a daily basis just so I could scrounge another cigarette or get protection from the big black guy with the stud in his face. I would harden, my skin would toughen, and I'd enjoy rough sex. Maybe it would define me or break me. Who knows? Who cares?

EPILOGUE

I got up slowly and picked up the muddy bomber jacket that Alan wears in the first scene, no doubt sourced from that hideous costume cupboard in haste by Phillipe. As I began to walk down the corridor past the office, I could have sworn that I heard a hiss from behind me. My conscience was playing tricks, I would ignore it. Maybe it was Rex's ghost. Maybe he would torment me forever, just like he had in life.

I stepped into the foyer and waited at the theatre door. I could hear the hum and bustle of the audience: "Where shall we sit?" "That's my daughter in the programme." "Have you seen him in anything else?" The buzz from the stage lights provided a small comfort, like listening to the patter of rain outside your window on a dark, miserable night or the sounds from inside your mother's womb. I felt protected and safe.

As the lights went down, I didn't feel nervous. I was Alan and I was about to walk into my stable and pat my horses, why on earth would I be nervous?

And that is what I did. The coughing stopped, the rustle of paper and the opening of sweet packets died down and the lights came up; they were blinding.

I didn't speak; I didn't feel the need to. I would speak when I was ready. Alan didn't want to speak, he was alone in the dark – he didn't have to speak. He could just sit until the moment presented itself.

But Alan didn't get the chance.

Aaron was a big lad and I didn't really have him down as someone who screamed like an animal getting mangled in a piece of farming machinery, but what reverberated down that corridor was a noise that sounded truly unnatural.

There was a momentary beat of collective confusion before anyone made a move, just like in a Pinter play. It was at that moment that I realised I had been discovered. He'd found the key and I was completely and utterly fucked.

Even in death Rex had got exactly what he wanted.

Clever, clever bastard.

Acknowledgements

Many thanks to my Editor: Kelly Owen

Cover Designer: Francesca Wood.

Special thanks to Thomas Cambridge for additional design and Lorna & Jude for telling me the truth.

Inner cover photo by Alex Edwards

Printed in Poland
by Amazon Fulfillment
Poland Sp. z o.o., Wrocław